Slave of the Huns

GÉZA GÁRDONYI

Slave of the Huns

TRANSLATED BY ANDREW FELDMAR

WITH A POSTSCRIPT BY GÉZA HEGEDŰS

CORVINA

First published in Hungary under the title *A láthatatlan ember* 1901
Postscript translated by Richard Aczel
Illustrations by Károly Csala, 1987

Printed in Hungary, 1987
Szekszárdi Printing House, Szekszárd
ISBN 963 13 2361 7
Second edition
CO 2536-h-8789

PREFACE
which might be read as an Epilogue

Ask anyone around Constantinople if he knows Zeta, and he will answer, 'Zeta? You mean the emperor's librarian? Priscus's friend? Yes, of course. A wise and honest man, they say, with a heart of gold.'

Well, I am that Zeta; and if you ask me, I say *nobody* knows me. True, I am the emperor's librarian; true that Priscus is fond of me. But – wise? No, I am not wise. I am not even always honest. And as for the heart of gold, it is nonsense to speak of it! Have I not killed? – yes, and not just one man but a hundred! I have thieved, and I've cheated too. But I'm being honest now, at any rate, in writing it all down truthfully in this book of mine. When you've read it, you'll be able to judge for yourself about my wisdom. Wisdom! – my foolishness, rather, for no man in the world has ever been such a fool.

After reading it, will anyone still say that he ever really knew me? Hardly, I think – not even my loyal Djidjia. It is only the face of a man that can ever really be known, and a man isn't his face: the real man is hidden behind the face. A girl taught me that....

I was twelve when my father sold me to be a slave, as one sells a chicken or a puppy or a foal. He had to, and at least he did it with tears in his eyes.

We lived in Thrace, in the Eastern Empire, and he was being dunned for his taxes. That was the time when the tax-collectors almost dug under people's skins for the money the Huns were demanding. The whole world seemed filled with that word 'Hun'.

'Hush – the Huns are coming!' was a mother's threat to a crying child.

'I've been dreaming of the Huns!' was the excuse of people who got up out of bed on the wrong side in the morning.

To prevent the cattle falling into the hands of marauding Huns, the authorities were rounding up and driving away all the poor Thracians' beasts; and it was just about this time that my mother died, leaving six of us children and one cow. My father had no choice but to take either the cow or one of us to the market, so he took me.

We sailed, then, to Constantinople, where my father white-washed my legs and stood me up in the market place, up on the plank among all the other slaves for sale. There were at least thirty other boys there of about my own age.

The first person to ask my price was an old-clothes man, next an old woman in a green shawl. My father said he wanted ten gold pieces for me, and they just laughed.

Then a rich man appeared, wearing a toga, a proud-looking man: two slaves beat a path for him through the crowd. From him, my father asked only two gold pieces, and this was agreed upon and the money paid. Whereupon my father burst out crying, and kissed me, and said, 'God be with you! Remember me, if you ever become fortunate, for I have sold you so cheaply to this gentleman because you are more likely to be lucky with him than with those peasants.' And that was the last time I ever saw my dear father.

My new owner was very dignified. He surveyed the world like an eagle, perched upon a rock; but his walk was self-conscious, like that of a Thracian lad going to church at Easter in his new sandals. His name was Maximinus.

As soon as we arrived at his home, they gave me a bath, first of all, and dressed me up in a nice white tunic, with a black belt. Then my master,

Maximinus, beckoned me to follow him into his garden.

Three boys were playing there under a plane tree.

'Well, here is your slave, boys,' said my master. 'His name is Theophil.'

The boys were about my own size, two of them somewhat older, one younger.

The grasshoppers scrutinized me with delight, and I too cheered up, thinking that I would be needed only as a playmate. I soon discovered the kind of playmate they wanted!

They made me stand up as a target, then threw lemons at me. 'Come on-- duck!', and I ducked, and it was fun as long as they kept missing me; but when they missed no longer, it was fun only for them. After a while, I burst out crying and threw myself on the grass; they began lashing my bare feet with stalks of poison ivy. I became furious and attacked the biggest boy, shoving him against a tree so violently that he knocked his head hard.

They were dumbfounded! The eldest turned and ran into the house, calling for his tutor. By now, I was ready to admit that to some extent I was in the wrong, but I thought, All right, go ahead, call anybody. I'll just tell them how you little devils were treating me.

In a short while the tutor appeared, and when he understood what had happened, he just stared at me.

'Sir,' I cried, 'these boys have been hurting me!'

'What of it? Aren't you a slave?' he bellowed in my face, and he gave me a dreadful thrashing. All the other slaves ran out of the house to see what was going on; one had a whip in his hand, and he beat me, too, so hard that he drew blood with every blow.

From that day on, my lot was to be eternal teasing and abuse. If I had managed to bottle up my suffering, they might perhaps have grown bored; but, remember, I was barely twelve at the time, and at that age one has not learnt to pretend. I could do nothing but bare my teeth in rage, and my rage amused them all the more: 'A slave, angry!' they thought. 'That' s very funny!'

Children sometimes tease chained dogs this way . . . .

They took care never to ill-treat me in front of their father or mother, only if we were alone, or if the other slaves were there. It was now that I saw to what an extent slaves can forget their humanity: not one of them dared to scold the boys; quite the reverse: they joined in their laughter. One of their favourite pastimes was to smear mud on my face, or they would tie a rope round my neck and play Hangman.

'Let's hang him!'

The bigger boy would then climb a tree and pull on the rope, while the two smaller ones held my hands behind my back. What amused them so much was my frantic howling. If we were by the seashore, they would throw their canes into the water, crying, 'Go fetch!' This wasn't difficult for me, since I could swim like an otter; but when I turned to swim ashore, they threw stones at me.

Often, in tears, I would plead with them, 'My little masters, let's play nicely, don't keep torturing me – I know lots of nice games!' And so I did; and so we played. But never for long. When they grew bored with the new game, they started tormenting me again, and my wailing was the one thing they wanted to amuse them.

I had been there for nearly a fortnight when one day I hurriedly gobbled up my lunch and hid myself in the garden: I wouldn't come out, I thought, until their teacher called them, so I burrowed under a thick tamarisk shrub and fell asleep.

I don't know how long I slept there before I was awakened by an excruciating pain – one of my feet was on fire! They had found me and put wood shavings between my toes and lit them. The three boys were positively shrieking with laughter.

I jumped out from under the bush, and flung myself upon them in a frenzy, shoving one to the right, another to the left, and the third I slapped in the face. All three fell down, while I rolled on the grass, crying and clutching my foot.

The shouting brought people running out of the house. My master, who was sitting on the balcony with a guest, shouted down, 'What's going on?'

In reply, one slave grabbed hold of me and dragged me under the balcony. 'This brat,' he said, 'has been beating the young masters!'

I saw the haughty lord turn pale; I saw how, out of consideration for his guest, he hid his anger; but he indicated with a nod of his head that I should be taken away, and knew that this nod meant also that I was to be whipped.

'My lord,' I cried, on my knees, 'they were burning my foot!'

But that didn't do me any good. I was beaten so severely that I could hardly move, but I couldn't stop crying. Perhaps four days passed before I could get up again and drag myself outside.

It was morning, and I thought that my young masters would be having lessons, and that the garden would be deserted at this time of day, so I went down and curled up on the lawn in the sun. Sick animals love the sunshine . . . .

As I was resting there, I caught sight of someone walking in the garden: it was that same rather portly stranger who had been talking with my master on the balcony on the day of my whipping. He walked alone, deep in thought.

'I won't get up,' I decided. 'He isn't from our house, so he won't hurt me.'

The stout gentleman stopped in front of me. 'Are you ill, little boy?' he asked.

When I heard his kindly voice my tears started again.

'Oh, my lord,' I replied, as if I were grieving to my own father, 'they've given me such a beating! My poor head hurts most of all, though my back aches horribly, too, and my feet are dreadfully painful.'

I let the shirt fall from my back: my body was covered with weals, black and blue from the blows I had received. And while he was looking at me, without a word, I went on pouring out my grievances with childish confidence.

As I was sobbing out all my sorrows, my master, Maximinus, appeared suddenly, and greeted his guest. They shook hands and the stranger said to him, 'Would you sell me this little slave?'

'Of course, with pleasure,' Maximinus answered. 'Indeed, you will oblige me greatly if you will accept him as small and worthless present from me.'

'No, I won't take him as a present,' answered the guest, 'but if you will agree to accept this gold piece as a token of our bargain–?'

'As you wish,' said Maximinus politely.

For a while they paced up and down the garden, talking. Then the stout gentleman took me by the hand and led me through three or four streets to a little two-storeyed house. It was only made of wood, but it was nice (and its base turned out to be made of stone after all).

I shall never forget that day. My good saviour was named Priscus, and he was the emperor's adviser and a teacher of history and rhetoric. He lived alone in the lower half of the house amidst his books and writings, with only a grey-haired Greek woman to look after him. The woman took me upstairs, where she put me to bed and rubbed me with oil from head to toe.

When I had recovered completely, Priscus had two suits made for me: one for special occasions, of white wool bordered with green silk; the other for everyday use, of ordinary linen.

Each morning, I helped the woman with her shopping, then went to school. In the afternoons, I would put on my better suit and accompany my master to the emperor's palace. Most of the time I followed him around, carrying scrolls under my arm, and I felt the proudest boy on earth! My master was a good man, and kind: now and again he would ruffle my hair,

or pat my cheek. For fun, he occasionally called me Zeta,* and when the woman heard this she began calling me Zeta, too. Eventually I was stuck with the name Zeta for good.

Later, as the woman grew older, my work increased. I had to clean my master's clothes and paint his sandals. I shopped in the market and the stores. It was my duty to refill the lamp, to sweep, dust, and even wash the dishes – and I did it all gladly.

My master liked me more with each year that passed. Especially, I think, because I took care of his books and papers, dusting and cleaning them with so much interest. My teacher once called his attention to my rare power of memory, and my master tested me. First, he read two lines of Homer to me, then four lines, then six – I repeated it all flawlessly. I don't know, myself, why it should be, but words stick in my mind so well that if I read or listen to something with attention, I never forget it.

In my third year, he set me to copying, and this benefitted me greatly. The Imperial Library was full of learned men copying. They helped me with lots of good advice, and I learned a great deal from merely listening to their conversations.

I learned from them, among other things, that a slave gained his freedom after eight years of service–though there were some slaves tied to their masters for ever. I didn't know to which group I belonged, but in any case I had no desire to be separated from my master. In the course of the eight years, we grew really fond of each other. My master loved me not just for my services, but also because I was able to talk with him on philosophy and history: I knew Plato, Aristotle, Herodotus, Plutarch, Suetonius, the philosophers and grammarians, and I had an inkling, at least, of all the sciences. My master always consulted me on place names, dates and so on, when he wrote. Even in the Imperial Archives I gradually became a kind of walking almanac, gazetteer, and index of names, all in one.

One morning my master didn't speak to me when I woke him. That in itself was strange: usually, while I shaved him and served his breakfast he would tell me his dreams, and though neither of us believed that dreams had any meaning, we would both make guesses as to what their meaning *might* be.

Well, as I was saying, one morning in early spring he didn't speak to me at all. I placed his morning milk on his desk and asked, 'How did you sleep, sir? What have you dreamt?'

* Zeta: the name of a letter in the Greek alphabet.

But even this he left without reply; he glanced at me occasionally, though, and the look in his eyes was thoughtful, almost sad.

What has come over him? I wondered. Could I have done something wrong? I had never fallen short in carrying out my duties before.

He spoke at last. 'How much money have we got, Zeta?' he asked.

'The same as we had yesterday, sir: seventy-five gold pieces and three-hundred-and-three sesterces.'

'And in the red leather bag?'

'Ninety-six gold pieces, or just a little over a pound in weight.'

This red leather bag was hidden in a special niche, concealed behind a wooden carving of the head of Jesus Christ. My master had once said about this bag that it belonged to someone he owed money to, though he never mentioned the man's name, and I didn't ask. It was always I who kept charge of all other money in the house.

'Bring me the red leather bag,' he ordered, motioning wearily towards it. 'Add four more pieces to it, to make it a hundred.'

I put the money in front of him on the desk, and he walked up and down the room, lost in thought while I stood beside the door and waited anxiously. His forehead was already lined for he was subject to headaches; when something bothered him, as now, the lines became deep furrows. After a while he paused, and looked at me.

'Zeta, my son, do you know what day it is today?'

'Saturday,' I replied readily, 'the third of April. On this day did Seleucus Nicator found the city of Antioch. On this day began the reign of Herod the Great's sons. And on this day, according to some, our Lord Jesus died.'

'True,' agreed Priscus, and he crossed himself, then continued pacing the room.

Finally he stopped again and said, 'There, among my diaries, you will find the year 440. Break the seal, and find April the third. Read it.'

I took out the bundle of papers, shook the dust off, opened the sheaf, and read aloud:

'In the morning the emperor called me to him. We had a long discussion concerning the Peace Treaty of Margus. The king of the Huns is not really bound by it – it is binding only on us! On us alone! Our Empire is lost if that barbarian turns his horses in our direction. In the afternoon I went to see Maximinus. I found a little slave there. They treated him inhumanly. I bought him and took him home with me. His name is Theophil.'

My voice faltered as I read the last lines. Confused, I looked at my master.
'That happened eight years ago today,' Priscus said, looking at me with damp eyes. 'Now you are free.'
I felt as if someone had hit me in the chest but gently, like an angel. I just stared, blinking my eyes – was I really awake?
Priscus picked up the leather bag.
'Here, I have put this aside for you. From now on you can wear a hat, you can marry, you can be your own master, or you can enlist as a soldier. From this day on, you need greet only those whom you wish to greet.'
My eyes filled with tears. 'Oh, my good master,' I said, sinking to my knees, 'don't send me away! Don't give me money! Let me stay as I have been!'
'Stand up.' The old man blinked, much affected. 'All right, then, all right...' He wanted to say something kind – I could see that in his eyes and in the motion of his lips – but he could only blink and smile and gently shake his head. 'Well, aren't you a foolish fellow!'
With tears in my own eyes, I answered, 'I can thank *you,* sir, for lifting me out of a state of wretchedness where I was a mere animal. I can thank you for the fine education I have acquired. *You* have never whipped me: you taught me with kindness instead. You gave me nice clothes, and allowed me to sit at your table. And didn't you teach me, above all, that only through the heart can anyone deserve to be called truly human?'
He kept nodding; then his face broke into a smile.
'Will you come with me, then, to the barbarians?' he asked.
'The barbarians?' My heart sank. 'To Attila?'
'That's right, to Attila, curse him,' answered Priscus, shaking his head, 'for in a few days we'll have to travel there.' He sat down and stared in front of him.
'To Attila?' I repeated, as if in a dream.
The news seemed incredible to me. My master had been sent by the emperor on various missions before, wherever a wise man was needed, but was he now to be sent among savages?
Soon, however, I began to see more clearly the meaning behind my master's words. A few days earlier Hunnish envoys had arrived to see our emperor, Theodosius. They were ugly, dark-complexioned men wearing tall fur hats. They wore tiger and leopard skins slung over their shoulders, and even their faces, deeply scarred, looked as if playful tigers had been on affectionate terms with them! But their many gold chains shone and jingled so beautifully on their breasts that it was a delight to watch them. There were five of them in

all. My master was called to the court every hour, or else someone came running to us–Chrysaphius the eunuch, perhaps, or Maximinus, the emperor's counsellor, or Vigilas, the emperor's interpreter–at times the palace seemed to be a madhouse! Everywhere I came upon dignified lords whispering together, their eyes clouded with doubts or bright with cunning.

The Hunnish envoys had brought a letter to the emperor, in which Attila demanded those fugitives from him who were hiding anywhere within the Roman Empire. He further demanded that the emperor's subjects should refrain from ploughing the land along the Ister (the River Danube), for it belonged, he said, to him, and as he had won it by fighting for it, so he intend to hold on to it. Finally, it was his wish that the market town should be not in Illyria, on the bank of the Ister, as formerly, but at Naissus on the border of the two empires, which was five days' journey farther inland.

I too was there in the palace when the Hunnish envoys handed over the letter. I stood behind my master, and saw the court turn pale as Vigilas, the interpreter, translated the letter sentence by sentence. The emperor sighed with relief when Vigilas reached the end of the letter, where Attila wished him good health. True, one did not have to be very clever to detect the evil humour hidden in this greeting, but the emperor wasn't interested in deeper meanings: the main thing was that Attila wasn't saddling his horse yet!

The emperor lifted his head and looked almost with servility at the five sinister Hunnish envoys.

'Did His Highness send any other message?'

Edecon, the chief envoy, a man with a dashing moustache, tossed his head proudly.

'He did. He says, next time you send envoys to him, don't choose ordinary people of no worth, but let them be from among the highest lords in your land – senators, or at least consuls.'

From the way the Hun spoke, one felt that *he* was the emperor, and Theodosius merely Attila's stable-boy!

The emperor nodded gracefully to everything, then placed the envoys in Chrysaphius's care, to be buttered up royally while the reply was being written.

The reply was in preparation for days, and my good master's few remaining black hairs turned white during the process. I saw what he wrote, since it was I who penned the final copies; and if letters of the alphabet were alive, these letters in our reply would have crawled before Attila's eyes on bended knee. Servility, thy name is disgrace! Civilized Europe was kowtowing to barbarian Asia!

The emperor humbly begged Attila to keep his people from making raids into the Roman Empire, and to send his supreme commander in order that a final and lasting peace treaty might be drawn up.

All this I remembered now, before I asked my master, 'And who will accompany you, my lord, if I may ask? Whom does the emperor send? Chrysaphius?'

Priscus shook his head.

'No, he is sending a finer man: Maximinus.'

My first master!

'I will follow you, my lord, wherever you go,' I told him with all my heart. 'Besides, those Huns may not be as black as they're made out to be!'

'Think it over. Even if you stay behind, you are free now, Zeta: I can't order you around any more. Think it over!'

'I have thought it over, my lord.'

'Those men drink blood, human blood! In battle they rip open their victims' chests, and with their teeth they bite out the still-beating heart!'

I could feel my cheeks growing pale – I always did abhor blood, even the mention of it. But I loved my master so much that I would have followed him even if he had ordered me to stay behind.

'I'll go with you, sir,' I answered. 'I'll follow you to the edge of the world, if necessary.'

'Well said!' The old man smiled. 'All right, then, my son, go and collect everything you think we ought to take along with us. Give my plants to the old housekeeper. We'll lock my room. Now, look, here's ten gold pieces: buy all kinds of spices from the Egyptian merchants, and a few crocodile-skins, and some red cordovan leather, copper rings, ear-rings–anything and everything that strikes you as possibly useful among those savages. But are you really coming with me?'

'Oh, my lord,' I replied, with all the warmth of my heart spilling out now, 'your own shadow will leave you sooner than ever I will!'

Spring was already full upon us by the time we led our horses to drink from the waters of the Ister. The willows and birches were already bursting into leaf; the fields and pastures looked like huge green velvet carpets on which a mile-stepping giant had scattered egg-yolk.

We had only ten tents. One belonged to Maximinus, who was the emperor's emissary. Another tent was shared by Priscus and me. A third belonged to Vigilas, the interpreter – a squinting, haggard man who had been to Attila before. The other tents belonged to the servants, and one to Rusticius, a merchant, who, with Maximinus's permission, had joined us in order to ransom a relative of his.

Ahead of us, about as far as you could shoot an arrow, the soldiers who guarded Attila's seventeen fugitives made their way; with them rode the Hunnish envoys, stirring up a cloud of dust before us.

On the way, of course, we inquired about the language of the Huns: how did those dogs bark? Vigilas and Rusticius taught the *gentlemen,* but I, being just a nobody, could ask them nothing – I just had to pick up what I could by eavesdropping at their lessons.

Vigilas was a clever teacher: he put his questions always in Hunnish, and the gentlemen had to reply by repeating the last words of the questions:

'What grazes there in the field?'

'There in the field a flock of sheep grazes.'

But at first, of course, he asked only for words:

'What's this?'–and he pointed at his cloak.

'Zees ees a clook,' answered Maximinus.

'Zees ees a clock,' my master offered.

'It's neither *clook* nor *clock,'* Vigilas would correct them, 'but *cloak.'*

'Devil take this barbarian tongue! Who could possibly learn it, unless he had sucked it from his mother's breast!'

But I felt I really *wanted* to learn.

I asked my master's permission to move up beside the fugitives: I'd make friends with one of the Huns – who could tell that it might not even come in handy some day to know one of them?

Priscus, himself, accompanied me to the captain and asked him to allow me to join the fugitives, to go with them and to talk to them.

Soon I picked out a small Hunnish youth with a scarred face – but all male Huns have scars on their faces. I could see, though, that he was young, and I thought that those of like age would understand one another more easily. For a while I rode beside him without a word, then, as kindly as I could, I asked him in Latin, *'Quid nomen tibi est?'* (What is your name?).

The Hun turned his tiny black eyes on me – I could see that he didn't understand. I had a slice of bread I was carrying, and I gave it to him–'This,' I thought, 'is how one would win over a dog!' Then I asked him, in Hunnish, 'What is this?'

The Hun smiled. 'Are you not Greek?' he asked, *in* Greek, though with a foreign accent. 'Why do you address me in Hun, when you do not speak Hun?'

'I want to learn,' I pleaded, in a friendly tone. All the same, it was good that he understood Greek – we could come to an understanding more easily: I'd help him with food and drink throughout our journey, and he'd teach me Hun. I would have liked to walk beside him, but this was impossible because of the smell of his clothes, so we went on conversing on horseback.

On the very first day, I took down about a hundred nouns, a few greetings and some idioms: 'Good day!' 'God be with you!', 'Good health!', 'God bless you!', 'Please', 'Thank you', 'Excuse me', and so on.

That same night I was able to greet Rusticius in Hun: *'I wish you good evening. Am I late supper for?'*

Rusticius couldn't help laughing. 'Just look,' he said to the gentlemen, 'this boy has mastered Hun in one day!'

'Just go on learning, Zeta,' said my master, encouragingly. 'Who knows when it will come in handy!'

So I kept on learning conscientiously. Oh, what a blind idiot I was! How fervently I worked for my own undoing!

In a few days I learned a good deal from my Hunnish friend. His name was Deel, he was the servant of a nobleman named Chath, and this Chath was the younger brother of Attila's commander-in-chief.

'Well, what on earth have you done wrong, then,' I asked, 'that you had to run away from such a good job?'

The lad sadly closed his eyes for a moment.

'I haven't done anything special.'

'Well, what?...'

'It was only...Chath has a daughter, you see...'

I smiled. 'Ah – and you fell in love with her.'

'I never even talked to her.'

He was unwilling to say any more. But after lunch I smuggled a bottle of wine to him; this was enough to open the lock of his heart.

'Tell me, Deel, how did it happen, if you couldn't even talk with her? You must have done something wrong!'

He sighed. 'No, nothing. I had a love-twig written, and sent it to her secretly.'

'Well, that was very foolish – but what *is* a love-twig?'

'Among us, only in the prince's court they use paper. ordinary people use twigs and write with the point of a knife. Well, I too cut a twig off a wild rose bush and took it to the shaman. “Carve on it delicately,” I asked him, “whatever a lad usullay says to a girl. Say that he who can’t even look at her, loves her.”

‘So the shaman very nicely carved this:

The grass loves the star,
But the star is so far!
Starry sky –
Heaven is high.
The grass below
Is soaked with dew.

Shamans know how to put these things well. I didn’t tell him the girl’s name of course, but I forgot to tell him, curse it, to leave my name out, too. That’s where the catastrophe began.’

‘It fell into her mother’s hands?’

‘Into her father’s. It was my luck that I happened to be hanging around the palace when I heard the master shout my name.’

Deel shook his head. ‘If it hadn’t been dark at the time I would have been food for the crows long ago.’

‘And is the girl beautiful?’

Deel gestured and raised his eyebrows as if to say that mere words could not express such beauty. I smiled at him: probably his beauty was just some fat little goose, I thought.

‘But look, Deel, my friend – if her father is such a high-ranking nobleman, they would never have given her to you. I am amazed that you could have done such a crazy thing.’ He was silent and blinked his eyes, then emptied his bottle of wine.

I went on. ‘What’s the girl’s name?’ (I asked only so that I would hear a Hun girl’s name.)

‘Emmo,’ he sighed sadly.

‘Emmo? A strange name...’

As we reached the border, Hunnish horsemen joined us in front to act as our guides through the forests and mountains. During the third week we reached a great plain, and from then on we never left it.

At last we arrived at Attila’s first settlement. I expected to see some huge barbarian city and lots of savages. But I was disappointed; in times of peace the Huns live scattered about the land – only the nobility gathers close to Attila. And the Huns don’t live in houses, but in tents; nor are they at all a vicious people.

We passed through many villages of houses, and saw tents in the yards among the buildings. The houses, of course, were not built by the Huns, but were found by them, deserted, when they arrived. Deel explained that they moved into the houses only during the most severe winters, and even then, only the women and the sick.

'I don't understand that,' I said to Deel. 'Houses are better than tents, whether it is winter or summer: warmer in winter, cooler in summer. Besides you can hide things better– keep your treasures safe.'

Deel shook his head. 'Houses tie people to one place. When I have to sleep in a house, I feel as if I'm in a crypt. Tents are better. A tent walks with me. Men with tents live wherever their fancy takes them. The world is big and beautiful. For me, though, it will soon be too small.'

Even Attila himself lived in a tent. We could see it from far away – splendidly decorated with golden spheres, it towered above the other brown and grey tents, and on its peak fluttered a white silk flag.

Bluish columns of smoke rose into the sky from cooking fires, and the smell of roast meat was strong in the air. 'Your people don't starve, I notice!' I remarked to my Hunnish friend. 'Is it true you live on horsemeat?'

Deel shrugged his shoulders. 'Sometimes – it depends. Horsemeat is good food, better than beef – though I doubt if I will ever have the choice again.' With a worried expression he scrutinized the tents. 'Look, Greek,' he went on after a moment, 'you have been generous with me on this journey, and I thank you; but I'd like to ask you if you do me one more favour.'

'Just tell me, and it's done, if it's at all possible.'

'Well... If you see me somewhere impaled on a stake, please come at night, and if I'm still alive, thrust your dagger into my breast.'

I couldn't talk to him again. They took him away, along with the other captives, in the direction of Attila's tents.

We reached a grassy hill near the settlement, and stopped there. For a short time we silently surveyed the plain–dappled with some ten thousand tents!

Children came galloping out to us on tiny horses, stared at us, and laughed cheerfully. Most of them wore garments of white linen and went without sandals or hats. They had quivers slung across their backs and carried bows on their shoulders or in their hands. Hunnish children, as I later observed, shoot at sparrows or swallows all day long. Until I grew used to their faces I thought the boys ugly. They all had their noses broken, and their faces were scarred as if, when babies, they had been scratched and bitten by dogs.

The little girls, on the other hand, were all the more beautiful because their noses weren't flattened, and their faces were smooth as rose petals. They wore red dresses, and they played with dolls, like our little girls; yet they walked barefoot like ducks.

Vigilas explained that Hunnish boys are made ugly on purpose. Fighting people are proud of their wounds. To them, the more beaten up a man's face is, the more handsome it is: a flawless face in a man is almost ugliness – except for princes and generals, for no weapon can harm them. So that's why Huns don't flinch from wounds in battle, like the people of other countries.

We laid out our tents on the hill but an angry Hunnish horseman galloped up to us and scolded us for daring to set them up higher than the king's. We realized only then how improper our action would have been... They then showed us where we *could* pitch our camp.

While we were busy, three Huns in leopard-skins and with bearskin hats rode up to us. Two of them we knew already: one was Edecon, with his dashing moustache, the other Orestes, also a nobleman and also haughty, though one could tell from his face that he wasn't of Hunnish origin. The name of the third we learned only later; it was Chath.

'What brings you here?' demanded Chath severely.

The lords' jaws dropped when Vigilas translated the question. Surely Attila must have known what brought us here!

Nevertheless, my master replied, 'The emperor has sent us to your king; therefore, we can answer only to him.'

'So you think,' Chath thundered, 'that we have come here just to parade ourselves in front of you! Our prince has sent us to ask your business!' he called Attila only 'prince' – not 'king'.

This Chath, by the way, was a big, wheezing and puffing tousled owl of a man, with the same dog-bitten face as all the other Huns. Around his neck he wore a gold chain of four twisted strands, and on it gold rings and coins glittered. His curved, diamond-studded sword alone was worth a fortune. (Well, poor Deel, if you fell in love with such a man's daughter, then it is unlikely indeed that you'll ever again have the choice of colt roast!)

'You yourselves must realize,' my master said, putting up a polite defence, 'what the custom is. When your envoys visit our emperor, would they give Attila's message to just anyone? They too would answer only the emperor himself.'

The Huns turned to one another, and exchanged a few words. Then, with a loud clatter, they trotted back to Attila.

We thought that Attila had sent the interrogators out of barbarian ignorance, and that after our lords' reply he'd slap his forehead and say, 'Quite right!' but things didn't turn out that way. Of the Hunnish lords, Chath and Orestes returned, and Chath again bellowed at us with cold dignity.

'If you have nothing more to say, other than what you have said so far, the prince sends you this message: go home!' Whereupon they left us.

Maximinus turned blue with anger. My master just stared after the horsemen in amazement. Vigilas almost exploded.

'And is this how we should go home? Take no other word back? Attila knows me – if I could have seen him face to face I could have talked him into leaving our country in peace!'

We had already packed our tent-poles on to the carts and were ready to depart when a new envoy came galloping up, shouting from a distance.

'The king does not allow you to leave during the night!' He called Attila 'king'. I found this strange, until I realized that he only used the word because we ourselves had used it.

So once more we pitched our tents, and Attila sent us a steer and a cart full of fish for our supper. Afterwards we prepared for sleep.

My master kept tossing throughout the night. He sighed and groaned. Eventually I asked what troubled him.

'Go to sleep,' he moaned. 'If you want to know, I am tortured by shame that a barbarian should so trifle with us.'

'Sir,' I said, propping myself up on my elbow, 'you are a wise man; don't you think there must be a *reason* for all this?'

'What reason could there be?'

'Just think back, sir, over our journey. Do you remember when you invited the five Hunnish envoys for dinner one evening and how, during the meal, when the talk turned to Theodosius and Attila, Vigilas's tongue ran away with him?'

'He was drunk.'

'He said, *"It is improper to mention a god and a man in the same breath."*'

'I tell you, he was drunk. The Hunnish envoy forgave him the next day.'

'Yes, they forgave him; but it doesn't follow that they did not tell Attila about it, and report what the envoys of Theodosius think of him.'

My master said no more, and I fell asleep. The next morning I saw him conferring with Maximinus in front of our tent. Then he called Rusticius over.

Rusticius, as I have said, travelled with us, though he wasn't a member of the delegation. He spoke Hun well. He was a curly-headed Greek about forty years old, and seemed always to be in a hurry.

My master mounted his horse, which I then led by the bridle, Rusticius picked his way beside us on foot in the bright spring sunshine, and so we came to Chath's tent.

I stayed outside with the horse, while the two of them announced themselves. What business could my master have with Chath? I learned later that he promised gifts if an audience could be arranged with Attila.

While they were inside with Chath, I marvelled at the two beautiful, sprawling, square structures of the tent, big enough to hold fifty people. One could see they belonged to a nobleman. They actually formed one double tent, made out of thick red-striped felt. The entrance was decorated with white horse tails and golden spheres the size of a fist. Above it an emblem caught my eye: it was of a red haircloth hand holding two real swords, both covered with tar, with a sun stitched in gold above them. Every tent had an emblem either hanging above the entrance or pinned to one side. A flag waved only on the king's tent.

The rear half of the double tent was evidently for the women. This was obvious from the white strings of pearls around the entrance, and from the white curtains covering the windows.

In front of the women's entrance stood a cart with four horses harnessed to it. It was being loaded with wooden chests and rugs. So the ladies were preparing for a trip! I had never seen such elaborately decorated chests. *We* leave chests their natural colour, just as they are – carved and shaped out of cedar; we cover them with a rug or cloth, but the chests themselves have no ornaments whatever. These barbarians, however, cover theirs with painted roses, tulips and peacock designs. Peculiar idea, I thought. If this was their taste in chests what, I wondered, was their notion of female beauty. What was that savage girl like for whom poor Deel was going to die? She must surely be some clumsy, pie-faced creature!

Beside the cart stood a double-chinned lady with crow's feet around her eyes. Her short ash-grey fur coat was exactly like those the men wore, and under it she had on a nut-brown skirt.

One could see by her haughty chins that she was no servant. She gave the slaves orders – what they should carry, and where – and watched as they lugged heavy things around, packed them on the cart, and mopped their perspiring faces.

After a little while a girl of about fifteen or sixteen stepped out: she had a delicate face; her coat was ash-grey, like that of the haughty-chinned lady, but her skirt was white.

I wondered if this could be she! Well, if it is, I don't like her at all, I thought. She's not exactly ugly, for she is as pretty as any healthy young girl must be, but she isn't beautiful either. There's no warmth about her. In Constantinople I've seen girls whose beauty hit like flames. And *our* girls are not so proud either.

While my thoughts ran on, the girl ordered a small, copper-cornered, tulip-painted chest to be put on the cart. Whether there was money or jewellery in the box I don't know, but it must have belonged to her, for she covered it carefully with matting. Just then the spring sun broke from behind the clouds and shone on her face, and she shielded her forehead with a grey ostrich-feather fan.

This movement of hers I liked – and suddenly she turned into a beautiful girl. Only the devil knows why from that moment I began to like her, but I did. Every beautiful girl has something that stays in one's memory for ever – with her, it was her eyes and her lips. It was as though she had come out of the workshop of creation simply because *someone* had to wear those dark dreamy eyes and that well-formed red mouth. Even now, when I think of her, it is her eyes and mouth that I remember.

'Mother,' she said, 'I'd like to go on horseback.' She had a sweet, clear voice like the sound of a distant flute.

'In that dress?' Her mother was shocked. 'How will your skirt look?'

'I can't simply sit and wait . . .'

'Come now, Emmo! . . .'

(Good gracious, so it *is* she!)

'I'll put on another skirt,' the girl said, 'if you'll let me ride.'

And then she looked at me. It was just a fleeting glance – like a ray of sunshine which, reflected from a mirror, glides across the wall, stops for a moment, then glides on, yet it shook me.

For me, this girl represented the spirit of death. We usually picture death as a human skeleton with scythe and hour-glass; in the land of the Huns it was a dark-eyed, red-lipped girl.

If she appeared to someone, he had to die.

She turned to her mother again and asked her something – I couldn't quite hear what. She started to go into the tent, then stopped, hesitant, meditating. Meanwhile her eyes wandered in my direction again and, perhaps because I was a stranger, they came to rest on me. Our eyes met.

I don't know if scientists will ever plumb the depths of the human eye and explain those invisible rays they emit – warm one second, cold the next, rays of ice and rays of fire, smooth as velvet, sharp as thorns, and sometimes striking with power of lightning.

The girl kept looking at me, and I stood paralysed.

*F*rom the men's tent Chath appeared and cast a glance over his servants who were standing out in front. I greeted him with a deep bow, but he didn't even look at me, just made a sign for his horse. He mounted and galloped away in the direction of Attila's tent.

I was surprised that my master remained inside, and I wondered anxiously if he had been arrested. But there wasn't time even to mumble a prayer before Chath was back on his clatter-hoofed horse. He jumped off and hurried inside the tent.

The next moment, Priscus emerged, Rusticius behind him, both looking highly pleased.

'Hurry up!' My master beckoned to me, then climbed onto his horse awkwardly, while the Hunnish children around hooted with laughter. Rusticius and I ran after him on foot, Rusticius much out of breath. The children followed merrily on their tiny horses.

'Attila will receive us,' my master shouted to Maximinus from a distance.

Our carts were all ready for departure, but these words suddenly changed everything. Immediately all the delegates washed and put their togas. Even our captain polished his sword and helmet, waxed his pointed moustache, and arranged his hair to cover his bald spot. And as they assembled, they began a heated argument as to how Attila should be addressed.

'Almighty king, the most honourable of all kings,' Priscus suggested.

Vigilas opposed this. 'It's enough to say *"almighty prince"*,' he said. 'Since Attila hasn't been crowned yet, he is no king – only chief prince.'

'It's all the same thing,' Maximinus answered. 'We had better address him ten ranks above his status rather than one below it!'

I didn't hear how the argument went on. I was thinking of that lovely butterfly of death, that slender girl who seemed to walk on air! What deep, penetrating eyes she had! And there was something so dignified about her. Oh, you poor, crazy Deel; young ladies like that are not reared for stableboys!

From among the tents Chath appeared, calling, 'Come on, then: the king awaits you,' and in his eyes one could read the proud thought, 'For this you can thank me and me alone!'

The delegation mounted their horses. Of the servants, I was the only one allowed to follow. My master's ink bottle and pens were tied to my belt, and I carried paper under my arm. I approached the royal tent apprehensively. So, I thought, I am about to gaze on the great cannibal!

In front of the tents, besides the guards with their shining weapons, there were some few people wearing crowns. What sort of kings were these? I only learned later, but they were *real* kings. At any other time Attila treated them as his friends, but when he gave audience to envoys they had to stand in front of his entrance, crowns and all!

When we entered I was expecting some dazzling sight. Attila would surely be dressed as some gilded barbarian god; he would be awaiting us on a throne made of gold bars, in ermine cloak, feet bare to display the diamond rings on his toes – I could hardly restrain myself from laughing.

But everything turned out differently from the way we imagined it. We entered a small, unornamented room which was filled with a cool smell, perhaps of Russian leather. In the middle, seated in an unpainted armchair, was a black-bearded man of medium height. He wore a brown hair-cloth jerkin and yellow boots. His elbow rested on a sword covered with black velvet. His dark glance from those small eyes was riveted on us from the moment we entered.

At first I didn't think this could be Attila, but it was. Around him stood his commanders: Edecon, Orestes, Chath, and three more, all of them ruddy, healthy animals; but Attila himself looked rather pale.

Our envoys bowed deeply in front of him – and remained in that position. They were waiting for him to say something, but he remained silent, and they didn't dare even to greet him. About as much time as it takes to say the Lord's Prayer passed like this: Attila sitting motionless as a marble statue – indeed, his yellow complexion was like marble, too – our envoys bent over, as if nursing a pain in their stomachs.

At last Chath said, 'Speak!'

Maximinus straightened up, and out of his toga produced the emperor's sealed letter.

'Almighty king, lord of nations, glorious prince . . .' His voice trembled – I wouldn't have believed it! The proud and haughty Maximinus, who always stood so erect, as if his spine were made of steel! 'Our lord the emperor,' he went on, 'sends his regards and wishes you good health.' Vigilas translated it all in one breath:' . . . wishes you good health.'

Attila, looking straight in front of him, said, 'I wish him exactly what he wishes me.' His voice was like the drone of a big wasp buzzing round and

round in a closed room. It was a fearful voice. Only months later did I understand the shadow that lay across his words when he said, 'I wish him exactly what he wishes me.'

He accepted the letter from Maximinus, and his eyes flashed at Vigilas.

'You insolent cur!' he exploded. 'It was you yourself who translated my will that no envoy should crawl to me until *all* the fugitives were handed over. How dare *you* come before me!' His voice was like a lion's roar now.

Vigilas almost collapsed with fright. The very poles supporting the tent began to tremble. Attila waited for a reply, but Vigilas could only stand there, wax-pale, shifty-eyed, his head hunched between his shoulders, and his palms pressed to his chest.

The dense silence was brokent at last by Edecon: 'Well, have you nothing to say for yourselves? Answer!'

'Almighty king,' stuttered Vigilas, 'the emperor *has* sent you under guard all the fugitives.'

Attila shook his head.

'Lying knaves! If I didn't respect the fact that you are envoys, I'd have you all impaled!' Then, glancing towards a thick-necked young Hun, he said 'Chegge, read the names of the fugitives!'

The scribe untied a bundle of paper scrolls, and in the tense silence read out from one of them about a hundred names.

'I demand these people!' Attila clanked his sword. 'I cannot tolerate the possibility of my own servant taking up arms against me!'

He stood up and walked away toward the inner quarters of the tent. The audience was over. We staggered dizzily outside.

'I don't understand,' said Vigilas, his teeth chattering. 'Attila always received me kindly before. I have never seen him so ready to bite.'

'But, look,' the captain said, choking with anger, 'we can't stand for this! I am a soldier – no one has the right to bawl at me!'

'Challenge him to a duel, then!' Maximinus flashed at him over his shoulder with angry sarcasm.

My master hung his head. 'Now I am convinced,' he said, 'that the barbarians have passed on to Attila Vigilas's remark, that drunken night.'

Edecon accompanied us to our tents. Then he took Vigilas aside, but what they talked about we did not know. Vigilas later *said* that Edecon attributed Attila's anger simply to the question of the fugitives, but in his face it was plain to see that he was lying and terrified.

An hour later, just as we were having lunch, two messengers came to us from Attila. One, with a bushy moustache, was an old gentleman by the name of Eslas. A servant accompanied him with two horses: one to ride on, one to carry baggage. He brought the king's order: Vigilas was to return immediately to Constantinople to collect the remaining fugitives. The rest of us were to wait until the commander-in-chief of the Huns returned from the Akatiri, for whatever presents we had brought for him we could not take back, nor could we give them to anyone else. Until then, Attila strictly forbade us to ransom any Roman prisoners or to buy Hunnish slaves–or to buy anything else for that matter except food.

Vigilas stopped eating. *Immediately,* the order said, so immediately it had to be. His lean, cunning face was pale with confusion. He talked a lot and mounted his horse in such a hurry that one would have thought his task was to make the round trip to Constantinople in fifteen minutes!

The following day the Hunnish camp moved on. We followed them due north. Attila was heading for his capital, but on the way, it was rumoured, he was going to marry a Hunnish girl called Echka.

The army stopped near the village where the Hunnish girl lived, but we weren't able to see the wedding, for Attila's order was that we should go on ahead.

Three Huns were our guides. I got talking with one of them, the very first day. I asked him if he knew what had happened to Deel, Chath's servant.

'Yes, I know,' he replied calmly.

'What, then?'

He shrugged his shoulders: 'They put him out to dry, the same day he arrived.'

'To dry? – how?'

The Hun laughed. 'Come, now, don't be such a blockhead. How is a milk-jug usually set out to dry? On a stake, of course!'

On a dull, gloomy night we came to a little lake. It was so shallow that even a child could have crossed it, but from the hoof-prints on its banks one could see that it was suitable for watering horses. Aged birches and poplars grew everywhere around.

We had hardly finished pounding our tent-poles into the ground when a strong wind sprang up and thunder began to rumble. The wind grew angrier and angrier, and tossed all our tents into the lake. Lightning sizzled, flash after flash, and the claps of thunder were so terrific that the earth trembled.

Frightening weather! Suddenly a thunderbolt struck in our midst with great flames and a deafening blast. It sizzled into the lake. We became so confused that we scattered in all directions, running into the darkness of the night.

I don't know how people picture the road to Hell. If I were a painter, after that night I would paint the damned being chased along in darkness by flashing lightning.

So we ran like frightened hens; and soon, by the flare of the lightning, I saw houses about me, houses with thatched roofs. Dogs rushed at me, barking angrily.

'Help!' I cried, and I could hear that the others were being attacked by other dogs, for they too were screaming for help.

From one of the houses a reddish light appeared; someone held out a bunch of burning reeds and asked, in Hunnish, 'Who are you? What's all the commotion?'

'Good people,' I gasped, out of breath, 'give us some shelter, please! The storm has beaten us to a pulp. Our camp was struck by lightning.'

By then, more and more people were peering out of their houses and tents, each one holding a similar torch made of reeds covered with pitch. They were all staring at us. For these few houses formed a small Hunnish settlement, and between the houses stood the usual tents; the people had retreated into the houses only because of the thunderstorm.

They received us graciously. My master and I were invited in by a Hunnish family with many children. The children were sleeping in the single room of the cottage; for us the master of the house made a fire on the porch, and we began drying ourselves.

My master could hardly stand up. Not only was he drenched, but one knee was bleeding, too; but the Hun had such a terribly angry, fierce look on his face that Priscus, despite his bleeding knee, pulled back from him quickly in terror.

But the man didn't bite. On the contrary, he offered us some bread and bacon, though we weren't hungry. My master wanted only to lie down, and I was busy drying my clothes. The Hun helped me: generously he kept adding reeds to the fire, all the while asking me questions as to who we were and what had brought us to this part of the country.

I learned from him that we were in the village of one of King Buda's widows – King Buda had been Attila's elder brother who had died just recently. He had been the head of the White Huns, as Attila had been head of the Black, but after his death the White Huns, too, had joined Attila.

'And what is the difference between the two?'

'Only the colour of the sheepskins they wear,' our host replied. 'During the summer there is no difference at all.' He himself, he told us, was a White Hun and his name was Zhadan.

That very night, the widow queen learned what sort of visitors the storm had driven into her village, and in less than an hour her servants appeared, bringing bed-sheets and dry bearskins, a jug of wine and a dish of cold wild-boar ham.

'What bliss!' said my master, meaning the warm dry clothing. As for the wine he could find no words to express his thanks, only raised grateful eyes to heaven. He wrapped himself in a bearskin and lay down, and so did I.

Next day, shortly after daybreak, we went back to the lake. There were our tents, swimming about in the water, our horses scattered around. But already the Huns were busy catching the animals and fishing out the tents. To our surprise we found we hadn't lost a thing.

'Well,' my master said, 'I have seen many lands in my time, but so far I have never met people more decent than these. Unpack my best toga: we are going to kiss Lady Buda's hands, even if she does walk around barefoot.'

So the lords set out. They took the queen three silver chalices, three pieces of fine soft leather, and a small casket of Indian peppers, cinnamon,saffron and coconut.

Meanwhile the rest of us cleaned the tents. Under the birches, wherever one stepped, lily-of-the-valley bloomed: I picked a small bunch for my master.

But as our lords stayed away a long time, we decided to poke our noses into the village ourselves. To watch strange people is always entertaining, and for a civilized Greek to have the chance to observe barbarians is a special delight: it is so pleasant to see how much better one is than other people!

In the village the only pretty building was Lady Buda's house. Even that was made of wood, and could be taken apart. It could have had four rooms at the most, but it was surrounded by ten tents, some of them tents of nobility. Among them was a square one with a shining golden sphere on top. Its door was covered with horse-hide, and above this, clutched in a red haircloth hand, were two black swords with a golden sun above.

My eyes opened wide–this was the emblem of the Chath family.

Oh, what was happening to me that my heart pounded so much? What had I to do with that girl? Had she been close enough for me to touch her dress, she would have been farther from me than the world's western edge from the east.

I turned my eyes away and began to scrutinize a group of Huns. Why, I forced myself to wonder, were they for ever on horseback? They talked and they laughed on horseback; they even stretched out full length on their horses, propped up on one elbow, just as we lie on a couch.

But suddenly I caught myself staring at the tent again. A white-bearded old Hun was sitting in front on a piece of bison-hide on the grass; his nose was so caved-in that only by courtesy could one call it a nose at all. One of his hands was missing, too. (Such mutilated veterans I saw often later.)

The old gentleman sat there while two small children played around him: one six years old, with a face already marked with scars; the other, perhaps three, was not yet disfigured.

The elder child had a small turtle-shell shield and wooden sword. The smaller, in nothing but a shirt, just rolled and tumbled around the old gentleman – for he must have been a gentleman, to judge by his hair which he wore in three clumps, one above the forehead, one at each temple. A guard stood in front of the tent, his spear was thrust into the ground and he was leaning on it.

And then I heard a voice from the window, 'Sunshine! My little ray of sunshine!' I felt a sweet tremor down my spine.

The smaller child smiled up at the window, at Emmo standing there.

And in a minute, she too came out; her step was so light she seemed to walk on air. She wore a white dress and red boots; her hair, in one thick braid, fell to her waist.

She brought milk in a small silver cup. Behind her, a barefoot slave girl, about thirteen years old, was carrying some bright orange cakes. The children drank the milk and devoured the cakes with gusto. Emmo sat down on the bison-hide and pulled the little child into her lap. She wiped his mouth clean with a white cloth, and covered his chubby face with loud kisses 'Darling! You darling!'

'Let's go!' I said to my companions. 'Let's go back!'

About midday, our masters came back, escorted by five heavily-laden Hunnish slaves, one carrying a calf across his shoulders, another, a bag of flour, a third, two hares. The lords were in good spirits.

'Zeta,' said my master when I greeted him with the flowers, 'I will release you from your duty of preparing the meal. Go and pick some more lilies-of-the-valley – a lot of them – and take them to the queen this afternoon.'

Well, in less than an hour I had picked a big basketful of the lilies. I picked some violets, too, and blades of grass and a few beautiful ferns, I made an arrangement in the basket, just for my own amusement: the big, shallow basket turned into a bridal bouquet the size of a cart-wheel!

'It's beautiful!' My master was delighted. 'Take it to her as it is, only pick a few more handfuls of grass so that it hangs over the edge and hides the basket completely.'

I was soon ready and placed the basket on my head.

On the way across I vowed that I wouldn't so much as glance at the Chaths' tent. This stood about fifty paces away from the queen's house, a narrow little path leading up to it, curving like a horseshoe. The path was all muddy from the rain.

What business of mine is that tent? I thought: No, I won't even look at it! But by the time I was half way there, I was arguing that there was no reason why I shouldn't look once more. I'd never see her again, anyway...

I lifted the basket off my head, as if I were stopping to take a rest, took it under one arm and turned towards the tent.

The young slave girl, who had brought out the cakes for the children in the morning, was there, scattering the path with dry sandy earth from a basket; but she hadn't enough, and her sprinkling covered only about a third of the path, so she returned to the tent for more.

It was then that Emmo stepped outside. She wore the same dress as before, though now her hair was covered with a long white veil that trailed behind her. She gathered up her skirt and, stepping carefully, started to walk along the path towards me. Towards *me!*

If I close my eyes, even today I can see those two little red boots stepping along so lightly and that tender little peachblossom face, with those beautiful dreamy black eyes... I can see her drawing near, and nearer, coming towards me, step by step...

When she came to the still muddy part of the path, she halted like a doe in the woods, her head lifted. She was waiting for the maid: to scold her, perhaps, for not having finished her sprinkling, or perhaps just to have it finished.

I felt as though someone had nudged me! I dipped my hand into my basket and scattered flowers in front of her. I didn't even look at her, as if what I was doing had nothing to do with her; I just went on, shaking the basket and scattering flowers over the mud of the path.

I had enough flowers to reach right up to the steps of the queen's house.

There I stopped. My face was burning, as if I stood at the mouth of a blazing oven; I could hear my heart pounding. I didn't dare look up, but stood there as if I were up before a judge for some crime.

Then I heard her approaching, over the flowers, and then I did look at her. She too looked up when she reached me.

The sun shines through the leaves of the trees like that. The rays from her eyes shone deep into my soul, and my soul filled at once with light and music. Sadly – but happily, too – I watched her, dazzled.

But her glance rested on me only for a minute; then she picked her way up the steps and I looked after her dazed. Only after she had disappeared did it occur to me that a Hun could have killed me with one blow for what I had done.

But no one touched me. The horsemen went on talking, unconcerned; the old guard had watched but he didn't seem interested. Perhaps he thought that I was obeying orders.

I started on my way back, feeling rather light-headed. At the edge of the village I heard a child's voice calling out, 'Hey, hey! Servant!'

I turned and there was the little slave girl who had been sprinkling the path for Emmo, waving to me.

'Do you speak Hun?' she asked, out of breath.

'I do,' I replied, like a man just waking, 'a little.'

'My young lady says come back. She'll give you something for your service.' She laughed. She was a homely, skinny little brown-haired girl, with a smudge on her face – a cheeky little thing!

'Tell your young lady,' I said, with all my dignity, 'that I am no servant. True, I'm not a gentleman, either – but I am *not* a servant. And my name is Zeta.'

With that, I proudly turned and walked away.

When I arrived back, the lords were already reclining at dinner, and the smell of roast veal filled the air. Priscus questioned me with a look. We knew one another's thoughts so well that at times we had no need for speech. His look asked, 'What did the queen say? Was she pleased with the flowers?'

Now, no lie had ever before passed my lips. Priscus had taught me so well that I had an abhorrence of lies. But, 'The queen,' I replied, looking over his head, 'though she didn't speak to me personally, sends her thanks.'

I was expecting the very earth to tremble, hearing my lie, or my tongue to be torn out by the root – but neither happened. The lords carried on gaily with their conversation, so I too sat down in front of the tent to have my dinner, feeling strangely confused and guilty.

That night, I slept poorly. My master was restless, too. He had been restless ever since we first came to Hunnish territory. Mine had begun only when I saw that girl, and since then I had no peace, day or night. Suddenly, about midnight, when I thought he was fast asleep, my master spoke.

'What's the matter with you?' he asked: 'Why are you crying? Has someone hurt you?'

His question took me by surprise, and for a few minutes I could say nothing. 'Oh, my lord,' I said at last, 'I am most unhappy!'

'Who has hurt you?' and as I didn't answer, he sat up in bed: 'I can assure you, whoever it was will be sorry!'

'No one has hurt me, my lord. I was only thinking about my lot in life.'

'Your lot?' he repeated, astonished. 'Is your lot really so miserable, then, that you have to cry about it?'

'Don't misunderstand me, sir! Your goodness is lifegiving sunshine to me, and I don't deserve a scrap of your attention. But when I think how I was sold into slavery as a child, I realize that you have given me my freedom in vain, and that, really, I am just a poor devil still...'

I stopped. I sensed my master's bewilderment as he listened to me, and I felt I was talking nonsense.

After a silence he said, 'I thought I knew you, Zeta, my son; for I have watched you grow just as I have watched that cypress which I planted the day I bought you. But at this moment, I don't recognize you, Zeta. I don't understand what is causing this turmoil in your soul.' He fell silent.

While he slept I lay thinking up lies for the next day. I'd say that I had a nightmare...

Meanwhile, I watched the stars through the opening of the tent. And I saw Emmo... For if I close my eyes, I see her always. I see her in a white skirt and red boots, picking her way with tiny steps along the path; and as she reaches me, she turns her beautiful, magnificent dark eyes upon me...

Dawn had hardly broken when the sound of horns woke us. Maximinus had decided to continue our journey at daybreak. With a headache after a nearly sleepless night, I tied our bedding bundles and helped with the packing of our tent; but after that I still had just enough time to go for a swim in the lake and I came back refreshed.

Then we mounted. We passed in front of the queen's palace, but I, of course, wasn't looking at any queen's palace. Carts stood in front of Chath's tent. The slaves were taking it apart and rolling it up on the long poles; the inside rugs had already been packed into huge bundles, weighing down the camels that stood waiting. So the Chaths, too, were coming! Perhaps they would take the same road!

At first I was jubilant; then I tried to knock some sense into myself. Had I gone crazy, devoting my soul's every thought to a girl who was practically guarded by the executioner himself? And yet, on the way, I fell behind again and again. At every turn of the road I stopped and looked back to see if they were coming. My efforts to talk sense to myself were in vain. Time after time I made up my mind to stay beside my master and just forget about the girl, yet in a little while I would feel an invisible hammer pounding in my chest. Just once more! Only once more let me absorb her with my eyes, as the sun absorbs the dew, so that even in the long night of my grave she could be my dream! Were they coming yet? I fell behind my master again and rode in the opposite direction – back to meet her! I just *had* to see her, even if it meant losing my master's trail! I *had* to see her – even if I ended up like Deel. I *had* to see her, once more!

I had been riding for about three hours. The sun was shining on the green spring world from an almost cloudless sky. Storks flew zigzag over the river. At last I caught sight of the Hunnish servants slowly ambling along with the carts. In front rode a few armed Huns, the sunshine sparkling on the studs of their reins like sizzling iron on a blacksmith's anvil.

Next followed a cart covered in velvety carpet, four horses pulling it. Lady Chath and the old Hun sat inside with the thin little slave girl and the two children opposite them. (I discovered later that Lady Chath was Emmo's stepmother.) Beside them rode Emmo on horseback and some twenty slaves followed.

I approached them at a slow pace, and when I reached them I dismounted and stood respectfully by the side of the road.

'What's the matter?' one Hun shouted: 'Have you lost something?' for from my clothes they recognized me as one of the Roman delegation.

'Yes,' I answered politely, 'we have lost one of our tent-fasteners. Have you seen it, by any chance?' And as the Chaths' carriage passed by, I bowed deeply. When it had gone by I raised my head and looked at the girl. She straddled her horse as a man would, but her skirt was so long that it covered the horse's body from head to tail. She had a turban-like headdress of some light material and a transparent white silk veil.

When I looked up she averted her eyes, and her horse moved slowly on. But that horse seemed to know whom it was carrying and picked up its feet proudly.

I continued to go back for a while, then I turned and followed them, examining the hoof-prints left on the road, pretending to myself I could tell which had been made by Emmo's horse. In an hour, the waters of the River Tisia once more glimmered in the distance, and the road almost vanished in the tall grass; the Tisia wound across the fields like an endless snake, and in places the water was hidden from sight by dense clumps of willows.

I was happy, because even from this far away I could keep Emmo in sight all the time. The lovely rider with the white turban proceeded among the company, floating like some sort of water-lily.

I noticed her suddenly wheel off the road so as to give her horse a run in the fields. For long stretches she would gallop, then just trot in circles for a while; she would rush ahead, then lag behind. Once she raced right down to the water and gave her horse a drink. And all this while my heart sang like an ascending skylark. I could feel that the girl was performing for me!

I stopped near the bank, where the willows grew, and – just as I hoped – I saw her coming straight towards me. She was almost flying, leaning forward in the saddle. Flying–in my direction!

I got off my horse, to greet her once more; and as I stood there with burning eyes, she arrived and reined in her horse.

I bowed.

'Slave!' She spoke haughtily. 'Is your name Zeta?'

'Yes, my lady.'

And so that her horse should not prance restlessly, I took hold of its bridle. She was looking at me. Her gaze was so majestic and so bewitching that my soul trembled within me like a sparrow caught in the hand.

Still looking at me, she asked: 'Was it you, then, who sprinkled my path with flowers?'

'The path was muddy,' I said, apologizing, 'the mud was very deep there.'

'And why wouldn't you accept a reward?'

'I didn't deserve one. And besides, I am no slave. I serve my master out of love, because he has been my father in place of my father...'

I stuttered all kinds of gibberish. She just watched me calmly, severely.

'But I cannot be your debtor,' she said. 'Stop by my mother as you ride past. I have already told her what you did; accept what she gives you.'

'Forgive me, my lady,' I said, bowing again, 'I would obey your word in everything, as an order – to my death, if you so wish. But *that* I cannot do. If you do not want to be my debtor... please let me touch the border of your gown with my lips.'

She made no answer; perhaps she was thinking what to say. So I bent my knee and kissed her gown with happy devotion.

And as my gaze fell upon her hand, I whispered dazedly, 'Oh, if I might only kiss your hand also – your lovely hand!'

'Insolent!' she snapped, lightning flashing from her eyes. 'Insolent dog!' – and with her riding whip she struck me across the face.

I fell backwards. The blow burned like fire; I could feel blood trickling down my neck.

The girl let her horse amble its own way, but I sat down at the edge of the road, just staring ahead of me stupidly, without thought. My heart had become a millstone going round slowly in my chest.

Whether I sat like this for half an hour or an hour, I don't know. The entire world turned topsy-turvy in my mind. What had I done wrong? Was it such a crime to kiss a hand? Even *her* hand was only a hand. Kissing someone's hand surely implied respect? I had grown a bit dizzy. Her beauty had cast a spell on me and I had wanted to kiss her hand – was that a crime? Our ways would have parted afterwards, anyway. Perhaps we never would have met again in this life; we would even have forgotten one another.

The pounding of horse's hoofs ended my reverie. At first I thought it was my own horse careering about, but it wasn't: he was still grazing. No, it was the girl returning.

She stopped in front of me, but I didn't look up. Anger flashed through me like lightning across brooding clouds. She had insulted my manhood! Had she been the daughter of Jupiter and I only a calf, she still had no cause to hit me as she had done!

'Zeta,' she said softly, 'you are a good boy. It's not your fault that you are stupid. In your country the customs may be different... Here, wrap this around your face –'

She tore off a piece of her veil and held it out to me.

I didn't reply. I didn't even look at her.

For a minute she went on holding out the piece of veil; then she threw it down, and I could hear her slap her horse and ride away.

Let her! What right had she to despise me so? The king of the Huns was no king of mine, the Hunnish lords were not my lords. And even if she said she was sorry for what she had done, the scar would remain on my face. No, *I* would despise *her* – and I trudged slowly to the water and washed the blood off my face.

The sound of hoofs again. I glanced up: she was coming back. I got up and looked at her, fiercely determined.

She approached and tossed back her veil.

'I came back,' she said warmly, 'because you are angry with me. I cannot bear the thought of anyone being angry with me – not even an animal. So... here is my hand: you *may* kiss it.'

'Thank you,' I answered proudly, 'but I do not wish to any more.'

All the colour drained from her. She looked at me darkly, proud and defiant, but I returned the look. And for a moment we stood like this. Then she tugged at the reins, slapped the horse, and slowly ambled away.

At noon the next day the Chaths' caravan caught up with ours. Probably they had strated earlier; we had been held up for a while because one of our horses had tired.

Our lords lined up the horses beside the road and greeted the Chaths with a bow. I stood not with the servants but beside my master.

As yesterday, Emmo was on horseback. The only change in her dress was in her turban – she had rolled it up higher and stuck three heron feathers in it.

If only I were a painter and could portray that graceful girl as she rode up on horseback! Her mount was a small, nervous bay. Her sky-blue silk cloak fluttered around her lovely figure. Her little red boots rested in small gilded stirrups.

I have tried to draw her often, on tables as well as on paper. I am not bad at sketching. I only become bad when I try draw *her*. I can never get it right – neither her nor her horse... And yet I can see her so vividly, as cleary as I see myself when I look into a mirror.

They passed by us, returning our greeting. Emmo, too, tossed back her veil and gracefully nodded in the direction of the envoys – and I could *feel* her eyes glide across the company and the shock when she looked at me, coldly piercing through me with her gaze. By then I no longer hated her. I was sorry that I had refused to kiss her hand. In a dream our meeting repeated itself, and there I *did* kiss her hand – it filled me with such delight as I had never felt before. The sweetness of that dream-kiss remained on my lips. Now, when I saw her, I felt the delight of the dream anew.

How oddly the human face is made! Hers was immobile, so was mine. When she glanced at me, she probably thought my impassive face hid hate. But what did hers hide?

After that we never caught up with the Chaths again.

On the seventh day, in the distance across a wheatfield, we caught sight of a group of people on the road, dressed in white togas fluttering in the wind.

'They are Romans!' we cried – with joy, though at home we wouldn't even spit on Romans!

They were, indeed, the envoys of the Western Roman Empire. Strangers. But in that infinitely flat Hunnish country we greeted them as if we were all the children of one mother.

'Salvus sis! Salve!'

The gentlemen embraced one another. The servants shook hands. The talk went on now in Latin.

The leader of the envoys was Romulus, a brown-haired gentleman with a hollow face and protruding nose. With him were Romanus, the chief officer, kindly and cheerful, with a jet-black moustache, and Promotus, governor of Pannonia, a grey-haired, balding nobleman.

Their mission was as troublesome as our own: Attila had demanded certain pieces of gold-ware from the Roman Emperor, and Valentinian* would have gladly given him as many as he wished; but Attila wanted only those which had disappeared during the siege of Sirmium. The thief had been one of Attila's own scribes, who had wheedled these golden treasures out of the Bishop of Sirmium on some far-fetched pretence, and then had pawned them with a Roman money-lender by the name of Silvanus. When Attila had learned of the theft, he had his scribe immediately impaled, then sent his ultimatum to Valentinian: either Silvanus or the gold-ware must be given up!

So the Romans we met were bringing the reply. Valentinian was sending word that Silvanus had paid for the things in good faith; and as they were the

* Valentinian was the emperor of the Western Empire as Theodosius was of the Eastern Empire.

property of the Church, he would like to offer money in exchange – if that were possible.

So the two delegations, conversing pleasantly, arrived together at Attila's chief city.

I call it a city, though it was unlike any of the world's other cities. It had no churches, no marble palaces, no stone buildings, no paved roads. Out of a multitude of tents, only two permanent structures stood out, both situated on hill-tops, and both built of wood. They were yellow and even had spires, but these were so slender and airy that only pigeons or kites could have lived in them.

'What are those buildings?' I asked.

'The first is Attila's house,' our guide told me – pronouncing the name 'Attila' with reverence. 'The other is the commander-in-chief's.'

The two palaces were surrounded by a multi-coloured jungle of tents. Ten thousand! A hundred thousand? A million? Nobody could possibly count them! Amid the tents a few houses showed white, but these were only made of mud, with thatched roofs, and no one lived in them – at least, not during the summer. Stacks of hay and straw towered around each tent.

On the outskirts of the town we saw a few hundred blacksmiths, dirty with ash: all day they were busy hammering away, shaping horseshoes and arrowheads in a pungent smoke of burnt hoofs and tar. Out in the fields countless horses grazed, along with flocks of sheep and herds of cattle. Dogs dashed out at us, and children kept getting in our way at every turn.

The commander-in-chief, for whose return we had been told to wait, was back already. A red flag waved from the top of his palace, a signal that he was at home – as those Huns explained who had ridden out to meet us.

Where were we to pitch our tents? The guides wanted to take us into the middle of the city, but our lords thought it more proper to stay outside until the right place had been pointed out by one of the Hunnish chiefs; so we halted our carts, and stretched out a sheet of canvas to give some shade.

The first thing to do was to find out when the commander-in-chief would grant us an audience, so three of us – my master, Rusticius, and I – mounted our horses and followed a guide into the town. Only then did I realize why Attila's town was so huge. The tents stood beside one another, but not at all close. They were spread out, with a good-sized clearing in front of each, as well as behind, where there were stacks of hay and straw and firewood. In the front, women cooked, baked, and nursed their children; often a cow and a couple of horses would graze there, too. In front, also, they dried clothes, and here was a pole driven into the ground on which they would hang their jugs and pots to dry. The tent itself served only as a place in which to sleep or to shelter from the rain; during the day the time was spent outside. The children played outside, women and slaves worked outside, even the old and the invalids lay about outside on the bare ground or, at best, on some animal skins.

But the men gathered in groups in the streets on horseback – always on horseback; they never worked, only talked, discussed politics, traded a little, hunted now and then, ran races, and organized war-games or drills for their boys. And of course they ate and drank a lot – mainly drank!

It was also interesting how, from the placing of the tents, one could tell how large a family inhabited it. Sometimes two or three tents stood in a group, close to one another: the smaller ones were occupied by newly-weds, one of whom came from the bigger tent – but members of the same family all used the same kitchen.

The closer we came to the king's palace, the more ornate and spacious the tents became. Made on four-, five-, or six-cornered wide wooden frames, covered with animal hides or thick hair-cloth, they displayed on their tops, or above their entrances, emblems or symbolic figures. These symbols consisted mostly of one single picture: a stork, a horse's head, a star, a rose, a cross, a circle. Sometimes the family's emblem wasn't embroidered on the tent but the object itself was hung there: an arrow, for instance, or a ram's head, or a horseshoe. From this it was obvious that here lived the Horseshoe family, there the Rams, or the Arrows. . . . Only when the emblem was hung out on a pole it was not the emblem of a family but the sign of a business: the cobbler hung out a sandal; the tent-maker, two crossed poles; the carpenter, an adze; the bow-maker, a bow, painted red; the furrier, a small sheepskin coat; the armourer, a sword; the blacksmith, a horseshoe – though many of the Huns never had their horses shod.

Crowds of slaves also milled about these central tents, and altogether the splendour here was dazzling – as well it might be: were not these people plundering half the world!

Among the horsemen were many with their heads or arms bandaged. One of them called out to our guide, 'God give you strength, Stag!'

'And health to you!' Stag answered. 'It's good to see you again!' They shook hands and talked.

'They've just got back from the war with the Akariti,' our guide told us as we rode on.

'And you?' I asked. 'Why didn't you go to war with them?'

'They wouldn't let me,' he answered. 'Only the worthless went to *that* war.

The cream of the fighting men had to stay at home, so that if our master decided to set out against the Romans there would be strength enough available.'

Hearing this, we shivered.

'Is Attila planning something like this, then?' we asked.

'He hasn't said so – but we know. Isn't most of the world under our heels already? All that is left standing is the Roman Empire.'

'And you think you'll be able to overpower it? It's not as small a nation as the Akatiri, you know!'

The Hun shrugged his shoulders: 'Small or large, it's all the same. The sword of God is in our hands – no man-made sword can ever defeat it.'

'What "sword of God"?'

'Don't you know? A sword was once dropped from heaven. It was found by a young herdsman. Whenever we start out on a big campaign, Attila takes along that sword.'

'But what makes you think it is really the sword of God?'

'What makes *you* think it isn't?'

'Well, but supposing it isn't...'

'Our shamans know that it is. That sword is so beautiful, no human hand could possibly have made it. Blue flames sprang from the earth all around that sword until the boy found it. Even Kama says it is heaven-sent.'

'And who is Kama?'

'Our head priest. Now *there's* a saint for you! – more of a saint than your pope, any day.'

The talk was drowned at this point by the skirl of bagpipes and the squealing of shawms. Sound of music rose from the tents in every direction. A Hunnish lad rode towards us, making his horse dance; three pipers followed him, two playing shawms, the third a bagpipe. The boy was singing, lifting his flask high, and generally enjoying himself.

'That one's in high spirits!' I said to the guide.

'Probably he's just sold a prisoner,' he answered, with indifference.

My attention was now drawn to the great amount of greenery arriving in carts, and as we reached the wide main road of the town, I saw that the tops and the doors of the tents were being decorated with green branches and the dusty road was being sprinkled with plenty of water. Also, trees were being set up in holes dug on either side of the road; the air smelled of wet earth and fresh leaves.

'Tell me,' I said to the guide, 'what are all these festive preparations for?'

'Attila will be arriving about noon,' he said.

Now I could view the two wooden palaces at close hand. Both were masterpieces of carpentry and wood-carving. Attila's was rather more ornate; close up, it proved to be a whole cluster of buildings. The centre one was the king's; the ones around it belonged to his wives, or to captive kings, to learned men, or to prisoners. A little way back stood a few quite plain buildings, and these were the stables: one for the king's horses, one for those of his wives, the third for the rest of the household's.

There were about thirty buildings altogether, twenty of them for the nobility. In the midst of the wooden structures stood a large, whitewashed stone building. My master marvelled at it, for in all our weeks of walking we had seen no stone or rock. Later, we found out that this stone house was a bath, and that it had been built by a slave from Sirmium, the stones having been brought here on carts from far away.

Between the commander's headquarters and the royal palace was a circular space large enough perhaps for holding horseraces. There was nothing within it except a very old linden tree beneath which stood a mechanical pump, and from this point, looking eastward, a wide street began. One could see down it to a forest of willows which marked the course of the Tisia.

We found the commander-in-chief in his yard, on horseback, addressing at least fifty young noblemen. They were in sumptuous costumes of fluttering white silk with close-fitting doublets of red, blue, or yellow, adorned with rows of gold buttons; even the horses were decked out in veil-like streamers. These young men were being briefed for the celebration; as soon as the commander-in-chief finished his speech, they set off from the courtyard at a fast gallop.

The commander-in-chief was a stocky, red-faced man, a grey-haired replica of Chath, but this brother was somewhat shorter, and his face was more friendly. He noticed us, rode up, and signed to us not to dismount.

'I have already been told of your coming,' he said shaking hands with my master. 'Be my guests. Stay with us and have dinner with us today. I've a thousand things to do: the king will be here by noon, and I've got to welcome him.'

By now I could understand every word that was spoken. I could have acted as interpreter in place of Rusticius.

My gaze wandered to the inner yard and was caught there. In front of the wide wooden buildings were the Chaths, unloading their camels and carts. Their house-servants were scurrying busily about, and that little brown-haired slave girl was shouting up at a window, 'Hurry down! Hurry!'

I saw Emmo, too. She was just dismounting.

A slave crouched on hands and knees beside the horse, and she stepped down onto him. She patted the horse's muzzle, and, light as air, walked into the house.

*T*he town was buzzing like a hive of swarming bees. Everywhere slaves were sprinkling water on the roads and scattering leaves and grass. Men and women stood in front of the tents, giving last-minute touches to their best clothes. The tails and manes of all white horses had been dyed red or yellow. Tents were being decked, on all sides, with flowered carpets. Everywhere, clouds of dust, scent of greenery, and manure, and the tinkling of horse-bells.

We hurried along with Maximinus to the commander-in-chief's palace – we must be on time! One of the servants led us to a big room on the second floor, and from the open window we could look down on the main road, and on the open space between the two palaces. I, of course, looked only from behind the backs of the gentlemen. The bustle out there grew more and more lively till, about noon, the horsemen cleared out the main road and white-clad women appeared.

The sun had just climbed to the middle of the sky, when a loud fanfare sounded from the steeple of the royal palace.

A few minutes later, three galloping horsemen came stirring up the dust and the commander-in-chief rode out to meet them. About thirty young Huns, all noblemen, followed him closely; among these were five lads who had golden bands on their hats – the youngest of them was about fourteen or fifteen, and he was dressed in sky-blue silk.

'The king's sons,' Rusticius told us.

The commander set out with them to meet Attila, and in about half an hour we could hear a glad murmur from the crowd in the distance. At first it was like the roar of the sea, but as it grew louder there seemed really nothing one could compare it with – as though the very earth had a heart that beat with joy.

By this time, a group of women had come out from the royal palace. They were all in white silk and riding horses all shades of brown like autumn leaves–each horse led by a page. These women gathered around a large gilded carriage, the shape of half a walnut shell, within which sat a queenly lady, pale and thin, with a little ten-year-old boy beside her. He too was dressed in white silk, like the women, and had long hair and a hat of sky-blue which contrasted with the fairness of his hair.

'The head queen: Lady Rika,' Rusticius whispered. 'The child's name is Chaba.'

The delighted crowd began to shout, 'Bless you, Chaba! Bless you!' (The Huns say 'Bless you!' as we say *'Vivat!'*–'Long live'.) The child Chaba, smiling, waved in every direction with his hat.

I heard later why they paid special attention to this particular prince. At his birth the priests had prophesied that though the Hunnish people would be scattered after Attila's death, 'like chaff in the wind', this prince, Chaba, would save the nation. And if no one really believed the prophecy, still the little prince was popular; everyone was glad to see the boy.

Among those fairy-like creatures riding beside the queen I recognized Emmo. Oh, my heart, ascend to heaven! It rose and soared as long as the carriage was in sight. Alas, they sped on fast enough, till the whole dream-group had vanished . . . .

Then the royal wedding procession came into view! Golden dust-fog billowed in the sunshine, and out of it came first a soldier with a curly moustache, carrying a large white flag on which fluttered an eagle embroidered in gold. Next, a band of musicians a hundred strong, on foot and all dressed in red. Their instruments were wooden shawms and drums, all kinds of whistles made of bone, two large brass cymbals, sticks with tiny bells attached to them.

Hunnish music sounds strange to a Roman ear, but it's good for marching to. I've so often heard the glad tune they played on the streets that day that it's not difficult to jot it down now.

A swarm of slave children ran around the musicians, capering and enjoying the music, one even turning cartwheels. On the heels of the band came horsemen, glittering with gold and silver.

'Bless you!' The noisy storm of joy swelled as Attila came into sight on his tall white horse. Little Prince Chaba now rode on the right of Attila, on his left, the commander-in-chief, with the other princes behind them. Then came the women: inside Lady Rika's gilded carriage sat the new wife, heavily veiled. Her green wreath was made of rose-leaves, but among them gleamed diamonds the size of hazel-nuts.

The women-folk of all the Hunnish leaders stood in front of the commander-in-chief's palace, under a wide green awning.

As Attila approached, he touched his hand to his hat and waved a greeting but did not smile.

Amid all the happy faces and shining eyes only Attila's remained unmoved like marble. A group of singing girls gathered around him and around the queens, and there was Emmo, smiling with the rest. She didn't look at me – she couldn't possibly have seen me, because of the linden tree that stood in front of the house – but in spite of this, because she was smiling, my heart was overcome with joy, so that I smiled, too. At that moment, I felt I loved Attila, loved the Hunnish people, the smell of horses, the merry-making, the sun and the earth – I would have liked to kiss everybody, the horses included!

Then Attila and the whole long wedding procession moved on.

The Chaths retired into the palace but went on watching the fun from the balcony. We stayed on too.

It was well past noon when Chath came out to invite our lords to dine with the commander-in-chief. The commander himself could not be with us at dinner, for he had to report to Attila on the late war, but his wife and family would be there.

'And so shall I,' said Chath.

Will Emmo be there? I wondered. My heart grew heavy, and I looked at my master: would he order me to stand behind him? During celebration feasts I had to stand behind him and he, according to Roman custom, would wipe his fingers in my hair.

God, be merciful! What if he should order me so to serve him now? How could I say to him, 'Sir, just this once, let me be absent!' I couldn't say that, because in public every gentleman has his servant as his chief ornament.

Priscus, as if he had understood my worry, called me to him and said, 'In an hour's time, bring in a plateful of dates on our most beautiful silver platter. Stand with it where Maximinus will be sitting – he'll take it from you.'

So he wouldn't be needing me after all!

I quickly arranged the dates, setting them neatly on bay leaves, with a few little flowers among them, then gave all my attention to myself: water, comb, and scented ointment! Let my master scold me for taking his finest nard, rather than have him wipe his fingers in my hair!

When the hour-glass showed that the hour had nearly passed, I picked up the platter and took it upstairs. The door of the dining-room stood open; the smell of roast meat drifting through it. There were at least twenty people at the table. The commander's wife was at the head, a blotchy-faced woman glittering with jewellery. On her right was Maximinus, on her left my master, then the other men and women in mixed order. Emmo was there, too.

For a moment, while I stood in the doorway waiting for my master to see me my eyes lingered on Emmo. A freckled girl next to her was chattering away while Emmo worked at a chicken leg with a mother-of-pearl knife. She had an air of great concentration.

My master made notes every day on all that he saw and heard. Later he would write a book from them which would be placed in the Imperial Library. The notes, naturally, were always in my handwriting: on little pieces of paper I jotted down everything that happened to us; my master would dictate occasionally, but not often. Once we got home again, we were going to arrange all the notes, and then I would make a fair copy on splendid white parchment.

This day there was so much to write about that I didn't even wait till my master got back, but started on my own. It was late when he did return, and it was a pleasant surprise for him to find me in front of the tent with my writing-pad.

'You are a good boy,' he praised me. 'How far have you got?' and from his pocket he produced a poppy-seed pastry the size of my fist; when I was still a child, he would often spoil me by bringing home a cake or pastry for me and I was always glad; but now, for the first time, his thoughtfulness made me sad – I was a child no longer!

'I've reached the point,' I answered, kissing his hand for the pastry, 'where Attila goes through the open gates of his palace, stops at the threshold, picks the new wife up in his arms and carries her inside as if she were a child.'

'Read me what you've written so far.'

So I read; and when I got to the part that described the Hunnish queen and her attendants, I began to read as if I were reciting poetry: 'They were like a large flock of white pigeons. Hunnish women are angels. There is one among them so beautiful that the earth trembles with ecstasy wherever she walks....'

'What sort of silly rubbish is this?' said Priscus with a grunt.

I could only stammer.

'Cross it out! Go on!'

Then, as he saw that I had gone scarlet to the ears, he looked at me very oddly.

'Watch out, my son!' he said more calmly, after a short silence. 'You are at a dangerous age. At your time of life many a butterfly will flutter about you. Watch your feet, so as not to lose your head!'

Then he began to talk to Maximinus – I didn't know what about and I certainly didn't care. My breathing began to slow down again, but my master's warning weighed heavily on me. It was all true: I knew nothing about Emmo's soul; it was merely her pretty face that had turned me inside out and upset my judgment. But that girl's body was God's most wonderful creation on earth, more perfect than a flower. No one who is human could turn away and refuse to inhale such a flower's fragrance.

*N*ext day we rose early to take the commander-in-chief his gift from the emperor.

I had to unpack it from its iron-bound crate. It consisted of masterpieces of the goldsmith's craft: five goblets, two large plates and five smaller ones. On the goblets was embossed the story of one of Alexander the Great's hunts, and if the five goblets were turned round and round simultaneously, the hunt came to life: golden people hunting golden beasts in a golden forest! The plates, too, were decorated with exquisite designs: on one, Adam and Eve under the tree; on another, the story of the Flood, and around the rim of each plate were tiny cupids holding hands. All these treasures were contained in a box made of cedar-wood and lined with white velvet, with several yards of pink flowered silk covering it.

As soon as the sun was up, my master, Rusticius, three servants, and I were already waiting in front of the commander's entrance, but the gates were still locked. The household must have been up late the night before, for the music had not stopped until after midnight. Emmo must have been dancing – I wondered with whom, and whether she had danced with the same young men before. I couldn't see into any of the windows of the house because they were covered with thick white curtains to keep out the sun. It would be all for the best anyhow, if that girl didn't show herself!

As we were waiting there, a black-eyed, middle-aged Hun approached. His shirt-sleeves were loose and his weapons ornate. He wore gold chains, like all the rich Huns, he had a tall black haircloth hat with a crane feather in it, his hair in three clumps, and his moustache was like the horns of an ox. A curved sword studded with turquoise dangled at his side – again, the weapon only of rich Huns.

From beneath his black eyebrows he smiled at Priscus.

'Khaire!' (Greetings!) he cried.

'Khaire!' Priscus was amazed. 'Who are you, greeting me in my own language? How did you get here? And how did you become a Hun?'

There were all sorts of nationalities living in the city, but few Greeks, and when we did see a Greek, he was only a slave – from the tousled black hair and torn clothing, one could always tell right away that they were slaves. But *this* Greek was a Hunnish gentleman, gold jingling all over him.

He smiled again. 'Why do you ask?'

'Because,' my master answered, 'you have greeted me in Greek yet your face looks Hunnish – although you have waxed your moustache...'

'Well,' said the stranger, fingering that moustache, 'I am a Hun – but I was born a Greek. They call me Free Greek now; when I was a slave they called me Greek.'

He sighed lightly. 'Truly, my friend, some lives are difficult, and one never knows where one will end up in one's old age.'

He told us how he used to be an oil merchant in Istria. But the Huns had overrun that place, sized all his possessions, and put him in chains. He had become the prisoner of the commander-in-chief, for noblemen like to keep rich captives for themselves. (Why? Well, for one thing, rich people are likely to have rich relations, from whom a high ransom can be demanded. And even if the ransom is not paid, it is still worthwhile to have gentlemen for servants: they are smarter, more attentive, cleverer than peasants. A household's air of nobility, its whole stature, depends very much on the presence of civilized slaves.)

'One never knows, indeed!' Priscus sighed. 'Civilization is dragged here and put in chains, the servant of barbarism!'

The Greek Hun shrugged his shoulders.

'Well... although my relations didn't ransom me, the good God himself did! My master took me with him to the war against the Akatiri. I fought beside him bravely, and a rich haul of loot fell to my share–whereupon I bought my freedom. I married a Hunnish woman. Now I have children–as fine and full of life as anyone could wish! And I sit at the commander's table. Whereas he used to address me by shouting, "Hi, you pig!" now he calls me "Friend", and that's what I am, his friend. And that's why I say, thank God for all the bad luck I had in Istria!'

Priscus shook his head. 'But if you became a free man, weren't you free to return home?'

'Yes – at any time.'

'Then why do you stay among these barbarians?'

'Barbarians, you call them? Why, they are better people than any I know; for when there is no war, here everyone lives at home among his own things undisturbed. I – I do what I want; I pay no taxes. No government official showes his face in at my door; no officer of the law, no bailiffs.'

'But you are at war all the time!'

'Even if we are, a man's life is worth something here, as it isn't with the Romans. In your Empire blood is shed even in time of peace. When you are not fighting wars you have trouble with bandits; and even if there aren't bandits, there are the *official* bandits; bailiffs and government officers. In the Roman Empire the rich and powerful live *above* the law; justice is meted out for money, and in the everlasting law-suits the judge and the lawyers bleed their clients white.'

Priscus defended the Romans as well as he could, but the Hun just waved and nodded: 'Have it your own way then! But it's still true that wherever a ruler turns himself into a god, the fate of the people is hell!'

He was a soft-spoken, kindly man; when he left us, he shook hands even with me.

Meanwhile a slave opened the gates and told us that the commander was about to come out, so instead of going in we waited for him in the courtyard. Soon his horse was brought out, then he himself appeared. It was only now that we noticed how short and bow-legged he was. But then Huns are most of them short and bow-legged: it's only on horseback they look so magnificent; on foot they waddle like ducks.

We bowed and Priscus stepped forward. He said that the East Roman envoy was here and sent greetings, and that in this cedar-wood casket was the emperor's gift. Now he asked that a time and a place might be chosen for a meeting.

I observed the victorius commander with interest: he had eyes like a watchful dog's, but his face was smiling, and it was an intelligent face.

'A time and a place? Well, if the business is so important, why not now, this moment, and at his own quarters?' he answered simply. 'You ride ahead, and I'll catch you up.'

Well, I thought, these people don't stand on ceremony as our noblemen do.

The commander-in-chief didn't even look at the gift, but had it sent up to his wife; we hurried away to give Maximinus time to put on his best toga – but there *wasn't* time: the commander arrived on our heels, shouting a friendly good morning.

Maximinus started to mutter some sort of welcoming speech, but the commander pushed him down into a chair, and when he understood that Maximinus was about to speak words in his praise he interrupted, 'Save your breath, my good man – I know who and what I am!'

Then, as if he were one of us, he began to describe some of his victories in the east, and told how, with the joy, a little sorrow had been mingled: Prince Aladar had fallen off his horse while fighting, and another horse had stepped on his arm.

At last Maximinus struck the right note, and with quite unpretentious words he said that the emperor would like a lasting peace, but that all this sending of small delegations backwards and forwards made agreement impossible. Couldn't the commander-in-chief himself come to the emperor? The treasures in the cedar casket were only samples of what awaited him in Constantinople.

The Hunnish dignitary blinked, then shook his head. 'That's not going to be easy,' he said.

'But my lord,' Maximinus went on, fanning the spark of interest, '*your* words would not be just empty chatter, like the speech of other envoys. If you could only come to us, the two empires might put a seal upon an eternal treaty. And this wouldn't benefit only our two nations, but your own family, too. The emperor would be your friend until death, and from his golden apple tree something would drop even into your grandchildren's laps.'

The commander shook his head. 'No. It's impossible. Even were I to go myself I could speak only with Attila's lips. If I said anything out of my own mouth, I should be forgetting that Attila is my master and that all Huns live together, even in the next world.' He lifted his head and looked us over calmly. 'Believe me,' he said, 'I would rather be a servant in Attila's shadow than a nobleman, however rich, in the sunshine of Roman favour. But in any case, I can be of more use to you here at home: it could even happen that if the king's anger turned against you I could channel it elsewhere.'

Then, apparently bored with politics: 'Do you really want to pitch your tents here? It's a long way from the king's palace, and if it rains the road isn't good.'

'We were about to ask you,' Maximinus answered, 'where we could set up our tents?'

'Nowhere! I will put you up. Your servants will find room in my courtyard, and for yourselves there are three big rooms you can share beside the dining-room.'

But our lords would not accept this favour. They asked permission to put up the tents in the space beside the palace on the big square, and the commander agreed.

As he left our tent, a group of young women with bows and silver quivers rode by us at a fast trot. I supposed they were going hunting, but later I saw just outside the city scarecrow targets had been set up for them. So girls too went for target practice.

Who they were, I don't know. There were a few lads with them, one of them with his arm in a sling: he greeted the commander with a sweeping wave of his hat.

'Prince Aladar,' the commander told us, smiling.

Then a smaller group set out after them, men and women together, their garments fluttering in the wind. The women wore veils, but I recognized Emmo among them. She greeted the commander with a wave of the hand. What a charming wave!

That instant, I don't know what got into her horse – perhaps the bit had slipped, or a fly had bitten him – he suddenly took it into his head to rear up on his hind legs. I was terrified for Emmo.

I had seen horses like that before to throw the rider, then drag him along with a foot caught in the stirrup. If the rider did stay on it wasn't for long:

when the animal came down on its fore feet and gave a fly kick he soon went hurtling over its head. He'd be lucky if he was only knocked unconscious and not crushed when the horse rolled on him.

But when Emmo's horse reared up, the girl held on like a panther. Her feet were firm in the stirrups, one hand clutching the mane, while the other pulled on the reins. Her body responded sinuously to every movement of the horse.

'Chelloe!' she cried, tugging at the bit angrily. 'Chelloe!'

The horse made about six steps... My heart misgave me as I watched, dreading the moment when he would buck or throw himself down on the ground... but as a result of the jerks on his bridle he at last lowered to all fours, prancing, jumping, slowly coming to order. Emmo stayed in the saddle as if nothing had happened.

While this was going on I noticed that the girl dropped something. Her companions galloped away. She fell back and stopped. Her riding whip was lying there in the dust – perhaps the very whip she had once used across my face.

But I didn't think of that now. Only too happy to serve her, I picked up the riding whip and ran to her with it.

'Thank you, Zeta!' she said warmly.

She removed her veil for a moment, then pinned it up again. Her eyes were shining; her face was red. She looked at me, wide-eyed.

Then she slapped her horse and flew away.

I don't know when or how the commander-in-chief left our tent. My face burned all day long, and the music of her voice rang in my ears: 'Thank you, Zeta!'

I wondered why she had moved her veil – to show me her face? Or her ungloved hand? – the most beautiful face and hand in the world!

*W*e ended up, then, living in our own tents, but near the Chaths' palace. It stood, as I said before, separated from Attila's by a wide empty space, broken up by nothing but horse tracks.

The palace of the Chath clan! – that colourful little two-storey wooden house fascinated me! The barbarian wood-carver must have been indulging his fancy when he made this little bird cage with its rows of tulips and camomiles carved all over it. Two posts painted green flanked the entrance and even these were covered in leaves and flowers.

In the morning, as soon as we were dressed, I was again engaged to carry gifts. 'Go, Zeta, and find the pitcher with the swan neck and the plate that goes with it; also the three large rolls of silk and the monkey-skin. Put on your best clothes, and sprinkle rose water on my toga. We are going to the queen: Queen Rika.'

I obeyed gladly.

Queen Rika was the head of all the women. Chaba was *her* son. She was the real wife; the others were secondary wives – so much live jewellery.

Our two lords discussed for a while whether they should both visit the queen, or only Priscus. At last they agreed that Priscus should go alone – he was the better talker. It was a matter of paying his respects and asking if the Roman envoy might be allowed to kiss her hand.

So Rusticius, Priscus and I set out. I covered the gold gift in a white cloth and carried it carefully. The rest of the gifts were in a carved cedar casket carried by a child slave.

Thus we went.

In the courtyard in front of the main palace a crowd was gathered: many wore steel armour, and had weapons glittering with gold and silver, but there was a group also of ordinary folk in coarse linen garments. Had it been winter they would have been wearing animal skins and reeking of the waxy smell of hides.

These common people stood around a colourful post with the figure of a flying eagle in copper on one side of it near the top: in one claw it held a sword, in the other, scales. At the foot of the post was an unoccupied armchair.

They answered our questions by directing us to an attractively carved two-storey palace which had its own white fence, which was cut to look like a row of wooden lilies, all the same height. The gates were guarded by four men wearing tigerskins. Farther in, a grey-haired, swollen-faced slave dozed on the steps with his head resting on his knees. He announced us, and in a few minutes took us in.

As soon as we entered the hall, a pleasant smell greeted us. I thought it was a mixture of mint and carnations, but I wasn't sure. The queen was sitting in the middle of the room on a low couch, surrounded by young ladies. I recognized her immediately, though she had on a different dress – soft, quite plain, made of butter-coloured silk, with sandals of the same material. Her grey hair was wound on her head in the shape of a snail shell, and fastened by

a pin with a gold head the size of a walnut. She must have been beautiful when young. Now only a withered old lady remained, but straight as a post.

There was no other furniture in the room but the couch, and a small table to the side. The walls were covered with a dark cherry-red material. The floor was spread with a thick woollen carpet under which there must have been something else soft–perhaps a thick rug made of coconut fibres. Some six women were sitting round the queen, all busy with their embroidery. Among them was Emmo.

I can't even remember what my master said in greeting. My eyes were only for Emmo. She too was wearing a plain white dress, round her waist with a finger-thick silk rope, something like the kind anchorites wear; her sandals were saffron yellow. Her hair down loose – like an angel's! And I gazed again at those lovely eyes, those perfect lips.

She too had an embroidery hoop, two handspans wide and was working with silk threads of red and gold. They all embroidered similar patterns: blood red double tulips, the edges outlined with gold.

As we entered, they looked up. Our gifts were examined – though not so much the gifts themselves as the ornaments on them: the elaborate sunflower decoration on the pitcher pleased them most of all. Right away one girl prepared some linen, and attempted to draw it with red chalk.

Emmo leaned over to watch. I too peeked curiously, not interested in the drawing itself, only what Emmo was seeing there.

Well, the girl was able to draw the middle of the flower after a fashion, but the ring of petals, drawn one by one, grew lopsided.

The girls laughed. The queen too looked over and smiled. 'It could be beautiful, though; the middle we could make chestnut-brown, the petals sulphur yellow. But first we need the drawing: who will try?'

A flame shot through me.

'If you'd let me, Your Highness!' I stuttered.

Priscus looked at me in surprise that I should have so misbehaved as to speak when not addressed. But the women weren't shocked. The next moment I had a piece of white linen and the red chalk and was kneeling on the rug, dotting out two circles with a shaking hand.

My trembling soon subsided. The thought that Emmo was looking at me and that here was a chance to show her something of my skill!... Soon the sunflower appeared and the women clapped. 'You are a clever boy!' said the queen. Then she had it translated to Priscus:'I envy you your slave!'

Again the blood rushed to my face. I looked at my master, expecting him to tell the queen: 'He is no slave, my lady, but a free man.' However, what he did say was, 'I would be happy if I could give him to Your Highness as a gift, but he grew up in my house from the time he was small and he is my son, rather than my slave. If Your Highness wished him to draw, however, he'll be at your service for as long as we stay in Your Highness's country.'

'Can you draw other things as well?' the queen asked, looking at me kindly.

'A thousand different things, my royal lady,' I answered, almost reeling with joy, for I saw how Emmo was looking at me in startled admiration and for the first time in my life I felt that I wouldn't exchange my lot for many a rich man's.

'All right then,' the queen said, 'I will rob your master for an hour of your service.'

Priscus bowed and left with Rusticius while I remained there, on my knees, among the women.

I had never before drawn things like this, only letters in the Imperial Library and at home.

When our scribes copy books, the first letter is always a picture, generally a flower. The scribe first sketches it out with a piece of tin, then paints it in colours according to his fancy.

'Will Your Highness allow me to draw a morning glory?'

'Draw everything you can!'

So I drew for them a morning glory twining round a stalk of grass, and the stalk bending under its weight. I drew four flowers, two completely out and two buds just about to open.

And they liked it. 'Beautiful!' they all said. And they twittered around me with compliments. But in all the praise I heard only Emmo's one quiet word: 'Lovely.'

'Your Highness,' I said humbly, 'this flower should be embroidered in a lilac-coloured silk, the leaves in green.'

'Draw flowers in place of the leaves!' said the queen.

So I changed my design and drew flowers side view and back view. The last and lowest flower I drew wilted.

They took my drawing again and marvelled at it, sitting or kneeling there around the queen. Only Emmo remained standing. Leaning on another girl's shoulder, she bent forward and looked at my drawing.

Then, when nobody was looking at me, I watched her; I devoured her with my eyes.

'Why did you draw a wilted flower?' she asked. 'Wilted flowers are sad.'

Her soul shone out at me from her eyes, and I could hardly answer. 'There *is* a flower like this, my young lady, that looks wilted, and yet if dew falls upon it, and morning sunshine, it comes to life again.'

She looked at me, thinking, then smiled.

'If that's the case, then draw it alive.'

A basketful of cherries was brought in for the queen. She took a handful, and gave some to each of the girls.

Just then I finished the drawing.

'That will do for now, my son,' the queen said benevolently. 'Tomorrow come again about the same time when you have your master's permission to leave him.' She dipped her hand into the basket again. 'Hold out your hands!'

She was all motherly kindness. But just at that moment I didn't want her motherly care and kindness. What did she think I was, rewarding me with a handful of cherries! And in front of Emmo!...

Outside, I gave the cherries to a child.

In the yard there were so many people, all standing so quietly, that I automatically turned to where everyone was looking. What was going on here?

I saw Attila sitting beneath the post with the copper eagle. It was him they were all listening to.

My master was craning his neck behind the crowd. Rusticius and Free Greek stood by him and the Roman envoys were there too.

Working my way through the crowd, I asked Free Greek what was happening.

'The king is administering justice,' he replied.

There was something ancient about that scene– the head of the people sitting there in a rough-hewn armchair. Even his beard radiated a magnificent calm. Before him stood two old and two young men; these were the plaintiffs. One was speaking, gesticulating with hat in hand. Some fifty old men sat or squatted on the ground and behind them stood the crowd of curious onlookers. All were bare–only the king had on a haircloth hat with the rim turned up.

'It is the custom here,' explained Free Greek in a hushed voice, 'that people are divided into families; if there is any trouble the head of the family deals with it–the father or grandfather. If two families quarrel, a tribunal is chosen from among neighbouring families in addition to the group of elders. If it cannot come to a verdict, or if the verdict is not accepted, the law-suit is brought before the king. In times of peace he sits here almost every morning. He doesn't need advisers. He listens to the disputants, puts a question or two, then decides on the true verdict. Right now there is a big squabble going on. One of the young Huns brought home a girl prisoner from the Akatiri; here he exchanged her for a horse and ten gold pieces. The girl prisoner, however, died the next morning; the other Hun now demands his horse back, saying the girl must have been sick!'

The speech of the old family head just barely reached our ears.

'I can tell you, my lord, the girl was as pale as of dough. I told my son right away, I told him, "You were crazy to exchange a horse for *this!*" I nagged and scolded him, my lord; I even said–'

'Enough!' said the king and everyone fell silent.

Attila spoke again. 'Falcon, when you offered your horse and money for the girl, did you notice that she looked ill?'

The lad hesitated, then answered, 'I can't say that I didn't, my lord, but I didn't see death in her!'

'Then who saw it? Let him speak up who saw death in the girl!'

The crowd was silent.

Again the king spoke. 'You purchased the girl; you purchased her illness as well. Warrior Tiny shall keep the horse, but to be honourable he will return you the ten gold pieces so that your loss won't be threefold.'

The petitioners left without another word. From among those sitting on the ground some six rose. This was a new case beginning so we left the administration of justice.

*N*ext day our delegation, my master included, was invited to dine with Attila. I was free to go to the queen again.

At the gates I met the Chaths' little nurse. She stood in front of me, and, as if we were old friends, said, 'Tell me, please–are you not an Avzon (Italian)?'

'No. I'm not,' I answered, surprised.

'I ask, because I am an Avzon.' She sighed. 'My mother was an Avzon woman, and my name is Djidja. Or, as they say here, Djidjia.'

(Ugly name! I thought.)

The girl went on. 'My mother was one of the Chaths' slaves, and I was born here. She died last year, though, may God rest her soul.' She crossed herself, blinking back a tear.

'What's all this got to do with me?' I barked at her.

She blushed and pressed her thin dark hand against her face, blinking and frightened. All in all she was an unappealing sight, poor thing – like a little boy in a skirt.

'What do you want then?' I asked, a little more mildly.

'Nothing,' she replied sadly.

I hurried on, almost running, to the queen.

The same women were there as on the previous day, but with two or three more; only Emmo was missing. I drew without spirit. Where could Emmo be? Was she hunting again? With whom?

The women again praised my drawings, but my heart no longer trembled at their compliments. I looked at them boldly enough now: I would have liked to discover one among them at least more beautiful than Emmo, so that I wouldn't have to think of that one girl all the time. But none surpassed her. With the exception of Emmo, Hunnish women are not as pretty as Greek women. Emmo was the morning star among stars.

About noon little Chaba was brought in–a pretty little rascal with sparkling eyes. He must have come straight from the bath, for his hair was still wet. He was dressed in a little snuff-coloured silk suit. The bottoms of his trousers were gartered with gold strings from his sandals to his knees.

The women all kissed the little prince but he only kissed his mother. Then immediately he came and stood beside me, examining with great interest the carnation I had drawn, then staring into my face.

'Who are you?' he asked with a child's open curiosity.

'I am a Greek,' I answered, smiling, 'from a distant country, where the land of fairy tales begins.'

At this he stared, even harder.

'Have you ever seen fairies?'

'I have.'

'And a hook-nosed warty old witch?'

'Yes, I saw a witch once!'

'Bet you haven't seen a seven-headed dragon?'

'I certainly have!'

'Live?'

'Alive, but with only one head.'

'One head? Was it throwing flames?'

'No.'

'Then what was it throwing?'

'Plates, at her husband's head!'

Chaba just stared, but the women laughed.

Even the queen smiled, then picked up her son and kissed him. 'Go, your horse is waiting for you. Remember not to go up to the visitors during dinner; don't stroke their beards or play with their gold chains. Sit beside your father; behave yourself, and act seriously as your father does.'

Chaba glanced at me once more, then they took him away.

At last I too was free to go. I walked all round the Chaths' house, but couldn't see the Hunnish girl anywhere.

I even ventured to look around the king's palace. Warriors stood about, clad in various uniforms. Some had hats made out of bison heads with the horns still on – most ferocious-looking: one was afraid of being gored. These were officers of the Saraguri, who had come as ambassadors.

It was late in the afternoon by the time my lords came out from dinner.

'Well, that was an unforgettable meal!' said Maximinus enthusiastically.

'Wonderful!' My master nodded his head.

'A dream-dinner!' stuttered the captain.

All the lords were red in the face but he was actually reeling a little.

Priscus immediately set me to my writing; he wanted to dictate how the dinner went while he was still in the heat of excitement, but Maximinus kept interrupting us.

'What a king!' He was burning with enthusiasm. 'If the emperor hears that Attila eats off wooden plates and drinks from wooden cups!...'

'It's only affectation,' shrieked the captain, who could hardly stand up.

'Nonsense!' Maximinus snorted. 'A man who sits down among his people to judge some stupid case about a horse is not affected!'

'But he scorns gold!'

'Try a sackful!'

'There is extraordinary intelligence burning in this barbarian!' my master put in, shaking his head. 'I can judge a man by the way he laughs. A cobbler guffaws. A man of learning only smiles. But what is one to make of a man who doesn't show the least crack of a smile, even watching that jester of his, that crazy Tzerko?!'

They all laughed.

'Well,' said Maximinus, 'I almost choked myself laughing – he was so funny!'

Priscus was still pondering. 'What I would like to know is whether he didn't find the fool entertaining, or whether he just didn't want to laugh.'

Maximinus didn't understand. He admired the physical man in Attila; Priscus saw the spiritual. And that day I, for the first time, saw the real difference between the two speakers.

*N*ext day it rained. The Huns turned their hides around, on both their tents and themselves, so that the hair faced out. I thought I was in a town full of bears!

In front of the king's palace, however, there were still as many people as on the previous day. From our tent it was possible to look straight over to the Chaths' house. I saw Emmo appear in the doorway, wearing a loose-fitting cloak made of swan feathers; she mounted a stocky grey horse, led by a thick-necked slave who ran beside it to the queen's palace.

So, suddenly, it became very urgent for me to go there also. I washed, dressed and scented myself, then I too rode over on a horse, so that my sandals shouldn't get muddy. I jumped off right onto the wooden step, then tied my horse to a post.

The queen sat with only two other women. She seemed surprised to see me. 'Have you come to draw? But the sky is overcast. Well, stay now, perhaps it will clear up.'

She sat on the sofa with an ordinary, unglazed earthenware pot on her lap, and all around her on the rug lay gold jewellery, chains, beads, brooches, pendants and buttons. I wondered why the queen kept all these riches in an ordinary pot, and not in some silver cup or box? I don't know. Perhaps because of superstition. Perhaps because that was the custom. Perhaps it was a remnant from ancient times when they had to hide their treasures under water or in the earth.

Emmo sat beside the window; its transparent membranes of stretched bladder looked like blocks of ice because of the cloudy skies.

All three of them were rubbing, brushing and polishing the jewellery. Even the queen was doing this. She had a wide belt of hammered gold in her hand, and held it out to show me when she saw me admiring it. It was fashioned as a chain of strawberry leaves with coral berries.

'Have you ever seen such a treasure?' asked the queen.

'I have seen the like at our goldsmiths,' I replied, 'but not as beautiful as this.'

'I have even more beautiful pieces,' said the queen, 'but look, I think it's getting lighter – try to draw this chain; perhaps it would make a good pattern for embroidery.'

Later, I understood from their conversation that the queen was choosing a gift from among her treasures for the new wife. It was the custom for the new wife to visit all the previous wives at the time of the first new moon after the wedding. The queen was planning to give her the gift then.

Queen Rika was a quiet and melancholic woman. She spoke rarely, and even when she was gay, a gentle smile was all her laughter. I looked up from my drawing as often as I could to watch Emmo; but if she happened to be behind me, then it was the queen I watched.

Emmo herself was more of a serious than a merry disposition.

The queen, looking with delight at an ivory bracelet studded with diamonds, suddenly turned to me.

'What kinds of bracelets do Greek women wear?'

'All sorts,' I answered tactfully. 'At least those who have any. For our country is not rich any more, my royal lady.'

'Do they wear necklaces?'

'Not often, my royal lady. They believe that gold necklaces belong on foreign men.'

'And the Greek girls,' asked Emmo, 'are the Greek girls beautiful? Do they wear dresses similar to ours?'

'Greek girls are all dark-haired, dark-eyed and white-skinned,' I replied, 'and are not as beautiful as Hunnish girls. Nowadays their clothes are not attractive, but there was a time when their dresses were most beautiful.'

'What were they like?' asked the three women in unison.

'Underneath was a blouse of silk or other fine material, and a short white skirt reaching the knees, or not quite.'

'Not quite that even?'

They were flabbergasted.

'That's right, for the younger ones especially. The outer clothing covered the legs a bit more. It consisted of a light, ample length of fine woollen material, held in place on the right shoulder with a clasp.'

But I could see they didn't understand me. 'My royal lady,' I said, 'that length of stuff made a truly beautiful dress! For it could be worn a hundred different ways. It lay against the slim body in finely draped folds, and allowed the lines of the shapely figure to show through.'

Then they had me draw hair styles. And because it didn't turn out too well, they had me show on Emmo how Greek women pile up their hair, leaving only one wave across the forehead.

My hands were shaking so as I touched Emmo's silken hair, I could hardly manage it. Finally, Emmo went into the next room to look at herself in the large steel mirror that hung there and she stayed so long that the queen had to call her back. 'Emmo, that mirror will get rusty!'

She came out then, and we looked at her in surprise: she was wearing only a shirt which reached to her knees and a white skirt. She had draped a cream-coloured wool bedspread around her shoulders; it flattered her lovely figure and left her arms and legs bare. Looking at her, I felt dizzy. She was like a flower, like a white narcissus growing in the sunshine.

She walked up and down the room, then came to a halt in front of me.

'Is this how those Greek girls look?'

'Oh, if only they did!...'

'Is anything missing?'

'A pair of pearl ear-rings, my young lady, and a palm-leaf fan for your hand, a green fan.'

Emmo turned to the queen. 'Am I beautiful, my lady?'

'You are, my child,' the queen told her, smiling. 'May your life be always as beautiful as you are.'

Emmo kissed the queen's hand, then went into the other room again to change back into her own clothes; after which she sat down and began embroidering one of my drawings.

'Sing to us, Emmo!' said the queen. 'I feel happy today; make the day complete!'

Emmo lowered her embroidery into her lap and began to sing in a warm, sweet, quiet voice:

The field is green now. The chestnut buds are out.
The spring rain washed away the road and all about.
When will my lover come back home again?
Of all the warriors he was best, of all young men.

She sang softly, looking straight in front of her as if the story she sang were actually taking place there. Then she leaned one elbow on the embroidery hoop, and swayed her head from side to side.

Oh – how I long for the spring to be over!
The spring season's passing, the long days of summer;
Sunflower's ripening, harvest days here;
Warriors' homecoming in the fall of the year.

At first I didn't understand the song and how the meaning of the words connected. But Hunnish songs are like that – like a broken necklace that has been restrung with some of the beads missing.

Forest boughs are bare. Leaves blow in the wind.
At last from distant the army has come home.
Only one man's missing; one man stayed behind.
All in vain I waited – he will never come.

Soldier Tarna, are you in the earth? or in the sky?
Be it sky, be it earth – remember me my love.
Come, take me with you to your blue home above,
Or lay me in your grave where the dark shadows lie.

What breaks the silence, knocking at the door?
'Come out, my dove, my sweetheart, I couldn't come before!
My horse in the moonlight gleams spotless white,
Like the mists of autumn that fade before the light.'

The girl puts on her best dress, all white; alone she stands,
A wreath of rosemary on her hair, a flower in her hands.
This is how they found her by the road when it was light:
With little red boots on, and dressed all in white...

As the song finished, her head was low, her eyes moist, and so were the queen's.

'Poor Rose,' said the queen. 'Couldn't she have found some other lad?'

Emmo replied, 'Some girls, my lady, are like flowers that blossom only once.'

Then, I became aware that I was the subject of conversation. The queen was asking me a question.

'Who were your parents?' she said. 'And who taught you to be so skilful with your hands?'

I shook myself out of my dream.

'My royal lady,' I replied, 'my parents were poor people who lived by the seashore. My father is a brown-haired man, with large eyes and a curly moustache. My mother was a thin little woman – may God rest her soul in peace. And I was never taught how to draw; I only noticed things, then tried to draw them and found suddenly that I could do it.'

I wondered again why such a golden-footed peacock as the queen should want to know about a poor little dusty sparrow like myself.

'And how did you get to know Master Priscus?' she questioned me further. 'Where do these people find such clever slaves?'

'I am not a slave any more, my royal lady. I serve my master of my own free will.'

'Of your own free will?'

'Out of love,' I answered.

'But have you left your mother and father for him?' asked the queen.

'No, my royal lady. When I was ten years old I had to redeem my family from miserable poverty. In our country we have to pay very heavy taxes; the state sells the right to collect it. The tax-collector gathers not only the money that he'll pour into the state's treasury, but also enough to stuff his own pockets. My father had a little bit of land and a thin little mottled cow. The taxmen, finding nothing left in the house to take away, were about to take the cow. My father was poor, he had six little children depending on him. I was the oldest. What else could he have done?...'

'Your own father sold you?'

She clapped her hands together and stared at me.

'With us this is not unusual, my royal lady,' I replied calmly. 'The Empire has been paying taxes to the Huns for decades now. Our emperor never sows, only reaps. The people harvest wheat, he harvests the people. At the time I was a child – I couldn't understand what slavery was; it only hurt when I had to say good-bye to my brothers and sisters and to my mother.'

My eyes were full of tears, but I went on. 'My mother lay there sick, and my father didn't tell her of his intention. As we were about to go, he led me in so that I could kiss her good-bye. My mother looked at my father, and from his face she could read what he was about to do. She cried out, "I won't let you! Wait until I get well, then sell *me!*" And even as she held me in her arms, pressing my face against hers – she died.'

The women looked at me with pity, Emmo too. The queen's eyebrows creased in a frown. 'So your father sold you after all?'

'We buried my mother, then boarded a ship. Next day there I stood, with whitewashed legs, in the slave market.'

The queen's eyes clouded. As she sat there hugging her knees, she kicked away the jewellery so hard that it flew against the wall.

'Accursed robbers!' she cried, her eyes bright with indignation, 'When will we finally break their rule and take it over for ourselves? When will the new order come to this world? How long will Attila wait before he steps on their necks?'

I froze in fear.

The queen rose and left for her bedchamber. The women accompanied her anxiously. The curtain dividing the two rooms fell behind them.

The handmaid called in two others who gathered up the jewellery and took it away.

I just stood there, turned to stone, like the shepherd of the tale. I didn't understand what had happened. What was I to do? Leave, or wait for their return? I couldn't leave without the queen's permission, or at least until someone told me that the queen required my services no more that day.

But perhaps I had said something stupid and would be scolded for it. Or I might even end up on a stake for making the queen sad.

One window was open; I walked over to it and looked down.

The rain was still coming down, dripping slowly, the heavy drops making bubbles on the surface of the puddles. A large crowd of people still stood getting drenched in front of Attila's palace.

A slave stood in front of our tent, squeezing the water out of a brown cloak. Judging by the horses waiting there, Roman envoys must be visiting us. The door opened and Emmo appeared. She came over to where I was standing.

'Your tale has excited and upset the queen too much,' she said reproachfully. 'You have committed an impropriety – or are you allowed in your country to talk to the queen of things that will make her unhappy?'

She talked in low tones scolding me – but I wasn't even listening to what she was saying; I only heard her voice, that sweet soft voice... How lovely she was as she leaned towards me – like a white narcissus bowing its head in the spring breeze! Those lovely little red lips kept talking softly.

'You suffered a lot,' she said after a while. 'Poor Zeta! But don't fret: Attila will crush the tyrants and then the Greek people will be just as happy as the Huns are now.'

'Oh, my young lady,' I breathed in ecstasy, 'I forget all my suffering when you look at me with such compassion.'

'The other day you spoke differently. You hated me then.'

'I shall always be sorry because...'

'I am sorry too for having hurt you. For you are a good boy, and you have a gentle soul. But now, go. We shall not be drawing any more today.'

'My young lady,' I whispered with a sinking heart, yet drunk with delight, 'may I ever hope that you will offer me your hand to kiss a second time. Heaven grant that you will!'

She looked at me, then smiled slightly, as one smiles at a child's foolishness.

'If that is your only wish–then heaven *will* grant it,' and she offered me her hand.

I took it in both of mine, as if I were fondling a bird, and, falling on one knee, I kissed it...

'Now go!' she said, pulling back her hand gently. 'Your are out of your mind.'

*N*ext day the queen did not receive me – though I was there, of course, all dressed up, waiting for Emmo. The sun came out, drying the mud to the consistency of dough; the air was heavy with the smell of damp earth and horse dung, and yet it felt clean and healthy in the lungs.

A brown-haired young man of about seventeen arrived on horseback at the Chaths'. He wore a gold chain of exquisite workmanship, and in his hat was set an eagle feather; two mounted servants followed him. I recognized him as Prince Aladar. His arm was better but he kept his hand tucked in between the buttons of his dolman.

He entered the Chaths' gate and in a little while reappeared with Emmo and the freckled slave girl. I was standing in front of our tent, so I bowed deeply to greet Emmo. I don't know whether or not she returned my greeting. Her stocky little grey horse danced fetlock-deep in mud; all I could see, for a moment, was her thin red sandal resting in the gilded stirrup.

The prince rode beside her, and the talk must have been gay, for all three were laughing heartily. For a second they stopped in front of Queen Rika's palace and asked something of the guard, who removed his hat and bowed three times. Then they rode on, and disappeared among Attila's buildings.

No one had ever plunged a knife into my breast, and yet I knew then exactly what it must feel like.

In the afternoon we visited the Roman envoys. The gentlemen conversed with the gentlemen, the servants with the servants. I talked with no one – I couldn't join the lords, and I thought myself better than the servants, so I just sat on one of the tent pegs and stared into nothingness.

As he was leaving, my master asked me, 'What's the matter with you?'

'Nothing,' I replied, surprised.

'You look pale,' he said. 'Perhaps something has upset your stomach. These Hunnish dishes... They are good, but you need the stomach of a Hun to digest them.'

The following morning, Adam, Queen Rika's old steward, came to see us, to invite our lords to dinner. It took place not in the queen's palace but in Adam's house, and the lords came home a bit tipsy. Priscus explained that there were many distinguished guests who kept toasting either the queen or each other, so everyone had to drink at each toast.

It was the same at Attila's dinner. Our lords liked this peculiar Hunnish custom, but it did affect them a little.

Priscus started to dictate the diary, but could only say that the queen was a charming woman, and that our Empress Pulcheria could only learn from her. In five minutes he made me cross out the remark about the empress and told me to write whatever I pleased.

Our lords, after so many days and weeks in Attila's city, were strongly urging the commander-in-chief to make a statement. They all would have liked to start out for home. All except me.

One day, at last, the commander visited us with a gentleman named Berki, who had been twice already at our emperor's court. He had a letter with him: Attila's reply. Our lords eyed the seal on the letter with great interest.

Early tomorrow morning, then, we were to start home. With a heavy heart I helped the servants pack. I asked Priscus to let me go to the queen for a quarter of an hour, but he said no. 'It wouldn't do for you to go there now: she might think you had come for a tip.'

I had never even thought of that.

In the afternoon about thirty beautiful steeds were brought to us, along with all kinds of weapons. This was the gift to our lords from Attila and the other noblemen whom they had got to know.

Our lords, however, accepted only three of the horses: Maximinus kept a bay, given by Berki; my master kept two greys, one from Attila and one from Chath; the rest they sent back.

While we took down the tents and rolled up the canvas, our lords paid the customary farewell visits. They visited the queen, Adam, and the commander-in-chief, the Chaths, Edecon and Orestes. My master dropped in on Free Greek too.

The queen did not receive them; she had a headache, but in the evening two of her servants appeared, bringing two horses from her – and a small silk purse for me.

I knew this man with the three silver stars on his hat; he used to stand guard at the gates.

'The queen sends you this,' he said. 'There are two big coins in it, and six small ones. She asked me to tell you that one of the big coins is yours, the other you should send to your father. The six small ones are for your six brothers and sisters.' (She must have forgotten that there were six of us altogether.)

I could have cried. I looked over at Priscus to see if I might accept the gift and he nodded his assent.

'Tell the royal lady,' I answered in a whisper gratefully, 'that I shall honour her name till I die, and that nothing would give me greater pleasure than to bend my knee in her presence once more.'

The lords did not accept the horses the queen had sent, declaring that they felt themselves unworthy of such generosity; it would be enough, they said, to take away a grateful memory in their hearts.

I withdrew behind our baggage cart and opened the purse. There were two big Egyptian gold pieces in it, and six small Roman ones from the time of Julius Caesar.

When our lords looked at them, they marvelled. The two big gold coins were as large as a child's palm.

My master said, joking, 'Why don't *you* hire *me* as your servant, seeing that of the two of us you are the richer?'

The eight gold pieces, of course, gave me new ideas. I decided that as soon as we arrived home, I would find out my father's situation, and if he still lived there in poverty, I'd visit him with two cows, clothes and all sorts of gifts. For the remaining money I'd buy some land and a house for him, and we'd have such a celebration as the village would never forget.

During all this I had kept looking around, hoping to catch sight of Emmo. When I thought of her, I couldn't even enjoy my wealth. I wished I were an eagle that might swoop down and carry her away like a dove, up, up into the clouds – and take her home.

But man is a miserable wretch, creeping along on the ground like a worm.

The sun was sinking lower in a cloudless sky and the town began to fill with the dust and mooing of cows returning home from pasture. The lords, nevertheless, sat out in front of the tent to eat their supper of cold roast and cheese.

'How could I get to the Chaths'?... If I walked through the courtyard, I might see her perhaps... Once more – oh, how I longed to see her just once more!

The gates were not yet locked and a few people were about. The guard at the door, a stout slave with a spear, yawned just then and stretched himself. Another slave was pulling out weeds near the gates. From the direction of the kitchen a slave boy ran out into the street with a covered saucepan, leaving behind a thick, curling trail of smoke.

Everyone looked up at that. For in the centre of the city no household ever asks another for fire; there are enough slaves to go around – there is always one to watch the fire, even at night, to make sure it won't go out. So while they were all gaping, I sneaked through the door in the fence. Perhaps I could see her from the other side of the house. The evening was quiet, they might be having their supper there by torchlight. If I could only see her – or her shadow even – just once, for the last time...

I walked around the house. There was an entrance from the back too, and the pillars were painted, the same as in front. On the threshold sat a whiskery Hun, holding a spear and looked at me.

'Is Lord Chath at home?' I asked, trying to sound matter-of-fact.

'No, he isn't,' he replied offhandedly.

'Well, the others, are they home?'

'They are.'

'Is my Lady Chath home as well?'

'She is.'

'And the young lady? Mistress Emmo?'

'She too.'

'You see, I have lost a silver button. When we were here last, I must have lost it. I'll be in trouble with my master when he hears about it.'

'That's your problem.'

I pretended to look for it, walking round the house. Then from a ground floor window the thin little slave girl, Djidjia, leaned out.

'Well, look who's here! Good old Zeta!'

'Is that you, Djidjia?'

I think I felt relieved.

'I've lost something, Djidjia. Only a button.'

'A button? I'll find it for you in the morning and bring it to your tent. I have to put little Sunshine to bed now.'

I noticed then that she was holding the little boy in her lap.

'By morning I won't be here,' I said. 'We are leaving.'

'Oh . . . really?' And she opened wide her large, honest eyes.

Someone called her name from within.

'Oh, someone is calling me!' she said, alarmed. She put down the child who was already asleep, then ran out of the room.

For a while I stayed there, straining my ears, then wandered back to the guard at the door. There at the back was a little garden, and on the first floor of the house a nicely carved verandah. But I couldn't see anybody there. Down in the kitchen a maid was singing and I heard the clatter of dishes. I didn't dare look up to the second floor, but kept staring at the ground as though looking for something.

The sun sank behind the distant poplars, casting its last rays on the house. I noticed red flowers in the garden, and a greengold insect circled about me, buzzing.

As I stood there with head bent, a rose fell in front of me. Startled, I looked up. All I could see in the second floor window was a fleeting glimpse of a hand. I picked up the rose and waited. The flower was fresh and its stem still warm.

But no one appeared.

The gates had already been closed. A slave blew on a horn and the last horsemen rode out into the twilight.

We started out at early dawn when the sun was hardly up. The city of tents reverberated with the bugle calls of cowherds and swineherds. We pulled up the last tent poles and packed them on to carts. The lords mounted their horses and so did I.

My eyes were almost torn out, I stared so long at that wooden palace, but the windows were covered with dark red curtains and not one of them moved.

But the rose was there, close to my heart.

Did *she* throw it to me? A hundred thoughts answered yes. Only one thought said, What if it fell by accident? What if a child threw it out, or one of the maids?

But *if* it was she!

I kept looking back. If I could only see her, even from a distance, if I could only wave good-bye with my hat!

But the tents were already blocking my view of the wooden buildings. Mooing cows and grunting pigs were running out on to the street from everywhere. Whips cracked and horns blared. The sun was darting golden arrows into the sky, and the world entered another day.

I would never see that house again – that birdcage of a house, nor the flittering little white bird within . . . Never, never! . . .

It would help if one could fit a dam into one's head, so that the stream of certain thoughts could be diverted for a few weeks and the wheels stop turning.

My wheels kept churning up thoughts of Free Greek: he was a slave once too, more wretched than ever I was. I had eight gold pieces, plus a hundred more. Free Greek had not had even the smallest copper coin. He had been older and clumsier and less educated than I was, yet he went to war and fought bravely, and they gave him his freedom; he became rich, and married a Hunnish woman. A Hunnish woman! . . .

This is where the dam would have come in useful. Ever since we had started on our homeward journey, the food, to me, was tasteless and I couldn't sleep. But how could I turn back? How could I part from my master? How could I tell him that I was returning to a girl who in all likelihood had been brought up to be the wife of one of Attila's sons? For I thought of leaving my hundred gold pieces in Constantinople–in Priscus's little bag – and sneaking back. Then I thought of secretly taking my hundred gold pieces out of my master's money. This thought I thrust from me in panic.

Then I thought I would lie down by the side of the road, pretending to rest – and so stay behind. Then I could have returned to Queen Rika and asked to serve her, for she knew that I was a free man. But what if she had forgotten our conversation? Or wouldn't accept me? For the last couple of days she didn't even receive me!

What if she thought that I was a fugitive, and sent me back under guard to my master?

At night, I watched the moon and wept. If I slept my dreams were full of tumult of battle, killing – or being killed. I, who couldn't bear the sight of blood, clung to the picture of becoming as big a man as Free Greek!

We were well beyond the Ister when we heard shouts, and there were thirty fugitives, on their way to Attila. We stopped for only a short conversation. Our lords acquainted the others with Attila's reply to the emperor and Vigilas told us about the fright and agitation his report of Attila's anger had caused at the court of Theodosius.

Then we parted; they continued on due north, while we kept plodding south.

At noon I had to prepare my writing instruments. A little way back we had seen three men impaled and Priscus wanted me to make a note of that, among other things. The sun's heat was strong, for it was summer now, so the lords lay down after lunch.

We rested in a forest and had our meal without pitching a tent, just in the cool shade of an oak. I sat in the shadow of a tree close by, paper and ink before me. I looked over at my master, who was asleep on his back with his arms under his head, while three slaves fanned him quietly.

I took out a clean piece of paper from my folder and wrote:

Respectfully, to Lord Chath,
My Lord, along the way I have been thinking what a splendid and kind-hearted man you are, and that it would be fitting for me to return your goodness. You have given me a beautiful steed, for which even the emperor might envy me. So now, I give you a slave, for whom Attila might envy you. He has half a year yet to serve; let this half year be yours.

This slave is worth a fortune. His memory is like wax. You can rhyme off a hundred different numbers to him, and he will keep them in his head. He can speak Greek, Latin and Hun. He is at home in history, philosophy, geography, grammar, rhetoric and calligraphy. His name is Theophil but I have always called him Zeta, and he is used to this name. Please, receive him as my gift.

Yours respectfully,
Priscus, rhetor.

My master's seal was in the small portable writing desk. I used it to seal the letter which I then hid in my bosom.

The lords were still fast asleep, the servants too.

So I wrote another letter.

To Priscus, rhetor, my master and father,
Despite my great affection for you, my master, I have to leave you now. I cannot tell you why, but I implore you, do not accuse me of ingratitude. For the memory of your kind, good heart will always bring tears to my eyes, and I shall always bless your name.

You were generous enough to make me a present of a hundred gold pieces. I have taken these, less one, out of your purse. Please, don't be angry with me for this. The one I left is the price of horse I have been using so far, and without which I cannot leave.

God be with you! Live happily!

Forever your loving and humble servant,
Zeta.

This letter I locked inside the drawer of the writing desk; the key I hid in my master's holiday toga, where he would find it when he got home.

It wasn't hard for me to put on a long face when I went up to the servants and told them that I had lost my money.

'It must have slipped out of my pocket when we watered the horses,' I said to them. 'But whether this morning or at noon I don't know.'

I could see by their faces that they were glad rather than sorry about my bad luck. They had always envied me–but I don't hold that against them.

'Tell my master,' I said, mounting my horse, 'that if I am not back by evening, he is not to worry. I'll sleep somewhere and catch up with you tomorrow or the day after.'

And I rode away.

As soon as I was past the bend in the road, I dug my spurs into my horse's sides. 'Come on, boy – as fast as you can,' I said.

I had caught up with Vigilas and his company within two hours. I told Vigilas that my master had sent me back with a letter of some importance, and wanted him to use me as his personal servant on the way, even though I was no longer a slave.

On this journey Vigilas had brought along his son with him to see something of the world. He was a spindly and ignorant boy who had spent his childhood sick in bed. He stuttered too, but he was an honest, serious lad.

Vigilas was surprised at my arrival. He questioned me closely for quite a while, trying to find out what business my master had with Chath. Then when I had convinced him that I didn't know, he gave up and rejoined the officer who was in charge of the fugitives.

I moved up front, but my head, almost mechanically, kept turning to look back. My face was burning, my heart was quivering like a jelly – and small wonder! I had stolen, cheated and behaved like a swine. I would never have thought myself capable of so much baseness.

*O*ne August evening we reached the Danube, the border of Attila's territory. The sun was on its way down, and Vigilas asked Eslas if it wouldn't be better to pitch camp on this side of the river.

For the opposite bank was used for the execution of fugitives caught trying to cross the frontier, their corpses were left hanging on trees as a public example. No fit sight to go sleep on!

Eslas, however, thought that Vigilas was merely afraid the Hunnish border guards might cause trouble and annoyance and he answered, 'No. The guards quake at the sight of me. Let's go across. We'll be that much farther on our way.'

He grabbed his horn and blew it, Hunnish fashion.

Nevertheless it took at least a quarter of an hour for the ferry to start out from the opposite shore, handled by two bare-headed Huns pulling on the rope.

'What the devil got into you!' swore Eslas. 'Your place is here at the dock! Where is your chief?'

'They are hanging,' the younger Hun offered as an excuse. 'We've been watching it.'

'What's there to see?' grunted Eslas. 'Your place is here!'

'They were hanging Roman fashion – on crosses,' the Hun said apologetically. 'You don't see that every day. Two of them...' and he spat into his hands and said, 'Those Romans really know a thing or two. They aren't cultured for nothing!'

The water flashed gold, shimmering away into the distance. The Ister is perhaps the world's largest river. I am always taken by surprise when I see that vast expanse of fresh water. But now I felt anxious as well as awestruck.

We stepped off onto the shore, where ten or fifteen Huns were already waiting for us. They all wore shirts and baggy pants. The chief ferryman turned up now, too, and asked Eslas if there was anything he would like.

'Roast a sheep,' ordered Eslas. 'But make it quick.'

Eslas was always eating and drinking, and he argued a lot too. But apart from this he was full of kindness.

The servants pitched the tents in a round clearing, which must have been a regular campsite because peg-holes had already been made there, and the earth was trampled flat. Two merchants were camping there besides us; they were on their way back to Constantinople.

As I looked east, I almost froze with fright: on a barren hill stood two crosses; against them, nailed, two men, naked, white.

I called Vigilas's attention to them and he too shuddered. 'Get into the tent!' he shouted at his son. 'Don't look over there!'

It hurt Eslas too, to look at the two crosses. 'What have they done?' he asked listlessly.

'Well,' replied the chief ferryman, 'there's so many fugitives, we can hardly keep up with 'em. If no one claims 'em in a week, we don't guard 'em here any longer. Till now we just threw the villains in the water, but sometimes, to make a stronger example we hang 'em from trees, so's anyone else who tries

to escape'll see where they'll end up. But those two were Romans, escaped slaves, so we decided to make the example in Roman fashion. Right away I had the crosses made; in the morning we put up the older one, in the afternoon, the younger one.'

One of the crucified was motionless by now, but the other still kept lifting his head and screaming. Vigilas and I approached him and asked if he had any message to anyone at home, but he was in no state to reply; he could only raise his head again and again, crying, 'Water! Water!'

About twenty Hunnish horsemen were observing the sufferer with interest. Occasionally they would make a remark: 'You asked for it, didn't you?'

There were even women and children there, gaping, one woman suckling her baby. But then, barbarians have no feelings; they are like a child who plays with a bird, never thinking that the bird might be suffering. Here these people found it amusing to see how a man died – nothing more than that.

He was hardly a boy, the one who was still living, moaning, calling for water. At Vigilas's command, the executioner climbed up the ladder leaning against the back of the cross, and put a pitcher to the lips of the tortured man. He drank. A little relieved, he noticed us, and, from our clothing, recognized us as Roman citizens.

'Have mercy on me!' he groaned. 'Kill me...!'

I couldn't listen any more, but returned to the tents, feeling as though ice-cold water were running in my veins. Shortly afterwards, Vigilas, too, came back. He asked Eslas if it were not possible to run a sword through the unfortunate man, but Eslas shook his head gravely:

'No, he is a Roman, and must die in the Roman way. And the Roman custom is to run a sword through the crucified only *after* death...'

We walked down to the river for a swim; for the sun was scorching and the dust of the road burning hot. By the time we returned, the horizon beyond the line of willows was hazy with dusk. The ferrymen were loitering about the fire.

'Hey, fellow!' I quietly called to a Hunnish lad with a pointed hat. 'I feel sorry for that crucified slave. Would you run a sword through his heart? For good pay?'

'I might,' he replied, squinting. 'What do you call good pay?'

'One gold piece.'

The Hun tried out the sound of the coin on a stone: then he disappeared.

For a short time we could still hear the moaning in the quiet of the night. Then suddenly all fell silent. One could hear only the grazing horses, as they quietly cropped the crisp grass.

I lay down in the open air, among the soldiers. The sky was cloudy and the moon had not yet risen, so we went to bed early.

But I couldn't sleep. I wasn't a slave again–yet. I could still turn back under some pretence or other. But what would happen to me once we left these shores if I changed my mind *then* about what I was doing? Neither Vigilas nor Eslas would be around; there would be no one to testify that I wasn't a fugitive slave. And what if I ran away from the Chaths after I had been accepted by them? How would I cross the border? Attila's guards circled his territory in a living chain; suppose there were other check-points where they treated a Roman in the Roman fashion! Drops of sweat broke out on my forehead.

But then I thought of Emmo, and the night turned rose-coloured. It had happened before in history that women of high rank had become the slaves of slaves. No human law could ever contain the human heart! The heart was a law unto itself.

The rose, wrapped in paper, was hidden in my breast. It was wilted now, but still smelled fragrant.

'This fragrance is your soul, Emmo – in this rose you have given me your soul.'

*W*e approached Attila's city by the same route we had travelled before. But whereas we had bought our food for money, now Eslas would not allow us to pay for anything.

'Wherever I am,' he said, 'everyone must be my guest!' and we thought this truly noble of him.

Only later did we realize that no traveller ever paid more dearly for his trip.

When we reached the bend of the River Tisia where I had my little quarrel with Emmo, I combed the entire area looking for that piece of veil she had torn off. But I couldn't find it. Either the wind had blown it away or a shepherd must have picked it up. At that time the fields had been green and dotted with flowers; since then everything had burned up in the heat of summer. At that time the crops were still standing; now, for weeks we had been riding through yellow stubble.

An aged, knotted willow stood near the spot where Emmo and I had met. Would it not be wise to hide my money beneath it? Who knew what would happen to me? And this place I could always find again. Nobody was likely to come nosing about here, digging in the earth.

I looked around. The others had gone on ahead and there was no one following behind. Only grazing cattle could be seen as white spots in the distance–and further off, herds of horses. We had seen herds of horses everywhere since reaching the plain. Nowhere else in the world are there so many horses.

There was not a soul around. I tied my horse to the willow, and with my dagger dug a hole at least two handspans deep.

The two gold pieces lacking to make up the hundred I replaced with two from the queen's gift, then pushed the money, in the leather bag, into the hole. I kicked a large lump of earth over it and trampled it flat, so that it wouldn't catch anyone's eye.

That was the first lucky idea I ever had in my life. It was this money that, a long time later, helped me back to Constantinople, where I now write these lines; and it was with this money that I had my happy little home built on the seashore.

*I*t was noon when we arrived in Attila's city. The sun was burning hot. The dogs hung out their tongues even in the shade. At the edge of town Eslas stopped us and sent a horseman ahead to report our arrival to Attila.

I began to take my leave of the company, but Eslas bellowed, 'You stay where you are!' His face was red and his eyes bulged with anger.

It was so peculiar to see this good, friendly man change so suddenly, we all looked at him aghast. Was he drunk, or had he gone mad?

In less than an hour a company of Hunnish soldiers galloped up to us. Seeing the silver stars shining on their hats, we knew that they were the king's bodyguard. They greeted Eslas, then seemed to be awaiting his command.

'You ten! Dismount!' Eslas ordered, meaning us. And as we got off our horses, he pointed. 'Tie up those there!'

I froze with fright and Vigilas turned pale.

'I object to such treatment!' he shouted. 'I am the emperor's envoy! Anyone who harms me harms the emperor!'

'Tie them up!' repeated Eslas and the soldiers tied us up: Vigilas, his son and me.

Our officer who was escorting the fugitives burst out, 'How dare you do this to our envoy? He is the emperor's person here! Haven't you been an envoy in our country twice now?'

Eslas had been drinking and fraternizing with this officer all along the way. His reply showed how little he cared. 'I'll answer for what I am doing!' he spat out.

'My lord,' I too objected indignantly, 'don't you know that I don't belong to Master Vigilas?'–for I guessed by now that that fox-faced Vigilas must have been up to no good.

But Eslas didn't answer.

'Search them!' he said, when our hands had been tied behind our backs.

They searched Vigilas first. They found in a leather belt under his shirt seventy gold pieces. His son had the same amount. From me they took the queen's purse and the letter addressed to Chath.

Then they opened Vigilas's crates. In one ordinary pinecrate, in the middle of the cart, they found a small iron-banded box, no bigger than a baby's coffin, but it was so heavy that it took two people to lift it out.

The other crates contained foodstuffs or clothing.

Eslas pointed at the iron-banded box.

'Where is the key to this one?'

'It's hanging round my neck,' said Vigilas choking on every word. He was pale, almost blue with anger. His breast was heaving like a bellows. 'Just wait!' he gasped. 'You'll be sorry for this! The Roman Empire is peace-loving, but that doesn't mean it is weaker than the Huns!'

The Roman officer,who had been standing with his back to Eslas, turned with a disdainful glance, and said harshly, 'I'll wait here till evening while the men and animals rest, and then I'll return and report to the emperor immediately. I shall tell him that if we are going to be friendly with barbarians, we'd better have stout clubs in our hands!'

These were fighting words. I waited for Eslas to turn on him: this thin-legged officer would have meant as much to that brawny Hun as a monkey to an elephant. But instead of crushing him, he replied in a friendly manner.

'And I will ask you to come with me!' he said. 'You are an officer and a man of honour. I will not take your sword away, but I will force you to come with us and convince yourself that *you* are the barbarians, not we!'

Then he gave the guards the signal to start.

The officer stood hesitating. But when Eslas mounted his horse and waved to him follow suit, he did at last, and rode up beside the Hun.

Silently we progressed through the main street of the town. Behind us on a cart they brought the iron-banded box and the gold they had confiscated from us. Eslas was as silent as the rest of us. Even our officer kept his foaming fury inside him.

About three o'clock we arrived at Attila's palace. On the way, of course, I kept looking up at the Chaths' windows, and at Queen Rika's palace. To my great relief I saw no one I knew among the ladies.

They took us straight into the palace and into a great hall with one side open to the east. It was supported by only six slender pillars. In the middle stood a brown, throne-like seat. On the walls there were no ornaments, only deep red, oriental rugs.

When we entered, Attila was standing between the pillars. He was dressed in ordinary white garments but of very fine linen, and over his shirt he wore a kind of sleeveless jacket of dark red silk that reached to the middle of his thighs. His hat was of white haircloth with the brim turned up. His sword hung by his side from a black silk rope. He was surrounded by the handsome Edecon, the puffing Chath and his brother, the sharp-eyed commander-in-chief, Berki, Orgovan, Macha the bullheaded one, Kason, Upor, Vachar, the usual group of noblemen, and a short old gentleman with a long beard and pointed ears – King Ardaric, whom I saw then for the first time. About five soldiers of Attila's bodyguard were there too, and a sleepy young scribe.

Eslas stepped forward, took off his hat and bowed. 'My lord,' he said, 'here is Vigilas. We have searched him. We have found this much gold on him.'

He turned his bushy moustache triumphantly towards the servants, who had already set down the box and opened it up. The gold was tied in one large leather satchel. As they opened that too, it all came cascading onto the floor.

Eslas continued. 'In the box is a hundredweight of gold, or about eight hundred pieces. He had this belt on too, also filled with gold, at least a poundweight, and his son had the same.'

Then he pointed at me.

'I had this slave brought here too. He is Priscus's slave. He joined us on the way. He also had six gold coins but this sealed letter too. It is addressed to Chath, but I thought we could learn something from it.' And he placed the letter on the mound of gold.

Attila folded his arms and looked at Vigilas.

'Why all this gold? What was it for?' he asked with cold gravity.

'My lord,' Vigilas stuttered, 'one needs so many servants and animals on a trip like this. From time to time one has to buy a horse or an ox. Then all the food... And also I wanted to ransom a few slaves...'

He was stuck. He looked pale and his forehead was gleaming with sweat; for Attila's face had changed and now he looked so angry that my breath caught in my throat.

'The truth!' he thundered, so that even the pillars shook.

I could see Attila struggle to regain his composure; then, calm, he continued. 'On the road you had no expense for food. Even if all your animals had fallen dead, one thousandth of this money would have been more than enough to replace them. And I am sure you remember that I have strictly forbidden the ransom of Roman slaves.'

In exasperation, he thumped the floor with his sword. 'Are you going to tell me why you have brought a hundred pounds of gold?'

'My lord,' whimpered Vigilas, 'I have nothing more to say...'

'No? Then we shall see.'

He signed to the guards. 'If you don't confess immediately, I will have your son hacked to pieces right here before your very eyes!'

Five guards pulled out their swords. A cold swish of metal... then silence... waiting for further orders... we all held our breath. I felt as if my blood had frozen, like a stream in winter. What dark secret was behind all this? What hellish business had I got myself mixed up in?

'Father!' screamed the boy, falling to his knees before Vigilas. 'Father!'

'My lord!' moaned Vigilas, also falling to his knees, 'I'll confess everything... only don't harm my son...not my son...'

'Speak then. But if you utter one false word, these swords will stab through your son.'

He ordered a chair to be brought, sat down and, resting his elbow on the arm, waited for the confession.

'My lord,' began Vigilas, his teeth chattering, 'this gold is the pay for an act of crime... It is the price of your majestic life...' He looked like a man standing under the gallows.

'Start at the beginning,' Attila ordered icily.

Vigilas swallowed. He rolled his eyes in agony, as if he were being strangled. But then he went on:

'When the lords Edecon and Orestes came to us the emperor put them in the care of Chrysaphius, to make sure they got suitable lodging and meals. Chrysaphius is the captain of all the guards, a powerful lord and in favour with the emperor. He decided to treat the envoys as his own guests. He took them into the city, showed them the sea, the walls of old Byzantium, the Golden Gate, the cemetery, the Hippodrome, the Saint Sophia church, the porphyry column of Constantine the Great and the lighthouse. Everything. I was the interpreter.'

Attila glanced at Edecon. With his eyes he asked if Vigilas spoke the truth.

Edecon nodded, smiling.

Vigilas, out of breath, gasped like a fish stranded on shore. Then he continued with a heavy heart.

'I'll tell everything to the very last detail, so help me. Only spare my son, Your Majesty!'

'Speak!'

'Edecon was impressed; he stared at the sights, especially the palaces and art treasures. "What beautiful buildings," he said. "Not for nothing are you a settled people staying always in one place – you know how to build houses!"

'Chrysaphius replied to this by saying, "Every snail has his house – what he makes depends on himself."

' "I don't understand you," replied Edecon. "No matter how industrious a snail I might be, I could never build a palace like that around me!"

' "Oh, yes you could," smiled Chrysaphius, "If you really *wanted* to, my Hunnish friend, you could own a palace like this – marble steps, gold roofs, a garden with cypresses...the sea below your garden..." '

As Vigilas spoke he looked like a corpse speaking. What horror was this confession leading up to?

' "Don't joke with me," replied Edecon. "A palace like this is valuable beyond one's dreams. How could I possibly come by one?"

'Chrysaphius smiled and told me in Greek to stay behind with Edecon and encourage him, saying that if he seriously desired a beautiful marble palace then he should come at noon for dinner, but alone – quite alone. At noon Edecon appeared. I accompanied him upstairs to the sitting-room. There Edecon was even more amazed. He touched all the curtains one by one, all the chairs, the materials of the couches; he stared at the paintings and the table legs carved like snakes – everything. Then, when he sat down at last, Chrysaphius spoke.

' "What is your position with Attila?"

' "We don't have positions," answered Edecon. "I am simply one of my master's trusted nobles, and I command his personal guard, as you do here."

'"Do you have free access to Attila?"

'"I do."

'"Even at night, when he is asleep?"
'"At all times."
'"Even at night, then?"
'"Yes, even at night."
Edecon smiled, and as Attila looked over at him just then, he spoke. 'How well the fox remembers.'

Attila leaned back in his armchair and placed his sword between his knees. Vigilas continued.

'Chrysaphius then turned the conversation to other topics. He suggested having dinner before further discussion. So we dined, but only the three of us. After dinner, Chrysaphius spoke to Edecon. "I swear on my honour that any palace could be yours if only you *wanted* it. And you could have treasures beyond anything you're capable of imagining now. But before I go any further, swear that whatever I say to you, even if you reject it, will remain a secret. Swear that you will never tell anyone about it as long as you live. Otherwise it could cause great trouble."

'Edecon gave his hand and the three of us swore that every word would be kept secret. But my lord... Your Majesty, I couldn't have acted otherwise. I am just a servant. Forty gold pieces is all my yearly salary. I have to translate whatever they tell me. I am just a tool, not even a human being. Of my own will I have done nothing against you.'

And he continued the confession. The secret seemed to break from him piece by piece. While Attila listened gravely, I felt the weight of a lead mountain pressing on my chest.

Vigilas went on. 'After the oath Chrysaphius asked, "If you have free access to Attila even at night, wouldn't it be possible to arrange for him to be reunited with his ancestors sooner than the laws of nature would have it?"

' "That is, could I kill him, " answered Edecon calmly.'

Attila closed his eyes contemptuously. The noblemen rumbled with anger. 'Go on!' he ordered. Vigilas continued, almost sweating blood in his fear. ' "I didn't say that," Chrysaphius corrected him. "I simply meant that there are stars in the sky and that some of them fall. Attila's star too could fall – if someone were to give it a well-aimed push..."

' "Let's talk straight," said Edecon. "You Greeks speak in I don't know what sort of flowery double-talk. The offer is clear: my part is to kill Attila, yours is to give me a palace and the riches that go with it. But what is your emperor's opinion about all this?"

' "The emperor?" replied Chrysaphius, speaking openly now. "The emperor speaks through me." '

Attila smashed his sword down on the floor.

'Villains!' bellowed Urkon. His sword was half way out already, when Attila stopped his hand with a glance.

For one moment there was absolute silence. A horse neighed outside. I could smell death around me. Vigilas, pale, continued.

'Edecon thought a while and then said, "This is no small matter. How much money are you willing to offer?"

' "As I said before," answered Chrysaphius, "you can choose any palace, any in the city, except of course the emperor's. But other than that – any. If you like, even this one, where we are now, as it stands – rugs, furniture, everything in it is yours. And so that you should have ample money thereafter, what we now pay Attila in taxes for one year will be yours – that is, about sixty hundredweight of gold. That should be sufficient treasure, no?"

' "Sufficient? Of course it is sufficient," Edecon agreed, "but I will need money before the assassination too – I'll have to bribe the guards."

' "We know that," smiled Chrysaphius. "That is all extra. How much would you need for that purpose?"

' "Fifty pounds would be enough," said Edecon.'

I thought I was going to faint. What would happen to us once Vigilas finally got through his story? This terrible man would crucify every Roman he could lay his hands on! – starting with all the Romans in the city. I looked at him. Like a statue of Hades he sat motionless, with a dark and silent face but what storms must have been brewing within his soul!

Vigilas was forced to go on. With every word he uttered the wretched man drove another nail into the cross on which he would be crucified. We could count our lives in minutes now.

'Chrysaphius got us,' Vigilas continued in a voice from the grave. 'He wanted to hand over the fifty pounds of gold right away. But Edecon held him back. "Let us not hurry with this," he said, "for my fellow envoys might get wind of so much gold in my possession. Besides, when we arrive Attila usually asks us how well we have been received. He asks for all the details – who gave us gifts and what and how much. If I were to say that this much gold was a gift, it would surely cause suspicion." '

'That is how it was!' agreed Edecon.

This Edecon was a handsome, beardless man. His face was honest, and his tiny eyes glittered with intelligence. He belonged to the king's innermost circle and had he been offered a country and its crown for one single hair from Attila's head, he would have reported that to his master. The confidants of a great man are strange people. They live with him as grass lives under a tree: the tree is their life and for them is no other. They know that if the tree falls, their roots will be torn out with it.

Still Vigilas went on. 'Edecon said, "No, I'll go home empty-handed; let this interpreter (meaning me) come with me, and I will send word by him how and when to forward the fifty pounds of gold."

'Chrysaphius was impressed with Edecon's sharp thinking. "Your words are wise," he said. "It will be best as you say. I will go to the emperor now and tell we have found our man. You will be my guest for supper. Your fellow envoys will also be invited. Then if opportunity offers, I will tell you the emperor's reaction to your undertaking." '

'That is how it was!' Edecon agreed, twirling his moustache.

'They never even asked me, my lord... Your Majesty, what *my* opinion was!' Vigilas went on. 'I am just a cur, my lord, shoved this way and that. I couldn't say no to anything, for I am just a servant, and my pay is only forty gold pieces a year.'

'Go on,' said Attila gravely.

So Vigilas continued talking. 'Chrysaphius went to see the emperor and he stayed all afternoon, till evening. The emperor called in Martialus also, who is his chief adviser. I cannot say what they talked about – I wasn't at their conference – but I was ordered to translate again later that evening when the Hunnish envoys were having supper with Chrysaphius. When we were out in the garden, and the other envoys were busy watching the sea and the bright lights of Chrysopolis on the opposite shore, only the three of us were left at the table.

'Then Chrysaphius turned to Edecon and spoke. "The emperor is very glad to hear of your undertaking, and is going to reward you as I said. What's more, he will honour you with a high position at court – higher than you now hold with Attila. But the emperor doesn't think that Vigilas is sufficiently high-ranking to accompany you; he will send Maximinus with you instead. He is a nobleman and very impressive. So he'll be the envoy, Vigilas simply the interpreter. But Maximinus doesn't know our secret and he must never know."

'Was it not like this, my lord?' Vigilas asked Edecon, almost crying.

'It was,' nodded Edecon with a contemptuous smile. Vigilas breathed more easily.

'Thank heaven that even you attest my innocence. So that is how we started out: Maximinus, Priscus and I. But after we had talked to you the first time, my lord, Edecon came to our tent, he called me aside and said, "Even chance is playing into our hands; you are the one who is being sent back to Constantinople for the remaining fugitives. When you come back with them you'll be able without suspicion to bring the money for bribing the guards."

'Well it was I, then, who had to go for the fugitives of whom I have now brought thirty, for this was your will, Your Majesty. And I had to bring the money, for that was *their* will. But instead of fifty pounds of gold I brought a hundred, for they said it would be better if Edecon were liberal with the money – he shouldn't be hampered on that account.'

So his tale ended – and now I understood his foxy, secretive behaviour, and Attila's anger on seeing him arrive with Maximinus. At that time already Attila knew of the foul play. It was clear now why he had insisted so much on the fugitives who, after all, were mere scum and hardly any of them Huns, anyway. He only wanted to give Vigilas an opportunity to go and come back again – alone.

My eyes were opened now; I saw why Eslas had forbidden us to spend any money, why we were his 'guests'. It was just a trap so that the true purpose of the hundred pounds of gold couldn't be explained away with a lie.

And this stupid fellow had even brought his son with him to see the great spectacle of the Huns burying a king!

To think that we call the Hun a stupid barbarian! Yet here were our high-minded, civilized lords caught by the 'stupid barbarian' in their own scheming net of intrigue.

But now it was my turn. Heaven and earth grew dark around me as Attila glanced at the letter and spoke.

'Let's see–what sort of writing is this?'

Oh, if this terrifying man were to examine me now! His look ripped you open like a lion's claws. One glance from Attila and there was no escape.

'This letter is from Priscus,' said Vigilas, 'and is addressed to Lord Chath.'

'This slave,' added Eslas, 'joined us on the way.' He held out the letter to Attila. But Attila did not take it. He called Chath over.

'It's your letter.'

'Perhaps we should read it here,' said Chath. 'I don't know what Priscus could possibly have to say to me.'

'Let's read it then,' said Attila, looking at the scribe.

The scribe was a bony, freckled man. Among the Huns he was called Rusti, short for Rusticius. Some time later I had a great deal to do with him.

He opened the letter, and read it straight out in Hun. Attila and the rest listened carefully. I was trembling all over.

'Strange!' said Chath, with a laugh, when Rusti had finished the letter. He

looked me up and down, then turned to Attila. 'Would you like to have this slave, my lord? The letter says he is a scholar.'

Attila didn't reply. Leaning to one side in his armchair, with both hands clutching the hilt of his sword, he looked at Vigilas darkly. Vigilas almost collapsed under the weight of that gaze. He could feel that, at this moment, his life and death were being weighed in the scales... in Attila's mind.

His son was still kneeling there, and feeling the danger, drew close to his father's legs. He was trembling like the leaves of an aspen.

This pause was so painful that at last Vigilas, like a drowning man emerging from the water, burst out, 'My lord, I only ask you to spare this innocent boy! This boy, please, don't... ! Poor thing, he's innocent!' Tears were running down his face and he fell to the floor, sobbing.

'What a despicable race of people!' said the commander-in-chief. 'I shall drive away all my Roman slaves!'

'We'll cut them all to pieces!' bellowed Urkon.

'On the contrary,' said Attila, 'let them be slaves for ever. It is proper and fitting that a worthless race should serve a noble one.'

Attila's every word was law. From then on the Huns would never free their Greek or Roman slaves. This edict set a black seal on my fate.

Attila stood up and turned to the others.

'This money,' he said calmly, 'is the price of my blood. I want you to distribute it immediately among the widows of those who fell in battle. You, Eslas, go back to Constantinople. Orestes and this boy will go with you,' and he pointed at Vigilas's son.

Then, speaking to Eslas, he went on: 'This leather satchel, which contained the hundred pounds of gold, you shall hang around your neck, and that is how you shall stand before the emperor. You shall say: Do you recognize this? And when they are all shocked and amazed, in my name throw these words in his face: *Theodosius is the descendant of a noble father; so is Attila. Attila has preserved his own nobility; Theodosius, however, lost his when he became the taxpayer and therefore the slave of Attila. But a slave who contemplates his master's assassination is not honest!'*

He made ready to leave, the others to follow him.

'And this boy?' asked Eslas, indicating Vigilas's son.

'The boy will bring back a ransom of fifty pounds in gold for his father. Until then his father is to be shackled and imprisoned.'

'What do we ask from the emperor? Nothing?'

'Oh, yes!' replied Attila darkly. 'I demand the head of Chrysaphius.'

*A*ttila left and the guards united our ropes. Vigilas embraced his son. They were both crying.

I didn't know which way to move. Chath had gone out with Attila towards the inner palace. I couldn't follow him there.

Eslas had stayed behind. He was waiting for a crate or sack in which to take the gold away and he kept looking towards the storehouses.

'My lord.' I addressed him. 'My gold pieces... As you have heard, those are not part of *that* money.'

'Your gold? Aren't you a slave?'

I understood: a slave had no money – whatever was his was his master's, be it money, child or beast.

'That is exactly why I am asking,' I said with determination. 'For I am Chath's slave. It is my duty to protest. Something that should be his is not to be mixed up with all the other gold.'

He thought about my words, blinking, then signed to me to pick up my purse. I walked slowly out of the palace, thinking I'd wait for Chath in front of the gates.

But I felt as if I'd been half beaten to death!

Outside, I noticed the well in front of the commander's house. I certainly needed a wash! Dust covered my hair, my face, my neck. I washed myself in the trough and had a drink too. The water was lukewarm from the heat of the sun, and green moss floated around in it; nonetheless I drank it.

I had to wait at the gates for more than an hour before Chath finally emerged. He was on horseback; I stepped forward and bowed as he approached. 'Follow me,' he said in a friendly tone.

Once we had reached his house and he had dismounted, he sized me up, thinking hard. 'What's your name again?'

'Just Zeta, my lord,' I replied sadly.

'Zeta...Zeta... Strange name. Are your parents alive?'

'My father may still be.'

'What is your father?'

'A poor peasant.'

He shook his head. 'What the hell am I to do with you?'

Some slaves were standing there in front of the house, among them an old man with a big head, big face, and white whiskers (though his chin was clean shaven) who had in his hand some keys on a leather strap.

'Chokona!' Chath called over to him. 'This slave was sent to me as a gift. No one will ransom him, and from now on that is forbidden anyhow. What can we use him for?'

'What can you do?' mumbled the old man, looking me over as if I were a horse.

'It was stated in the letter my master received,' I answered uneasily. 'History, geography, philosophy, grammar.' Did he want to hear more?

The old man looked at me like a sleepy elephant.

'Can you curry horses?'

'My lord!' I turned to Chath as if I had been hit. 'Couldn't I be the tutor of your two lovely children? I have seen that you have two fine little boys, and there is never a tutor with them.'

Chath cast a sidelong glance at me but went on thinking.

'Well, we shall see,' he said, and turned to the old man. 'Give him something to eat. Then let him rest, for he has come a long way.'

True, I was tired, and probably looked it.

The old head slave led the way without a word and I followed. He took me around to the back, into the kitchen, and there they gave me some bread and cheese. I looked at the cheese suspiciously–I was sure it was made from mare's milk; I wouldn't touch it. But the cook was a morose, mustached woman whom I didn't dare ask about it, so I took a bite of the bread, then drank lots of water.

The maids examined me curiously. A dusky-faced girl, scrubbing a copper dish, looked up suddenly and asked, 'Can you understand Hun?'

'I can,' I replied wearily.

'Where do you come from?'

'Constantinople.'

'Will you be ransomed?'

'No.'

They all stared at me in amazement, but didn't say anything. In the corner one of the women said something in the Avzon tongue to her companion. 'Handsome boy. It's a pity his neck's so long.'

Old Chokona returned, and took me into the stable. It was a large wooden building which obviously housed many horses and cattle in the winter. At that time, however, only two horses were there, standing looking bored, by the manger.

In the corner at one end of the stable were about ten straw pallets piled in a heap. Tattered winter clothing hung on the wall covered with spiderwebs. Awful smell. Lots of flies.

I was horrified at this disgusting place. Was it to be my new lodging? At home, in Constantinople, I had slept in a bed with sheets, on my master's clean little verandah; there had been flowers in the window there and portraits on the wall of Constantine the Great and Theodosius. The air was clear, and smelled of the sea. I'd had mesh curtain, too, to protect me from the flies.

'Couldn't I sleep–' I asked the old man, 'I mean–would you allow me to sleep outside? If you'd give me a blanket, I could lie down outside.'

'Blanket? H'm. You can't do without one, eh?' So he gave me a rough horse blanket, and I spread it out beside a stack of hay, in the shade, then stretched out on it.

What was to become of me if Chath wouldn't accept me as tutor to his children? Was I to be thrown among the stable-boys?

In the evening, seeing I wasn't asleep, the old man shuffled up to me.

He had a thick slice of dark bread in his hand, and some cheese.

'Well,' he said goodheartedly, 'have you had a rest?'

'I will, tonight,' I replied. 'May I sleep out here at night too? You see, I've never had anything to do with horses, and I've never slept in a stable. I would rather be out here...'

'Well...you can,' muttered the old man kindly, and he sat down beside me. From his pocket he took out a salt shaker carved of wood, and began to eat.

'Where are you from?' he asked.

I told him what I could. Then I asked him, 'How is life around here at the Chaths, Uncle Chokona? – if you don't mind my asking about the household?'

'Well...' He shrugged his shoulders. 'It depends. The lot of a slave is bitter everywhere.'

'Yes, but I mean, how are the slaves treated here?'

'Depends on the slave. According to merit.'

'Who is better, the master or the mistress?

'Well... the master has a heavy hand. And the mistress keeps track of even sparrows' eggs. But I'd rather serve here than anywhere else.'

'And the young mistress?'

He shrugged. 'We have nothing to do with her. She is still a child.'

We fell silent for a while. I stared at the ground; he munched his cheese. He was a Saraguri, born among the Huns, but by now he had forgotten the language of his ancestors. As a young man he had been a stable-boy with the Chaths; now, in his old age, he had been ordered to do service around the house.

I broke the silence again.

'But there must be enough to eat for all?'

'Well... there is. You can even grow fat if you want to. Though certainly not many sheep will be skinned for our benefit.'

'Must one eat horsemeat too?'

'No one will force you!'

'But that cheese, it's made of mare's milk, isn't it?'

'No, it isn't; this is made of ordinary cow's milk.'

Just then about twenty pigs dashed through the gates and headed for the sties. Maids and servants hurried past, carrying swill in huge buckets.

The old man stood up, put away his pocket-knife and salt shaker, then he too shuffled towards the sties.

At daybreak I was awakened by the mad din of a barbarian city: nowhere else is there such a blowing of horns, cracking of whips, grunting of pigs, mooing of cows, whooping of people. People here rise with the sun. At dawn the whole city is astir. Horsemen dash about, watering their horses at the well. Tousled women chase pigs, maids stretch themselves, sparrows chirp in the dewy trees, pigeons flap around the city, and swallows dart hither and thither as they begin their hunt for flies.

I had found myself a good little spot in the hay, and although other servants slept there too, nothing more than a few mosquitoes disturbed me.

I brushed bits of hay off me and shook the dust off my sandals as best I could. I noticed with dismay that one was coming apart at the side. Slaves went barefoot in summer. No one around here had sandals as nice as mine. If they wore out on my feet, would I have to let Emmo see me walking barefoot?

I washed myself, then tidied my hair as well as I could without a comb. After that I stood by the gates, thinking that when my master awoke, he'd send for me, and so it turned out. In an hour I heard some servants calling me.

'Hey, Greek! Come along in. The master wants you.'

The family was sitting on the first floor verandah. On the table were milk, butter, bacon and burnt wine. Emmo was sitting beside the two children, and Djidjia was there too, and another old, hook-nosed maidservant, dressed in a red silk jacket.

All this I took in at a glance as I entered. I bowed, then stayed beside the door with downcast eyes, as a slave should in front of his master.

'What's in your hand?' asked Chath.

'My money.'

With that I stepped forward and handed the purse over to him.
'Gold pieces!' Chath was amazed. 'You are that rich, eh?'
'Priscus allowed me to know the meaning of the word *mine.* I know that the custom is different here.'
'But father,' Emmo broke in hotly, 'Queen Rika gave the money to this Greek!'
'What do I care?' replied Chath merrily. 'It's not good for a slave to have money.'
'What a slave owns, his master owns,' added the lady of the house.
I went back to the door.
'I have thought about what you told me,' the master began. 'It is a strange custom with the Romans to hire a tutor for their children.'
According to strict etiquette I should have answered with a yes or a no, but what was politeness to a barbarian like this, who ate horsemeat and could take away the purse of a poor slave?
'A man only becomes a man through education,' I said, raising my eyes. 'The two little boys seem to be clever.'
'But what in the name of damnation should we have them learn?'
'First of all the alphabet, my lord. Letters are the key to the treasury of the mind.'
'The treasury of the mind? And what might "the treasury of the mind" be?'
'The riches of the soul, my lord. The thoughts, knowledge, wisdom and memory of thousands of men, all collected in books over many hundreds of years.'
'So you'd teach them how to read, then.'
'To read and write, if you so wish, my lord.'
'You're crazy, lad! Can't you see that I am a rich man? I can hire as many scribes as I like. Why should I or my sons know how to write?'
Since he said this with irritation, fully convinced of its truth, I didn't dare contradict him.
'Well, then, perhaps mathematics.'
'What in the name of damnation is that?'
'The science of counting, my lord.'
'What's the good of that? I have never counted my livestock, and yet I notice if a horse or cow is missing. Chickens are sometimes more, sometimes less, why bother to count them? That's what the steward is for; let him keep count. What else would you teach?'
'Geography, history, philosophy – anything you wish, my lord.' I was beginning to grow worried.

'Don't use all those Greek words to me – speak Hun.'

'Geography is the science of the earth. A clever man can make use of his knowledge of lands, mountains, waters; where what people dwell; what other cities are like; where mines, mountain passes and castles are located; where the various different industries are found and so on.'

'Yes, that is a good science,' he nodded, musing, 'but not for children; only for a king. The king takes his people wherever he wishes, and the important thing is that the place should be good pasture and near fresh water. What else do you offer?'

'History, or the past. That, my lord, concerns those who lived before us. What sort of people they were; who their kings and leaders were; how they struggled; how they became strong; or how they grew weak, but learned from their own misfortune.'

Chath shook his head.

'That's the job of bards and ballad makers,' he said. 'My sons are not reduced to having to learn this. If they'd like to hear such things, they can call a bard and have the stories told to them. What else?'

I began to feel uncomfortable.

'Philosophy, or the science of wisdom,' said sadly. 'The lives and teachings of the seven Greek seers, especially those of Aristotle, Epictetus, Plato and Socrates...'

Chath waved his hand.

'Let the Greek devil take them all! I have never learned any wisdom out of books, and yet I am a wise man. My sons won't be any worse off either.'

I didn't dare say more. I felt numb with disappointment – they wouldn't use me inside the house.

Emmo didn't even look at me. I was deeply depressed.

Chath emptied his silver mug. 'Well,' he said at last, 'we'll see what I can use you for. For the time being, your duty will be to go with me wherever I go. Be off now.'

What a relief! So I wasn't just to be tossed to the horses! Chath must have thought me a cut above the others. So I bowed and backed out as if the Emperor himself had dismissed me. The old maidservant with the hook nose caught up with me in the passage. She gave me a shove and looked at me contemptuously.

'What an ill-mannered idiot you are!'

I was astounded. 'Why?'

'You enter – no greetings. You leave – again no greetings. I am surprised the master didn't give you one across the face!'

In fifteen minutes Chath stepped out of the house. His horse was harnessed and waiting. All the servants nodded and gave him greetings.

'Top of the morning to you, sir. Hope you slept well, sir.'

Chath looked around. 'Bring another horse. Is Smoke in the stable?'

'No, sir,' replied the groom. 'I let him go with the others, because –'

'Well then, bring old Balkan!'

'Saddled?'

'No.'

They led out the other horse – no saddle, no blanket, no stirrups. Chath signed to me to mount, then started out. We plodded through the long street. People greeted him from all sides; he just lifted his hand to his hat.

Then he shouted back, 'Zeta!' and slowed down his steed. I hurried to catch up with him.

'Have you been to the Imperial Palace with your master?'

'Yes, my lord; often, almost daily.'

'Tell me about them. What sort of people are they?'

'If I am not mistaken, my lord, you have been there yourself as an envoy, three years ago, when you brought away six thousand pounds of gold from the emperor.'

'True. But every word is a lie there, my son, and every gesture play-acting. They put on honesty as they would put on their best clothes. I'd like to hear about their everyday faces. Tell me.'

I told him that Theodosius was a weak, helpless person. It was his older sister who ruled in actuality, but even she only with the brains of a few advisers. I could see now that my job was to keep him company by talking to him. During a pause in our conversation I brought up my own affair.

'Allow me, my lord, to speak of something that does not concern the topic of our discussion. After I left you, my lord, the maid called my attention to the fact that I hadn't greeted you. I apologize, my lord–I didn't know the custom. With us a slave cannot speak unless spoken to.'

'Doesn't matter,' he waved good-naturedly.

We reached the place where all his horses grazed and he picked out a short, grey horse. This was Smoke; from then on he was to be my mount, for Chath wouldn't allow a slave to sit as high as he did.

On our way back Chath stopped at the gates and gave me his hat. 'Take it in,' he puffed, 'and ask my wife for the *palace* one.' So I galloped into the yard, and ran up to the first floor.

In the passage I met Emmo coming towards me. She was dressed to go visiting: white dress, red sandals, veil and a riding whip in her hand.

As soon as she saw me I thought she was going to attack me; her eyes flashing anger, she whispered, 'How did you get here? Why did you come back?'

I was engulfed by that same fine fragrance from her dress that I remembered at Queen Rika's. She looked at me wide-eyed, like an angry cat, so that I could only stutter, not knowing what to say.

She took hold of my arm and pushed me roughly through a half open door into a room. It was the clothing room with furs hanging all along the walls. Three suits of Roman armour were fastened to a pole.

'Why did you come back?' she repeated angrily, leaning so close to me that her nose almost touched mine–as if she expected my eyes to answer. My heart was pounding.

Resolutely I replied, 'I wanted to.'

'You wanted to? You, yourself?'

'Yes, I myself.'

'But why? You were free. My father says Priscus gave you to him as a gift. Why are you a slave?'

'I put myself into slavery. To you I confess, my young lady, that I ran away from Priscus. I wrote the letter in his name. All so that I could come back.'

The girl fixed me with a stern look. 'I don't understand you. Why did you do it?'

'Simply to find out,' I said, reaching into my tunic, 'if you gave me this rose.'

Staring, her eyebrows drawn into a frown, she looked at the rose. Then her icy gaze fixed itself on my face again.

'No.' And she hurried out of the room.

I went out, reeling. The whole world seemed confused in my mind.

During the following days my feelings suffered worse shocks; I was constantly being hurt.

The servants received me indifferently. They were accustomed to seeing slaves come and go. At most they were interested in finding out if I was of noble origin and if I expected to be ransomed.

As soon as they learned that my father walked barefoot and no one would ever think of ransoming me, they looked on me with contempt. They said things like, 'Your hands look like a gentleman's. Well, they'll soon get rough here.' Or, 'He puts perfume in his hair. Kopi, make sure he has the finest almond milk to wash in every morning!'

This Kopi was the water carrier, fire watcher, and generally a jack-of-all-trades.

They all guffawed at such remarks, thinking them very funny.

'Good people,' I pleaded with them, 'I don't mind you making fun of me as long as you don't do it maliciously. But I don't make jokes that hurt. I am my master's servant, but I'll be yours, too, if you will only bear with me.'

They were quiet for a minute. Then the water carrier spoke; he was always ready with a joke.

'You speak so fine, like a student. Perhaps you even know how to write?'

'He knows everything,' the hook-nosed maid butted in. 'You should have heard him telling the master how he knows everything, yet he didn't know how to give a proper greeting.'

And now they were all laughing at me again.

This rough sort of joking turned to positive spite when they saw that Chath took me everywhere with him and for days none of them would speak to me. If I greeted them, they didn't answer. If I approached them, they turned away. Once, when I sat down with them for dinner, Raba the cook said in a wondering voice, 'What are you here for? I thought you ate with the master today!'

'A dog's place is at his master's table,' said Uzura the doorman.

'He knows all about flattery,' went on Karach, a dark Kidarite with a bashed-in face. 'He bows to the master like some Roman senator.'

I just sat silently. I am not going to argue with them, I thought. Uneducated people are like dogs; they can't stomach strangers until they get used to them.

And yet I couldn't quite ignore the cook – it was she who ladled out the food onto my plate. So, no matter how gruff she was with me, I always answered kindly and thanked her for whatever she gave me.

Then she came in for cutting remarks too: 'Go ahead, Auntie Raba, give him the best part!' Uzura would shout. 'He thanks you so nicely, he'll soon be kissing your hand.'

'He'll marry Raba!' whooped Kopi.

They all laughed. Raba was quite old; she had a moustache and a voice like a man's, and weighed at least three hundred pounds. They laughed for days at Kopi's remark.

This is a sad chapter. Comfortable people, reading it, may wonder why I didn't just get up and leave or do something for myself on my own. But remember, eating is a *need,* not just a *habit.* If one is hungry enough one will eat the bark of trees and drink the water out of puddles. I am not surprised that the prodigal son in the Bible ate from the same trough as the pigs.

Oh, I can see now that I ought to have laughed at myself whenever they laughed at me. When they cracked jokes I should have gone one better, then all their arrows would have bounced off me. But my spirit was so broken at that time that I could only writhe like a snake beaten with a stick. Everything hurt, even stupid remarks.

So I just took it all in silence till I could get away. I didn't mind sitting outside with poor lame Kopi. I couldn't be angry with him because I could see he meant no harm. He joked to cheer himself up.

There was no dog around the house, for one of the children had been bitten once, and Chath had had all his dogs killed. Among the chickens which pecked in the yard by the kitchen I noticed a black hen with a crippled leg; when it was still a chick, someone had stepped on it. They didn't kill it, of course, but likely it wouldn't have ended up on a spit anyhow because of its colour. Black chickens were usually given to the shamans, but because it was lame, they had no use for it even that way.

Well, I was eating there on the threshold when my eyes came to rest on that poor little feathered creature. She was ugly and sad, and always looked frightened. Her comb was pale. All the other hens pecked her and drove her off. At times she was almost screeching with pain.

And yet she managed to stay alive – while all the other hens were scutting around the stables, merrily scratching the ground, she would stay there alone near the kitchen, hopping away when someone approached. So I threw her some of my bread.

At first she was startled, and jumped away. I could see she thought I was throwing stones at her. In a few days, though, her fear disappeared and she dared to come closer.

She began to look more trusting. She knew that from me she could expect only good.

So while my fellow servants ate inside, I would chat to my little hen.

'Come, Blackie, don't be afraid. Here! Catch! Pick it up!'

She was soon eating out of my hand and would come running up the minute I appeared, would give me a knowing look, quite without fear, and duck when I spoke to her. Later she even sat on my lap and let me stroke her, though birds don't usually like to be handled.

This hen grew to like me so much that I used to find her perched by my bed every morning, waiting for me to wake up.

Summer had passed. The city of tents was changed. Beside every tent now stood stacks of hay and straw and between the stacks, stalls had been built for the horses–just hurdles placed so that the north and east winds wouldn't chill the horses. Even the tents were set so as to protect the animals from the winds.

More skins had been put on the tents and the openings were covered with horsehides or cowhides, pulled aside during the day, but let down at night.

The people looked different too: the ample, fluttering shirts and breeches were covered now under hairy leather clothing – wolfskin, bearskin, deerskin, calfskin – all with the hair left on. Their light haircloth hats had been replaced by tall fur ones – lambskin for the common people, foxskin or beaver for the others. Attila's hat was made from a lion's mane, the commander-in-chief's and other dignitaries' – including my master's – of bearskin. Only the slaves continued to go bareheaded.

I still followed Chath around and I had got used to sleeping in the stable, though it was hard for me and there were times when I wept; but when the weather turned cold the warmth of the animals was comforting.

I saw Emmo every day, but she never so much as looked at me, except very rarely when we met when nobody else was about; then she did say a word or two, casually; but at least she did speak to me.

She asked me once if I was satisfied with my lot.

'My young lady,' I sighed, 'I am the world's most lucky unhappy man.'

She should have asked me why I called myself both lucky and unhappy, but instead she just shrugged her shoulders.

'Too late now for regrets.'

'If I can only see you,' I replied, 'nothing else matters.'

'Don't you know,' she demanded threateningly, 'that you are playing with your life *for nothing.*'

'To you nothing, yes – but for me everything.'

She turned angrily and left me.

Once, I saw her leaning out of a window overlooking the garden. It was a grey autumn evening and the moon had just come up. I walked by and greeted her.

'*Your* slave wishes you a good evening.'

She just looked at me, her face calm; and though I stopped for a moment, thinking she might say something, she didn't.

Another time, I was sitting by the door feeling sad, and so preoccupied with my thoughts that I didn't even notice people walking about me, when I caught the scent of her dress and looked up to find her standing there.

She had on a coat made of wildcat fur with a matching hat.

She was waiting for her horse.

I stood up and bowed.

She spoke to me then. 'Are you well?'

'Thank you.' I bowed again. 'I am dead but breathing.'

We never exchanged words again, in spite of the fact that whenever it was possible I looked for an excuse to get inside the house. I was always trying to please the children, making toys for them, or taking them flowers or fruit. But other slaves were doing the same, and women know better how to talk to children. There were at least ten female slaves.

I *could* talk with Chath; that's why he kept me–to marvel at me, as if I were some finely-cut gem. I was his slave, therefore my culture and education were his. He trotted me around the way he wore his chains and rings. He could sense my value, but didn't know its worth in gold.

So I became his favourite dog. The slaves saw that he didn't kick me away from him, so their attitude towards me changed. If they had any wishes they wanted made known, they entrusted me with them, since I could always weave them skilfully into my talk with the master. But on my own behalf I seemed to be only stupid and unlucky. In vain did I keep bringing up the fact that the carpets didn't hang in quite the correct order in his dining room, or that he should have me clean his treasures and weapons. He asked me what I suggested, then had me teach one of his other servants. It was obvious that he thought of me as a valuable companion, and that all knowledge interested him. Wherever he went I was to follow him, bareheaded, on my unsaddled horse, and was to talk about anything and everything.

His ignorance was beyond belief. At times, when I thought he had understood me, he would ask such a ridiculous question that I could hardly refrain from laughing. I couldn't resist inventing outlandish scientific theorems, historical events that had never taken place, and descriptions of nonexistent countries and peoples. He believed everything: dog-headed men, headless people, one-legged ones – to him they were all credible.

This helped to keep up my spirits, this constant feeling of intellectual superiority; without it I might never have recovered from my desperate sadness.

It grieved me especially that my clothing was getting tattered. I wasn't afraid of the cold as much as of the impression I made on Emmo.

The slaves in the courtyard – or, as they called them, the *outside slaves* all went about in ragged, dirty clothes held together at times only by their belts. They scarcely washed themselves or combed their hair.

Periodically I washed my own clothes, and mended them if they tore. I washed and combed regularly. But I still wore my Roman garments, and my sandals were so torn that I was ashamed in front of Emmo. If I saw her approach, I hid myself or turned my back to her, trembling for one glimpse of her, yet avoiding her so that she wouldn't see me.

When the first snow fell I rode beside my master, shivering; my hands were blue, my nose red. He must have sensed that it was an effort for me to talk.

'Devil take your hide!' he barked. 'What are you shivering for? What's all this shaking? Why don't you ask Chokona for something to wear. You'll perish in this cold!'

'Oh, my master!' I replied sadly. 'Old Chokona gave out such awful clothes that I was afraid to put them on for fear that people would speak ill of you on account of my shabbiness.'

Chath reached for his sword in anger. 'Who dares to speak ill of me? No man has his slaves walk around in silk!'

All the same, when we reached home Chath called me upstairs and himself rummaged through his own garments to pick out some that would do for me.

For a long time I had wanted to wear Hunnish clothes. I wanted to *be* a Hun, since a Hun meant being one step closer to Emmo. But in any case I came to like their style – the white shirt, wide trousers, and the hat with an eagle feather. Only I still didn't care much for their winter outfits. People looked like the distant relatives of animals – like bears on horseback.

Amid much grunting and puffing and swearing Chath chose a pair of foxskin pants, a wolfskin coat and some calfskin boots.

His wife chided him. 'Have you gone crazy?' she said. 'Giving good clothes to this slave!'

'Shut up!' Chath growled at her. The woman scuttled out.

The garments were really nice. The coat fastened with gold chains in the shape of lion's claws; Chath cut those off, of course, giving me short leather thongs instead. Nonetheless it was a lovely coat – slightly moth-eaten, but only on one side. The breeches were faultless except for a little wear on the seat, but the coat would cover that up.

'My lord,' I said with gratitude and also a little hypocrisy, 'I don't deserve this. Perhaps you could find shoddier clothes than these!'

'Shoddier than these I won't find,' he muttered. 'I'd give you a hat too, but then they'd mistake you for a lord, so you won't get a hat. But if your head gets cold, put a kerchief around it, like the others.'

So I thanked him for the clothes with all my heart. Oh, when Emmo sees me! I thought that was my greatest joy in them.

All too soon I had to come down to earth again. When I tried on the garments, I realized that Chath was a much wider and taller man than I. Everything hung on me. I stood in the coat like a bear on its hind legs. I pulled it in with a belt, but the female servants laughed when they saw me emerge from the dressing-room, and as for Chath, he guffawed and he called the rest of the household to come and look. His wife laughed and oh, if only Emmo hadn't!

I tried hard to laugh myself, but my eyes filled with tears. I would have liked to throw down the animal skins and run away somewhere to hide.

'My lord,' I said once when I found him in a particularly good humour, 'there are so many furriers in the camp; couldn't these clothes be altered a little?'

'What an idea!' My words shocked him. 'Do you think I am going to give you new garments every year? You can grow and fill them out! You'll wear these till your death, Greek!'

When winter got really cold, I understood why Huns wear furry clothes: for no other reason than to be able to turn the fur inside. Fires were kept burning in the tents, but for cooking and baking only. The men still stood around in groups in the open all winter long. The horses had blankets thrown over them. People put on gloves if the weather got really crisp, and pulled their hats down over their ears, but winter could never get cold enough to penetrate those fur garments.

In winter the women wore furry hats, boots made of soft rabbitskin or catskin, reaching above the knees, and dresses lined with the fur of martens and weasels.

My hair had grown to my shoulders. My head never even felt the chill any more, although, when it snowed, the snow would sometimes freeze on my hair.

Attila had a visit from one delegation or another almost every week. Even kings among them at times. Of course, these weren't statuesque kings of marble like the Roman emperors, but greasy-faced barbarian royalty who lived in tents and rattled half a ton of gold on their persons. They were uneducated, but dignified, and knowing nothing of luxury, they didn't seek it. They willingly accepted Attila as their overlord.

Well, whenever royal visitors arrived, there was always a noisy supper at the palace; around dawn I had to lead my master home with someone's help. The Huns drank like mad. It was said that even Attila became merry on occasion.

There were weddings too; six the same day, sometimes. And again people drank, and danced to music. Once it was rumoured among the servants that Emmo was to be married to Prince Aladar, but nothing came of it. The prince married the daughter of a commoner. I saw the girl; she wasn't as beautiful as Emmo.

I wouldn't wish those days back again.

I soon gave up standing around waiting in front of the palace when my master had luncheon with Attila. I knew he wouldn't be back before sundown. If he had luncheon with the commander-in-chief, I knew that I didn't have to call for him before midnight. So on afternoons like that, I camped in the kitchen.

In one corner was a large, wide fire-pit not higher than a handspan, for boiling kettles and cauldrons. They fed it with big logs of wood during the winter, and it was good to sit there on the warm stones in the afternoon, just staring into the fire.

Sometimes, during the long winter nights, there were as many as ten of us sitting around the fire – horseherds and also cowherds who had brought their animals back from the fields, free Hunnish servants, myself, and Chokona, the old steward. We would all sit looking into the fire. For the Huns this is a sort of pious entertainment. Even on summer evenings they make fires in the fields, then just stare into them devoutly with dreamy eyes.

Once I was sitting there alone. It was wash-day for the women, and they were hanging up the wet clothes in the loft. The sun was about to set, and snow and sleet were coming down.

Djidjia entered the kitchen flashing her smiling dark eyes at me. 'Good old Zeta,' she chattered, 'I'm glad to find you here.'

She sat down beside me, stretching her hands out over the embers.

'We don't meet often, do we?' she twittered, 'and yet there's so much I'd like to talk to you about. For my mother was a Roman subject too, you know, and would you have guessed that I'm fourteen already?'

Well, no, I wouldn't, but then it didn't interest me, either.

The girl didn't even look thirteen, and there was nothing feminine about her – she looked like a boy in skirts, a rather spiritless urchin. Whenever she saw me she always smiled and greeted me. But I didn't like her–if she hadn't existed perhaps they would have entrusted the children to *me!*

'The way we keep track of my age is this,' she prattled on: 'the young mistress was born when Attila was elected king. I was born two years after that. Look at this little jacket lined with weasel fur–it's hardly worn; I got it today from the young mistress.'

She got up and drank from the servants' pitcher. Then she sat down again, somewhat closer to me this time, and faced me. She had on the jacket Emmo had been wearing last week, but her legs were bare and red from the cold.

'The children are asleep,' she chattered gaily. 'The young mistress is at the palace–there's dance there tonight.'

I don't know what else she told me, but all the time her eyes never stopped wandering over me, and at last she hitched closer to me again, leaning forward as if she were going to rest her head on my shoulder.

'Get out here!' I growled at her.

She got up, frightened and embarrassed, and brushed off the ash from her dress. Then she glanced at me sadly and sighed.

At last, ashamed, she left the kitchen.

*O*ne morning in December, horsemen in Greek robes arrived in our courtyard. One of them I recognized as Vigilas's sickly son, another as Nomus, a patrician who had often been the emperor's guest.

Chath was still asleep at the time. I was squatting under the eaves of the gates. The snow was coming down in huge flakes.

As soon as I recognized the Greeks I began to feel hot and uncomfortable.

My God! What if Priscus were with them! I'd die of shame! They had three servants with them, and an interpreter. I knew them all by sight.

'Is the master in?' asked the interpreter in Hun.

'He is,' I replied, also in Hun.

I was surprised that they didn't recognize me.

A servant announced them, and led them up. They took a gift in a small crate, and stayed with Chath for about fifteen minutes.

Left alone there under the gates, I still felt hot and uncomfortable.

At last I addressed one of the servants in Greek. 'Are there many of you here?'

'There are quite a few of us,' he replied, surprised to hear his own tongue spoken.

'Who among the lords have come?'

'Master Anatolius, and Nomus, with a scribe and an interpreter.'

'Maximinus hasn't come?'

'No.'

'Nor Priscus?'

'He hasn't come either.'

I breathed more easily. I straightened up and demanded like an interrogator. 'What about Chrysaphius's head?'

'Chrisaphius's head?'

'Yes, his head. Where is his head?'

'Where else? On his neck.'

'That means trouble.'

'Where there is gold, there is no trouble. We brought lots. We have three crates full of gold with us. That should be enough to pay for a man's head!'

Then they asked me who I was, though they had seen me often enough in Constantinople. I don't know if it was my clothes that altered me so much, or whether the change was due to my moustache and beard that had sprouted quite vigorously in the past few months. I didn't satisfy their curiosity.

'I have no time now. It would take too long to tell my story. Some other time, perhaps.'

They had hardly left when my master called me in and asked me to run over to the royal palace and get the scribe Constantinus to come over immediately. I saw a letter on his desk with the seal not even broken.

Well, I was so scared that I lost my head. 'My lord,' I offered eagerly, 'I'll read you the letter if you wish...'

'No,' he said coldly. 'Priscus sent it. There could be something in it concerning you.'

So I turned and left, and came back with the scribe. 'Sir,' I begged the man on the way over, 'if there is something that concerns me in the letter, please leave it out! I appeal to you as man to man...'

'That's difficult,' he said, shaking his head. 'Your master will have someone else read the letter also. No, it's impossible.'

Well, I felt as sick as a dog.

'Stay here!' My master motioned me back with his head. 'Perhaps there will be something in the letter that will need your explanation.'

He tore the letter open, and gave it to Constantinus.

'Read!'

This Constantinus was of Roman origin. He was a haggard-looking, small, brown-haired lad, but clever as a snake and cold as a turtle.

He glanced through the letter, and then read it out, translating into Hun.

My Honoured Lord,

God grant you all that is good. I trouble you with this humble letter because my dear servant, Zeta, has left me and journeyed back to your country. To this day he has not returned.

I brought that boy up, and taught him from the time he was little. My goal for him was to obtain a position in the Imperial Palace, which he deserves, for his mind is excellently keen, and his integrity is unsurpassed.

But something must have disturbed that boy's mind. He escaped from me and now he must be wandering around somewhere in Attila's territory.

I ask you, please, have him sought out, and send him back with these envoys. If someone has captured him and he is now being held as a slave, send word to me who has him and for how much I could ransom him. If the ransom is not too high, I will do all that is in my power to free him.

The envoys are carrying a vase made out of silver and covered with gold. That is my small gift to you.

Accept it with good will.

Your servant who honours you,
Priscus, rhetor

Chath looked at me with wide, round eyes. His wife was examining the vase near the window. Emmo listened while the letter was read, then ran into the next room.

'I don't understand,' mumbled Chath. 'I don't understand. Read it again, scribe!'

The scribe started again, from the beginning: *My Honoured Lord.*

'I don't understand!' said Chath, annoyed, raising his bushy eyebrows. He blew through his nostrils as if there were a storm locked up within his chest.

'Wasn't Priscus who gave you to me as a present? He even wrote a letter! Hey, Mother, go find that letter. Thin, yellow, smallish. It's under the rafter in the big room.'

The woman looked suspiciously at me, and hurriedly shuffled away for the letter. I could hear the faint creaking of the floorboards in the next room. Well, here it was, then: no way out of it for me now!

'My lord!' I began to speak, feeling as if I were pinned beneath the weight of a huge rock. 'I owe you a confession. That letter was not written by Priscus. I wrote it.'

Chath stared at me. 'You wrote it?'

'Yes, sir.'

'Then that letter was a forgery?'

'I don't deny it.'

I had forgotten that I was talking to a barbarian, not to a civilized man. Suddenly the animal that was Chath began to roar. He waited for no explanation. It was enough for him that I had dared to deceive him. He picked up a chair.

'Villain!' he bellowed in a voice that made the whole houseframe tremble. 'Why, you dog! You villain!...'

He swung the chair above my head.

I raised my arm to defend myself, and under that terrible blow my arm broke. The chair broke too, so that in Chath's hand only the leg remained. But with it he hit me over the head so hard that I fell unconscious.

When I came to, I saw skirts hanging from a nail: I was in the cook's little room. Women stood about me. One bent figure was crying, at the foot of the bed, and I recognized her; it was Djidjia.

There were tears on the faces of the other women too. They had all thought me dead. But as my eyes moved, they too came to life.

'He's alive!' Raba cried out. 'Bring some water!' She pulled my coat off and held my head in her lap.

Gently, they washed me. How big my head wound was and what had happened to me I didn't know; I could only see that the water trickling into the bucket was as red as wine.

Later a shaman, a priest of the Hunnish religion, entered. Shaman Bial was a good man. He brought with him bark, earth and raffia. He fitted my arm into splints of bark, packed it with earth, then bound raffia around it so beautifully that it was a marvel to watch him do it.

Djidjia was still standing there, crying her eyes out.

'Come, now! Stop bawling for nothing!' the shaman rebuked her. 'He's not dead – no need for mourning!'

He cut off my hair and dressed my head with bandages.

When he left, I could hear him through the thin wall talking to the servants.

'He had a thorough beating! It will be a wonder if he ever walks again.'

I thought his nasal voice had something of a sneer in it; later when I knew him better I found out what an honest soul he really was.

I felt as numb as stone, perhaps from my injury or perhaps from the darkness that had fallen over my soul.

Raba found herself another place to sleep, and the servants nursed me in shifts.

The servants...I have to pause here. I hadn't talked much with these people before, not even after they got used to me. For me humanness began with the knowledge of the alphabet. Anyone who hadn't read Plato or at least Virgil was just an animal as far as I was concerned.

Well, that's how I looked on these people. Their thoughts simply revolved around their daily tasks and each other. I despised them. My master included.

But there was still Emmo; I didn't quite know how to place her.

I often thought that she was just an animal like the rest, only she had received a beautiful shape from the workshop of nature. But I had seen beautiful shapes before; what's more, if the epitome of feminine beauty were in statues carved of marble, I had seen some more beautiful than Emmo.

I often wondered what it was in that face that enchanted me so much. I took it apart in my mind... but found no answer. After a first glancc, no one would look again. But hearing her words, that unique musical voice–that was what caught a man. Then she became beautiful. From then on, even if she was silent, she remained magically beautiful. So what if she wasn't versed in the sciences! Doves can't read, and yet we love them. If we hold a dove in our hands we cannot help but kiss it.

But the others I had always looked upon as animals; I realized only now how little I knew the people around me.

All the women were interested in my welfare, as though I had been their

own brother. One look from me was enough to tell them when I wanted water, food, quiet. I imagined at first that this was because they thought of me as a gentleman after all, a tribute to my culture and knowledge. But no. I was simply suffering; they only saw a man in need of their care.

The wound on my head must have been large, for I couldn't lift my head at all. It felt as heavy as a mountain, and as if a river of fire, big as the Danube, were flowing within it. Or as if I were being tossed on boiling waves with a sensation of hovering, then sinking.

I cannot tell for how long I lay like this. After a while the violent tossing subsided, and I opened my eyes. There was no one in the room except Kopi who had just brought some water, and when he saw my eyes on him, 'Thank God!' he said.

'Kopi,' I whispered, 'my little black hen... is she still alive?'

'Of course. Why wouldn't she be?'

'Do you give her food?'

'Of course we do. Why wouldn't we?'

'Bring her to me, please.'

Even today I find it strange that the hen should have been the first thing I thought of. I was so glad to see her and I hugged her as if she were my sister!

'Oh, Blackie, little Blackie!'

The hen had been terribly frightened when they brought her in, but as soon as she heard my voice she calmed down at once. She sat beside me and looked–right eye, left eye, the way hens do – and clucked away happily: we talked together as we had before I was ill.

I asked her, 'Do you get enough to eat, my dear? Do those wicked hens still beat you up? Do you still sleep under my bed?'

And she answered it all in her own hen talk. 'Kla-kla-kla...'

During those days I slept a lot. I would wake for an hour or two, then fall asleep again like a baby.

Once, as I woke, I felt something pleasantly cool on my forehead, and, opening my eyes, saw Emmo sitting beside me; it was her hand that felt so pleasant.

Djidjia stood beside her, and they were talking quietly. The room was light; the parchment window was yellow with sunshine.

But as soon as she saw my eyes open, she drew back her hand and stood up.

'Don't leave,' I whispered. 'Stay a little longer, beautiful dream!'

She looked at me, hesitating, then turned to Djidjia and said, 'Go and fetch some fresh water in the bowl,' then sat down again. 'Are you better?' she asked kindly. 'We were so afraid you were going to die.'

'If I see you, I am not ill any more. I feel as if spring has come and you are a narcissus–a narcissus turned into a girl. When you speak I hear angels singing.'

She looked at me deep in thought, then closed her eyes for a moment.

'My father feels sorry for you too. But you know how quick-tempered he is. Whatever made you tell him that you forged the letter? Sometimes you are wiser than the shamans, and sometimes you are such a child that I wouldn't trust you with a milk jug.'

'I never learned to lie.'

'That's too bad. Lying is self-defence. It's necessary. Men carry weapons, but women and slaves can only lie; it's our shield. You could have said that your master was drunk when he gave you to my father, and that by the time he sobered up you were well on your way here.'

She paused and listened to make sure no one was coming, then she spoke in a whisper.

'I'll send you some wine. Drink it and you'll soon get well. And then, promise me you'll go home. My father will discharge you without ransom. He has already sent word to Priscus that he will do so.'

'I'm not going home.'

'You are not?'

'No. I don't care how much I have to suffer but I cannot live without seeing you!' Tears came to my eyes.

She gazed at me listlessly and sighed.

'But you must be mad. Don't you know that...'

'Yes, I know.'

'If they catch one careless glance from you, within the hour my father will have you executed by the most horrible death.'

'I know that too.'

'And I have never given you the right to hope for...'

'No, you haven't given me the right, but then you cannot forbid it either. I am a slave, so you can impale me, crucify me whenever you want to. But no power on earth can forbid me to dream my dreams.'

She gazed at me fixedly, her eyes moist.

'And if I ask you leave... if *I* ask you?'

'Why should you? I will never be a burden to you. If I see only your shadow, I feel happy. If I see your dress hanging on a nail, I touch it in secret.

If some water is left in your cup, I drink it, and that water tastes as sweet to me as the nectar of the pagan gods. I know, I know that you can never be mine. Only tell me one thing. Was it you who gave me that rose?'

She became stern and serious, and shook her head.

'Why do you deny it?' I kept pleading with her. 'Even though I know it might not be true, it would make me so happy.'

She shook her head again.

'It wasn't I who gave it to you.'

Djidjia entered then. She put a wet cloth on my forehead and by the time she had done arranging it, Emmo had left us.

*I*t was Djidjia who stayed with me most of the time. She sat beside my bed, ready to jump up at my slightest wish. She talked and twittered whether I listened or not.

Whenever she had to leave, she stroked my hand and said good-bye. But she was back again, just as soon as she could be. She was almost glad that I was ill.

One day I said, 'I don't know what's the matter with me, Djidjia, but I am extremely thirsty. Please, put a handful of snow into my water.'

'Snow?' she repeated astonished. 'Where am I to get snow?'

'Is there none outside?'

'Outside? Why, the apple trees are in blossom!'

Had I really spent so long in bed? I could hardly wait to get out into the world again where everything was green. In the yard, brood hens clucked, ducklings nibbled at the grass. The skies were blue. Swallows flew to and fro carrying tiny beakfuls of mud for building their nests.

I asked to be helped out onto the fresh grass and my little black hen followed me, cackling away happily, 'Kla-kla-kla...'

What is it in the sun with such amazing healing power that every invalid yearns for it? As I lay there in the blessed sunshine I felt as if I myself were snow being drawn up by the sun, dwindling and dissolving into eternity in an annihilation that was sweet.

That day my shaman came to see me for the last time. He took the bark off my arm, and felt it to see how the bones had knit. He was pleased and proud of his job.

'Well!' he said, 'can Christian priests do such a good job?'

'Good Bial,' I replied with gratitude, 'let the first movement of my bad arm be a grateful handshake. I know I am a slave and you a gentleman, and so my wish is not proper, but we are both human, after all...'

'All right, all right!' He smiled and squeezed my hand gently. 'You are a sensible and honest fellow. I hear you can also read and write. If you gain your freedom, come and see me: I'll make such a shaman out of you that you'll even be able to make rain.'

'If I gain my freedom,' I replied, 'the first gold piece that I earn shall be yours.'

'And I,' he said, 'will give you my daughter in marriage.'

He washed the earth off my hand, gave my head a last look too, then patted my cheek.

'Just lie in the sun!' was his final advice. 'The rays of the sun are fire on earth, straight from the hands of God. That's why it heals. If at any time you don't feel well, just send for me. If I treat someone with incantation, he'll get well for certain, God willing. My father was a famous doctor also. Attila still drinks out of a cup he gave him. That's why no harm can ever touch him.'

'Tell me something about the beliefs of the Huns, good Bial! What sort of god do you have?'

'What sort? Why, have a look, if you have good eyes!'

'Where?'

'In the sun. You can see him in the sun. His hair is gold and his beard is gold; his eyes are diamonds, but everything else about him to the tips of his toes is sparkling gold. He rises in the morning to view his world, and retires in the evening. Then, under the cloak of darkness comes Evil. His hair is pitch, his beard is soot, and his eyes are green like a cat's, although you rarely see them flash from under his dark brows...'

But I felt weak as I listened, and fell asleep as he talked.

Later I tried my feet again. All I could do, of course, was just wander about the yard. Chath's wife gave me two suits of summer clothes made of fine linen, and this made me very happy. I twirled my freshly-grown moustache into points, and sat out in front of the palace, hoping to see my other beautiful sun should she decide to appear.

But all I saw was Chath peering out of his window.

'Is that you, Greek?'

'It is, my lord.'

'Come up.'

Well, I thought, it's my own fault for showing myself. If he flies into another rage, Shaman Bial will hardly be able to stick me together a second time!

Chath received me sternly enough.

'Let us continue our conversation,' he said. 'Tell me why you made a fool of me with that letter?' Chath's wife and her father were sitting there in the room, and Emmo too, flitted in from the next room, and against the door, looking at me anxiously.

'My lord,' I replied sadly, 'soften your anger towards me. I am not as black as I seem to be. While I was here with my master I got to like the Hunnish way of life. And then, one day Free Greek came along, wearing splendid Hunnish clothes, and greeted us happily; he seemed so jovial, and lively. He told us that he had once been a slave but then had gone to war with his master and distinguished himself, so that now he shared the table of his former master.'

'That is true,' said Chath benevolently. 'So this is what was in your head?'

'Yes, sir.'

Emmo's face lit up, her glance touched me with its warmth.

However, I saw Chath blinking suspiciously again. 'But Priscus had made you free, and brought you up to fill a gentleman's post!'

'My lord, I didn't trust the court. It is ruled by women; here, men rule. I saw you, my lord, and from your face I discerned that you must be a good man. I thought I would be one of your slaves, and then as soon as war broke out, I would fight beside you.'

Chath looked at me as he walked up and down the room. 'He's crazy but he's honest!' he said, shaking his head. 'This is what you should have said in the first place instead of being deceitful. All right then, I won't return you to Priscus. But you should have come straight out with all this.'

'I was afraid that you'd send me back, my lord.'

'All right then. But you'll remain a slave, since you yourself chose to become one. Free foreigners are not allowed to live here anyway. But as you are not a purchased slave, nor a captured one, I'll return your money. Woman!' He turned to his wife. 'Give this boy back his purse.'

'Please, sir, keep it for yourself,' I told him. 'I don't want to buy anything; there's nothing I need except your mercy and good will. At most I'd accept one gold piece to give as a gift to Shaman Bial...'

'Horse radishes for him, not gold!' shrieked the woman. 'What next, indeed! He was given a calf for treating you! That's enough for him!'

The woman was Emmo's stepmother. Chath was more afraid of her, perhaps, than of Attila.

From that day on I went every morning with the fourteen- and fifteen-year-olds to shoot arrows, throw javelins and learn military horsemanship. Of course, I did only those exercises which I could manage with my good arm. They had teachers who showed me everything from how to twist a bowstring to how to face about on horseback. The horn signals I had to learn especially well. For every movement, every manoeuvre, there was a signal. These are heard by the Huns from the time they are children, so it is easy for them to respond; for me it was all new. I had to make notes, and study them at home.

It was rather humbling to discover on the very first day that there were things the horses could teach me. They all knew which horn signal meant *gallop!* which *turn!* which *stop!* and so on – the one they knew best, of course, was the one meaning *feed the horses!*

Well, the Hun's military horsemanship is a difficult science. I had supposed I should not have to learn how to ride – for in the dirty streets of Constantinople we rode horseback most of the time. But an unsaddled horse is another matter entirely: those wild runs and jumps and turns that I had to master, out in the fields of the Huns – why, I felt that I was always just about to break my neck.

For galloping we always started in a tight group and fanned out as we went along. The 'enemy' was frequently a clump of birches that had been specially planted for the purpose. We had to shoot our arrows as we passed the patch; then, when we heard the horn signal, we suddenly turned and roared back.

The teachers, all experienced veterans, never tired of telling me that in real battle to be in full control of one's horse was absolutely essential. To pretend to the enemy that one is retreating, so that, gathering courage, he begins to give chase and his lines break up in places – then to turn suddenly, to shoot off fresh arrows, to head right into the midst of the enemy now confused by the arrows, and, catching up with them, throw javelins – these were the basic essentials of a soldier's training; and, for the rest, sword, pick-axe, spear, club, mace – and courage.

One rainy day when we didn't go out for training, I visited Shaman Bial. The shamans had pitched their tents behind Attila's palace buildings. A horse skull mounted on a pole marked each tent as the home of a priest. In front of each entrance stood a small rectangular stone altar on which a tiny fire smouldered. Pleasant smells of roasting meat floated along the row of tents. For, of course, the animal used as sacrificial offering becomes the property of the priest. If anyone else were to eat it, the offering wouldn't be accepted.

'Hey, child! Which tent is the wise Shaman Bial's?'

'Over there, where that young white goat is jumping around.'

'Thank you, little friend.'

'I am no "little friend" of a slave!'

In the tallest tent lived old, blind Kama who had begun his priestly career in the time of Balamber long, long ago, and he was a very wise man indeed, always there among the nobles whenever important matters were to be discussed. His thin grey beard hung down to the middle of his chest; on the left side his long thin moustache stuck out about a handspan, while on the right it usually drooped. This was because he usually meditated, resting on his left elbow. He had the reputation of seeing into the future, but he wasn't allowed to divulge all, because for every hint he gave, he lost a day from his life, from the hundred years that had been allotted him in this world.

The tent was covered with white horseskins all the way around. So were those of all the other shamans for that matter, but his was more spacious. Skins were stretched out in front to provide shade, and many children – all his grandchildren – played there, the blind man listening to their joyful noise all day long and smiling.

The priests' tents stood around a grassy clearing, each tent with its own special duty and its own list of visitors, depending on what each priest could do. They all knew something extraordinary.

Old Kama was the head priest and chief seer, storm-quieter and army-blesser. With a touch of his hand he could bring to life those who had been hanged. The storm lessened if he twirled his magic stick at the sky, and it ceased completely – if God also was willing.

Old Iddar was in charge of the sacrifices. He was seventy, with a large head and broad shoulders. His voice boomed, and his glance was so powerful that it could stop the enemy's arrows in mid-flight, making them drop harmlessly – if God also was willing.

Young Zobogan was in charge of praying and singing. His voice was as strong and loud as a horn; his song possessed magical powers, and reached to one's very marrow. It was said of him that he knew a prayer that dulled the enemy's weapons and changed even steel to lead – if God also was willing.

Shaman Bogar, a fat, fair-haired, jovial man, was the priest of fire and the scribe of the people. If anyone needed a letter written, he drew those absurd

Hunnish characters; and he was well paid, of course. I didn't hear anything supernatural about him. They said that he could handle hot stones from the fire, but that wasn't too hard to do. In our courts every street magician could play with red hot iron.

Shaman Gyorhe could dispel curses and charms. He wailed at the funerals of common Huns, and at their weddings he prayed for the happiness of the newlyweds. At sacrifices he cut out the animal's tongue and held it in a spoon while the head priest prayed.

Shaman Bucha was a doctor for eye diseases. At sacrifices he cut off the animal's head and stuck it on a pole to frighten evil spirits away.

Shaman Bial was the master of healing broken bones. At sacrifices he caught the blood of the animal and poured it out for Evil into a little cavity beneath the altar.

Sharmand could successfully cure plague. He was also a ritual dancer, charmed weapons and could put a curse on the enemy. He only had to let one drop of water fall on a baby, and it was certain that the child would become immune to all charms and curses.

Damonogh prayed during births, and his special art was the blessing of arrows for those who were setting out for distant lands. He gave advice to lovers; he chased away hurricanes with a wave of his arm; and he could turn curses back upon the curser.

Shaman Vitosh was a very old, very pious hunchback; he had spells to cure domestic animals, and he gave out drugs too. He had an ointment which, if rubbed on a horse's muzzle, would, in battle, drag the enemy off his horse to be trampled to death.

All the others too had some skill that provided them with a living. They earned most, I think, by selling charms. There wasn't one Hun without something hanging around his neck – under his robe, of course. Even the new-born baby, as soon as it was bathed, had a red string tied around its little wrist to prevent the evil spirits from harming it.

I could only laugh at this religion. The young laugh easily. After all, every ship, small or large, blue or green, with oars or sail, navigates by the same star. That star's name to us is *Theos;* to the Goths, *Gut;* to the Huns, *Isten* (God).

Shaman Bial was at home. He and Shaman Zobogan were sitting under the wide canvas of his tent, with a small table in front of them on which were a flask made of pumpkin and two silver cups. I stopped in front of them at a distance of about five steps and respectfully waited for them to address me.

'Is that you, Zeta?' said the shaman cheerfully in his nasal voice.

'Yes, my lord,' I said, bowing. 'I have come to see you to thank you again for what you did for me.'

'Well, that's fine! But don't just stand there in the rain. Come on in! Hey, children!' he shouted into the tent. 'Bring out a cushion.'

I protested that I wasn't worthy of such treatment, but they made me sit down.

Zobogan was kind to me too, even though he was a great priest and rich too – the master of at least fifteen slaves.

'I have heard of you,' he said, giving me his hand. 'Priscus sent you here, and you are a wise man. You are a Christian, of course, like all the Greeks?'

'Yes, I am a Christian,' I replied, 'one of those Christians who look at even other religions through the heart of Jesus.'

'How is that?'

'His main teaching is that we should accept and love all peoples.'

'He was a great and holy man,' said Zobogan, nodding. 'I've heard of him, and spent a few sleepless nights on account of him. But no man can live the way *he* wanted men to live.'

This Zobogan was thin and had a drooping moustache. He was about thirty-five, dreamy-eyed and slow-moving. And, incidentally, he was old Kama's son.

'Judging by what you say,' I said, 'there must have been missionaries around here.'

'One or two always come with the returning army,' said Zobogan, 'among the prisoners; then they try to convert us, though not with much success. As soon as a Hun hears that he shouldn't fight, he leaves. This is not for us.'

Bial too smiled.

'They have never yet converted a Hun. Only the foreign slaves get baptized sometimes. But other missionaries come too–yellow ones from the East, who teach us not to wish for anything and not to want anything. This doesn't even appeal to the slaves.'

'Then, oh honoured priests,' I asked humbly, 'may I know what *your* opinions are on war?'

A Hunnish woman approached us just then, carrying an eight-year-old boy on her back. She was looking for Shaman Bial, because a cow had stepped on the boy's foot. They brought out a bench from the tent and laid the small patient on it. He wasn't making much fuss – but I knew from experience that a broken bone doesn't hurt a lot the first day.

Zobogan answered my question. 'You ask me how we judge fighting? It's necessary, my son. If it were not necessary, there would be none of it.'

'Is this to say then my lord, that everything bad is necessary?'

The priest shrugged his shoulders.

'What is bad? The mother of good. Everything that is good in this world is born of something bad. If we were practising Christian, we would have to throw all our weapons into the River Tisia. And if we did this today, the nation of the Huns would be exterminated tomorrow. By the Christians themselves! And after that there would certainly be neither good nor bad for the Huns in this world.'

'But let us suppose,' I replied, 'that all nations were to accept the Christian faith.'

'Impossible!'

'Why impossible? Forgive me, my lord, I am not saying this to contradict you, only to help us find the truth.'

'Go ahead!'

'It's just that if individuals can get along without fighting, why couldn't whole nations? A nation is only a large collection of individuals!'

'But the human race today is only in its childhood. Where have you seen the child who doesn't fight? Everything in all creation fights. The strong always subdue the weak. Life is struggle.'

'But we are not animals!'

He closed his eyes and, smiling, made a humming noise through his nose.

'We are not animals. H'm. You say that we are not animals. H'm. But what if the animals are also people?'

'People?'

'People, living in bodies of various shapes and forms.'

'Excuse me, my lord, I don't understand.'

'Before you became a man, you could have been a blade of grass, a flower, a tree, a fly, then a may bug, wolf, horse, lion – anything, everything.'

'Is this certain?'

'Is it certain that everything has a precedent? Everything springs from something else?'

'That is certain.'

'And that precedents must also have precedents?'

'That is also certain.'

'It couldn't be otherwise. Do you not feel within yourself now one animal, now another?'

'No my lord, never.'

'Do you not know people who are always ready to pounce on their prey, or who weave intricate webs just like spiders?'

'Yes.'

'Do you not know people who gather and hoard like squirrels, who are blood-thirsty like lions, who are cowardly like rabbits, or ready to serve like horses, or treacherous like snakes? What else could cause this, if not a remnant of a previous life?'

'But what purpose would it serve, this travel of the soul through many forms?'

'What purpose would it serve? Only he who started it all knows the purpose. I can only think it matures us; by it our intellect grows stronger like the brightness of a growing star. Every death is a moulting. After each moulting, we live until the next rung on the ladder.'

'And what happens after we have been human?'

'We go on still a rung higher; we enter a body of even more perfect form. One thing is certain: we never decay into idleness. Life is motion. The Creator himself moves ceaselessly. Man too must move, create, struggle – in all his forms, even though in different places and among different adversaries. But our understanding gets more and more enlightened; we become more and more compassionate, and our actions more and more noble and generous.'

'But I do not *remember* what I have been, nor what experience I may have had when I was, say, a grasshopper.'

'Why should you remember? Are you interested in the reasons for your tears when you were two? Or why you laughed then? Or what you used to play with? Or how you thought?'

'I have heard a few of your sermons, my lord; do you ever preach on this topic?'

The shaman shrugged his shoulders.

'The common people wouldn't understand. Not even you understand, and you are an educated man. Perhaps in a few thousand years . . . People today still need magic, and signs visible to the physical eye. The soul's eyes have not opened yet in you.'

We had to break off our conversation, for Shaman Bial had put on his magical hat, and with pious concentration began to mumble at the child out of a black book.

*O*ne summer day, we heard the news of Theodosius's death. A woman – Pulcheria – was to take his place upon the throne.

Attila didn't wait for Pulcheria's envoys: the stout Eslas had to mount once more and ride down to the Sea of Marmara. This time they picked all the men with the most savage faces to go with him – Hardo, Kesi, the bull-headed Macha–and as for the servants they took with them, *their* faces would have frightened even the Greek horses!

Attila's message was just this:

If, this time, my envoys do not return with the head of Chrysaphius, I am coming to get it myself!

Chrysaphius may have had some strange dreams at this time.

Up till now, only gold had been sent – not Chrysaphius's head, and the Huns were talking of setting out soon for Constantinople; they were discussing it everywhere.

The nobles spent their time from noon till midnight hanging about Attila. A gigantic map of Constatinople was spread out on a table in the largest room of the palace with every important building marked. The sea was coloured green and dotted with ships; on the royal palace was a crown.

Edecon, Chath, Berki and Orestes explained which building was which. I didn't see that map until two years later; I marvelled at how accurate it was.

Everywhere around the city youngsters milled about noisily. From morning till night they practised shooting arrows, galloping and wrestling. Chath freed me from all my duties so that I could go out with the others for training.

Even to this day I don't know for sure what Chath's purpose could possibly have been in allowing me to do that. Perhaps within that hardened man dwelt a good soul that was flattered by my trust. Attila had in his entourage at least ten noblemen of foreign origin who had risen from slavery. Perhaps Chath wanted to put a potential nobleman under an obligation. Maybe he thought that if I became a gentleman I could help him or his children later on.

Now I never got back home until late in the evening. By then Emmo was in the sleeping quarters, and I myself, very tired, just gobbled up my supper and fell sound asleep.

For weeks I didn't set eyes on Emmo.

At last the delegation returned. Three days before they actually arrived, word reached us of what they had accomplished, and yet their arrival was still exciting. Horns blared from the steeple of the palace, and galloping horsemen shouted in triumph: 'Here is the head! They are bringing the assassin's head!'

And there it was! At the outskirts of the city they had taken it out of the honey, washed it and stuck it on a javelin; that was how they brought it to Attila.

Every day Chath had midday meal with Attila. At first I thought they were just carousing, for I believed that barbarians found their greatest pleasure in eating and drinking, but once again I was wrong.

On special occasions, when Attila had guests, those luncheons might be noisy and festive but mostly they were not so much a meal as a conference.

In this way the king united the Hunnish nobility into one family circle. Everyone could express his opinion and differing views were fully discussed. The words of the elders carried considerable weight, and it was Attila who gave the final decision.

They dispersed after luncheon – sometimes late, sometimes early – each to pursue his own affairs. Attila too either visited his wives, viewed the youngsters' war games, or received emissaries of which there were always several from some far corner of the world.

One rainy October evening I was sitting in front of our blacksmith's shop while the smith (who mostly shod horses and made arrowheads) was working at the other end of the yard. At this moment he was occupied with burning distinguishing marks into the shafts of some arrows. The sign was the same as the family's insignia: two swords in the hand, and the sun.

I too used arrows like these. After exercises the boys would gather up the arrows that had been shot, and, according to the markings, dealt them back to the owners.

My arrows were made of fir, but my master's were of slender bamboo. The blacksmith made arrows for the older Chath boy too, but of course only out of light reeds from beside the River Tisia.

Well, as I was watching how skilfully the smith fixed the flight feathers, Kaza, a servant from the court, ran in all excited.

'Zeta! Zeta! To the palace immediately! Attila wants to see you! Hurry! Hurry!'

I felt stunned, but, as you can suppose, I hurried. I changed my clothes and ran to the palace.

What was calling me, I wondered, good luck or bad? My head was spinning. Oh! – what if Priscus had come!

I was led in. With awe I saw that about fifty men were sitting around Attila at the table, near the back of the room, the air was heavy with the smell of wine. On the king's right sat Barcza, his uncle; on the left, Aladar. Chath with his alert, watch-dog eyes, and Edecon, with his handsome moustache, the other Chath, the commander-in-chief, Dorog, Macha, Kason, Vachar, Upor, Balan, Madaras, cat-eyed Urkon, Zhogod, Chomortan, the old one-armed Barakon (Chath's father-in-law), Shallo, Kontsagh, Hargita – noblemen, all of them. A white cloth covered the table. Servants were lighting the wax torches mounted on the pillars. Kamocha, a round-headed, thick-necked Hun, was standing, addressing the company, and his eyes flickered towards Attila with mischievous amusement. All the others around the table were red in the face with laughing.

Kaza made me stop beside the door. We were to wait while Kamocha finished his speech. My master too signed to me to wait, and soon Kamocha lifted his cup high and said, 'Now I toast you, my royal lord. Your magnificent, newly-acquired state of betrothal calls for a toast! Nor must I overlook your betrothed.'

Loud laughter followed these words. Even the elders were laughing in their halting way. Old Barakon banged the table, shouting, 'That's it! Well said!'

Attila himself smiled.

That was the first time I saw him smile, and it seemed strange to me. A grave man smiling is like a green apple turned red – both seem transformed beyond recognition. Yet only his eyes were smiling, those terrible black eyes which could make even the mountains tremble.

It took a few minutes for the waves of merriment to subside. Then my master motioned me to step forward and he stood up and led me before Attila.

'Here, my lords,' he said, 'This is the slave I mentioned before. He does not lie even if you hit him over the head.'

My heart almost stopped beating. What sort of an introduction was this: *'even if you hit him over the head'?....*

The company quietened down. All eyes came to rest on me. I didn't know what the custom was, so I bowed, then knelt down; I thought that was what a slave should do.

'Stand up,' said Attila. 'Do you know of Princess Honoria, the sister of Emperor Valentinian the Third?'
The room was quiet; only the crackling of the torches could be heard.
'I have seen her only once,' I said, hesitating, 'when she was still being held under lock and key in Constantinople.'
'Is she still alive?'
'When I left, she was. But by then she had been taken to Ravenna. There too she was under guard.'
'And why are they holding her under guard?'
'Because, my lord, sixteen years ago she sent you a ring of betrothal.'
I thought I detected satisfaction in Attila's eyes. He glanced at the lords. Soft murmurs and shifting. Then silence again. The torches crackled.
'And what sort of creature is that lady?' Attila interrogated me further.
'It is said of her that she is mad.'
And now laughter broke out. It erupted, exploded like the volcano Vesuvius. I looked over at Chath, wondering why they were laughing so. He motioned with his hand, that I had said the right thing, but he too was helpless with laughter. Prince Aladar bared all his white teeth in his glee. They laughed so hard that one would have thought they had gone berserk. Only Attila sat calmly, his eyes glittering with mischief.
He asked me further questions.
'And how does the princess look – her face, for example?'
Total silence. A few snorts of laughter. Lips tight together. Attila gazing at me, his eyes full of devilish mirth.
Good God! What's going on? What am I to answer? I had no time to think.
'I only remember that she had a long nose, like all the descendants of Theodosius the Great, and that her face was withered.'
Again explosions of laughter. Long-haired Dorog was writhing and rocking in his seat. Attila's uncle, Barcza, had big tears rolling down his face, and his fat body shook in his chair.
Attila leaned back and smiled that squinting smile.
Only I stood there without a smile, feeling like a fool. From the chaos of voices I tried to catch some reason for this hilarity, but in vain: fifty people were laughing and talking all at once. At last Attila raised his finger and everyone quietened down.
'Boy,' he said, serious once more. 'Tell me, how do they think of me? What do they say about me in the Roman Empire?'
The question was asked amiably enough, and yet I trembled on hearing it. I had no idea what to say. In the midst of all the merriment I stood alone and

ignorant of what was happening. And I was not supposed to make Attila wait.

'At the court they think of you, my lord, as a special breed of lion which they have to feed with gold lest it tear the world to pieces.'

'I didn't ask about the court. They know me, that gang. But tell me – what do people in general say about me in that great empire?'

I looked at my master. He was positively beaming with delight as he looked at me. He nodded for me to go ahead and speak freely (as one might incite a dog just out of mischief), so I spoke with reckless honesty.

'Nothing good, my lord.'

'Be more explicit.'

'The opinion is, my lord – please forgive me, it is not my opinion, but as you have ordered me to speak the truth...'

'Only the truth!'

'Well, the opinion is, my lord, that you are the terrible child of witches, like every Hun. They say your head is bald, your nose is like a pig's, your ears hang down like a hunting dog's, and you cannot speak, only growl, like...'

There was such a storm of laughter in the room that I was afraid the building might collapse. I myself could hardly keep a straight face.

People were heaving and writhing. Eslas howled, his face turning blue. Berki guffawed, and as for Edecon, his very soul seemed in danger of being shaken out of his mouth. I have never heard or seen such hooting, braying and howling in my life. Some of them fell off their chairs and lay writhing on the floor in spasms of laughter.

I kept looking at Attila. Across his face glided that same fleeting smile that I had noticed earlier. That face was just as pleasant when a ray of mirth shone forth from his eyes as it was dark and fearsome in its usual Pluto-like seriousness.

I began to be worried lest I found myself taking up crazy Tzerko's profession – I wouldn't have regarded that as a stroke of luck, even though I was only a slave. Attila waved, however, and I was allowed to leave.

It was evening before my master returned home. I waited for him in the doorway, hoping he'd say something. I felt ashamed because those barbarians had found my openness so funny. I still didn't know what they had been laughing at so wildly. I was planning to go over to Kaza the next morning and ask him to explain.

Chath sat on his horse, his face shining with happiness and perspiration and still with a beaming smile. He jumped off his horse and slapped me on the shoulder.

'Well, boy, you stood the test! Tonight you'll eat with me! You are a slave, but you'll eat with me!'

This was a privilege which no slave in the Chath household had ever earned before.

During supper he told his wife how bravely I had behaved before Attila.

'For days we have been racking our brains,' he said, 'over how to provoke the Roman Empire. We would have started out long ago had they refused to give us Chrysaphius's head, but the cowards just handed it over! Attila was smouldering with anger for want of a pretext to take up arms. At last it came to him that fifteen years ago some foolish princess had sent him a ring of betrothal. He sent for the ring and it was found. Then he sent for Rusti. They read the old documents and found that the name of this princess was Honoria. Well, you see she is a Christian and Attila a heathen; and there in the Roman Empire they believe Attila to have the face of the devil, snorting and grunting and eating raw meat. So tomorrow Attila will send envoys to Rome for his betrothed.'

Suddenly everything made sense to me. What cunning and frightening people these Huns were! I felt a chill in my bones.

'This is what we've been laughing at all day today,' Chath continued, 'and that fox, Edecon, with a perfectly straight face, raised the question what would happen – good God! – if they actually hand over the princess? What if they send her?...' and Chath laughed again, and so did his wife.

I glanced at Emmo and she was smiling.

Then Chath repeated word for word, not forgetting a single detail, all my reply to Attila, and he remarked on how calmly and bravely I had stood there – 'He must be of noble origin, this Greek!'

I sat quietly at the end of the table with my eyes cast down, taking a bite of food now and then out of politeness. All the while Chath was praising me I could feel Emmo's eyes resting on my face.

*I*n three days a delegation of five, headed by Edecon, set out for Ravenna to see Valentinian, the Roman Emperor. Kamocha, bald Madaras, Macha, Betegh and Upor accompanied them. They carried a letter, and during one of our rides Chath told me what was in it.

Greetings to the Emperor Valentinian!

With indignation I have received the news that my betrothed, your sister Honoria, is kept locked up by you.

I will not suffer my betrothed to be held in prison; I demand her immediate release and that you send her to me, and with her the inheritance her father left her.

This inheritance is one half of the wealth Constantinus left behind, plus one half of the Roman Empire.

Attila

While this letter was on its way to Ravenna two strange delegations arrived to see Attila.

One consisted of two brown giants with rings in their ears and ostrich feathers in their hats. They wore tightly fitting leather clothes that left only their arms bare. They were handsome, black-eyed men with legs like huge pillars, Vandals from Africa. King Genseric had sent them with a crate filled with gold dishes.

The other delegation was made up of ten blond, blue-eyed men. Their clothes were made of fine soft yellow leather and their hats of red velvet. Their weapons were an alloy of silver and steel, and on their breasts shone gold buckles. These were Franks from beside the River Neckar. Hunnish women rode in groups to the tents of these men to stare at the whiteness of their faces, and to chatter about their long, loose yellow hair.

The leader of the Franks was a banished prince – a pert, handsome lad who wore such a long eagle feather in his hat that its end touched the tops of even the tallest gates. He quickly became a friend of Aladar, and from then on they went everywhere together.

Both delegations had come to solicit Attila's help in military matters.

The Vandals at one time had had their nest in the forests of the Carpathian Mountains, but eventually they had grown so numerous that they flooded across Europe. They crossed over from the tip of Iberia and conquered Carthage, and now the shores of Africa were their home. The Vandal king was suggesting to Attila that next spring they should attack the Roman Empire from two opposite sides. He would cross the sea and strike from the south while Attila invaded from the north. They would meet in Rome.

'Why should I wait for spring?' Attila had replied with a shrug (so Chath told me). 'The European half of the Roman Empire makes hay for my horses *this summer!'* He was only waiting for the reply from Rome.

Well, it too arrived. A multitude of gifts – pearls, cloth of gold, velvet and silk came with it. The court of the Roman Empire sent word that Honoria had already married.

Now Attila unfurled the red flag. He sent horsemen to rally the armies from every corner of the world.

And from that moment life was different.

Wherever I went I saw preparations for war. Everyone was polishing or repairing weapons, sharpening swords, making new maces, braiding bowstrings, reinforcing their battle jackets with metal scales, lining helmets, putting new leather on saddles, hammering away at camping tents. Thousands of knife-grinders! Thousands of bow-makers and harness-makers! And the blacksmiths' anvils ringing everywhere.

The women had smoked the meat of countless cows, pigs, and sheep all through the summer; they had dried heavy, kneaded dough. Now they ground up the meat into a powder, and tied the dried dough into bags.

Menfolk practised throwing javelins even among the tents. They made small hillocks of earth, pounded them solid, and from a distance of twenty or thirty paces threw their javelins into them.

Young people exercised out in the fields in huge swarms. Horns blared out signals. A long falling note meant a retreat. Two long rising notes meant an about-face in mid-gallop and shoot.

This manoeuvre I simply could not master. The Huns had been practising from childhood on; when their horses were galloping so fast that they were swimming through the air, the riders would turn themselves round, lie on their stomachs and shoot their arrows far behind them. Some even shot lying on their backs.

There are no officers in the Hunnish army, at least, not like there are in the Roman army; there are only commanders, and zoltans who ride very fast horses and distribute the orders of their commanders.

Divisions are formed according to families and tribes; each chooses its own leader and standard-bearer. The standard is only reeds, a sword, a horse tail, a buffalo head, a moon or some other such emblem is visible.

By autumn the Alans had arrived from the north. They came like a moving jungle of reeds with their long javelins. Their king was a stocky man with blazing eyes; he wasn't young, but certainly was agile. His people, however, were not at all stocky. Most of them were tall, long-necked men with arched eyebrows. They passed through the city with a great racket.

Soon the Nubades appeared; for days they kept coming. They were all clad in wolfskins. Even their music was a howling of horns. The Huns said that these men could actually turn into real wolves.

Then came the large army of the wild, bearded Blemmyes, who used slings instead of bows, and of course sharp stones instead of arrows. They came singing and playing fifes.

On their heels, when the first snow had fallen, the painted Gelons came with their innumerable horses. They were all armed with scythes, and they wore vests made of human skin. Their faces were so ringed with red and yellow paint that we had to ask them how they recognized one another if they changed the pattern.

On thundering carts came the Bastarnes from Asia. (Their womenfolk, also armed, came with them, but only the younger ones.) These troops wore towering helmets of copper and shields made of woven reeds. Their swords were made of bronze, wide and heavy, and their arrows were poisoned. I saw one extremely beautiful girl among them with a tiger kitten beside her in the cart.

The flood of the Akatiri lasted for about two days; they had been conquered by the Huns just the previous year. Their bows were half again as tall as themselves; they had to lie on their backs to pull them taut with their feet. They were a handsome, brown-skinned people, but had very low foreheads.

Then on deep-chested horses came the eagle-eyed Rugi, many of whom had red hair. Their long coats were blood-red too. Their main weapon was a double-edged hatchet which they could throw accurately even from a distance of twenty or thirty paces. Usually they aimed for the head of the enemy's horse and when the horse collapsed they went for the rider with their long javelins.

Then came the Sciri – a white-faced, haggard, large-boned people. They too had wide hatchets hanging down from their saddles, and their bows were double-curved. They brought no women with them.

The Tuncassi came on foot, carrying round shields and short swords. Even the day after they had passed through I could still smell onions. Their swords were of polished copper – beautiful weapons. It was said of them that they only entered the battle once the Hunnish horsemen had already engaged the enemy.

Then came the Heruls, the world's fastest horsemen. They showed no mercy for anyone, but then they asked for none themselves. Their flag was a pattern of skulls.

From the west came a fraction of the Kvads. These were large, bushy-browed archers with bows so strong their arrows would penetrate even thick wooden planks. Their coats were of furry hides, but I wondered who made them, for they stunk to high heaven.

Then immediately after came the large-nosed blue-eyed Swabians, with copper sheets across their shoulders with spiked battle flails which could fell a horse. Only a few thousand of them came; the rest, they said, would not start out until the spring.

Then various tiny clans arrived, remnants of disappearing or scattered peoples – from south and east, from north and west. Horsemen came, foot soldiers came, giant handcarts and noisy wagons came, and clattering horses came in an endless procession. Almost all of them brought along their gods, made of stone or wood or copper or gold – devilish faces all. Some were on a special cart, some on a pole but all were carried with reverential awe. Everyone trekked through the city to pitch their own camps just beyond those who had last arrived.

For days and weeks the flood of armies flowed to the sound of horns or fifes, or the dull clattering of hoofbeats and rattle of drums. The commanders saw Attila for a moment, announced their arrival, took their orders, then went on with their troops.

At Christmas came the Ostrogoths on foot. Their boots reached above their knees, and in place of helmets they wore skins from animals' heads, complete with manes or horns. Their swords were long and straight. The brothers Valamir, Theudomir and Widemir were their three leading princes. The Goths were a fearfully large nation. At one time half of Europe was theirs: their flocks grazed from the River Volga to the Baltic Sea. But then came the Huns: Balamber tore this strong people in two. Half of them fled to Gaul; these were called the Visigoths, or western Goths. The other half gave in to the Huns; these were called the Ostrogoths, or eastern Goths. Their army took days to cross the city.

In their footsteps came the Gepids, whose king, Ardaric, lived in Attila's court almost constantly. The Gepids were foot soldiers too; glittering with copper and gold, they crossed the city singing.

Next, the Saraguri, skirted, speaking the same language as the Huns, and, likewise, a short-necked, stocky people. Their javelins were made from the horns of animals. Armed women too came with them, singing cheerfully; they were muscled like leopards and had eyes like cats. Their shields were made of the skins of cranes, and their helmets were made of wood. The Saraguri drank horse blood as we drink wine. They too smelled of animal skins, like all the rest.

Then came the Saraguri's kinsmen, the Roxolans, who were also a nation of mounted bowmen. From each saddle, on a string or a strap hung a human skull – this was what they used for a drinking-cup. They brought their families, for their home is always wherever they happen to pitch camp. Their smiling women were peeking curiously out from their spacious wagons which were all hooded with skins, while their children rode along beside them. These troops took a week to pass.

Next, the army of the Jazyges swarmed through. They were actually Alans, who a long time ago had been assimilated by the Huns, and now only their clothing differed. In battle they wore scaly garments, the scales being carved from thin slices of bone; their horses too were covered from head to hoof in a similar manner. Though these men clad in scales looked somewhat like fish, they were certainly handsome: brown-haired, tall and strong, every one of them. They are the best archers in the world.

Finally, the flood of all the Huns began to pour in, Black Huns and White Huns, Hunugors, Hungars, and Magyars. I saw then that the White Huns are called white not only because of their clothing, but also because their skin and hair are lighter. The Black Huns were all black-haired, black as coal. Chath's first wife must have been Hunugor, for Emmo's hair was chestnut brown. Oh, my beauty, where is your lovely chestnut hair now!...

These Hunugors were all armed with two swords – a one-edged blade on their right side, a double-edged on their left. Often one saw lariats on their saddles–ropes of animal hair, used for wrenching the running enemy off his horse. They kept pouring in, with gay music, as if they had come for a wedding.

Following the Magyars' carts of fodder, hay and oats came the Ugors on foot. They made their living by fishing, and were more suited for guarding the camp than for fighting. Also, whenever there was a lake or river on the way, they provided fish for this huge army of a million stomachs!

The mustering of the Huns took until the end of January. Each Hun brought along an extra horse. Group leaders and zoltans had three horses, while commanders and princes galloped into camp with five to ten extra horses each. And what fantastic horses!

The tallying lasted for days. Ten thousand here, twenty thousand there, fifty thousand of the Jazyges alone, eighty thousand Gepids, sixty thousand Goths. We counted them for a week, just by taking their leaders' word for how many of them were there. When we passed the half million mark we left off. To this day I don't know how many people were gathered there, for to the men counted one would have to add the hundreds of thousands of camp followers. There must also have been more than a million horses and thousands upon thousands of carts.

All this multitude of people didn't even know where they were heading!

It was perhaps the first day of February when the heat of the sun made the icicles on the eaves start to drip. In the afternoon Attila rode out from his palace, accompanied by his commanders and noblemen, and toured the infinite armies.

Meanwhile his tent had been packed into carts in front of the palace. It took twenty-two large carts to carry this one tent alone. A smaller tent of his, used on the way for shorter stops and one-night stays, was packed on a single gilded cart, with large wheels.

At night it fell below freezing again. The sky was clear and without a cloud. As soon as the sun had set below the horizon, an enormous bright comet rose from the east. We watched it with awe for at first it resembled a sheaf of wheat, but then it grew thinner till we saw in it the sword of the Huns.

*N*ext morning Kason, Attila's bugler, climbed to the very top of the royal palace, lifted the huge ivory horn, and with a resounding blast began to blow the march. And as if thousands of horns had awakened, heaven and earth were soon filled with their calls. They all played the march; whole orchestras of fifes began to play; music and noise rose from every part of the city.

Everywhere throngs of people milled about in battle array. Smoke curled out of every home as the last breakfast turned on the spits. I saw many women crying.

Our tent too had been ready for the last couple of days, waiting out in the yard. It was a large, strong, square tent, made of leather and lined with red felt. On its sides were flaps of yellow leather that could be extended to form smaller tents; that was where the servants were to sleep – myself, Karach, Sabolch-the-big-eared, Lado and Baczon.

In the tent were the master's hammock, a folding table and folding chairs. Packed in crates were two complete suits of steel armour and five different kinds of leather battle cloaks – for winter, for summer, for rain and for heat. One was made of hippopotamus hide, and had holes in the shape of flowers. Then there were all sorts of weapons, kettles, mugs and pans, and five thousand arrows for the master alone. The weather was freezing and the straw around the haystacks was frosty, but the sky was clear.

'Good omen,' they said, 'if we start in sunshine.'

Following a horn signal, everyone harnessed and saddled the horses. My master got dressed, then called me in to see him. He gave me two swords, a javelin and a bow, and a battle cloak made of pigskin. It was lined in front with fine wire mesh.

He embraced and kissed his wife, daughter, father-in-law and children a hundred times.

He too said, 'The sky is clear. That's good omen.'

Then he added, 'My dream wasn't promising, but... dreams are just foolish anyway!'

I too approached and kissed his wife's hand, then old Barakon's, and my eyes filled with tears when I turned to Emmo. She gave me her hand silently; I bowed and kissed it. I felt her squeezing my hand.

Chath had trouble saying his last good-byes.

'That damned dream! But it's just nonsense! All dreams are nonsense!'

Then he turned back once more from the threshold. 'My gold chain, the one with the large links...' he said to his wife, '...or some money...ten gold pieces should do.'

The woman began to cry.

'Why did you turn back? That's bad luck...'

I stood in the middle of the room, Emmo and I were alone.

'If I return,' I said in a low voice, 'and can achieve the same status Free Greek won for himself, can I hope...that you will be glad to talk to me then?' She looked at me sadly in silence.

'Even if you return,' she replied finally, 'I cannot promise you anything, Zeta. You are good, but in this hour you stand so far away from me...and always and for ever you will stand from me... But if you do not return...if you do not return...'

'I will die for you, and that will be the end of it.'

'It may be so,' she said thoughtfully, then, stepping up to me, 'You may kiss my cheek.'

Perhaps I was not supposed to touch her, except to lean over and touch her face with my lips, but my arms moved of their own accord and I gently caressed her. For a moment her face rested on my breast; I thought I could hear the beating of her heart. I kept holding her, my lips pressed to her velvet, petal-soft cheek, while she closed her eyes and endured my kiss in silence.

I could say nothing to her except one word: 'Narcissus!'...

For that is how she looked, like the spring narcissus: all gentleness... whiteness...poetry...

In the next room Chath's heavy steps could be heard again. We separated.

Emmo passed her hands over her hair. Her eyes were calm as a mountain lake.

How easily a face can hide a person's secrets!

By the time we all got outside, the red cart – the one carrying the tent – had already rolled out of the yard and the servants all stood in a line from the door of the house to the gate.

'May God bring you back soon!'

At the gate Djidjia was crying her heart out. She too kissed the master's hand. Then suddenly she jumped at me, threw her arms around my neck and kissed me, wetting my face all over with her tears.

'May God save you! May the angels of heaven protect you!'

Well, at any other time I would have slapped her, but now I swallowed my anger and hurried after my master.

The sun was already climbing the sky. As we came outside the city a tall column of smoke rose in a spiral towards the clouds from the fire of the shamans, who were sacrificing a white horse and howling the sacred song. Old, blind Kama stood before the bonfire, holding up a bloody sword; then reached out towards Attila with his hands, sending blessings, while his blind eyes stared into heaven.

Thousands of swords snapped forth, and the armed thousands shouted with their blades in the air: 'God! God! God!'

Then they set out, heading west.

*O*ne half of the army crossed over to the other side of the Danube, and spread out like a flood. Divided thus into two, we kept going north and then west. On the southern bank of the Danube Attila led the way, on the northern bank, the commander-in-chief, Chath.

My master travelled with Attila. The two armies didn't meet until spring; they joined in a wild, forested area where the Danube had its source. But we were still advancing through Attila's territory, for it stretched from the Volga to the Rhine. Not even Attila himself knew all the land, the people and their kings, and yet this vast area was all his.

One morning I was riding between two of Attila's scribes, Mena-Sagh and Chegge. These two were always glad to talk to me, even though I was just a servant, and I was only too happy to relieve the boredom of the journey by talking with them. Mena-Sagh was forty-five, bearded, bald and red-eyed – one of the White Huns. Chegge, also a White Hun, was my age; he had a thick neck, and a squint. He had been taken prisoner as a child by the Romans, and it was they who had taught him to write.

'Could you tell me, my lords,' I asked them, 'why Attila is not taking us straight toward Rome?'

'Because he is a wise man,' said Mena-Sagh, blinking. He smiled when I looked bewildered. 'I mean,' he went on, 'world affairs are too complicated for us, I don't pretend to understand.'

'Then how can you say that the reason for our heading west is that Attila is a wise man?'

'Until now Attila has never done anything stupid. Therefore even if he is doing something that we do not understand, it is certain that he is doing the right thing.'

'Priests say this about God!'

'So, he *is* God – God on earth. He never loses a battle, and he keeps the nation together.'

'He is no mere man,' said Chegge enthusiastically, 'He is a mortal divinity here among us!'

I shrugged my shoulders.

'Do you not think that he is great?'

'Attila? Without a doubt! But the halo of legend is for dead heroes.'

Mena-Sagh spoke again. 'I think Attila is heading west because the border of the Roman Empire is there. Europe is inhabited by small tribes; most of them are nomads, and will probably follow this tremendous army of ours. If they refuse, they will be forced to; if they resist, they will be wiped out. So we proceed like an avalanche. And when we have grown as big as we possibly can, then we'll turn south and crush the great Roman Empire.'

'*That* will be the funeral! *That* will be something the world has never seen before!' said Chegge, with fire.

'The funeral of civilization,' I whispered, with a shudder.

'Its renewal,' said Mena-Sagh seriously. 'Look at those rich green spots all over the field. They are the places where campfires once burned. After the fire is gone, a bare spot remains, but next spring new life begins.'

He rode on, deep in thought, not saying any more. It was Chegge who spoke next.

'If only that Aetius didn't exist! I might be a bit afraid of *him*... if he dares to stand up against us...'

'Not even he could possibly hold out against Attila,' I said, with confusion in my heart.

'All the same, he is a dangerous man! A childhood friend of Attila – you know they held Attila as hostage when he was a child? And Aetius, in turn was held hostage by the Huns a few years later. They spent their years of adolescence together. Aetius knows all the Hunnish tricks. Once he himself led them in a campaign – and won!'

Chath was riding ahead of us. He looked back. I slapped my horse, but he motioned that I should stay with the others. He waited for us to catch up with him, then joined us.

'What are you talking about?'

Chegge told him in a few words.

'You are quite close to the truth,' Chath said, 'Attila's aim *is* to annex the Germans, Kvads, Swabians, Franks, Burgundians and heaven knows who else to our army. But most of all he wants to win over the Visigoths. If they are not willing, he'll break the dogs. They are a large nation, and strong. And you can't overlook the other half of the Alans or the Franks, either. If these three do not join us, but join the Roman army instead, Aetius could probably stand up against us.'

'Against *us,*' I shouted in amazement. 'Against this sea of people? I should think, my lord, that if all the people living in the world marched against us, followed by all those who had died long ago and had risen for this occasion, even then this army could not be overpowered!'

Chath looked highly pleased.

'I must tell this Attila,' he said, laughing. "If all the people..." How did you say it?' Then he galloped away.

We were joined by Rusti, the blond chief scribe with the freckled face.

'What did you tell Chath?' he asked curiously.

Chegge told him our conversation.

Rusti listened intently. A sour sort of smile played over his face.

'Sir,' I said, encouraged by his grin, 'if that Aetius is such a dangerous man, wouldn't it have been better to write to the Romans that we are going not against them but against some other nation, instead of declaring war on them directly? Aetius would have stayed home then!'

'Your idea was born too late,' replied Rusti. 'Attila thought of it already.'

'Too bad it wasn't in time.'

'Oh, but it was! Before we set out, we wrote to the Romans to say that we intend them no harm, but are going to fight the Visigoths. I wrote the letter myself, but it is no secret in any case. The Visigoths by rights are Attila's subjects, but they didn't want to pay taxes, so they fled and settled in Gaul. We are going to punish them. That's what they understand in Rome.'

'But why then did Aetius take up arms?'

Rusti smiled.

'Why? Because they too have some brains. If Attila clears his throat, it's enough to make them jump under their shields for fear he'll spit fire at them.'

'And if we defeat Aetius, what then?'

'Rome.'

'And after Rome?'

'Constantinople.'

'Then all the rest of the world!'

'No, we'll found our own permanent country, and only use our swords to wave at our tax-paying subjects.'

'You think Attila will remain peaceful? If a lion swore to eat nothing but grass, who would believe him?'

'Attila is not blood-thirsty. You are wrong if that's what you think. Don't you remember how our envoys visited Theodosius little more than a year ago to talk about trade around the Danube?'

'Don't tell me that Attila will ever settle in one place! He won't stay long by the River Tisia.'

'Oh, yes, he will! He'll never move into any emperor's palace. And if he does yearn after imperial marble palaces, he'll have them put onto carts and brought to the River Tisia.'

'I don't understand.'

'Our people can only live in a grassy land. There isn't as much pasture in one stretch anywhere in the world as there is around the Danube and the Tisia.'

At this moment Hargita waved to him, and Rusti moved away on his horse to see what he wanted. Hargita was a nobleman of fifty who always looked angry, though he wasn't really angry at all, it was just something about his eyes.

Chegge and I plodded along side by side in silence. I heard him heave a deep sigh.

'Where is that sigh flying to?' I asked jokingly.

He smiled, and said, 'I'll tell you. I'll tell you because you know her. She is lovely, and has the most beautiful eyes. It's for her that I'm going to war; I shall have the scribes write up at least ten people killed by me.'

A horrible feeling took hold of me; I could hardly speak.

'Who is the girl?'

'You know her. Of course you do! How I have envied you, living in that household!'

'Djidjia!'

'Oh, no! She is only a child! And you don't think I would take my skin to the death-market for a raggedy little nursemaid like her!'

'Emmo?'

To this day I am amazed that I could utter that name so calmly when the heavens themselves turned black.

'Yes, that's who,' he said warmly.

I didn't dare look at him. I felt myself go pale. That one moment was enough to induce a deep hatred within me for this man. My hand clutched at my dagger–I'd kill him! I'd kill the cross-eyed pig!

But I didn't kill him. On the contrary I turned to him with a smile, and slapped him on the back in jest with my riding stick.

'Hey, you dog! What do you mean by squinting at such high-class young ladies? You've even talked to her about this, I suppose...'

'No, not quite,' he replied with an air of self-importance. 'You know that fellows like us can't pay court to young ladies like her. But isn't that what wars are for–so that each can show what he can do? The Huns look at a man's own merit, not his father's. Remember, in the fighting, to aim for the enemies' heads, and cut them off and hang them on your saddler. You don't even have to show them to the scribes, just show them to your master, for if the nobles see them, that's good enough.'

I knew all this, but I let him chatter: it gave me time to pull myself together.

'And did the girl agree?' I asked, patting my horse's neck in as casual a manner as I could command.

'The girl? Oh, yes, of course,' he answered gaily, though I could sense from his voice that he was lying.

'And how did it all begin?' I went on probing.

'How did it begin: Well, as a matter of fact, it didn't. We loved each other before we ever exchanged a word. Womenfolk are very clever; they only have to look at you, and they can read all your inmost secrets in your eyes.'

'But tell me, where did you talk the first time?'

'The first time? At Queen Echka's. A Roman glassware merchant had come, and they needed an interpreter, so Attila sent me over.'

'So that's where you met?'

'Yes. It was after sundown, and Prince Aladar and I escorted Emmo home. Aladar began to have hiccups on the way. He was embarrassed in front of the girl, so he turned back. Then in the shadow of the palaces–'

'Yes–?'

'Well, I discussed things with Emmo–in the twilight...you know...'

'What things?'

'Our secret.'
'Your secret? What secret?'
'Well–that we love each other.'
'You love each other? H'm. But so easily?'
'Of course. She spoke first. She said, "At last I can talk to you, Chegge. I have understood you for a long time now. Go, fight like a hero in the next campaign. You know how they divide up the plunder according to how many men each has killed. You could become a gentleman around the palace in no time. And then..."'
I coughed so that my flushed face wouldn't give me away.
'And Prince Aladar?' I asked, still coughing.
'He was courting her, wasn't he?'
He shrugged his shoulders.
'Can I help it if she prefers me?' he replied gaily.
'Have you met often since then?'
'Oh, yes. But only on the way home to her house.'
We came to a hill, from which we could see all the towns in the valley. Chegge enjoyed the sight; I stood behind him, dark and bitter.
I knew he was lying, for Emmo never went anywhere alone, and she was always home before the sun went down; but even if a hundredth of his story were true...if it were only true that Emmo had once looked at him warmly, even then...
Chegge could not return home alive!

Throughout the journey I could see Attila a hundred or so paces ahead of me.
His two older sons, Aladar and Ellak, rode with him, also the Frankish prince, Aladar's friend, and Eudoxius, the doctor who had fled to us in the autumn from the Roman courts. Other 'stars' were Valamir, the chief prince of the Goths; King Ardaric; the king of the Alans, and the king of the Akatiri, but only stars from a distance: close up they were nothing but tallow candles. Of the Hunnish nobility, Edecon, Chath, Orestes, Berki, Upor, Vachar and Balan were there. (The rest of the noblemen were leading separate units of the army.) Zobogan and the head priest Iddar were also in Attila's camp. Two of Attila's wives travelled in a silk-covered, scarlet-upholstered cart,

which was always surrounded by all sorts of servants, among whom one could sometimes see Tzerko the jester wandering about.

The servants of all the lords followed in one group, the scribes in front – those who weren't free men yet – the cooks and stable-boys and other house servants. My master had two stable-boys, one shield-bearer and a footman. We servants never cooked. Every day forty or fifty people sat around Attila's table. Behind each lord stood his servant; I stood behind Chath and served him. He always left me something – a chicken leg, or some fish, cheese or fruit. I couldn't complain about him.

The army poured westward like a river in flood. They burned the towns behind them, and anyone they could catch they chained as a slave. Rugs and clothing ended up on carts – and the carts also were plunder. Gold and silver treasures were locked in special iron crates which were watched over by the scribes and treasure guards.

One day we arrived in the still smouldering ruins of a burnt-out town where much worse destruction had taken place. Everywhere dead bodies lay around – men, women, babies. The air was heavy with the smell of charred skin. In front of the church I saw a dead man, very old, tied to a pillar. He had no clothes on, and his head lay in front of him in a puddle of blood, a white mitre close by.

Nauseated, I stopped on the steps of the church, where I saw on the marble slabs wide, bloody footprints–perhaps the footprints of the bishop's murderer. What sort of wild beast could he have been? No Hun, certainly. Huns are only wild in battle: they do not try to prove their bravery with defenceless people.

A woman screamed: one of King Ardaric's Gepids was dragging a young woman along by hair through the dust. I had seen hundreds of such scenes before. At first it had upset me; later I didn't even look. But now it upset me again.

From where I stood beside one of the pillars I glanced around to see if anyone was watching me. Hundreds and thousands of human wolves were milling about the streets, and in and out of buildings, all intent on looting.

The Gepid was sweating, his face red, as he dragged the screaming woman. She, poor creature, tried to clutch hold of anything she could–grass, trees, stones, corpses.

I drew my bow tight, aimed, then shot. My arrow pierced the Gepid's side. He jerked and let the woman go, fell to his knees, then full length on the ground. The woman stared at him incredulously. When she noticed the arrow she looked around, then collapsed face down among the dead.

That was my first murder.

If anyone had seen me, I would have been beaten to death, but I didn't care. I felt no pangs of conscience whatsoever.

It was past noon when we left the town. Beyond it Attila's tent had already been set up, and food waiting. I still kept seeing that headless bishop; I felt quite sick, as stood behind my master.

Dinner began in an unusual silence, for Attila was morose and dispirited.

We were eating wild boar meat – boiled, with nothing but horse radishes. Attila ate off a wooden plate, as always and drank from a coconut cup; the nobility had silver, and washed down their meal with red wine out of silver goblets. At last he spoke. 'Who is killing women and children wantonly?'

'The Gepids,' said a hesitant voice.

'No, not the Gepids!' snapped Ardaric.

'The Roxolans,' said Chath. 'I've seen them with my own eyes.'

'The Gelons,' said Hargita.

'What can be done about it?' muttered Balan, who was a kind-hearted Hunnish gentleman, revolted by this savage slaughter.

Three messengers arrived.

One brought news of an earthquake in Gaul where buildings had fallen, and the inhabitants had fled.

The second report was delivered by a Gelon whose face was painted bright red. Their leader had died and he was asking for another man.

Attila looked across to Hargita. 'I'll trust them to you.' And Hargita bowed. From the look on his face he was not going to spare Gelon blood.

The third report was brought by a Frankish horseman. He informed the blond prince that his brother, the king, had been banished; a delegation was now on its way, bringing him the crown, which would be presented to him with great ceremony.

We were at the second course – geese roasted on the spit. Where so many geese had been found only the good God knows! When Chath gave me a drumstick I took it to Chegge.

But why to Chegge, of all people? Because by being friendly I wanted to make sure that he'd be close to me in battle.

*T*he first major stop, where we rested for a week, was at the town of Augusta.

This was the first time they assembled Attila's big tent. The gilded, richly decorated structure dazzled me with its pillars and plates of gold. It wasn't so much a tent as a multi-storeyed, spired wooden palace with walls of fabric.

On the first floor lived the two queens and all their women servants. The ground floor was a spacious dining room which served as council room as well.

Attila was now walking among us in clothes glittering with gold and diamonds. I couldn't comprehend what had happened, but the scribes explained later that on campaigns Attila always surrounded himself with luxury, especially when he was expecting nations to pay him homage.

By now thousands of Marcomans, Kvads and Swabians had joined us and were marching with us. They had attached themselves to the army led by the commander-in-chief on the opposite bank of the river.

Near the Rhine the Thuringi tribes joined us; so did the Burgundians from beyond the Rhine. The Franks from the banks of the Neckar also joined us, bringing their prince the crown, and reporting the demise of his brother. I expect they had beaten him to death.

While these new alliances were being formed, the ancient forest of Hertz-berg rang with the blows of axes.

The army had to cross the Rhine, but where in the world were enough bridges, ferries and rafts to carry this multitude across?

'Cut down the forest!' Attila had ordered, and in less than half an hour began a murmur like distant thunder which was to last for many a day and night. All the axes, adzes and hatchets that were in the army were felling trees and making bridges and ferries.

Next day the vanguard and hundreds of leaders crossed over. Our spies had crossed long before that, of course.

If this flood of people could have been viewed from the vantage point of the sun, it would have provided a sight unique in the history of the world. Millions of ants thronging and swarming through mountains and valleys, all coming together and concentrating at the Rhine. For days – for weeks even – ceaselessly, one would have observed glittering human ants embarking in small groups, all crossing the river on narrow yellow willow leaves. Then they all spread out again, some to the north and some to the south, and like hunters beating in a wide sweep to cut off their quarry, the multitude spanned a distance of one or two hundred miles.

Before them, well ahead, moved another great crowd. Who were these

people whom Attila's army kept pressing due west, little by little? These were the Roman garrisons that had fled the towns we passed through; they were looking for Aetius's army, to join him. Among them also were the Salian Franks, who, having already sipped at the cup of Roman culture, preferred the Roman way of life.

Only nomads – the peoples of the tents – joined Attila. Those living in stone houses fled, and kept on fleeing before us until they reached the Roman army. But where was that Roman army? Westward, they were told, towards the setting sun.

But one Burgundian tribe was worthy of honour in their mad recklessness. Their king, Gondikar, defied Attila. 'What's Attila to me?' he cried. 'What are earthly gods to me? Attila won't see *my* back!'

He commanded some eighty thousand men, all of them heroes and all of them mad. Within one hour the hoofs of the Hunnish horses were red with their blood and eighty thousand souls were ascending through the clouds.

At the foot of a rock lay a grey-haired man covered with wounds. Neither sword nor helmet lay beside him. His head was staved in, and his grey beard was bloody. Looting hands had left hardly any clothing on him. He was pointed out as King Gondikar.

I took off my hat.

We journeyed on. Attila received spies, messengers and delegations day in and day out.

'The Roman armies are heading south,' the spies reported in March.

'The Visigoths will not join the Roman army,' they said in April, 'for their king, Theodoric, cannot come to terms with Aetius.'

Then again, 'Aetius is on his way. He's at the foot of the Alps already. He is bringing the main body of his army from Rome – one hundred thousand armed men.'

'The king of the Alans, Sangiban, has joined the Romans.'

'Theodoric has sent a message to Aetius, saying that since it was the Romans who conjured up the storm, now it is up to them alone to weather it. Aetius is torn by doubts.'

So we came to an endless plain dappled everywhere with white bones: the bones of horses, and human skulls. A broad, very shallow stream wound its way across the fields. In the blue distance the gates of a little town stood out white against the horizon.

This town was Catalaunum.

Attila ordered a rest for the army, and with his commanders rode around to survey the plain. For hours they galloped up and down, stopping only occasionally. When they returned, Attila marked out a hill for his tent. The ordnance officers took care of the rest, deciding where to set up the tents of the nobility and the bodyguards, and which nation should camp where.

It took days and weeks for all the scattered peoples to assemble.

The little town was empty, like all the small tows we had passed through. Only the occasional dog barked at us, terrified, on deserted streets. Attila designated this town as one end of the semi-circle of armoured carts, which they set up in two rows. This was the main camp; this was the line we would defend once the Roman army arrived. Those regiments that had carts were to collect fodder, flour, cattle, sheep, cooking fat, bacon and vegetables. Dams were to be made across the stream–such thousands of horses needed plenty of water.

During those days of settling, the commanders conferred ceaselessly, trying to decide which to attack first, Paris or Orleans.

Meanwhile envoys had been sent to King Sangiban of the Alans, asking him to come to Attila. At the time, he promised to meet and join us at Orleans; but later – heaven only knows why – he took Aetius's side after all.

So we set out for Orleans.

By then we knew that Aetius was in Gaul, and that he too was collecting allies on the way. He had already gathered a huge army. One day news came that this proud Roman commander had decided to go himself to the Visigoths and personally ask them not to join Attila, but to follow him.

'That will give us about five weeks,' said Attila.

So he set up the battering rams around Orleans, and the stone-throwing catapults and the ballistae which hurled iron beams. And the siege began.

This fortress was the strongest I had ever seen. At the least noticeable movement on the walls, the Huns' arrows flew up in a cloud. The replying cloud was scanty indeed–but those walls!

We erected large mechanical slingshots which threw rocks weighing a ton over the walls; the rocks crashed inside with a noise like thunder.

Then began the work of the battering rams, secured on pulleys and beams. Heavy tree trunks with iron capped ends were pulled back by one or two hundred men hauling on ropes. At a horn signal they all let go, and the long, thick beams thumped against the wall so that even the earth beneath them shook.

The noise of battle subsided only late that evening. In the still of the night we heard psalms being sung deep within the town.

Ut quid Domine recessisti longe, despicis in opportunitatibus in tribulatione!

The men's voices came from near the walls, the women's from farther in – thousands of women singing in the starry night. It was magnificent! A chill ran down my spine...

Arise, O Lord; O God, lift thine hand!...the poor committeth himself unto thee... thou wilt cause thine ear to hear:

To judge the fatherless and the oppressed, that the man of the earth may no more oppress.

The siege roared up again at dawn: stones rumbled, the walls thudded, and burning clumps of oakum fastened to arrows flew from a thousand directions at once into the fortress. From within, stones from slingshots whistled among us, along with copper-tipped arrows. A thump now and then as someone's leather shield caught an arrow.

High above the smoking town a hundred thousand ravens whirled.

Meanwhile, news kept coming in.

'The Bretons have joined Aetius.'

'Damnation swallow them all!' said my master.

'With them have gone the Laethian Teutons, the Laethian Batavians, the Swabians of Le Mans, the Franks of Rennes, the Saraguri of Poitiers and all of the Teufles – all to fight under the Roman eagles.'

'Damnation...'

At last came the news, 'Aetius has won the support of the king of the Visigoths.'

That day Attila emerged from his tent with a gloomy expression. He sent word to the citizens of Orleans that they had better capitulate, otherwise he'd heap a forest around the walls and drown the town in a sea of fire in which all would perish. The residents of the town had invested all offices in their bishop: he was mayor, general, and head of the church. Next day a delegation of three proceeded through the gates, bringing gifts, and a letter.

'What is in this letter?' asked Attila angrily.

'Some of our humble conditions,' whispered the envoy.

'No conditions!' Attila snapped, throwing the letter at the envoy's feet. 'I didn't come here to correspond, I came to conquer. If you do not open the gates, our fire will do the job.'

Thousands of carts stood ready, laden with wood, at the foot of the walls.

But there was another reason for Attila's impatience: the Roman army – a terrifying multitude–was getting near. Attila's spies kept reporting on their advance mile by mile.

But the people in Orleans, of course, knew nothing of this. 'My lord!' the three envoys begged on their knees. 'Only give us three days for our people to prepare to leave. We will leave the town, or, if you assure us that you will receive us among your peoples, we will put all our treasure at your feet.'

'I will wait until tomorrow morning,' Attila replied.

The next day was June 14th. The gates of the fortress opened, and the bishop's envoys brought out to Attila the keys of the town on velvet cushions.

'I do not desire your blood,' said Attila, 'but the army needs food.'

He sent there thousand empty carts into the town and looting began. We stayed close to Attila, and from a hill watched the troops enter with the carts.

The roofs were soon filled with people seeking safety from the looters, but of course these savages broke through everything and found their way up to the roofs too.

But by noon some Gepids, all bloody and exhausted, reported to Attila that the vanguard of the Roman army had engaged some of our troops on the flank and scattered them.

Attila gave the signal to retreat from the town, and sent some Alans to cover the gates.

From the steeples of the town, however, one could see far into the distance, and the inhabitants must have noticed the huge cloud of dust rolling in from the west, and within it the Roman legions' glittering eagles.

By then the horns were wailing all around.

'Retreat! Retreat!'

Now the people on the roofs began to stir. With the fury and joy of approaching freedom they threw stones and beams on the enemy milling in the streets. Prisoners tore themselves free, and fought with whatever came to hand.

There was also a great commotion outside, around the town. Our troops clashed with the Romans without command of discipline. Men and horses kicked and jostled in the bloody waves of the River Loire. A thousand horns kept calling, 'Retreat! Retreat!'

Those who had already got involved in the battle kept fighting furiously, but the main body of our army continued the retreat which they had already begun the day before, back to the Catalaunian Plains.

The skirmish continued only around the fortress, while the Huns made off with all their spoils; then they left the empty hive to the Romans.

The return to the Catalaunian Plains took several days, of course. Dust and filth; clouds of flies on troops and horses; jingling and clanking and rattling of weapons; the hurrying clatter and creaking of wagons. Shouts, horn signals, and horror at every step.

The army looted every unwalled city on its way and trampled all the green crops, leaving not a blade of grass standing in their wake.

One town, however, Troyes, kept its gates shut. The vanguard halted. What on earth! – The huge wooden gate with its iron studs and brass was locked. The multitude began to dam up, forming a lake of men and horses, waiting for Attila's command.

We could hear people singing psalms within the walls. The bishop appeared on top of the gates, wearing his mitre, and a white silk chasuble ornamented with gold flowers; he held up a silver crucifix.

'Who amongst you can understand Latin?' the priests shouted down to us.

There were many who could. In our army there was someone from every nation in the world.

The bishop wished to speak with Attila.

We were only too familiar with such incidents by then. The bishop, in full pontificals, would emerge leading the town's clergy and nobility, and would beg mercy of Attila (or of the commander-in-chief) as if he were some sort of deity. Attila or the commander-in-chief would always reply that the town would not be harmed provided it surrendered in due form – which meant handing over all stocks of food and fodder within the walls. They were also to guarantee that they would remain loyal to the Huns.

And how were they to 'guarantee' this? Three prominent citizens of the town, along with their families, would have to move to Attila's headquarters. The bishop would return to the town; the gates would be locked; the population would confer, pray and lament. Not one of the prominent citizens would agree to go and live as hostage in the lion's den. They would hoist the red flag and defend the town – as long as it was possible.

It was never possible for long. Eventually the church, and the wealthy families would bring all their gold and silver, placing it on the altar. Then they would raise their eyes to heaven.

'Oh Lord, have mercy upon us!'

But the heavens never replied . . . (What is man's brief life span in the eye of eternity?)

At Troyes, however, everything turned out differently.

The bishop did emerge leading his clergy (some thirty priests), the mayor, the magistrate, the councillors and other dignitaries. Attila was passing by just then, so this time it was he who rode up to the gate. When the psalm-singing had ceased, the old bishop just remained standing there, stock-still.

He raised his head and stared at Attila silently. Suddenly, as if at some horrible apparition, he shouted at him in Latin:

'Who are you, that you demolish thrones, ravage countries, and oppress peoples? Where does your power come from? Who had bidden you turn the world upside down? Who are you?'

We were breathless with astonishment.

I was even more astounded to hear Attila reply in Latin. He thumped his chest, and his voice carried like the blast of a horn:

'Ego sum Attila, flagellum Dei!' (I am Attila, the scourge of God!)

'If that be so,' the old bishop replied with tears in his eyes, 'if you have truly been sent by God, then I can do nothing against you. Come and do your work on us as you have done on others.'

And the gates opened. The white-bearded old man took hold of the bridle of Attila's horse, and with tears in his eyes led him inside.

Attila seemed to be moved by the old man's majestic simplicity. He spoke one word to Kamocha, and rode through the gates, followed by his retinue.

Kamocha remained by the gates. He ordered a few of the zoltans to stand beside him and keep shouting to all the warriors streaming in: 'Don't harm the citizens! That is the king's command!'

When we arrived at the market-place, Attila gave a horse to the old bishop.

'You are a holy man,' he said, 'and you bring luck to the people you live among. You will have to spend a few days with me. I will spare your town, but you are to tell your priests that all the supplies of grain and flour in this town must be loaded onto carts and delivered to the Huns. We must also have all the fodder.'

So we moved on. The army passed through the town in an orderly manner. Only the clatter of hooves and the rattle of weapons could be heard. Of the inhabitants not a soul showed himself except for a few very old men here and there. The houses were silent; the people must have been hiding in cellars and attics. The zoltans formed lines along the main street to ensure that no one forgot the king's prohibition.

When we reached the eastern gates, we saw some of the town's inhabitants fleeing on horseback, in carts or on foot, heading for the woods to the north. The women carried little children on their backs, and the older children were weighed down with baskets and bundles. They were all heading for the forest and the reeds of the marshes, as refugees did everywhere.

As we crossed a bridge, we noticed a woman in rags who had fallen behind; she was stumbling across the field with a baby on her back, and holding on to a child with each hand. Beside her ran five little girls, all barefoot, and two pretty blond girls in their teens. Each was lugging something – rags, worthless nothings, even a whitewash brush. In their great panting hurry the first one would trip and fall, then another, and all were moaning and crying.

'Oh mother!'

'Oh, my sweet little one!'

And as she glanced back, the mother saw that all her efforts were in vain. She stopped at the bank of the brook, her tearful face pale with fright, and stared like a mad woman.

Attila stopped his horse and asked Urkon to bring the woman to him. The bishop too hurried along with Urkon, encouraging the woman and telling her not to be afraid. Dragging her children with her, she knelt down in front of Attila; she was unable to speak, but her trembling hands and flowing tears craved mercy.

'Are these all your children?' asked Attila.

'All of them, my lord!' sobbed the woman. 'I am widowed; if you kill me I shall leave ten orphans behind to starve.' The bishop translated what she said.

Attila motioned for his treasurer, Upor, and said something to him. Upor pulled a purse from his bag and counted some money into it, all in gold pieces. There must have been about three hundred of them.

'Return to the town in peace,' said Attila to the woman, 'and take this money. Use it to raise your children.' And he ordered one of his bodyguards, Botar, to accompany her back to the town.

I had noticed already at Orleans that many of our men were sick. Some of them staggered along, looking very pale and with blue patches around their eyes. They would sit down and vomit blood, then suddenly drop dead. It was not the heat that was to blame, as I first thought; it was plague. People fell like flies in autumn. The smell of the army was monstrous in any case.

By the time we turned back, there were dead bodies lining the road on either side. Here a Nubade, there a Herul, a Swabian, a Marcoman – all lying together. Anyone who fell down was left behind, by the side of the road. If his weapon was valuable someone took it. If he was wearing a good pair of boots, they took those off. If his cloak was usable, they turned him out of it. They took away everything, leaving him behind alone.

Attila became so morose that it was frightening just to look at him.

One afternoon, as I was riding beside Chegge, a Tuncassi wearing a leather jacket swayed and fell right in front of us.

The man wore a copper helmet with a crest. He must have picked it off the head of a Roman around Orleans, or perhaps he had taken it with the head inside. We had noticed that helmet before.

As the man fell over, the helmet rolled off his head. Chegge jumped off his horse and picked it up, putting it on his own head.

I envied him. It was such a fine helmet with red garnets set in the crest, and a movable visor, it must have been worth two gold coins even in times of peace. But how much more in war! One only had to cover the copper crest with a piece of felt or leather, put one or two feathers in it, and the Huns would know the wearer was one of their own.

Next day Chegge complained of headaches. The third day his nose bled. 'I am finished,' he said, pale.

By the fifth day there was swelling in his armpits and around his throat; by night he was ready to die.

He asked me for some water. Everyone in the camp was asleep. I went for water and gave him some to drink.

'Thank you,' he panted. 'I have a few valuables at home – a few suits of clothing and a book: I leave them to you.' He gave me his hand.

I held the torch so that I could see his face; leaning closer to him, I said, trembling, 'Chegge, don't you want to send any message to Emmo?'

He looked at me and replied faintly, 'No.'

'But why not?'

'What for?'

'Chegge,' I said, squeezing his arm, 'don't go to the next world with a lie on your conscience! Tell me what you babbled about Emmo was all a lie! You never talked to her! I would have seen you! Tell me, in truth – you were lying!'

I looked into his eyes. He didn't answer.

His eyes were glassy and his forehead was covered with sweat. In a sudden spasm his fingers dug into the grass. He breathed with more and more difficulty. Then he opened his eyes and looked at me, questioning, wondering. But he never spoke again; his dead glance froze on me.

*A*ttila's tent faced the west, so all the other tents were set up the same way. Aetius, however, had not led the army to where we expected, but further east.

So the River Vesle, which flowed behind our camp, suddenly was in front of us as we faced about.

Chath growled softly to himself. 'What in the name of damnation...!'

Attila had stationed Ardaric with his Gepids, at the River Aube to cover the gathering armies, and to force the Romans to come against us from the west – so that they would have the early morning sun in their eyes.

The explanation of Aetius's strategy arrived at the same time as the first Roman horsemen; Aetius had stormed the Gepids and broken through our lines, heading east. We lost fifteen thousand men in that clash.

Attila sent the remaining Gepids behind the walls of Catalaunum to defend it, if it ever came to that.

Just when we had to turn around to face the enemy, I noticed a small hillock some distance from us. It lay between the two armies. By the time I thought this through, four detachments from our army also sent a mighty regiment of horsemen. It was plain that their men were more numerous than ours. They came together with a great clash and our men were pushed back.

'Bad omen,' Shaman Bial murmured beside me.

'Why is it a bad omen?' I turned on him, disappointed. 'If we had started out sooner and with more men, the hill would be ours now!'

'That is exactly why it is a bad omen!' the shaman's voice snapped in my ear.

'What is?'

'That we didn't start out sooner and that we didn't send more men.'

All the shamans had changed for the worse during the time they spent with us. Whether this was because of their fear of the plague or because they were always praying, I don't know, but they had all turned morose. In their black garments they looked like the servants of death.

'I am afraid,' I said, annoyed, 'that you superstitious priests are counting the bad omens far more loudly than you ought to. Forgive me, but that is not a wise thing to do.'

'What is superstition?' he said with a shrug. 'You are a Christian; to you our faith is superstition. Our faith is Hun; to us *your* beliefs are superstitions.'

Hearing him talk thus, waving three fingers as if he were ridiculing the Holy Trinity, I grew angry.

'There is only one God! There is no Hun god, Roman god, or Greek god! God is God–the common father and master of all peoples! He is not fighting for hills, either with us or against us!'

'Ignorant slave! I am not going to argue with you!'

'Because you are afraid of me!'

'Of you?'

'Of my words, of the truth!'

He looked at me darkly from beneath his dusty eyebrows. We were standing on my master's cart, by the side of our tent.

'What if I prove to you,' he said quietly, 'that the Huns' God is not the same as the Romans'?'

'That you will never be able to do!'

'Would I not prove it if I told you right now what is going to happen?'

'That would only be fabrication.'

'But what if it comes true?'

'I will give you my head as a gift.'

'Thank you. I do not accept worthless gifts.'

'It's not worthless to me.'

'Promise you will never divulge what I say.'

'Here is my hand. But what if your prophecy doesn't come true?'

'You can make me your slave. You can christen me. You can sell me. You can do anything you like with me.'

'I am listening.'

'Take heed: the signs today have shown that Attila is going to lose this battle.'

He said this with such conviction that his words sent shivers down my spine.

'Impossible!' I said in dismay. 'It's true that we are decimated by the plague, but the army's so huge, it's invincible. Attila has never lost a battle yet. And have you forgotten about the sword of God?'

He sat down on the wheel of the cart and wound his white and yellow beard around his hand, staring before him gloomily.

*T*he lords stood about on the turret of Attila's tent from morning till night, viewing the Romans at work pitching their camp.

I looked about too, but only from our tent. It was extremely hot throughout the day; one could see far across the plain. I listened with interest to the older warriors' remarks.

'Hey,' said one of them, 'the Romans are putting the Alans in the middle.'

And, true enough, one could see how Aetius had lined up the army, the forest of moving reeds in the middle was Sangiban's forces. Perhaps Aetius was suspicious of that irresolute man... or perhaps he meant their long javelins to defend the main body of the army. Who knows? And was it really the middle? Where was the middle in a multitude of that size?

'There are the Burgundians,' said another, 'and over there are the Franks!'

'But what the devil are the Romans doing on the left?'

The glittering Roman helmets had indeed appeared on the left flank. Mechanical bows and stone-throwers were being set up in front of them. Those with good eyesight could see it all.

'They want to surround Attila,' one of the bodyguards said, with a laugh. He glanced at me and noticed Chegge's helmet on my head. He yelled at me gaily. 'Look at that! Don't tell me you're going to fight, too!'

'I've not come all this way to do the cooking!'

'Will you fight by your master's side?'

'Not by yours, anyway!'

'Have you ever been in battle before?'

'No–and nor have you–not in such a battle as this one is going to be!'

'If you give me that helmet, I'll teach you something useful.'

'What's that?'

'How to come through the battle alive.'

'If I give you my helmet I shan't come through alive. You keep your advice and I'll keep the helmet, thank you!'

Everyone around us laughed, while the bodyguard rubbed his back against the tent pole, scratching like a pig.

'This Greek is a bit of a fox,' said one of them. 'You can't fool him so easily!'

This was the sort of soldier's talk we had throughout the journey. One said that a warrior should always trust his horse above all else. Another said that it is the horse one must be most wary of–many horses stumble and fall, or get frightened, or jump into danger.

Some of them wore time-tested amulets with magical powers. Others relied on swords that sent a hundred enemies to death. Some rubbed their horses' noses in human blood. Others put their trust in the cry: *'Yea, God, my Lord–let the Devil take the enemy!'*

All I knew was that my horse was one of Chath's best. And though my arms might not be as strong as some, I still had my wits about me. If I saw an unhealthy situation developing, I'd pull my horse away. If by chance I got carried into the midst of the Romans, I'd pull the leather off my helmet's crest, and the feather off my visor button, and I'd scream in Latin. But if I saw that *we* had the enemy on the run I'd shout like a true Hun: 'Hee-yah! Hee-yea! Damnation!'

And of course I would lay about me diligently, taking care only that there was a witness, or a head, to attest each deed.

That day, however, when I saw the enemy–that vast sea of people–a cold breath of intuition touched my ear: Zeta, you'll never get out here! Many thousands of men will stay here forever; how can *you* be sure that you'll come out of this peril alive?

In the afternoon the Roman army was still shifting about. We saw the lines of the Visigoths with their leather shields curling forward like a brown snake. They too were being sent into the front lines. But suddenly our camp began to stir also.

'Hiryit! Hiryit!' (Here! Here!) I could hear shouts of the Goth officers, and the Goths started to move forward, winding their way in a long line from among the tents. One officer after another appeared: dark Akran, blue-eyed, eccentric Eysarn, smiling Fiskya with the curly moustache, and young Skura, with his hat on one side as usual. Only the day before he had danced to the tunes of bagpipes.

After the Roman army had taken up its position, Attila stationed his Alans opposite the Alans who fought with Rome, and his own Ostrogoths directly opposite the Visigoths. Brother against brother! The Visigoths hated the Ostrogoths because they did not join them when they were fleeing Attila. The Ostrogoths hated the Visigoths because, to them, to have surrendered and then to have escaped was foul play! Enemies in battle may come to be reconciled, but never brothers who fight. Cain's weapon is the deadliest of all.

It remained for the Huns to fill the centre position: Black and White Huns together. Ardaric and the Gepids took up their positions on the right according to Attila's orders, and with them the Akatiri, Jazyges, Kvads, Rugi and Saraguri.

'I don't see the Heruls,' said Free Greek, who was standing beside me.

'Attila sent them north along with the Magyars,' replied my master, wiping the sweat from his brow. 'They'll attack the Romans from behind.'

With a great clatter a spear-shooting machine was dragged past us, drawn by six oxen. The war machines were being brought up on all sides and made ready: spear-shooters, wooden catapults, stone-throwers and mechanical bows. The nations with slingshots positioned themselves on the tops of carts. They could work quite cheerfully on top of all the overstuffed bags, kegs and bundles. In front of the carts sat the Alans with their javelins, and the Gelons with their scythes. These were to join in and start reaping only if the enemy pushed forward as far as the line of carts.

I thought that we would begin the fight that very day, but we didn't. All day long men kept taking up positions, exactly as Attila ordered.

Night fell–so dark, it was as if the sky had been painted with soot. Watch fires were lit before both camps. Guards from opposing sides stood so close that they could have shot arrows at one another. The last order for the night was that all bugles and fifes were to be silent, and everyone was to sleep early.

*O*nly in Attila's open-sided tent were the torches still burning. On the table steamed the chickens which the town of Troyes had sent out to Attila.

The Hunnish noblemen and other kings ate without a word. Among them sat Bishop Lupus from Troyes. Even here he wore his mitre and golden chasuble and before him lay the large silver crucifix. He hardly ate at all, but only stroked his beard and at times glanced at Attila with a worried expression. Now and then he gasped from a twinge of pain; the poor man suffered from gout. The leaders of all the various nations stood around in front of the tent, waiting for orders. Throughout supper Attila kept asking Mena-Sagh to show him the tablet–this was a black wooden panel with small coloured pieces of linen pinned to it on which thė groupings of the two camps were shown. Attila examined this ceaselessly, giving orders even while eating.

Spies arrived intermittently, and also reports from our own most forward posts: over in the other camp nothing was stirring. That was to be expected; in the dark no army can move. There was no moon, and clouds covered the stars.

At the end of the supper they served cheese, and fruit boiled in wine.

Bishop Lupus rose and set down his goblet in front of him.

'Mighty king! King of kings!' he began solemnly, speaking in Latin. 'Allow this servant of servants to speak. Fame writes your name in bloody letters. Across the skies a comet signalled your setting out. The earth trembles where your shadow falls, and courageous men pale at your glance. But let them call you the wolf of the world, or a blood-thirsty devil! If I appear at God's throne before you, I will tell Him that you led your mighty, world-trampling host through my town, and yet tonight its inhabitants sleep in peace.'

Gratitude shone in his kindly old eyes. The lords didn't follow his speech, of course; at most Orestes did, and perhaps the young king of the Franks from the River Neckar, and I, but his voice was solemn and his speech exalted like a psalm.

Attila leaned back in his chair. His prominent brow cast a shadow over his eyes, so I couldn't see whether or not the bishop's words pleased him. For only his eye ever revealed a bit of his soul; the rest of his face was expressionless like a statue.

The old man went on. 'The world is uneasy now, like a stormy sea. Every nation is a great wave, and all the waves pass towards the west. It must be God's will.'

Attila motioned to Orestes. 'Translate for my guests what the old man speaks!'

The bishop was silent while the interpreter repeated what he had said thus far; then he continued with a radiant face:'The people of the old world have come together here to oppose you, and perhaps as soon as tomorrow you will measure your strength against theirs and much blood will flow. But it is the moral of history that humanity is born anew always in a sea of tears and blood. In every great storm there is much damage, much wrecking and death. Crops are crushed into the mud, flocks are scattered, trees are uprooted, rocks fall and kill the living. Destruction and ruins–how much there is to mourn for! But once the storm subsides, the air will be filled with a life-giving force. The roots of the uprooted trees will grow anew, thrice as strong, and human souls will take up their lives again with new zest.

'Mighty king, Attila! You are the scourge which God has set loose on humanity. Your fame alone is like thunder; your sword is lightning; your people are a raging storm. God wishes it so, for nothing can happen that is against His will. Because you are a good man, I respect and honour you, even though I view your giant rage with terror. May God grant you the happiness of seeing the rebirth after the storm; even as God has scourged the world with your hand, so may He bless it with your hand.'

He stepped closer to Attila, who stretched out his hand. The old man wanted to kiss the hand but Attila embraced him.

'Blessings!' cried the Huns.

'Vivat!' cried the foreigners.

'Hoch!' cried the Goth leaders.

And they all drank to Attila's health.

The king, remaining seated, replied in Latin with a slight Hunnish accent.

'I believe that our lives do not begin here on this earth, and that they do not end here either. We wander here and strive, not quite knowing why. But there is one who knows. I was sent by the God of the Huns, who is also the God of the entire world! He placed a sword in my hand–I shall never put it down! Who could possibly withstand me?'

The Huns broke out in enthusiastic toasts and blessings. Attila, his eyes alight, raised his goblet to the bishop with a stately gesture, showing that it was to his health he was drinking this time.

*S*ome of the company left; the rest stayed on. The servants folded up and carried out all the portable tables; the chairs they propped up against the sides of the tent, working hurriedly.

During supper I had noticed that there was a strange coming and going and restlessness in front of the tent, but the conversation at the table held me so spellbound that I had not attended to what went on outside.

Afterwards I saw that they had planted a birch tree with its full foliage, and were pounding down the earth around its trunk. Ten paces from the birch the apprentices lit a bonfire. The shamans were all there too, puttering about: Gyorhe was holding on to a white ewe and a black ram; Bucha set a seven-cornered altar stone in its place, and Sharmand brought a round black stone. So there was to be a sacrifice–that was what the lords were waiting for.

The fire shone its blaze on the figures of the priests moving around it. Kama and Iddar were in white, Zobogan, Bogar and Gyorhe in red, and the rest of them in black; the helpers wore their regular fighting clothes, but also long, pointed sacrificial hats.

Three half-naked ceremonial musicians squatted down under the birch, two of them with long cylindrical drums; the third had a long fife with a funnellike mouth–*tárogató* (shawm) in Hun.

The lords took their places on low chairs around Attila. Beyond the bonfire, outside, stood a crowd of spectators, mostly leading elders.

The drummers sounded a roll, and the man with the shawm began to play a painful, horrifying, howling melody. One priest lit a large white wax candle; another splashed the back of the ewe with water or something from a bowl held high. The ewe trembled for a moment. Zobogan bowed before it as if it were a person, and suddenly his knife flickered–he thrust it deep into the animal. Shaman Vitosh did the same to the black ram. The sheeps' bleating mingled with the music. The blood of the white ewe was caught in a silver bowl, the black ram's in an iron one.

The priests worked diligently. Bogar and Gyorhe rolled up their sleeves, and with broad curved knives swiftly skinned the two animals. Damanogh heated a hatchet in the fire and with it separated the black ram's horns. He handed them to Vitosh, who fitted them into the rim of his hat so that the horns stood out above his ears.

Then the music stopped.

Old Iddar climbed up the birch on the footholds that had been cut in the trunk, and stopped when he reached the first boughs. There he spread his arms and chanted in a shaky voice: 'Silence! Silence! Silence!'

Every man took off his hat–even Attila.

Zobogan cut out the white ewe's tongue, placed it in a large silver spoon and raised it high before the fire.

Iddar, in the tree, turned to the east and cried into the skies: 'Our Creator! Our Lord God! Master of the sun and moon! Master of earth! Master of water! Master of the star-filled skies! We make this offering to you in fire, in flames!'

Zobogan threw the tongue into the fire. The priests cried in unison, 'Help us, our Maker, our God! Be with us!'

Iddar descended from the tree and took hold of the sacred spoon in which the white ewe's heart showed red. He raised it high and prayed:

'You, almighty ancient father, who live above the clouds, you who command the lightning, set heaven thundering and earth trembling! As this heart burns in the fire, our hearts burn no less in their love of you! Be with us!'

'Be with us!' murmured all the shamans, and with them the people.

Iddar threw the heart too into the fire. The sacred music started up once more.

Now Vitosh stepped forth. A muffled roll came from the two drums. He placed the tongue and heart of the black ram in an iron spoon. He spoke in a hollow voice, looking at the ground.

'Lord of harmful spirits! Powerful Evil! Master of devils! Source of sadness and trouble! Black Evil! Do not harm us!'

'Do not harm us!' everyone murmured.

He threw the tongue and heart into the pit under the altar stone, then emptied the blood from the iron dish there too. Only the embers were glowing now.

Iddar tossed the two stones into the embers, and on each he placed a blade bone. Throughout the rest of the ceremony he stood motionless, with his hands stretched out in the direction of the bones.

Dry grass was thrown on the fire, and flames shot up. Now blind Kama turned to the fire, and, holding two swords high, formed a cross with them. The music stopped.

'Bow down!' Iddar chanted.

Everyone bowed deeply.

Kama began to sing in a tremulous old voice: 'Our Lord God above, we call upon you. Your will has led the Hunnish people here; your sword is in Attila's hands. Pour your strength into us from above! We beg you–help the son of Balamber, the leader of the Huns, your chosen Attila!'

'Help Attila!' murmured the people along with the shamans.

I stole a glance at Attila. He sat motionless in his chair. With his black beard, pale face, and eyes sunk in shadow, he looked like the spirit of the night.

The shaman continued.

'Our Lord God, who has brought us from far in the east to the plains of the Tisia, and from the plains of the Tisia to the lands of the west, strengthen our swords so that steel can cut through steel! Let each blow be like storm lightning!'

Iddar took the swords from Kama, giving him two arrows in their place.

The fire flared up again and Kama sang, calling upon God to bless the arrows of the Huns.

After this Kama took reins in his hands, and prayed to God to give strength to the horses.

The people echoed the last words of each prayer.

Next, wine was poured onto the fire. For a moment darkness covered everything. Then new flames rose, and the hissing fire made the tall column of steam glow red.

Holding the sword aloft and brandishing it in the light of the fire, Kama invoked the spirits of all departed Huns, calling by name all the heroes of the nation.

'From fire and water, from sky and earth, come forth! Come like the breath of one asleep! Come like clouds frayed by trees high on the mountain! Come like shadows in the night! Come forth and help us!'

'Come forth and help us!' murmured the people.

Iddar stabbed the two swords into the trunk of the birch and above them stuck the arrows. Then he fixed the burning candle there and hung the reins over a branch.

Attila rose, and the people began to leave. The high priests, princes and nobles followed Attila into his tent where they sat along the walls, leaving the middle of the room empty.

A few thick wax torches hissed and sputtered on the central pillar of the tent. The camp was drowned in quiet–the soft sound of sleep and horses grazing–like the monotonous murmuring of the sea. Only a few camp dogs barked in the distance, and the bonfire crackled there in front of us, making the priests' lengthy shadows dance on the walls of the tent.

The two drums now thumped angrily as the drummers hit them with their fingers and palms. The fifer placed the shawm to his lips and blew one tune endlessly repeated.

Now Shaman Zobogan stood up in the middle of the room. He turned his face to heaven, spread his arms wide, and started walking in a circle, gradually increasing speed. Soon he was running, jumping and leaping around as if he wanted to escape from the tent. The thunder of the drums became more and more wild, the leaping became more and more breathless. His hair steamed, his whole body whirled. Then he began to slow down, and at last tottered round, weakly, his eyes turned up so that only their whites flashed at us. His face was purple-blue; then he turned yellow, then pale. At last he lost his balance and, foaming at the mouth, collapsed in the middle of the room.

The other shamans knelt down around him. The music stopped. He gasped a few words as he twitched spasmodically.

'Field...flowers...horses...swim...'

Attila sat in the armchair, watching with eyebrows drawn together.

Kama turned to Attila.

'The field will yield blood-flowers. Horses and eagles will swim in the same dust.'

We stared silently. Some shrugged their shoulders, others were lost in thought. Attila sat staring before him from the dark depths of his eyes.

Zobogan was helped up by two others and carried away. I thought he must have drunk the juice of some poisonous plant, for he was like a madman.

The music started up again.

Now an Alan priest stepped to the middle of the rug, dressed from head to foot in black mourning robes. He shook various coloured rods onto a piece of white felt. Around him a completely naked figure, painted white, was summoning spirits by turning cartwheels and leaping about with grotesque, angular movements, while the priest kept shouting God's name, and tried to find a pattern in the way the rods fell.

The Alan priest's prediction was more sweet-sounding.

'I see the enemy as a seven-headed dragon. Its angriest head drops into the dust. The Roman sword is white, the Hunnish sword is red.'

Attila moved his head. The Hunnish nobles then whispered wonderingly.

'Aetius...'

Then the Goth priests came, performed their rites and made vague prophecies. Those present listened spellbound, scarcely breathing.

At last the Hunnish shamans dragged in the two glowing-hot altar stones with iron tongs, and placed them on a heap of embers in the centre of the room. A devout silence followed.

With gold-handled silver pincers Iddar picked up the charred bone from the round stone and held it up to the torchlight. He examined the cracks with a worried expression.

'Nothing discernible,' he said at last, turning to the blind head shaman. 'Nothing but one great crack.'

'Understandable,' Kama replied.

He turned to Attila.

'The leader of the enemy will die in battle.'

Attila remained motionless. 'Let's see the other one,' he said.

Shaman Iddar picked up the second bone. Tense silence. He began to read it syllable by syllable: 'All...the...Hun...nish...spi...rits...will...fight...be-...side...you...'

The lords jumped up. Everyone hurried to the bone, Attila foremost.

The cracks in the black shoulder blade, as Shaman Bial drew them for me later, actually spelled out that sentence in the Hun alphabet.

Cheer brightened every face. Only the old bishop sat in his place, calm and sleepy. Attila turned to him.

'Are you not going to prophesy my future? Do you not have the power to consult the Christian souls?'

The bishop rose and answered humbly. 'No, no my lord. Our religion knows one prophecy only.'

'Tell me.'

'All will be according to God's will.'

'That is good, then!' said Attila, clapping his hand to his sword. 'If it is God's will that this sword should hang by my side, then it is also his will that it should strike.'

He nodded to the lords and retired upstairs.

I lit a torch and set out in front of my master. Sleeping men lay everywhere. My master followed behind me with the commander-in-chief; neither spoke. Only when we reached our tent and the older brother mounted his horse, did Chath ask, 'Well then, it won't be we who start?'

'Probably not,' replied the commander-in-chief in a sleepy, unconcerned voice.

'The signs are not so transparent then?'

'No. Attila will likely review the positions once more in the morning.'

I was surprised by the commander's words. I realized later, however, that Attila, because of the foreign princes present, had purposely pretended that the signs were all favourable.

'And what if they start early?' asked Chath.

His brother shook his head. 'I don't think they will. Sleep as much as possible. I will set out this very hour.'

'To the south?'

'Yes. Two of our spies volunteered to set fire to the hay carts if there was any wind. The Romans have set them up close to one another. With God's help I'll get them from behind. Take care of the stream where the reeds are.'

The brothers shook hands.

Chath stepped into the tent deep in thought. He stopped as if debating something, then yawned so widely that his jaws cracked. I stuck the torch into the iron holder on the tent pole, and stood ready to help him undress.

'Tonight we won't undress,' he said. 'You too lie down in your clothes–and keep your sword!'

He reached into a crate and took out two small goatskin flasks the size of a hog-bladder.

'Take them out,' he said, 'and hang them on the back of the saddles, covered with wet cloths. Put one on Lightning, the other on the spare horse. Wait!' he said, searching in the crate again. 'I'll give you one too.'

In battle one gets very thirsty.

He pulled out the cork and tasted the contents.

'Damnation! It's turned to vinegar! Taste it! It's sour!'

'No wonder,' I replied. 'You know, my lord, we did not bring the cellar along!'

'Why didn't the king's spoil?'

'They brought his in kegs kept under wet hides.'

He climbed into his hammock and fell asleep immediately.

The horses stood beside the tent in full trappings, with Karach, the stable-boy, for company. A copper-covered mace of cornel wood hung from each saddle, along with a quiver stuffed full of yard-long bamboo arrows.

'Throw something to the horses,' I said. 'We won't be doing anything before morning.'

Karach yawned. 'Can't you see that they have their feed bags on?' he replied. Then he stretched out by the side of the tent.

I got into my bed which was hooked to the tent poles under the leather flap of the door.

I couldn't fall asleep for a long time for wondering about the morrow. Would I have another night in this world? Was I seeing the Big Dipper for the last time? How different this night would have been had I never met Emmo–I'd be sleeping at home in Constantinople, in the lap of the still, sea-scented summer night, instead of here in the midst of this sleeping hell, listening to my horse munching oats unconcernedly, though perhaps tomorrow I would ride him into the world of the dead.

Around midnight, however, sleep came at last. How long I slept I do not know. In summer the sky becomes light at three in the morning. I woke to clattering noises all around me. The ground shook with the hoofbeats of many horses being led down to drink.

I climbed up the tent pole with the footholds on it to view the enemy. They too were milling about. At the streams between the two camps were millions of horses. Would there be enough water for them all? And would we start the battle today?

My master got up, washed his face with a splash of water, and wiped his moustache and beard in his hands. I held his leather cloak for him; he jerked it on, then hurried over to Attila.

The Huns were all on horseback by then. The younger ones went without saddles, sitting just on their coats, or on pieces of hide or blanket. They all kept turning their heads in the direction of Attila's tent. From the fields farther out they shouted to us again and again. 'What's happening? When are we starting?'

The young men were just itching to fight. The older ones too thought the dry sunny weather ideal for battle. It's better in the morning while it's not too hot! And it's always better today than tomorrow!

I felt restless too. While my master was with Attila I once more checked the buckles and straps on the reins, the stirrups and my battle cloak. My dagger and sword I polished on the sole of my sandal.

Like all the others, I tied a leather pouch stuffed with horsehair on each knee.

An Arabian merchant made his way among the Huns, selling lion fat. They made fun of him, asking if the lion used to neigh or grunt, but many bought some.

At last Attila sent word that everyone should eat and drink, and that horses should be fed too. So campfires flared up everywhere. On all sides oxen, calves, sheep and lambs were herded through the pathways between tents.

'So we aren't going to fight today, then?' asked one another, annoyed.

'Perhaps in the afternoon.'

'Afternoon? Who the hell ever heard of such a thing?'

'Can't you see that right now the sun would be shining in our eyes?'

But then why didn't the Romans attack? The sun wasn't shining in their eyes.

Our spies reported that Aetius was still waiting for one more army. He was planning to start the following morning.

'This afternoon we fight,' said Chath, as he took his battle cloak off and gave it to me for safe-keeping.

It was hot. Over the fires on yard-long spits turned the energy that would fight in the afternoon.

*T*he noon shadows of the tents were still short when Kason, the bugler, appeared on the peak of the royal tent and blew into his great white ivory horn:

Thousands upon thousands of horns blared, and repeated these three terrifying howls. If there had been no other sound, one could have heard how these three calls flew through the camp to the farthest limits of the army out of sight in the distance. But weapons clanked noisily, and a chaos of shouts suddenly filled the camp: names, signals and commands were yelled in great confusion.

Everyone mounted. Everyone was tying or adjusting something–his leather hat or helmet, his breastplate, shield, quiver, sword or javelin, his horse's girth, or the string on his bow. The Saraguri and Roxolans pulled on their helmets–animal skulls with skin and horns still on. The Gelons stuck human skulls on their spears. The Marcomans fastened their ox horns to their hats; they looked like devils.

In front of the army the smoke of sacrificial fires billowed in thirty places at once. The priests of all foreign peoples were preparing to make sacrifices. The Hunnish priests would offer up a white horse, the Saraguri and Gelons, men.

From the distance an unknown horn signal sounded; it came from the north–shrill, and long and winding as a snake; it was something I did not recognize.

'They've started closing in from up there,' said a stable-boy.

The guards withdrew from the field. Now the zoltans kicked up the dust of the pathways between the tents, galloping in every direction. All the flag-bearers had their flag-staffs anchored in their stirrups by now. The fifers stood up on the mechanical bows and catapults.

Every movement was quick. All eyes shone. Everyone talked and shouted boisterously.

I felt I must be the only one pale and silent. A chill ran through my body, as if an invisible hyena had licked my face. I had only one thought in my mind, frozen and fixed: you are setting out to die.

I was still standing in front of Attila's tent among the stable-boys who were holding the reins of his and the noblemen's horses. My horse's breast was protected by a leather apron, and my mace hung from my saddle. I was wearing my grey battle cloak, and on top of it a cape–to look more like the lords. The copper helmet on my head was made up to look like leather; at my right side hung the sword, and at my left the quiver with about a hundred yard-long lightweight arrows in it. I carried another quiver on my back. My bow was in my hand.

The horn blared for the second time from the peak of the tent.

Again thousands of horns caught the call and sounded it across the length and breadth of the camp.

All the chains which linked the carts were undone, and the horsemen began to pour out onto the field between them with a great din and clatter.

Zoltans on nimble steeds darted back and forth in front of the multitude, crane and ostrich feathers in their hats. With loud shouts they summoned the horsemen to form groups according to clans and families. The first rows were taken up by those whose horses' breasts were best protected. These men were all seasoned warriors, and were entitled to a double portion of loot after the battle.

In the middle of each division the youngest man, sometimes hardly fifteen, held up the family's emblem on a long spear.

All right arms were bare. Some had their left arms bare too, but then they had a silver or copper serpent twined round the arm to protect the muscles. Only the chest was heavily protected, and the head. Steel helmets, however, were rare–most men wore leather.

The White Huns mingled with the Black Huns in colourful little groups in between the lines. Behind all stood the foot soldiers.

A loud roar of greeting rose from the direction of Attila's tent. He rode out wearing a gilded helmet and a cape made of lionskin. Gold protectors spiralled around his brown and muscled arms. He was surrounded by his chief officers and bodyguard, and before him fluttered a large white silk flag with a shining hawk embroidered on it in gold.

When Attila's flag appeared a storm of joyous shouts thundered through the endless camp.

The king put spurs to his fabulous white horse and flew by the rows; heading out into the field, he turned to survey the army, the like of which had never been seen by the sky's old sun since the time of Xerxes.

The cheers that greeted him were like roll upon roll of thunder.

At this moment, at all the altars, they began the slaughter for the offerings. Attila paused at the altar where blind Kama was offering his sacrifice.

The ceremony was short. The priest called to the Hunnish God in a loud voice, then reached out his arms in the direction of every tribe and nation. He dipped a broom made of birch twigs into the blood, and with it blessed the army.

The priests then quietly continued their offerings at the altars; they would do so as long as the battle lasted.

Attila sped by the divisions at a fast gallop. Sometimes he stopped to exchange a word with the leaders or shout encouragement to the warriors.

When he came to our division I heard him shout: 'Huns! Today we shall show the world once more what it is to be a Hun!' Those flashing eyes! That movement of the head! It was all sheer excitement from that moment: the man seemed hardly a man at all, but rather some lion-god in human form!

Everyone shouted back enthusiastically: 'We'll show them!'

But from my throat the shout came huskily.

Beside us stood the army of Berki. Attila shouted to them, 'God will fight on our side! We have never yet lost a battle!'

'Nor shall we now!' The army thundered in reply.

And Attila flew on. Wherever he spoke we heard an answering cry and saw a raising of spears. But the battle line was so long that the two wings were lost in the distant plains. To them Attila only flashed his sword. That meant as much as a speech: *Look, this is the sword of God!*

A distant murmur and a flash of arms showed that they had understood Attila's gesture; his soul burned in everyone, like the rising sun in the waves of the ocean.

Meanwhile our enemies were taking up their positions.

They didn't really want to fight today, especially in the afternoon when in a few hours the sun would be in their eyes. But what could they do? They had heard the horn signals and seen our preparations–they had to accept the challenge.

I was full of cold shivers.

Beside me was an old Hun with a face as lined as a cantaloupe. 'Well, this will be a vicious fight!' he blurted out.

'Why?' I asked, snatching at his words for my ears devoured all that was said around me.

'Because if we start now,' replied the man, 'we'll go on throughout the night. Nothing is worse than night battles.' 'That's all for the best,' Sabolch with the big ears said proudly. 'At least we shan't sweat!'

We watched the enemy swarming out. The silvery, glittering stripe on the other bank of the stream was the Romans; the yellow one with the red patches was the Franks with their leather shields; the one patched with white was the Burgundians; the moving reeds were the Alans; the multitude waving like acres of wheat were the Visigoths; and the small, brilliant group galloping up and down before the armies consisted of Aetius and King Theodoric with his son, King Sangiban, and Merovius, the king of the Franks, and Gondibo, the Burgundian king, and all the other leaders.

They too marshalled their army as Attila had. One or another silvery regiment of horsemen changed places, flowing across the plain like a river. Then the group of leaders dispersed. Now in the far distance one could see the Roman army all on the left wing, facing our Gepids and our various wild peoples with their painted faces and animal skins.

The Visigoths on the other wing would fight our Ostrogoths. The Franks, Burgundians, Alans and other mixed peoples stood opposite the Huns in the middle.

Attila's commanders also dispersed, each taking up his place.

The heat was great; everyone was sweating profusely.

Behind the Roman camp a great cloud of smoke rose in the distance. Were the hay carts burning? Had the commander-in-chief begun his attack from the rear? High in the sky a stork circled above the two camps.

Attila stood up in his stirrups and examined the enemy–he was still looking for something.

He signalled to the Goth king with his sword. The Goth army began to move. The horsemen fanned out, heading at a fast gallop for the hill that was held by Thorismund. Their shouts became one overwhelming roar. Flying weapons glinted in the sun.

Dust enveloped the horsemen. From then on the Goths' horsemen were like a yellow mist moving close to the ground. A cloud such as the first gusts of a gathering storm stirred up on a road.

But now, to the left of us, the Romans too set out. Like the overflowing Tisia they flooded towards our outermost armies. They were so far away from us that we could only hear muffled hoofbeats, like the mutter of distant thunder.

Everyone was silent, watching. The heat was terrible.

'Damn him!' Chath swore at his horse. 'We haven't even begun and he's sweating behind the ears!'

Now the drums began to roll in our division, and the horns began to shriek and the music of the fifes started up. But the mad noise of final preparations drowned out all the horns and fifes.

Chath looked back to see if I was there. His eyes were bloodshot and his face was so shiny from sweat that he looked as if he'd been lacquered.

The cold shiver of death ran through me. My muscles waited for the release from tension like the taut string of a drawn bow.

Attila again rose on his horse, looked back and with his sword gave the signal to follow him.

Three hundred thousand throats screamed the battle cry: *'Hooy-raah!'* and the horses were away, rushing straight for the middle of the Roman army.

'God help us!'

The earth trembled. The air was a storm of voices. Everyone galloped after the group leaders, crouching low. One group after another separated, forming a pattern like a chessboard with empty spaces in between. These were soon taken up by the armies of Berki, Orgovan, Dorog and Macha.

Once in the field, they spread out more and galloped on. The best horses were already ahead like the fingers of a glove–there was no holding them back. A short distance behind them, the armies of Upor, Balan, Madaras and Kamocha started out; after them came Urkon, Betegh, Aladar and Zhogod.

Now it was our turn. Up till now we had stood tense as a bow drawn to the limit, waiting for some space open before us. When those who had left last were far enough ahead, Chath gave out a yell and shook his bow.

'Hooy-raah! Lord God!'

And we too were starting.

Were we really going forward? Or was the earth running backwards under us? I had to grip hard with my knees to stay on the galloping horse.

'Hooy! Hooy!'

I was not supposed to lose Chath. Lado rode beside him on the left, carrying a huge leather shield. His only duty in battle was to watch out for the master–to stop all spears and blows coming from the left with the large shield. Close on their heels followed Karach and I. Karach was leading a saddled horse beside his own: in case the master's horse caught an arrow or a spear, he could immediately mount another.

'Hooy! Hooy!'

We galloped on–in my case thanks to my horse, for, to tell the truth, I was paralysed again for the first few minutes. That infernal yelling, the horses' frightened snorting, the drumming hoofbeats, the rising cloud of dust...it all felt like the apocalypse.

'Hooy! Hooy! Hooy-raah!' The words burst from my breast like flames.

But it was only the pressure of the first few minutes. Then suddenly I gained such strength as I had never felt before. All the shouting, those angry yells–that was what strengthened me.

The horsemen rushed on, fanning out more and more, like water from the rose of a watering can. Soon a dust-filled space opened up around me, giving me room to grab my bow. I threw the reins on the saddle horn, then pulled the bow taut and awaited the order to shoot.

The grass was all torn up under the hoofs. I could hardly keep an eye on Chath for the cloud of dust.

'Hooy-raah!'

A horn signal: 'Shoot!'

The world grew dark as a cloud of arrows–our arrows–obscured the sky.

What a noise as they whirred and whistled, frightened horses blew and men shouted with rage!

But now came a cloud of arrows from the enemy. I held up my shield. One arrow hit the wood of my saddle, and in a moment another one struck my shield. Oh, my God! If only my horse could escape without being hit!

We galloped on.

Through narrow openings in the great rush I could see the dense ranks of the enemy, all behind their shields. The breasts of our horses pushed them back with a grinding crunch. Maces with sharp nails crashed noisily. Shouts of *hooy-raah* changed into strange howls and yelps. I could still see only our horses ahead of me, but my horse was already jumping over corpses. Pull the spears out of them! These are the Alans! Step on them, my horse! Trample the writhing worms!

There in front of me was a wounded man, still alive, trying to pull himself up–but Chath knocked him over. Ah, but here was another to take his place–an Alan with a tousled beard,in armour, his spear broken. He struck someone to the right with his wooden mace. I too kept chopping right and left wherever I could see a head. There was terrific strength in me; I could have demolished buildings! There! You dog, take that! –and something fell on my thigh. It was easy–nothing to it! But look! Chath suddenly pulled back his horse, his hand to his face. Those who were behind galloped past us, screaming.

We were all panting; we must have been fighting for over an hour. The horses too were puffing. Sweat poured down between their hind legs in white foamy streams. It would have been good to shorten my stirrups so that I could stretch higher to strike. If only I had time! My lungs were being torn to shreds with the heaving and gasping and I was parched with thirst.

I looked at Chath. What had happened to him? He spat out two or three bloody teeth; swearing terribly, he shook the tears out of his eyes and shouted over to Lado: 'Give me the battle axe!'

And he grabbed it. The Alans stood dense as wheat before harvest; they concentrated on spearing the horses. Mountains of kicking horses and writhing men protected them like a bulwark. We had to veer to one side to get at them again. But from the cloud of dust, red-feathered Frankish horsemen came pouring out–straight at us.

The two divisions of horsemen clashed like an explosion. Shields thudded and helmets smashed–yells, screams, the snorting of horses. It was a battle in hell! A blood-drenched Frankish horseman charged toward me. I hit him in the chest with my mace and he fell off his mount. The horse lurched against mine–I hit that too, in the head. I could hardly see because of the dust. Then, to my surprise, I heard the horn signal to return, so I reined in my horse. The enemy's horsemen were forcing us back. The crowd was so thick that I couldn't even turn round. But as more space opened up behind me, my horse turned, rearing high, and took off after the rest.

'God bless you, you clever animal!'

Another division continued the fighting where we left off, and we regrouped once more, panting–well, thank God, I was still alive!

Everyone was covered with blood. Chath's horn blew the signal to fall into order, then we rested for a space. The sweep of the Frankish horsemen had been so strong that it had pushed us back a thousand paces before Orgovan's army arrived and attacked them from the side.

We rested, caught our breath and dried ourselves off. Thirst stuck in my throat like a sharp knife. Chath was still spitting and swearing, but others were bloody too. They kept turning their arms and stretching their legs–as long as everything moved, nothing much could be wrong. The bleeding didn't matter; indeed I was proud to see that my thigh and chest were bloody. If I could only have adjusted my stirrups! We all rose in our saddles now to see how Orgovan was doing. They were pushing through, due north, fighting all the way. It was a riddle why the two armies engaged in battle kept moving north. Perhaps the initial push made the horses move that way. It seemed as if tiny white lightning bolts flashed ceaselessly above the multitude. A space about as wide as the Danube now lay between the fighting multitude and us.

'I've cut down eight of them!' panted Lado. 'You all saw it?'

'I've killed five!' I shouted.

'I saw it!' replied Lado. 'And you?'

'A thousand!' shouted Chath angrily. 'I'll kill a thousand single-handed!'

A great din behind us drowned out even the tumult of the battle.

'Attila!' cried Chath, amazed.

It was he, mounted on his big white horse and surrounded by his glittering bodyguard, leading a vast throng of some twenty thousand Huns. As he approached us, he waved his sword as if to say, 'Huns, why are you idle? Is there anyone who doesn't fight to the end when *I* lead the battle?'

And he thundered past with his mounted warriors, his flag like a white ghost above the galloping army.

So our division was filled with new strength. Inspired by Attila we threw ourselves once more into the attack.

'Right in their centre!' yelled an ostrich-feathered zoltan immediately in front of me. 'Attila's order! We'll break the enemy right in their centre!'

But who the devil could tell in this chaos where the middle of the enemy was? It must have been where Attila was leading. And in a little while we too were where the dust rose highest. Through it all we could still see the flash of swords ahead of us, and always Attila's white flag fluttering. The earth and the very sky rumbled with the bloody fury of that fight. Once I thought I caught a glimpse of Attila's shining yellow helmet, the lightning flash of his sword. Now the enemy consisted mostly of Alan horsemen and their yard-long spears flew among us like birds–once more we were in the midst of hell's whirlpool.

The first man I encountered was a broad-shouldered Burgundian with bloodshot eyes. Chath's mace had smashed his shield, but Chath himself had dashed away from him to fall upon some other victim. As the Burgundian's injured left arm dropped, my spear crashed through his chest with a crunch. A moment of terror ran through me, and I forgot to jerk back my spear. The Burgundian turned over and slid off his horse like a sack.

I had no time to look around and see if anyone had witnessed my kill–my horse carried me on. Lacking a spear, I grabbed my sword. Oh, those stirrups! If I had only had time to shorten them!

'Hooy! Hooy!'

My horse was jumping over dead horses now, and stepping on human corpses, and instead of *hooy-hooy!* there were shouts of 'There they run!'

Now horses piled against horses. The Alans with their spears had not been able to withstand the terrible pressure of the Huns, but the storing, densely packed hundred thousand Frankish horsemen stood fast. Swords would never cut a way through them, only spears, daggers and maces.

The Hunnish and Frankish horsemen met in a deadly melee. It was impossible to see anything clearly, only an angry, bloody swirling, the glitter of weapons, horses prancing and shying; a storm of curses, thudding maces, ratting and snapping swords and spears. Now and then a horse collapsed, dragging its rider down with it; but above them other horsemen instantly dashed, and in a few minutes, where that one horse had fallen, only a moving, writhing bloody heap of horses and men remained.

For a moment I too got entangled in just such a turmoil. I had lost sight of Chath long ago. White Huns, common soldiers all, were wielding their long-handled battle axes all about me. One of them, right in front of me, was hit in the chest with an adze by a bloody-bearded Frank. The Hun fell backwards off his horse and I was able to catch his battle axe as it flew out of his hand. In the next moment I had struck the Frank on the head with it with such force that his skull caved in and the man fell lifeless.

'Who saw that?' but I couldn't even hear my own voice in that hellish din.

'Get into the thick of it!' shrieked the zoltans. And as one wide-mounted zoltan stood there shouting like that, on top of a heap of horses, it seemed as if not just his mouth but his entire body was yelling–a shout become human! The nightmare of a sick imagination.

The horses sneezed and snorted because of the dust. The froth of their saliva flew like white rags over their heads, spattering the horsemen.

Another Hunnish army attacked the Franks from the side and drove them away from in front of us. An empty space opened up before us, and again we had a pause in which to catch our breath. I raised the visor of my helmet: the sweat was pouring off me so profusely, it would have watered three flower beds at home. My horse was sweating too and covered with foam–bloody foam. Never before had I seen so many red horses...

A few blood-drenched warriors from among those who were fighting fell behind, and, turning their horses towards our group, left the scene of the battle. There was one with an arm hanging limp, like a puppet's arm; another man fell off his horse on the way, and was dragged along the ground with one foot caught in the stirrup.

My stirrups were still too long. My face was burning with sweat. I pulled out a kerchief to wipe it off, and as I took away the kerchief, I noticed it was full of blood.

'*Hooy,* you miserable murderers!' And as the field began to fill with a division which was backing up, I spurred on my horse, and with my battle axe attacked three Franks at once.

I thrashed about, blind with rage; I hardly looked where I was hitting, but more Huns came and helped me. Two Franks fell over among the horses; the third was carried away by his horse into the open field and there thrown off.

'Magnificent, Zeta! What a blow!' shouted a voice behind me.

I turned–it was Badalo, the Hun who taught the young people at home to throw spears and javelins. He was so soaked in blood, I wouldn't have recognized him if his sweat hadn't washed his face clean. But his praise put new spirit into me!

The next moment the Armoric army rushed us–different battle-cries, different weapons, different people–as thick as locusts. They charged us and it was as if a mountain had fallen on top us. One Hun after another fell off his horse, while those who couldn't get at them yet, shook their battle axes and swords, shouting.

The bugler sounded the retreat.

Our horses turned without being directed–they knew the signal; they turned and galloped away a short distance. The Franks and Armorics followed us in a great screaming swarm, but our gallop gradually slowed: it was a trick. Even while escaping we grabbed our bows and drew them tight. At the new signal we turned and let our arrows fly.

The front line of the enemy didn't have a chance! Some of them turned into porcupines! They fell, horses and all!

'Now your battle axes!'

But the enemy seemed numberless. Foaming horses' heads heaved and tossed like waves in a choppy sea, and always in place of those who fell, a new wave of people exploding against us. The live horses jumped over the dead ones and once again the field was alive with devils.

'Hooy-raah!'

A broad-shouldered Frank, wearing a black, pot-shaped helmet, rushed towards us and struck Badalo, who was just ahead of me. He slashed across his neck with a broad sword with such force that Badalo's head went spinning away among the horsemen.

This, I could feel, was my fatal moment; the dark moment of death! Badalo's killer was saving his second blow for me. But how fickle is the luck of battle! A Hunnish horseman loomed up in front of me, shouting and shaking his spear.

'Hooy-raah!'

He pushed me back, away from there and after him came another, then another. They belonged to a fresh army attacking from the side, engaging in battle for the first time. This was plain to see, for their garments were not yet bloody, and all of them still had their hats. I was pushed farther and farther back with Badalo's army; red rings of fire played before my eyes.

I would have liked to return to our camp and find out why the blood was pouring down my face. But behind me another battle was raging. Horsemen hidden in clouds of dust milled about in a vast, unending crowd, blocking the way back. I only had time to jump down and seize a long-handled steel axe that lay on the ground and to shorten my left stirrup by quickly tying a knot.

The next moment we were all galloping due south, over dead men and horses lead by a zoltan carrying a javelin with a flag of red cambric tied to it. By now the shouts and battle cries were only a loud rasping from hoarse throats, and every mount was a fountain of foam splashing our faces.

We attacked a group of Burgundians – about five hundred of them–from the rear. It was their bad luck that they had broken away from the main body; now they were squeezed and beaten and massacred from all sides by the Huns, though they fought back with rabid desperation.

'Surround them!' sounded the horn. 'Surround them!'

I got behind them so that their backs were toward me. I don't know how many I downed, though my arm grew tired. One was about to strike back, but his broadsword hit my horse as it tossed its head up high and the horse swayed and collapsed. I jumped onto a Burgundian horse, but noticed that it too was wounded. There were many riderless horses around, though, and they were squeezed together so tightly that one could have run across their backs. Seeing a Hunnish horse among them, I grabbed its mane and swung myself up.

'Surround them!'

How long the massacre lasted, I don't know. I only saw that the Burgundians grew fewer and fewer, until the last one fell, and the Huns' tight circle closed in on a mountain of corpses.

Now the horns blared a turn-about. New groups formed. We galloped after our leaders and zoltans. Attila's white flag was waving in the distance, perhaps in the middle of the enemy's camp, and we followed in that direction. But my strength was almost gone. I was bleeding profusely. All down my right side there was not one clean spot, and the reins were so bloody that they slipped through my hands. I would have liked to return to camp, or at least to rest for a while and drink a lot–a pailful of water. Impossible.

We reached the enemy's carts. From the north our painted Gelons rushed to meet us in a great swarm, screeching angrily. The next minute they overran the carts, breaking the chains and forcing their way between them.

Suddenly the air was full of flour; in the midst of it Franks on foot defended the carts, pitting their swords against the flashing daggers of the Gelons. We rushed by them, and once more our horses got caught in a melee, struggling, snorting.

Today I cannot think back without horror to that killing, all that blood in which our horses slipped again and again, all those corpses lying in heaps everywhere, horse and man on top of one another. But as I said, I wasn't human then. I was a wild beast. I killed and killed with the ferocity of a tiger, hating all my foes. I never thought of my own death.

But it was there, as we battled against a particularly strong division, that one blow after another fell on me too before finally I was hit over the head by some sort of a flail; the world grew dark about me, and I fell off my horse dizzily among the dead.

*I*f there is anyone whom necessity – or madness like mine!–leads into battle, let him take comfort: death is not painful.

In all the breathless excitement the body seems to lose every scrap of feeling: neither blows nor cuts nor thrusts hurt; they feel like mere touches. If the wound is fatal, one falls asleep as one does every night.

A man who is fighting neither feels nor thinks. He only has a will: to kill! Even his movements of self-defence are automatic: we put out our hands when we fall, or close our eyes if something whizzes past them. But most wonderful is the fact that the greatest blows and wounds do not hurt.

I asked others too, some who had been knocked unconscious – they all said it didn't hurt.

When I came to, it was getting dark. Only a few clouds, touched by the sun's dying fire, smouldered high up in the sky. I was cold.

Where was I?

In the field the battle was still raging, just as it was when I had left off, only farther away. Was that thunder? Or was it horses pounding the ground? My ears were numb.

I lay between two dead horses, on my back, in bloody mud. Above me lay dead men but my head was free. I lifted it as much as I could, and listened to the muddled angry shouts of thousands of warriors, the clatter of steel, the snorts of horses, the thuds and shrieks. The noise of hell could not be uglier! Were they coming nearer? No, they were still moving farther away. Suddenly I thought: so we still haven't won! Were we going to? Why had Attila joined the fight? He usually stood on top of his tent, viewing the struggle of all his divisions, and shouting his orders from there to the zoltans who waited beside the tent on horseback, ready to take the orders to the various groups. The mile-long fighting army had him for a brain; he directed the limbs, saying which was to advance, which retreat... Why, today, had he joined in the fighting?

It was dark now. In the distance the bugles sounded the retreat. But within a minute, even in darkness, came another Hun signal, and two enemy armies clashed again; the struggle was renewed.

Oh, God, please don't let them trample me to death!

I let my head drop back into the blood-soaked grass. Where was I wounded? I had felt many blows, but perhaps my pigskin cloak, and my helmet and shield had warded off some of them! Could I climb out from here? – I felt so weak.

I lost consciousness again. When I came to because of the cold, the noise of battle sounded very far away, like the repeated drone of distant thunder on summer evenings.

Then everything fell silent. Around me I could hear only the moaning of the wounded, and the coughing of horses. In the distance a rattle of arms...a dog's bark... But all this was silence compared with the terrible tumult I had moved in for hours.

Total darkness–as if the sky had laid a veil of mourning over the battlefield.

I was so thirsty...

The voices of the wounded grew louder, their shouts and moans forming a peculiar hum of pain. The world became chaotic with shouts of agony.

With great effort I propped myself up as best I could. I pushed one corpse off the horse and tried to climb out, but I felt a stabbing pain in my right knee. I reached out to see if an arrow was lodged in it. I could feel that my knee was bloody. When I touched a large wet wound I almost fainted again.

Perhaps all that kept me conscious was that I saw fires moving over the battlefield, tiny red lights meandering to and fro. First they were far apart, scattered in all directions, then they gathered together in a group.

Men with torches were walking in the fields.

Hope for life came back to me. Gathering all my strength, I tried to shout, but only hoarse sounds broke from my throat: 'Over here! This way!'

And then I began to fear that perhaps those people were not Huns. If they were of the enemy and found me, they'd surely thrust me through with their spears.

Close beside me from the other side of the horse on my left came a faint call: 'Hey! Come this way!'

The men with the torches were still far off.

'Who are you?' I called over to the Hun.

'Ochod,' a voice moaned painfully. I didn't know the name. 'And you?' he asked in a little while, with a voice sadder than I had ever heard before.

'I am Zeta,' I replied, 'Chath's servant. Do you think they'll find us?'

'I don't know. Oh, my God...! Someone important has died and they're looking for him!'

'Attila?'

'No, not Attila.'

'But surely it must be–'

'No weapon can harm him!'

I almost swore out loud–what he said was so inane.

A burning thirst tortured me. I felt the saddles for flasks or water bags or goatskins but could find only weapons. From the shape of the saddles I could tell both horses were Frankish.

In the meantime, the men with the torches were coming closer. From the glitter of their helmets I saw that they were Romans and Visigoths. So they weren't Huns – then I was to stay there, among the dead. I would probably bleed to death or die of thirst! The thought made me weaker.

And why was I lying there in a pool of blood, among dead horses and the bodies of strangers, to be dead myself by morning? What had brought me there?

To suffer for a worthy cause – for religion, for one's country, for learning – that is something. But to suffer to no purpose – for a mere kitten, a female Hunnish child so uncultured that she didn't even know the alphabet, so barbarian that she ate lard for breakfast and never even gave me a loving glance...

Whereas I, with all my philosophy, my -ologies and- isms–I might just as well have studied how to bray!

Oh! this terrible thirst! I sat again painfully. The light of the torches moved and again came nearer. Holding onto one saddle, I scrutinized them. Who were they? Thieves? Or was there perhaps a Christian priest among them?

Now they no longer spread out and searched alone–they came in a group, in a long, thin straight line in our direction. On a stretcher improvised from spears they were carrying a dead body.

Following the dead man walked a bare-headed young man; he covered his eyes, crying. As they passed by us, I saw more weeping men, mostly Visigoths, and on the stretcher lay a white-haired man dressed in glittering gold. He had a long white beard and his helmet, carried by one of the men, had a crown on it.

Who had won? Who had lost? This question kept churning in my mind whenever I was able to think of something other than my deadly thirst. If we had won, I hoped my master would send someone to look for me...

'Ochod!' I called out to the Hun. 'Who won?'

'It's not over yet,' he said, even more weakly than before.

'How do you know?'

'Both camps are quiet.'

'Then they are asleep.'

'No–they are watching one another. Or trying to surround one another. I am dying of thirst.'

'Will we go on fighting tomorrow then?'

'For a week if necessary. The horses will trample me to death here...'

I shuddered with horror.

'You think they won't fetch us, then?'

'Perhaps, in the morning.'

'But it's not certain?'

'No.'

'But they must collect the wounded!'

'Yes, in places where there is no fighting.'

'What's wrong with you?'

'A spear...'

'Where did it get you?'

'In the belly.'

'Is the wound large?'

'It came out at the back.'

I didn't say any more to him. He was as good as dead. In a little while he said in a whimper, 'Give me some water!'

Near and far, from all directions, I could hear this same moaning; occasionally someone gave a desperate shout, or wept aloud. 'Water... Water...'

Suddenly someone groaned in Latin near me, past my head.

'Aquam! Aquam!'

Water, yes...If only there were someone to pull me out, so that I could crawl from horse to horse until I found some water somewhere. The dry thirst that burned within me was the most fearful pain I have ever felt.

'Aquam!' I heard it again, but now from near my feet. The voice was the same as before, so the thirsty Roman could walk, or at least move.

'Amice!' I yelled to him.

'Aquam!' he moaned in reply. *'Da mihi bibere!'* (Give me something to drink!)

'Can you walk?'

'I can, a little. But I cannot see. I am blind in both eyes.'

'It's so dark no one can see.'

'But an arrow put out both my eyes. Give me some water–if you believe in God!'

I could hear the clink his scabbard made, and I guessed that he was feeling his way in my direction. 'This way!' I urged him. 'I'll give you a drink if you can pull me out of here. I have a wound in my leg, and I am stuck between two horses. I don't even know if I still have the lower part of my leg. It may be broken under the weight of this horse.'

'Have you any water?'

'No, but I'd go and look for some.'

'Where? the stream is far away.'

'My horse fell somewhere near here. There is some wine on the saddle.'

While we talked, the Roman reached me and felt me with his hands.

'You are a Hun!' he jumped back with fright.

He must have felt my tunic.

'Don't be afraid,' I replied. 'Both you and I are wounded. And both of us are dying of thirst.'

'You won't harm me, then?'

'I am a Christian.'

He was silent. A few minutes passed. 'If you were a Christian, you wouldn't be here,' he said suspiciously.

'What about yourself?' I said, annoyed. 'Let us say simply that we have both been christened; the main thing is for you to pull me out of here.'

'You won't kill me?'

'I swear to Christ.'

He took hold of my two arms and tried to pull, but he hadn't much strength and gave up in tears. 'When I fell,' he said, 'the horses trampled all over me. I feel as if every bone is broken. The blood is still trickling from my eyes, and I shall die here.

'Oh, my dear Julius, my dear and only son!' he went on, weeping, 'why does a soldier ever marry!'

'If you could try from the other side, perhaps you could free my left leg. I cannot move it. Come this way where you can hear my voice.'

He found me. Trying together we managed it. In a little while I could feel that I could move my leg. Gathering all my strength and holding onto one of the saddles, I was able to lift myself with great difficulty, enough to lie on my stomach across the horse's flank. Oh, but the pain in that knee!

'Come on, then!' said the Roman.

I didn't reply, only sucked in my breath and groaned heavily with pain.

'Come on!' the man urged me on. 'Are you moving yet? I've done what you wanted.'

'I can't!' I was able to speak at last. 'I can't even move. There is a horrible wound in my knee...'

I fell back.

'At least tell me where your horse is!'

'Oh!... I don't know – just feel every horse around here... The wine is hanging from the back of the saddle.' In a few minutes I called after him. 'If you find it, bring me some too!'

As the pain subsided I again touched my knee. Now I could feel that what I had previously thought to be a wound was no more than coagulated blood. The leather padding was missing. Suddenly I touched something hard near my knee, and again the torturing pain shot through me. Minutes passed before I could gasp away this new pain. Then I reached down to my knee again, this time very carefully. After many groans and gasps I finally realized that the broken tip of a spear was lodged in the bone.

If I could only jerk it out, the pain it was giving me would surely end. And if then I could find some long halberd or spear or handle of some sort, with its help I could hobble into camp by morning, or close to camp, anyway. At least at daybreak they wouldn't trample me to death when the battle continued.

But I was weak, and fever was sapping what little strength I had. I don't know why, but for a moment my hen came to mind – my little lame black hen. I could just see her limping towards me... *'Kla-kla-kla...'*

'What would you like, chickie?' I whispered. 'You funny little shrimp. Want some water? I haven't any myself!'

I moved to get up, but the pain in my knee hit me again. That brought me back to my senses. After a while it eased again and I wiped away my tears. I had to get out of here somehow! Keeping my leg stiff, I pulled myself up onto the body of the lifeless horse. Then in the darkness of the night I saw that within two bow-shots of where I lay there were many torches moving to and fro in a long, long line, and eagles sparkled in the torchlight.

So I was near the Roman camp.

I heard the monotonous clinking and clattering that one was used to in a camp on the move. What were they up to? Were they setting out against the Huns in this infernal darkness, a weapon in one hand, a torch in the other?

Carefully, I took hold of the spear tip.

'Christ, help me!'

I shut my eyes, gritted my teeth, and yanked it out.

*O*h, blessed sunshine, blessed daybreak! And blessed dew refreshing my parched face!

Was I waking from a dream, or had I fainted? I don't know. But my eyes drank in the sky's beautiful red glow! I was alive! My head was so heavy I could hardly lift it. Perhaps because of my helmet... Yes, it was still on my head. But my hands too seemed to be made of lead. I had to muster all my strength to take the helmet off.

I had a headache and my throat and stomach felt as if I had eaten fire.

The helmet, I saw, was caved in; something had broken through it. I felt my head. My hair was sticky with blood. I could tell from the way my helmet had been cut that someone must have hit me with a broad sword from behind. I didn't dare to feel my skull.

I looked about as much as my sore neck would allow me. Franks, Huns and Burgundians, all lay motionless around me. Two of them lay face up. On the other side four armed Huns lay dead, one on top of another; a fifth sat on them as if on a sofa and seemed to be asleep with his head bent low, but he was pierced through with a javelin.

I yelled over to him.

'Ochod!'

He didn't answer. Didn't even stir.

The battlefield was strewn with corpses. Men, horses and weapons lay jumbled in complete disorder. A bare arm lay near me, all by itself. Someone had severed it right from the shoulder. On one of the fingers was a gold ring. A Roman, black with blood, sat on the ground not five paces from me, his skull split like an oyster.

No one moaned or groaned any more. The air was cool, but my head was burning.

I looked myself over. Blackened blood covered my torn clothes. I tried to pull myself up. My left leg felt all right, but a sharp pain in my right one made me pause. The knee was very swollen.

With the help of my left leg and arm, however, I managed to raise myself. A Frankish warrior without a head lay there on his back beside the horse, even now gripping his spear with stiff fingers. I had to twist it to get it out of his hand.

With the spear's help I managed to sit on the horse's rump. I could see the far distant fields now but there wasn't a square foot of clear space anywhere, nothing but dead horses and men.

When the morning mist lifted, I could see the Hunnish camp. The carts surrounded it like the walls of a castle and mounted guards stood everywhere in front of them.

Then I looked at the Roman camp, or rather, I tried to, but I couldn't see it anywhere.

My head must have weighed a ton. My tongue was as dry as tinder. I would have given half my remaining life for a glass of water!

About fifteen minutes passed before I heard the sound of horns and a great commotion in the Hunnish camp. But the signals called for moving on, not for more fighting. The hubbub sounded most unusual. Horsemen broke away and rode out in different directions, some towards me.

I waved to them, shouting, 'This way! This way! This way!' But they kept galloping to and fro, only stopping sometimes to scrutinize the eastern horizon.

One rode close by me without so much as glancing at me. They kept galloping up and down as if they had all gone berserk.

Now and then I could hear their shouts: 'They've slipped away!'

More and more horsemen came jumping over the corpses, all across the field.

The camp buzzed like a bee hive and the fifers struck up a gay tooting. Now I understood: the Romans must have moved away during the night.

Thanks be to the God of the Huns! At last was something pleasant in my wretched state. Now they must certainly come and collect the wounded!

I waited patiently, though my thirst was unbearable. If grapes had feelings, only they, when they are being dried into raisin in the heat of an oven, could feel as I did then.

In half an hour, however, I could see a flood of priests and women of all nations come pouring out from behind the carts, along with the Ugor fishermen. A few noblemen showed themselves too.

Now in the battlefield arms and hats moved, and the shouting began.

'Here! This way! Here! Here! Hey! Water!'

'Aaaah...' The groaning grew louder.

A shield woven of bamboo lay near me. I stuck my spear into it and lifted it high. 'Here! This way!' When would they get to me!

The horsemen were all noblemen as far as I could see. They were merely inspecting the bloody battlefield. Oh, if only my master would come, or someone from his people!

Then at last they did come my way.

'Help!' I shouted.

Sirtosh, a Hunnish nobleman, stopped his horse and stared at me–or the large groups of corpses around me.

'They'll come for you soon,' he said good-naturedly, to cheer me.

'Your water bottle...'

He reached behind his saddle.

'I haven't got it with me!'

'Why doesn't everyone come from the camp?' I asked, complaining. 'There are so many of us here wounded.'

'Attila has forbidden it,' replied the horseman. 'The Romans may yet turn up behind our backs.' Then he rode on.

Another horseman called over to him. 'Who was that king they buried during the night?'

'Theodoric,' replied Sirtosh. And his horse, weaving its way through corpses, carried him on.

Then for a long time no one came near me.

More and more people came out from the camp in large groups, some of them with carts, collecting all the treasures and weapons of the dead. Other groups picked up the wounded. Everywhere in the camp the music of fifes and bagpipes could be heard.

My arms got tired waving, and it seemed an eternity before help arrived. They gave me something to drink and put me on a ladder from one of the carts, then took me to the stream where all the other wounded were being carried.

The stream was still the colour of red wine. Countless dead lay all around its banks, and probably more were in the stream itself!

The priests, Saraguri women and Ugors washed us and bandaged us; the rest were out on the battlefield, collecting valuables. I heard that of saddles alone they picked up enough to fill several hundred carts; even so it was less than half of what lay scattered about. They built fires in the field to burn the corpses of those who had been noblemen or group leaders or standard bearers. Some fires were made entirely from broken spears, wooden shields and parts of carts. The dead who had relatives in the camp were also taken and burned.

My only wounds needing dressing were on my head and leg. My leg wound was a horrible sight, but I had no right to complain, for I saw others with wounds so terrible that I had to close my eyes. Those good heathen priests! God bless them. But thousands of wounded were awaiting treatment; I couldn't get anyone to carry me to Chath's tent.

In vain I shouted–they left us all on the bank. For pillows they put saddles under our heads, or a horsehead or a hat, and told us to suffer patiently until it was our turn.

The healthy ones, of course, either made merry or were out looting. And there we lay in the scorching sun, fighting off flies and fearing that suddenly the camp would pack up and leave us behind for the ravens.

Old Bishop Lupus busied himself with the wounded too. I called out to him in Latin, *'Heus domine!'*

He came over to me, and promised that when he returned to camp at night he'd leave word for Chath. But he didn't return to the camp; he slept there among the wounded.

Next day Attila rode across the battlefield. He too looked us over, his words consoled us and gave us new heart.

'Your wounds are your glory! You will all recover on the way home, and will arrive healthy as ever!' Even those who were about to die were content when they saw Attila.

But my master wasn't with him. Was he dead? Or was he wounded? I didn't know.

By this time I was consumed with fever. I raised myself on one elbow and vomited blood.

A zoltan by the name of Estan was sitting beside me; both his legs were broken. He yelled at me.

'Good God, man, you've got the plague!'

By then I had realized this myself. My neck and armpits were all swollen. I had escaped death on the battlefield, but now I had the plague.

*N*ext afternoon they came to collect the wounded and take them all to camp, but I soon saw that everyone was avoiding me, they were going to pass me by. The plague was burning within me now with an ever-growing fire. I pleaded with them. 'Please, don't leave me behind!'

No one so much as replied.

I called them by name. 'Tarosh, Tzobor!'

Tzobor stopped, but just shrugged his shoulders. 'How would it help you, even if I did take you along? You've got the plague, don't you understand?'

'At least I'd die among people and not among ravens.'

He shook his head, spat, and then went on. I was left alone, a horse's head for my pillow, corpses for company, and ravens my wailing mourners.

Bonfires of saddles and wooden shields–funeral pyres–began to burn in the field and the smoke rose in tall columns. The dirges of the shamans started up with long-drawn-out notes accompanied by the rattle of drums, the drone of horns: according to the Hunnish faith, the souls of the slain rose up from the flames, taking with them as servants those they killed in battle.

I don't know how many fires were lit, nor how many people were burnt thus. Probably only a few received this special honour. A forest would have been needed to burn all the Huns who had fallen.

Then the singing stopped; soon the only sound was the distant murmur of the camp and the cawing of ravens circling in the sky. And I lay there among the dead, without food or water, deserted by God himself.

Intermittently I lost consciousness, then again revived. When night fell and the stars began to glitter in the summer sky, the thought of death weighed on me with infinite sadness. I didn't want to die at night. I wanted to see daybreak once more, the red of dawn and the rising sun! And once more, just once more in my life I wanted to drink.

Water! I would have drunk any water, however foul, for within me burned the embers of hell!

The stream was only ten paces away and I was dying of thirst! Then something unexpected happened.

For some time I had felt an uncomfortable pressure in the small of my back. I had been only aware of it during the night out on the battlefield, but I was too preoccupied with the wound on my knee to think of anything else. Well, as I was lying there, feeling the hour of my death approaching, I reached behind my back with an automatic movement. It might be a swelling caused by a heavy blow, or perhaps I was lying on a stone. If I was going to die, at least my last minutes needn't be made worse by a stone, if that was what it was!

But look what I found! My goatskin flask, filled with the wine which my master had given me before the battle!

Suddenly I remembered that in the midst of all the confusion I had tied the flask behind my back on my belt, instead of on the saddle, thinking that if my horse fell, my wine shouldn't be lost with it.

Nothing seemed more certain than that I wouldn't live to see the morning, and yet a feeling of real joy flared up in me; it was like a dying fire suddenly showing one last spurt of flame before going out completely.

I tore the cork out with my teeth and drank. I drank with a greedy, infinite thirst. I drank and I drank. That sour, strong wine–or vinegar, rather–tasted like poison, and I felt it course through every vein and artery. My whole being drank. My bones and marrow sucked up the wine, like a sponge. I drank it all to the last drop. And immediately I fell asleep.

How long I slept I don't know–possibly for a day, maybe two. I woke to feel heavy rain on my face and heard the rumbling of thunder. Then I noticed that it was daylight. My clothes were soaked with rain. It was as if someone were pouring water down from the sky. But in half an hour the cloudburst stopped and the sun came out. I felt water lapping round my foot and realized with fright that the level of the stream had risen, and the water was flooding the banks–filthy, scarlet water from the battlefield!

With the greatest pain and difficulty I pulled myself higher up onto the horse's head, propping my back against it. I watched the rising waters, and

the corpses bobbing up and down; hats, wooden shields, saddles, wooden helmets, arrows, spears, bales of hay, all were being carried downstream.

The water kept rising until it was sloshing under my waist and lifting my legs.

Well, my bad luck certainly had sent me several forms of death from which to choose.

The dead floated past in a ceaseless stream, turning this way and that.

When one corpse got caught in an eddy, others bumped into it and they circled together. But as fast as the company gathered, so they broke up and dispersed again.

Then the remains of a wide, shattered bridge came floating towards me. I thought that perhaps this bridge might take me down to the camp, so as it slowly approached I gathered all my strength to grab it.

The next minute, I too was floating in the cool current, travelling with the bridge alongside the dead. For an infinitely long time, I rocked and bobbed onward with waves lapping against my face.

When I reached the place where I thought the camp should have been, all I saw was an empty field. Not a tent, not a cart in sight. The only traces of Attila's camp having been there were the black remnants of fires. I saw a wolf drinking from the stream. It must have had plenty to eat, for it was drinking greedily.

The flood carried me on.

At last, in the evening, I saw some people on the bank. With long poles and grappling hooks they were pulling out corpses, wooden helmets, weapons and wooden shoes.

I yelled to them: 'In God's name!...' They pulled me out and stood around me, gaping at me in amazement. 'Have mercy!' I said. 'Give me shelter, give me something to eat!' They only gaped the more.

Then I realized that I was speaking in Greek, whereas they were Catalauni–not Franks, not Burgundians, not even Goths. At last I noticed a priest standing among them and addressing him, I moaned in Latin, *'Reverendissime domine!* I am the slave of Bishop Lupus...'

I don't know what happened to me after that.

It's crazy ever to despair. Death had attacked me in so many different ways; it even crept inside me–and yet here I am.

But how I survived plague, I shall never know. Sometimes I think it was the power of my youthful blood which saved me. Sometimes I think it was that strong red wine, turned into vinegar, which must have cleansed my body like medicine. Then at times I think that fever I had because of my wounds must have scalded the poison of the plague. Let the doctors figure it out!

Bishop Lupus must have been surprised when they took me to him and told him that I had declared myself to be his slave. But he was a holy man and didn't send me away from his house. I woke up in a clean white bed with soft bandages on my head and leg. The air of the room was fragrant with incense, and the walls were covered with pictures of saints. Across from my bed was a huge fireplace, with a low armchair covered with animal skins drawn up in front of it.

'Pater sanctissime,' I said with gratitude, when I was able to speak. 'Is there any human language with words to express my thanks for your goodness?'

'Since you have turned up here, God must surely have sent you,' replied the old man. 'Don't worry about the rest.'

I could see in his face, though, that he was amazed that I should know Latin.

'I thought you were a Hun!' he said, smiling benevolently. 'But let us not discuss this further. The trouble is over; the Lord's name be praised!'

'Amen,' I answered, and my eyes filled with tears.

The roast chicken they brought me after my long starvation melted in my mouth like butter. Never in my life have I eaten with more delight. The smell of it was a joy to my very soul, and the meat became strength even as I chewed it!

Then I drank a glass of wine, and I felt that I had surely come to the happiest hour of my life–a happier one I'd never have.

The old bishop had about twenty priests under him–some canons, some seminarists; they all lived with the old man. After the church services they shed their habits and one canon became the cook, another swept the grounds or worked in the garden, and a third looked after the cow or chopped wood. A few were teachers, and a few looked after the laity. Each had his duties.

As I began to get well, the old man marvelled more and more at my knowledge, for he and his priests didn't wear out too many books. Of secular works he was familiar only with Ovid's *Fasti.* As for his priests, they had just barely mastered reading. When I regained my strength, I sat among them like the twelve-year-old Christ amidst the doctors, and we questioned each other. I had never studied eccleasiastical matters, yet I knew more than they did. Only the old man himself was a theologian of great knowledge; when he was present I rarely argued. But he found great pleasure in me.

'My son,' he said, 'you were truly sent to me by God. If only you would learn the language of the Catalauni and how to say mass, I'd ordain you to be my successor.'

The priests all looked at me askance. But I said that I had no ambitions in the clergy, and wished to be nothing but the humblest of servants. I had to keep saying this, for at first they didn't believe me, but later, when I was able to walk about and could help with the housework they accepted me. Oh, I could be most humble! Slavery is the greatest master in teaching humility. Gradually they grew to like me. Soon they didn't even mind that the old man treated me as if I were his own son, his very shadow. I accompanied him to funerals, and I sat beside him at weddings and feast-days.

'God gave me this boy,' the old man would tell everyone. 'You'll see–he will be a holy man one day!'

Well, there was enough of the holy man in me never to do anyone harm, and if someone gave me an angry look, I showered him with so much affection that he simply had to grow fond of me. But this was all a game for me. I despised people who were wrapped up in their own petty affairs, domestic problems, gossip or superstitions. I loved only the old bishop with true filial affection. He was truly a holy man.

Some people dress in velvet and silk, concerned to display their rank and status, yet when we speak with them we feel at once that under their high show they are nothing but animals–human animals. Others can dress in threadbare tunics and walk around in painted cloaks and worn-down sandals, but they only have to say one word and we feel at once that they are angels living in animals' bodies.

Some people retain a dull mind regardless of how long they stay at school or how many books they read. They know words, titles and dates, but ask their opinion and they give an amazingly stupid answer. Others, even if they cannot read or write have a sharp intellect and keen insight. It is a blessing just to be with them.

My bishop, poor soul, was one of these threadbare old angels. He walked about in a black habit made of hair. In summer he was bareheaded and barefoot; in winter he wore a hat and boots.

In his room there were no ornaments except pictures of Jesus, Mary and St Paul. His bed was only a mat. Sheets and other linen he had only because women brought him some. He didn't know what a shirt was. It was the Huns who invented shirts.

There were many rooms in the house, but he lived in only one. The two adjacent rooms were occupied by two very old canons and five orphan boys. About five rooms stood empty where beggars slept when they passed through the town. He gave all he had to old beggars, even the income of the church. He gave them new clothes, looked after them, and sent them on their way cheered.

When the first snow of winter fell the old man gathered together all the children of the town, and we all began to teach them. I taught the oldest ones Latin, especially those who planned to become priests. My textbook was the Bible.

In principio creavit Deus coelum et terram. (In the beginning God created heaven and earth.) This was the first lesson. I suggest to all teachers of Latin that they start their teaching with this chapter of the Bible. The sentences are easy and their content is beautiful.

At night, when the orphans had gone to bed, we all gathered in front of the large fireplace in the old man's room, and talked.

Occasionally he had visitors – then we were very busy cooking and baking. Even the old man himself helped clean carrots or chop wood or turn the spits. After supper I would read them the legends of the saints by the light of two fragrant wax candles, and after that we sang psalms. One priest, Gad, could sing a few sacred songs by himself in an exquisite baritone. Sometimes the old bishop would entertain his guests with stories of his experiences in Britain.

Nevertheless, in the midst of all this happiness and wellbeing I still felt sad.

Winter had come before I finally got out of bed, and my strength returned only very slowly. My knee had healed, but it still didn't bend. They would have let me go if I had insisted, but how could I have ridden with a bad knee? Nor would I have dared to face all those pacles of wolves that roamed the plain. It was as if the world's entire wolf population had congregated here– birds of prey too in unusual numbers: eagles, ravens, crows. Whenever one looked up, there they were circling in the sky and we heard nothing but screeching and cawing.

It was rumoured at first that the bishop planned to bury every single dead body. The devout citizens of the town had gone out with spades and hoes, but they had soon returned. 'There are more than a hundred thousand dead,' they said, shaking their heads. So praise be to God who created the wolf, the hyena, the raven and the wind.

But how could I set out into a world like that!

So I was sad. I was glad to work because then I didn't have to think. But at night when I went to bed, I couldn't sleep no matter how tired I was. I wondered what would be happening at home? Why did it have to be me who couldn't return? At times the longing for home took me with such force that I was ready to rush out and start my journey bareheaded and on foot.

The bishop often asked me why I was sad. Was there anything not to my liking? If I didn't care for simple meals, he'd gladly have something special cooked for me, he said. If I needed clothes, I had only to ask.

So one day I told him the story of my love for Emmo.

He just listened, without saying anything–just listened. When I came to the end, he shook his head.

'It is strange that such an educated, clever man as you could be so much the prisoner of an unschooled, foolish girl. I was young once – I did crazy things myself! I climbed walls, swam rivers, to stand around on bitter windy nights under the window of my fairy queen while she snored unperturbed, but I would never have handed my life to her on a platter like a name-day present.'

'I can believe it,' I said with a sigh. 'But the girl wasn't Emmo; there is only one Emmo.'

'One has to pass through this stage, my son. It's just like teething,' he said, trying to console me. 'That girl will surely be married this winter, and by the time you get home she'll probably be a mother.'

Oh, how I wished he hadn't said that! His words ripped out my heart. As I sat there by the fire on an upturned basket, I collapsed onto the floor, and, crying, I cursed the hour when death had passed me by. The old man was frightened. He sprinkled my temples with holy water and took my head into his lap, stroking it as if he were my mother.

'Poor boy,' he said compassionately. 'Your sorrow is great! And even greater is your immaturity! You see, I was once a married man myself, and had a happy marriage for six years. Our love was infinite. But since we spent our lives in prayer, I said, "It would be more pleasing in God's eyes if I became a priest and you a nun." And that is what happened. We separated, and now I am a bishop and she is a nun. But we still think of one another every day with love.'

Misery is like a balloon: if it is stretched too far, it explodes. When I heard the story of this holy man I burst out laughing.

*T*he snow was gone but plague came. Every day more people died. The bishop ordained me on Easter day because he needed someone to help him with confessions and burials. And I resigned myself to becoming a priest.

What should I go back for, I thought. I have fought like a hero in the battle and all for nothing. I didn't take any heads to show to the scribes. Who could testify to my conduct? Perhaps at most Chath would make me a free man–if he was not being eaten by the crows on the battlefield – but I wouldn't receive any money or honour to enable me to ask Emmo's hand in marriage. *There* I'd be just a nobody, but here they kissed my hands and called me a gentleman. It would be a quiet, peaceful life. I might even hope for the mitre and become a bishop while young, for in these parts a better educated man than I was not to be found.

But the plague!

When the death-roll exceeded twenty a day we no longer gave them extreme unction. There were only three of us – we couldn't keep it up. All our fellow priests had either died or left for the mountains to stay among the people who were still hiding out there. There were at least a thousand refugees from Attila up in the mountains, not daring to return home. The bishop hired a cook and maids so that we wouldn't have to worry about the house, but we just couldn't do everything.

In May we were having fifty, sixty or seventy die every day. There were houses that stood empty; there were entire streets with hardly a soul left alive.

When June came the strength of death had somewhat abated, but by then only the two of us lived, the old bishop and I; the good psalmist had died. The dead were piled in front of the church. We gave them a general absolution, and every second hour we buried some of them.

It was a July day when a wealthy burgher died, and the bishop brought the joyful news that he had left all his wealth to me.

'To me?'

'Yes, God's name be praised! What good you will be able to do with it!'

Next evening we had a look at my inheritance: a beautiful one-storey house, three horses, many beautiful paintings, excellent weapons, some furniture, and seven hundred and ten gold pieces.

I gave the money to the bishop to put in the poor-box. The house and everything in it I entrusted to the mayor of the town; he was to look after it as the plague stayed with us then sell it and use the money to help the poor.

But when we came to the three horses, I didn't say anything. I felt something stir near my heart as though a tombstone had moved. That night, when the bishop was asleep, I left the house and, going straight to the mayor, I knocked on his window.

'Get up, my lord, and bring the key to my house!'

He came out barefoot, half dressed, frightened.

'What has happened?'

'I have to leave for Paris this very night. Our bishop sent there for some priests, but they haven't come, so I'll bring some back with me. I'll return by tomorrow afternoon.'

I entered the house and from the weapons chose a magnificent sword, a javelin and a bow. I hung a bag around my neck and I changed into a cherry-coloured suit made of beautiful velvet. There was a fine pair of sandals there which laced up to the knees; I put those on too, and golden spurs. One cannot ride without spurs.

The mayor didn't find it at all peculiar that I should go heavily armed – the area was still infested with wolves.

I picked out the best steed, and headed east!

*I*t was autumn, and everything was turning yellow when after an eventful journey I arrived one evening at dusk at the banks of the Danube and sounded my horn. In a little while I could see the barge approaching with a tocky white-bearded Hun at the tiller. But even before the boat reached shore, the old man drew his bow.

'Who are you and what do you want?'

'I am a Hun like yourself,' I replied. 'I am returning home.'

'Why are you returning home?'

'That is my business. It is your duty to take me over.'

'My duty be damned! Don't you know that I could shoot an arrow through you?'

'Why would you do that?'

'Because you are a worthless deserter!'

'Deserter? *I?* Look, we obviously don't understand one another. I've come from the field of Catalaunum–last year's battle.'

His mouth dropped in surprise.

'Then you're not from the Roman expedition?'

'No. Why, has our army gone to Rome, then?'

'Yes.'

Now *my* chin dropped.

The Hun paddled up to me and he examined my clothes and face.

'I'll take you over,' he said, 'but you'll have to take the consequences.'

'What consequences?'

'Well, you can enter, but if you ever want to leave again...'

I didn't argue with him. I would have ridden on, but my horse was tired, so I had to ask for shelter from the ferrymen. At supper we warmed to each other a bit, for I told them a lot about the battle. And, of course, I asked questions myself.

'When did Attila set out for Italy?'

'Soon after he returned from the west. He hardly rested–only a few weeks, barely enough to get the horses in condition. As soon as the worst of the winter was over, he set out.'

'Do you know anything of Chath? Is he alive?'

'He is.'

'And his family?'

They didn't know anything about them. The ferrymen and borderguards were mostly Ugors. A few disabled Huns lived among them, fishing and hunting. Every hundred feet stood a hut made of reeds: no spies can penetrate the land of the Huns.

I started on my journey quite early the next day, and by night the steeples of Attila's palace were twinkling before me. I cannot describe my confused emotions. My heart was full of rapture one minute, the next it fell with broken wings, worrying: is she still unmarried? How will she look upon me when I stand before her?

My heart was pounding with excitement as I rode on towards the River Tisia where I gave my horse a drink. I myself got down and quickly had a bath and beat some of the dust off my clothes.

Then I entered the city on horseback. How silent and deserted it was! Only women and children loitered about.

Before the royal palace, however, there were a few armed horsemen. That was the queen's guard: disabled warriors, old rankless Huns, and two-thirds of Attila's army of servants.

I rode through Chath's gates with a heavy heart. The servants and slaves looked up at me all agape, but coldly, as if I were a stranger.

'Good evening, Uzura!'

Uzura dropped his spear in surprise.

'Master of the heavens,' he stuttered. 'Is it you, Zeta?'

'Of course it's me!'

He yelled into the house. 'Zeta is here!'–as happy as if I had been his own son.

The servants and slaves all rushed out. As I dismounted, a girl suddenly flung her arms round my neck and kissed me noisily.

'Zeta! Zeta!'

I looked again... Well, if it wasn't Djidjia! I hardly recognized her she had grown so much.

But all the others embraced me gladly too. They shook my hands and patted my clothes, all asking at once where I had come from, and if I really hadn't died. Then I was pushed and dragged upstairs to see Lady Chath and the old gentleman, Barakon. The two children, also glad to see me, ran up to me, and I asked permission to kiss their hands.

Only one person was missing, the one I would have liked to see most. My heart was bursting with dark premonitions, so I could answer the mistress and the old gentleman only in stammers.

'Is everyone in the family healthy and well?' I asked at last, awkwardly.

'Yes, all of us, Zeta.'

'The young l-lady too?'

'She too, Zeta.'

'And the young l-lady, Miss Emmo–she is not s-sick, then?'

'Why should she be? She is out hunting with Queen Rika. Tomorrow the queen will surely invite you to see her, for she has mourned for you. My husband came home with the news that you had died of the plague.'

A great burden fell from my heart. If Emmo had married, Lady Chath would have corrected me by saying, 'She is no Miss any more, young man!' instead of telling me that she was out hunting.

'And did my master return unscathed from the battle?' I asked, 'I thought *he* was the one who died!'

'Oh no! He doesn't usually die!' replied the lady, laughing.

'Will he be away for long? Do you not think, my lady, that it would be best for me to follow him?'

'Follow him? No! It's autumn already. By the time you got there, they'd be coming back!'

'Did my master mention anything about my deeds in the battle?'

'No, Zeta. He said that right after the battle began he lost sight of you.'

This saddened me. I would remain a slave, then. I who could have been a bishop would remain a stable-boy, cleaning sandals–no better than a two-legged dog.

That night there was a big celebration in the kitchen. The slaves and servants all gathered together to hear my story. Raba made a roast and put wine on the table. She sat me down in her own armchair, and called me her 'dear son'. They had Djidjia sit beside me and this annoyed me, for the girl had put on her best dress, and picked some Michaelmas daisies to put in a mug for me.

Well, I told them all about my adventures, about the battle, about my escape. I showed them the scar on my knee, and the one on my head.

They just stared devoutly.

'Well,' said Jonji, a maid, 'then it wasn't in vain that Djidjia prayed so much for you!'

I shrugged my shoulders.

'Why did she pray? What am I to Djidjia? And what is she to me? I thank you for it, Djidjia, but I don't understand you. It is all right for you to be concerned for my welfare – I am not against that – but it wasn't all right for you to jump on me and hug me when I arrived, as if...well–God knows what! Please, don't act like that again. You are a grown-up girl now; you should be careful how you behave.'

Djidjia sank back in her chair, all colour drained from her face, but I pretended not to notice. I slapped my hand on the table top.

'And my hen, my little black hen! Where is she?

They all smiled and looked at Uzura, who blushed and scratched his head.

'Well, tell me –'

'Well... 'It was Raba who spoke at last. 'Uzura sacrificed the hen in your memory. When he heard that you had died, he killed it and we burned it, so that it could be your hen in the next world too.'

*N*ext morning the queen did send for me. I was ready. My fellow slaves–good fellows that they were, competed with each other seeing who could work the hardest cleaning the clothes I had arrived in from Catalaunum. They painted all the leather straps yellow, brushed the velvet, rubbed the golden buttons till they sparkled, and wherever there was a tear, they sewed it up. In short, by the time I woke up–in my old room–they were bringing me my clothes, all clean and ready.

My mistress was generous too: she gave me a beautiful wide collar of fine linen. When I put that on too, general opinion in the house was that anyone who didn't know me would take me for a prince in exile.

I always had liked nice clothes and clean linen, even if I had to do my own washing. I always managed to have perfume, too, or a few fragrant herbs. But never before had I dressed so elegantly as now, when after such a long absence I was to appear before Emmo once more.

I was still worried a little. My face had changed–I had grown a beard, black and bushy. The slaves and servants said that I looked better with my beard, but what would Emmo think? I twirled my moustache into points, Hunnish fashion. I didn't knot my hair the way Huns do, for I still was a slave, but as it fell to my shoulders neatly, I didn't mind.

So I stepped into the palace, holding a wide-brimmed hat in my hand and wearing my sword and my sandals with golden spurs. I wore cherry-coloured trousers, a wine-red velvet jacket, and the linen collar, and from my shoulder on a silver chain hung an ivory horn two handspans long. I wouldn't have changed my clothes for those of one of their tousled princes.

When the servant pulled aside the curtain covering the doorway, I entered like a prince. My glance swept over the women; there were some twenty of them and among them Emmo in a white dress with red flowers on it; her hair was braided behind her in one plait as before. My eyes rested on her for only a fleeting second, but I could see that she hadn't changed one whit. They were trying a new blue and white dress on a blonde woman I hadn't seen before. My entry startled them.

I bowed deeply, and, sinking on one knee, waited for the queen to address me.

'God bless my soul!' she cried, clapping her hands together. 'Is that you, Zeta! How you frightened us!'

'I beg your pardon, my royal lady, but I have no other clothes than these, the ones I arrived in. But please be assured of my humble obedience–I am ready to serve you even in these frightening garments.'

'Come closer! Well, well! Look, girls, what a handsome young man this boy has become! Tell me all, Zeta! Everything! We were told that you had died. I wept for you.'

'Thank you, Your Highness,' said with a bow, moved. 'Had I known in those difficult hours that you would grieve for me I would have felt consoled.'

'Tell me the whole story. Where have you been? Where did you live? Why didn't you come back last autumn?' She moved over onto the divan and looked at me, propping herself on one elbow. All of them were watching me with interest.

The fair-skinned blonde stranger sat at the queen's feet and examined me

14

coldly. Emmo took an embroidered pillow to sit on and leaned back against the queen's divan. I don't know for sure if she was smiling, because I didn't dare look at her but I could feel that I was being looked at kindly.

I don't usually get embarrassed. Only very rarely can anyone's gaze confuse me. But now, seeing Emmo again and feeling her eyes resting on me, I could hardly say a word. I just stood there not knowing where to begin.

'My royal lady,' I said at last, 'I cannot know what most interests you, nor how many of the events I witnessed...'

'Everything interests me, everything! Bring him a chair, or sit down on the carpet. In these clothes you are as formal as if you were about to recite your New Year's greetings. Throw your hat in the corner and don't stand on ceremony!'

So I sat down among them on a low hassock and put my hat on the floor. I soon felt less shy, realizing that I was among children, for women when merry are always children. Only Emmo's glance disconcerted me a little, but sweetly.

'My royal lady,' I said, 'if you leave it up to me completely, I am afraid that my tale will be lengthy and boring. Where would you like me to begin?'

'Here, at the outskirts of the town, when you mounted. Then tell us about the long journey, the battle and all your adventures.'

A Hunnish woman with impish eyes added, 'And give us especially the details that you would most like to be silent about.'

They all laughed. Only the fair-skinned blonde girl remained serious, her eyes filled with wonder. It was only later that I found out that the woman with the impish eyes was Queen Echka, and that the fair-skinned blonde did not understand Hun: she was of Germanic origin and her name was Ildiko.

'Well, I shall begin where you wish, your ladyship. It was dawn when we mounted, and the head priest blessed us all. We all felt very sad, for not one of us knew if he'd ever return to this city, or if he were setting out on a journey to the land of souls. The king himself seemed sad; I saw tears in his eyes too.'

'Your king always looks sad, but if he were to cry, it would be without tears.'

'That is possible,' I replied, bowing. 'It is possible that there were tears in my eyes, and that's how I saw some in the king's.'

My glance flicked across Emmo's face. She was looking at me without blinking, her eyes thoughtful. Her face too was like Attila's – no one could guess what was behind it.

'Nothing extraordinary happened to us on the way. Until spring we advanced along the valley of the Danube. Armies were advancing in front of ours, and they ransacked all the Roman towns. The first incident worth mentioning–it certainly made *us* think–occurred as we were about to cross a swampy bog. As we were moving on, in rushes and mud up to our horses' knees, suddenly a ragged, thin old woman slipped out from among the reeds. She had great dark circles under her eyes and from her skinny arms hung wet shreds the colour of moss. Before we even had a chance to stop her, she popped up in front of the king, snatched his horse's bridle, and screamed in German:

'"Back, Attila! Back!"'

'She was dragged away from the king and driven off until she disappeared again in the bog.'

My audience grew pale–Emmo too, I could see.

'Several other omens, just as full of foreboding, occurred later,' I continued. 'In one place we saw a hermit standing among some rock. When the king approached, he raised his arms and yelled: "I know who you are! You are the sledge-hammer of the world! The earth trembles wherever you step, and the stars fall wherever you stop to sound your horn. But know this: even as God has sent you out into this world, so He will recall you!"'

'Prophets are just as stupid everywhere!' said the queen with a serious expression. 'Heaven and earth, everything foretold disaster for Attila, and then how did it all end?'

'I still do not know, your ladyship. I remained alone on the battlefield.'

'It ended with his return late last autumn healthy and rich, and bringing a pack of princes and princesses as hostages, to force the western nations to remain faithful. Look at this marvellously beautiful girl!' She pointed to Ildiko. 'He brought her from the west too. She is a princess, and a very charming one.'

She embraced Ildiko, and kissed her.

Then I told them about the battle. When I was describing the scene where Attila stood in front of the troops with his sword drawn and led them into battle, they held their breath and listened with shining eyes. I was surprised to see that Emmo, too, whose face I had never known to be anything but immobile was watching me with burning eyes. It was easy to see that my story had captured her soul.

I judged that this was the right moment to speak of my own heroic deeds, but the curtains opened and a servant announced that a messenger had arrived from the king.

As if lightning had stuck into their midst they all leaped up. The queen herself rose.

'Is he in mourning?' she asked anxiously.

'No, my lady, he brought good news.'

'Let him in. Call the steward!' And she sighed with relief. 'How he frightened us!'

The messenger, Igar, a Hunnish warrior, entered the room covered with dust, and from a kneeling position handed Attila's letter to the queen.

'What news have you brought?' asked the queen. 'Are you in Rome yet?'

'No, my royal lady,' replied Igar. 'Rome came to meet us.'

'I do not understand you.'

'The Roman pope, the greatest master of the Christian world, came to meet us in full regalia. He threw himself at the king's feet and begged him to spare the city.'

'And?'

'We are on our way home.'

Queen Rika gave a start.

'Why did he spare them? Why did he not sit on the throne of the Empire?'

Her eyes blazed and she drew herself up. How that woman changed! Now she was indeed Attila's queen.

All this was only for a moment, however–an unfamiliar landscape exposed by a flash of lightning. Then she gazed at the ground and in a tone almost of boredom she asked, 'Nobody put up any resistance?'

'No one, my lady. Who would dare oppose us?'

'Aetius?'

'Aetius had spread the report that *he* had won the battle of Catalaunum.'

'I have already heard that. But where is he?'

'We do not know. The mighty victor cannot be found anywhere, but on the other hand, the loser has put a yoke on the world's greatest city, humiliating it by levying taxes.'

'Then there were no battles at all?'

'No, my lady. As soon as we had broken Aquileia's resistance, the whole of Italy was at our feet. We are bringing home thousands upon thousands of carts filled with treasures. Immeasurable quantities of silk, velvet, pottery, paintings, gold and silver are being brought, and an impressive army of young slaves.'

'And the plague?'

'The same as last year, my royal lady. I would guess that that was one reason why the king did not enter Rome.'

'But he is healthy?'

'He is, praise be to God.'

'Tell me,' asked Queen Echka, 'what sort of man is the Pope?'
'An aged, thin man,' said the messenger, smiling. 'His nose is wrinkled and his expression frightened.'
The steward arrived. The queen retired into an inner room with him and Queen Echka to have the letter read.
Meanwhile we waited quietly in the large hall. The women whispered amongst themselves; I had no one to talk to, but when nobody was looking at me, I devoured Emmo with my eyes.
Emmo addressed Igar. 'Is my father in good health?'
'He is well, my young lady.'
'Have you any message for us?'
'Only in words.'
'Can you tell it to me?'
'It's only that he is healthy and that the two young masters shouldn't be given any unripe fruit.'
Emmo sat down on the divan and, embracing Ildiko, pressed her face against hers.
'Isn't this girl beautiful, Zeta? Have you ever seen a girl more beautiful?'
'I have, my young lady.'
'Where, then?'
'By the banks of the River Tisia, my young lady. There I saw one once; she was on horseback, in a dress the colour of turtle-doves, and she was wearing a veil.'
Her eyelashes fluttered, but her face remained indifferent.
'You are beautiful,' she said to Ildiko warmly. 'You are beautiful. Do you understand?'
Ildiko nodded, smiling.
'Understand: you bootyfull.'
And they laughed.

I was again in Raba's room. She wouldn't hear of letting me stay anywhere else, but moved into a smaller room herself instead.
I was tired. I asked the old steward not to assign me any work for the just yet. So after lunch I retired to my room and lay down.
The little room was pleasantly cool. A wilted wreath hung on the wall. It

had been Emmo's at one time, for some wedding ceremony or other. When they had thrown it out, I had picked it up and kept it.

That was the only ornament in the room. Everywhere else hung the ironed skirts of the cook, filling the air with a starchy odour.

I wasn't quite asleep yet when I heard the wooden doorknob click quietly. The door opened a little, and Djidjia peeked in shyly.

'Are you asleep?'

'No. What do you want, Djidjia?'

She was pale, and more serious than usual. She entered and stood in front of me, like a pupil before her teacher.

How tall this girl has become! How she has grown! I thought. When I left she was a mere child; now she is a woman ready for marriage. She was tall and full-breasted, and her face too had filled out. The other servants jokingly called her 'young lady', perhaps because she wore Emmo's old clothes. It had always hurt me a little to see this.

'I would like to talk to you,' she said anxiously. And she stood beside the door, one finger against her cheek, as if afraid that I'd chase her away. I pointed to a dilapidated straw chair and told her to sit down, which she did.

'I only want to ask...' she whispered, 'only...what have I done to you? Why do you hate me?'

'I? Hate you?'

'Didn't you humiliate me yesterday in front of all the others? Oh, I thought I would die!' Her eyes grew moist. 'Why?'

'You humiliated yourself, my girl. It is very peculiar that you ask me to justify myself, as if you were a judge!'

'I am not asking you to justify anything, Zeta. Mine is only a humble question. I would like to know how I have hurt you–because I want to understand and never do it again.'

That the girl should speak so reasonably surprised me.

'I am glad,' I said, 'that you are so sensible. Now we can at least clear up this business. It was nice of you to greet me with such enthusiasm when I returned home, and it felt good, but you went too far! What would you say if when Attila returned, I rushed out and kissed him?'

'You are not Attila. And I always... felt...as if you were my brother.'

'Thank you. But, you see, people cannot know what you feel, and could easily misunderstand. That wouldn't be good for you or for me.'

She pressed her hands against her face, and I saw that she was weeping.

'I didn't mean to hurt you, Djidja. But let's not talk about it any more. We are both slaves, and our lot is sad indeed. Come, tell me instead, what all of you have been doing for the year and a half I was away. What did the master say when he returned?'

Djidjia wiped her eyes in her apron.

'He said that he last saw you when the battle began.'

'He mentioned nothing of my deeds?'

'No, he said only that you were last seen among the wounded, and that you had no wounds but were ill with the plague.'

'And Chath thought me dead?'

'Yes.'

'Was he sorry?'

'He was.'

'How did he show it? What did he say?'

'He said that it was a pity, for your mouth alone was worth as much as the hands of others, and that you were very skilful, and that he would have had you design the gold engraving on his new shield.'

'What about the mistress? Was she sorry?'

'Yes, she was.'

'How? What did she say?'

'She said that it was silly to take a slave like you away from the house. No one could bow and greet and speak as well as you. A slave like that was a house's greatest ornament, like silk curtains. She actually quarrelled with her husband for taking you and losing you.'

'And what did the young mistress say?' I said, stifling a yawn. (How well it came off!) 'What did she say?'

'Nothing.'

'She didn't feel sorry for me?'

'Yes, she did.'

'But how? What did she say?'

'What? Oh, yes, I forgot, once she did say something like "Perhaps it is better for him this way."'

A long silence followed this. I forgot that Djidjia was still there. Her words were spinning around in my soul like a whirlwind.

'Aren't you going to ask me anything else?' she said at last. 'Aren't you going to ask how *I* felt?' and I could almost hear her heart beating.

'No,' I replied, closing my eyes. 'Go away!'

Emmo came home in the evening. She was using a small horse these days, a nice, tame little brown animal, always grazing somewhere near the house; if anyone called it, it came running–like a dog.

I knew that she would tell her mother what I had said to the queen, and that I would be summoned upstairs after supper.

It crossed my mind that she might even call me upstairs to talk to me herself.

In front of the doors stood two tamarisk trees with thick red foliage. (I don't know where they had come from; perhaps Chath had brought them for his wife from my own homeland!) I always used to sit under one of them when I waited for my master, and that was where I sat tonight, ready in case I was called.

I wasn't disappointed. Even before they had quite finished their supper, I heard Djidjia call down from the first-storey window:

'Zeta! Have you seen Zeta? Tell him to come up!'

They were sitting at the table. Beside the two children sat a young ladylike woman I hadn't seen before. The old grandfather's face was like red felt from the wine.

'Zeta,' said the mistress, chiding me, 'do you talk only to the queen?'

I offered my excuse. 'Oh, my lady, how can I talk if you do not order me to? A slave has to keep silent!'

'But you are not that kind of slave. You have to talk!'

'Thank you. I'll always gladly talk if you call me, my lady. But to tell of the battle would take a week. And to tell of my master's heroic deeds–why, one evening wouldn't be long enough for that either.'

'Then you did see my husband in the battle?'

'Indeed I did! My lady, he was a storm in human shape!'

'But he didn't see you, he said. He lost sight of you immediately.'

'A master is not duty bound to keep an eye on his slave, but it is the slave's duty to watch his master. I fought always either beside him or just behind him.'

And while I told of Chath's deeds, I sadly remembered that the queen had made me sit down, but here I was to speak standing up.

My leg still hurt me, especially if I stood or walked too much. Even today, if the weather changes, my knee reminds me of the plains of Catalaunum.

That evening I talked only of Chath. I realized that in the Chaths' house, Chath would be the most interesting topic. The mistress listened to me ardently and the two children were so absorbed, they left their mouths hanging open. Only old Barakon kept blinking beside the wine jug, shooting his bushy white eyebrows up and down.

'Well,' he blurted out once, 'I have been in the thick of forty-five battles, but never said as much of the whole forty-five of them as this babbler says about one! Everyone is a hero now! A man has only to catch one tired enemy on the point of his sword, and it becomes a long story!'

The children grew sleepy and heavy-eyed and the old man too kept his shout a little longer after each blink. Only the mistress and Emmo wanted to hear more and more.

'Keep your tale for a while,' said the mistress. 'The children had better be put to bed,' and she led them out.

From the next room I could hear one of them, Dedesh, pleading to come back, but they talked him into going to sleep: 'Djidjia is going to tell you a story about the red bear and the fairy prince.'

The old man fell asleep. Now Emmo and I were alone. She looked at me, leaning on one elbow. Only the three silver oil lamps sputtered now and again. I broke the silence.

'My young lady... have you nothing to say to me?'

'When my mother returns, speak of Attila. It must have been wonderful to see him appear in front of his army in his golden helmet... Oh, how splendid that man must have looked–like a god treading the earth!'

She stared into space.

Lady Chath returned–and I talked of Attila. I gave so many tiny details of that scene that I might have been describing it to a painter. Emmo put her elbows on the table and drank in every word I said. Her face was tinted pink by the light from the lamps and her arms were rounded like the arms of a nymph in marble.

Attila arrived three weeks later.

The city donned its festive colours. Carts by the hundred brought pine branches from the mountains to decorate tents and roads.

The queens went with their retinues to the edge of the city to meet him.

The first divisions of the army arrived around noon–the Jazyges and the Goths, all waving their arrow-torn flags proudly and leading many slaves. What a sad scene: young men, young women and girls, all herded together.

They were brown-haired, short, and tattered, and all were sad. Huns and Gepids accompanied them.

Towards evening the horns sounded to herald the approach of Attila himself. We could hear the music of the fifes from a great distance. Everyone in the city was out, waving hats and veils and shouting joyfully above the music.

'Blessings! Blessings!'

The king greeted his women with a wave of his hand. He kissed only his children.

After that the men broke ranks and order gave way to confusion. Every Hunnish warrior embraced his wife. The children carried their fathers' bows, spears and shields victoriously. Every tent was the scene of a glad homecoming–even the horses had their share of kisses. Some of the warriors who had received their share of spoils on the way were examining their new slaves lined up in the courtyard.

I was ordered to stand beside our two children, for, of course, we too had gone out to meet Chath. Of the servants, only I followed behind the family and for this occasion I had to put on the clothes I had brought from Catalaunum, except for my hat, which I had to leave behind.

Chath was certainly surprised when he saw me. He could hardly believe his eyes.

'How dare you come before me,' he bellowed with mock anger, 'when you are dead?'

'Oh, my good lord!' I bowed politely. 'This only proves my faithfulness–I have returned from the dead to serve you.'

He was gentleman enough to shake my hand.

That night the city was filled with noisy comings and goings, ringing and clanging, and music. The streets were lit up everywhere with torches, and the people cooked and baked and made merry by large fires in front of the tents. Singly or in pairs, the bards sang the ballads of victory. The fifes tooted, the Kvad musicians played their bagpipes, and the town whooped and sang and reverberated.

Around midnight Attila came out from his palace, and, accompanied by happy music and bodyguards carrying torches, he rode through the city. Occasionally he stopped at a particularly bright and crowded tent and drank from each goblet that was offered to him. He shook the older people's hands and rode on amid stormy shouts of 'Blessings!'

Next day the main body of the army arrived, along with the carts filled with booty. The line was endless; it lasted from morning till night, one cart after another. Even next day they still kept coming.

Chath summoned me that evening. His wife and Emmo were present.

The hour has come, I thought with a thumping heart. Chath will free me from slavery.

Well, he did mention the issue.

'My son,' he said, 'I know that you have fought on the plains of Catalaunum, and in a few days we are going to examine your merit. Now, however, Attila needs you–there is a lot to do. I have given you to him as a present. So pick up your belongings, and report to Rusti or Mena-Sagh.'

I stood there, stock still, as if struck by lightning. What good would it do me to be free if I were to be transferred into the king's service as a scribe?

'My lord,' I moaned, downcast, 'please let me tell you... It is very hard for me to leave you all...'

'I'm sorry to let you go, too,' he replied. 'God knows, I would rather have paid for someone else to go, but it's no use. The plague took three of the scribes, and there is a lot to do, dividing the booty.'

My despair was so immense that I just stood there as if my feet had taken root. My tearful eyes turned to Emmo. The girl was staring into the flame of a candle, musing, indifferent...

*T*he carts loaded with booty–hundreds and thousands of them–all stood there in a long line on the main street, in the square and in the king's courtyard. Booty was piled in great heaps in front of the scribes' room–everything that had been-brought in bundles by horse, mule and camel. This mostly consisted of rugs and all kinds of fabrics. We had to count them and catalogue them all. The work was going to last for weeks, and it was boring–at least for someone who had no claim to any of the riches. I was utterly dejected.

In the king's courtyard we worked in ten groups, as fast as we could, under the spacious porches. The slaves opened up the booty, and the valuers appraised it with one glance. All we had to do was to write it down, give a number to each object, and make a note of its value. But this was done only for those objects that seemed to be extremely valuable–for example, some dishes from Egypt, silk materials, brocades with gold and silver embroidery, chasubles, pearls and other jewellery. Ordinary things were marked on stick only–so many rugs, so many cloaks, sandals, weapons, linens, belts, leather cases, tunics, hoods, works in coral, scarves, ribbons: so many of this, so much of that. The horses were valued somewhere else, and their number too was tallied on sticks.

The currency in Attila's land was most often Roman money, so we wrote everything down in terms of the gold pieces. It was called the *solidus,* and was the smallest gold coin. In Hun it was called 'zsoldos'.*

Once everything had been catalogued, the booty was to be divided, so next we had to calculate who deserved how many gold pieces. Commanders and group leaders were entitled to ten portions each. Zoltans got five portions. Widows too received five. Any other warrior usually got as many portions as the number of heads they had cut off. Now, however, since there had been no battle, each received only one portion. Those who had distinguished themselves in the siege were to have first choice of the horses and slaves.

We catalogued and numbered the slaves in the same way as we did the objects of value. Well-born prisoners were taken by the Hunnish nobility right there on the spot. There was a painter among them, an Avzon from Naples. He was kept busy, for all the Huns wanted pictures of their horses.

I have never laughed more than during those sad days, doing that sad work. The valuers constantly made mistakes. For example, a valuable collection of some four hundred cameos fell out of one crate. They were marvellously carved on snail shells.

'What the hell are these?' said the valuers. And they were put down as 'assorted buttons: one solidus for fifty.'

Next they emptied a box of theatrical masks. Turzo, the chief valuer, picked up one of them, and dictated:

'Devil's face to be worn in war. Good for frightening the enemy. Value– ten solidus.'

I burst out laughing and my fellow scribes joined in, for they were either of Roman or Greek origin themselves and knew the true value of the masks.

Old Turzo blinked at us angrily. Then suddenly he drew his sword and screamed:

'Oh, you white-faced worms, serpents-pawn! You dare to laugh at me, you dogs?'

If the other valuers hadn't held him back he would have come at us.

In the midst of this struggle Attila stepped onto the porch. He stopped and looked over the entire group inquiringly.

* The word later came to have the meaning of 'mercenary' or 'hireling'. – Tr.

'My lord,' said Turzo, red with anger, 'these good-for-nothing slaves!... One of them should be hanged as an example!...'

Attila still looked at us inquiringly.

The scribes remained silent, shivering but at last, I spoke, in Latin.

'My lord, there are some valuble cameos here, each worth a small country, and Master Turzo, your chief valuer, declared them to be worthless buttons. He told us to list them at the rate of fifty for one solidus.' I picked up a handful of cameos and held them out to the king. 'Judge for yourself, my lord. I took these at random, and look! Here is a picture of Venus as she emerges from the foam of the sea. Look at the fine details of the carving! Even the foam on the waves is shown. This should adorn the crown of a king!'

Attila took the cameos in his hands and examined them carefully. 'These cameos,' he then said, calmly, 'should be deposited in my treasury. You–what is your name?'

'Zeta, my lord.'

'You, Zeta, must help the valuers in judging valuables like these. Whatever is rare and outstanding I want to buy for myself. And you, old Turzo, if someone laughs when you are angry, teach him manners even if you have to use your sword!'

'Croaking ravens, damn them all!' the old man mumbled. 'I would have cut them up if they hadn't held me back!'

It took a little while to calm the old man down.

'Look, my lord Turzo,' I said, 'there is no man on this earth who could know everything. You have never seen such things, so no matter how clever you are, you couldn't possibly know their value.'

'That is true, of course,' the old man said, 'but I won't stand for anyone sniggering at me!'

Next day it was too wet to work. That afternoon I visited the Chaths. I looked carefully but I couldn't detect Emmo's horse's hoofprints in the mud.

She was home and when she saw me making for their house, she sent word that I was to come up.

Attila had given Chath a female slave in my place. The woman was the wife of a patrician of Milan, and had been captured as she fled. A sizable ransom was expected for her.

I was asked upstairs to write a letter to the woman's family, and I did it gladly. There were no writing materials in the house, so I had to send a slave over to the royal writing-house. Meanwhile I sat down beside the door and wondered if I would be able to talk to Emmo.

The master was not in, and Lady Chath was visiting somewhere with her elder son.

There were only three of us in the room, and Djidjia too, part of the time.

I began by asking the captured woman what she wanted me to write.

'They are asking a hundred pounds of gold for me,' she said, crying, 'but how can my husband pay that much when all we own has been ransacked? Our wine, our crops–they took everything! They didn't leave as much as a pillow in the entire house!'

She was somewhat withered, and had a dusky face. She kept weeping incessantly, and for this reason it was impossible to tell whether or not she had once been beautiful. Djidjia could understand her too; it was usually she who translated for everyone what the woman said. The woman didn't have a rough life with the Chaths, for all she had to do was sew dresses, but still, tears kept welling up in her eyes.

'My lady,' I said, trying to console her, 'give thanks to God that you have ended up in this household. Elsewhere they would have shut you in with the cows, perhaps, or given you the babies to mind. Don't you know that usually, the more ransom they expect for their prisoners, the harder the work they torture them with!'

'You are taking their side!' she burst out at me. 'I cannot accept anyone as my master–it's against my nature. I only have one master, my husband, and even then, *I* order *him* about!' And she went on abusing the Huns and lamenting the loss of her pearls.

'My lady,' I said, trying to calm her, 'you are unjust, for your treasures were once plunder too, like the plunder of the Huns, except that you came to them a little earlier. When the Romans and Greeks held sway they did the same. Did not Alexander the Great ransack Persia and Egypt and Julius Caesar plunder Europe? At present it is the star of the Huns that shines, but the wheel of time will turn again, and the Huns' riches will be taken by another people.'

'Oh, if they had only left my pearls!' she wailed. 'I ought to have buried them!'

I realized then that philosophy of history is not for womenfolk.

I wrote the letter–as neatly as I could, since Emmo sat there, watching me.

There was silence all the while, only the scratching of my pen on the paper. Then, in the quiet, I heard Emmo's voice saying softly, dreamily: 'How are you getting along at the palace?'

'Surely you don't have to ask, my young lady?' I replied, grateful for the question. 'I am alive, that's about all. But I will live only as you remain unmarried.'

'You will likely live a long life.'

What did she mean? Her pensive face did not betray her thoughts.

In a short while she spoke again. 'Do you see Attila often?'

'I do. He talked to me just yesterday!'

'He did? What did you talk about?'

Her face had brightened, and she looked at me eagerly. Oh, those enchanting eyes of hers, so mysterious and wonderful...!

I told her what had happened out on the porch, ending, 'Attila has grown old since I last saw him. There are some white hairs in his beard. You will see, my young lady–in three years he will be an old, old man.'

'Never!' she said, smiling. 'Not even when he is as white as a dove! Attila will always be young! He is like the Greek gods walking the fields! He is like–look, there on our tapestry!– Ares, who descended from the clouds and donned armour to fight armies! Don't you see the strength in his eyes? They are like no other man's. If he is angry, the very leaves on the trees tremble! If he smiles, even the clouds disperse!'

I would have liked to say that on a rainy day like this he would have had to smile for a long time, but I didn't say anything. I was used to people worshipping Attila. Today, I thought, he is king, tomorrow dust. If there weren't people like myself to record his name the wind of the centuries would blow him away, along with all his glory.

From then on I visited the Chaths almost every week. The patrician's wife sent one letter after another to her home, to every one of her relatives and to the Pope.

The letters were carried by envoys who journeyed back and forth ceaselessly. Almost every week a delegation was either arriving or leaving. Now they brought ransom for captive nobles, now a letter from the Emperor or Pope, now taxes or gifts.

Attila's all-seeing eyes soon recognized what a useful man he had in me. Whenever an envoy arrived, he summoned me as well as Rusti and Constantinus and asked me to interpret, sometimes even to give my opinion. It wasn't long before I realized that I wasn't only the first among the slaves, but that I was also the most outstanding among the free scribes.

This was a happy period of my life. The slaves greeted me as they did their masters, and the free scribes behaved as if *they* were slaves and *I* were free. Everyone prophesied that Attila would give me freedom and wealth. I would become rich and powerful like Orestes, who used to be a tattered slave himself once; now he was strutting like a peacock among the Hunnish nobility – yet, compared to me, he was as stupid as an ox.

I was always asked to the Chaths in the evening, after I was free of my official duties. At times we talked and always about Attila–who visited him, what was said, what he replied. If I praised Attila, Emmo's eyes filled with joy. Once as I was leaving, she held out her hand. 'You may kiss it.'

The patrician's wife, seeing how much pleasure this gave me, magnanimously held out her hand too. 'You may kiss it,' she said in Hun.

We laughed at that till tears came to our eyes.

I was never able to speak with Emmo alone, however. There was always someone in the room – her mother, or Djidjia, or some other maid; or the boys were playing around us. I had to be satisfied with just seeing her and hearing the music of her voice.

When I was leaving, it was most often Djidjia who accompanied me downstairs with a lamp to lock the door behind me. I always left Emmo with a happy feeling in my heart, for when I wished them good night, I kissed their hands one after the other (including the hand of the patrician's wife!) and so brought away with me the warmth of Emmo's fine little hand. Usually I left in such a daze that I didn't speak to Djidjia on the way down the stairs–I only came to myself when she said good night.

Once she said, 'Zeta, you take everyone's hand when you leave, but to me you show your back.' She said this with so much sorrow in her voice that I smiled and said, 'Please forgive me–I don't do it deliberately, it's merely absent-mindedness.' And I shook hands with her.

Once a month, at the full moon, Attila gave a banquet to which the men brought along their wives and daughters. Those who had more than one wife took the one who had borne him the most sons.

That winter I too was called in to attend the first such banquet, not as a guest but to interpret for the distinguished, aristocratic prisoners. There were some six hundred present at that feast, and that was where I first saw the king's wives. He had about ten of them. On his right sat Queen Rika, on his left his loyal old friend, King Ardaric, and beyond were seated the rest, according to rank and status, the women opposite their husbands, the girls interspersed among the young single men. Beside the queen sat the visiting kings, and the captive princes who had been brought to Attila's court as hostages.

The women wore white dresses and gold jewellery as at Attila's wedding and the men wore silk, satin and velvet of various colours, with red boots.

A thousand candles reflected in dishes of silver and gold. But Attila's place was laid with a wooden plate and mug, for he despised all luxuries. His dark clothes were unadorned–and he never even wore rings.

Dinner began quietly, but the atmosphere warmed up after the first course, when Attila lifted his wooden mug and spoke.

'I drink to my family! My family is the Hunnish nation! May God always love us!'

Then everyone stood up and drank to the king's health.

There was music during dinner, but it was continually interrupted, as first one lord, then another stood up to propose a toast.

After the third course the music stopped. The room buzzed with gay, quiet conversation.

My eyes, of course, were on Emmo. She was talking to the foreign princes on either side of her.

Then the servants took the tables apart, and while this was going on the young couples walked around in twos and threes, and the musicians played quietly. Then, at a sign from Attila they struck up a dance.

It was always he who began the dance, choosing his partner at random, not by rank. That night he offered his hand to Emmo.

The guests followed suit, dancing with those nearby.

Hunnish dancing is not like that of other nations. It begins with quiet, smooth and dignified steps, the dancers at first only holding hands; later they face one another and sway to and fro, looking into each other's eyes.

I could see that Emmo was ecstatically happy, gazing deep into the king's eyes. She was serious; so was he. Never had I seen people dance so seriously. And if Emmo had never before enchanted my soul, she would have then as she danced with Attila, like some unearthly figure from a dream.

The men kept changing partners with the one nearest them. Emmo was taken by Todomer, the commander of the Goths; Attila gave his hand to Ildiko, the blonde German princess whom I had seen at Queen Rika's.

I leant against a pillar at the side, watching them all. It was a beautiful dance, for it seemed not just a physical thing–their spirits danced, too. As Attila passed in front of me, I saw that Ildiko's large blue eyes looked at Attila with a happy sparkle, and Attila smiled back at her.

*N*ext day it was rumoured in the palace that Attila had sent envoys that morning to Ildiko's father on the banks of the Rhine, asking the girl's hand in marriage. It was true that some noblemen had left–among them Chath, Dorog and Orgovan–but no one knew their destination.

I didn't give the matter much thought. I had to write letters to the princes of the Swabians, Kvads, Rugi, Saraguri, Heruls and others who were spending the winter by the shores of the Adriatic with their peoples, saying that as soon as the worst of the winter was over they should immediately set out for the lower Danube and there wait for Attila; we were to start out for Constantinople in the spring.

The new Emperor, Marcian, a thick-necked old soldier, had refused to pay taxes even before the expedition to Catalaunum. He had sent to Attila saying, 'I give to my friend only. Others can expect steel.'

To this Attila gave an even shorter reply: 'Steel will be met by steel.'

That was nearly two years ago when we were just setting off to the west. Marcian could wait. Now his turn had come.

'A year from now,' said Attila, 'we are going to have lunch in Marcian's palace, and he will set my plate before me himself.'

Well, as I said, that day I had a lot to do.

In the evening the wife of the patrician again sent for me, and though I was tired, I gladly rushed over to see them.

Chath really had gone. Emmo looked listless and Lady Chath, tired from the night before, went to bed early.

Emmo, however, stayed with us.

I wrote the letters slowly and made them long, hoping for an opportunity to speak to Emmo.

I wanted to boast of my prosperity and prospects, how I earned one or two gold pieces every day, and my fellow scribes foretold great things for me. Certainly in Constantinople I was going to be even more needed and important. And I would be fighting beside Attila! This especially I rehearsed–I saw myself saying to Emmo, 'I will be fighting beside Attila.' She would know what that mean: a rosy future–riches, honour, and heaven!

I was in a good mood, and joked, hoping to make Emmo more cheerful. I put down her paleness to the fact that she couldn't have had much sleep. I praised her dancing, her dress–meanwhile getting on with the letter to the patrician. It made me smile, because I had to describe how much she suffered, how, if the ransom didn't arrive soon, she'd pine away in her misery...

'My lady,' I said, mischievously, 'since you've been here, you have put on weight. Can you really be pining away?'

She yawned. 'I don't know why it is,' she replied, 'but I *have* noticed that my dresses are beginning to feel tight.'

At last the letter was finished. I dripped sealing wax on to it and the patrician's wife pressed her ring in it. Djidjia took the smaller lamp and walked the woman to her room. For a moment we were left alone. Emmo's eyes opened wide, and she looked at me with a strange, melancholy gaze, the way a woman might look kneeling at the scaffold, gazing up for the last time before bowing her head beneath the executioner's sword.

Then she spoke.

'Zeta, what is sadder than death?'

I could only stare. What possible answer could one give a question like that? But she answered it herself. Still staring into space and rocking to and fro.

'Life!'

I was speechless.

Her eyes were swimming in tears. What was she trying to say? I couldn't tell. I could only wait for her to explain. What could be the matter with her? But Djidjia came back, and Emmo rose and, without saying good-bye, left the room.

On the steps I talked to Djidjia.

'What is troubling your young mistress? She is extremely sad.'

'The same thing that troubles me,' replied Djidjia.

'And what's wrong with you?'

'Who cares about that?'

I was irked by this answer. 'What on earth is going on? Now you too are talking in riddles! What's wrong with your young mistress?'

She just looked at me thoughtfully, shrugging her shoulders. I couldn't make her speak. I trudged home very disconsolate, and all night Emmo's words hummed in my head–'What is sadder than death?'

Shortly after this the patrician's wife was ransomed. Her husband himself came for her. He looked me up in the writing-house, and asked me how much my ransom would be.

'I do not know, my lord,' I said, shrugging my shoulders. 'I didn't ask.'

'Well,' he said, 'if it's not too much I will ransom you and take you with me: I can get you a title among the nobility. Your letters were a marvel even to the scholars. You have painted such a heart-rending picture of my wife that even strangers wept on reading it. I'll ransom you!'

'Thank you,' I replied with a haughty humility, 'but I would rather be a slave here than a nobleman in your country, my lord!'

He looked at me with astonishment. No doubt he still shakes his head to this day whenever he thinks of me.

Spring came early that year.

By the end of February the Hunnish girls had violets in their hair and the fields were green. From all the allied armies came messages that they had started out, to wait for Attila at the lower Danube.

Perhaps even more people were gathering now than had taken part in the western campaign. Attila's star shone high in the sky. After the battle of Catalaunum no Hun doubted any longer that the entire world was his.

We heard that Marcian was already beginning to whine and change his tune. He'd soon see that he'd have to kneel down before Attila and give up his crown. What else could he do? On this earth there was only one king fit to rule.

In the writing-house we discussed the rumours going about that Attila was planning to move to Constantinople. A marble palace was due to the ruler of the world, and a city on the seashore to the nobility of the mighty Hunnish people.

All we were waiting for was the wedding; the day after that Attila would probably start out, taking his new wife with him.

One spring day the wedding was duly celebrated. The priest gave his blessings at noon. There were bonfires in the main square and a white horse was sacrificed. The city was filled with flowers and the smell of incense. People roasted oxen and sheep, wine flowed, music played, spurs jingled, and the bards sang songs to the lute.

Attila invited a thousand guests to his palace. The main room was newly decorated for the event. Huge carpets covered the walls and pillars and in the corners stood the white marble statues of Greek and Roman male gods brought back from the towns of the Roman Empire. (The Huns did not tolerate female statues and even the male statues must be clothed ones and be adorned with a Hunnish hat.) A carved barrel hung from a chain in the centre of the room–the gift of the Roman Pope, it contained the most ancient *Lacrimae Christi.*

I was not at the feast, of course. I watched the horse racing in the military practice grounds and the tight-rope walkers, Avzon comedians, Alan knife-throwers and Greek clowns who entertained the people. In the square in front of the palace, Tzerko rode a broom and mimicked the noblemen.

I was already familiar with his jokes, but the people were seeing them for the first time, and they found his performance hilarious when he strutted with a pot belly like Eslas or pulled at his moustache like Chath.

When dusk fell hundreds of thousands of torches were lit everywhere. The people gathered in front of Attila's palace and clamoured to see their king. He appeared on the balcony, with his new wife, to be greeted with a deafening ovation. Men waved their hats, women their kerchiefs. Every face glowed with joy.

I, who can remain detached from all sorts of excitement, could not help sharing the mood of the crowd that evening. I too waved a torch and bellowed with the Huns.

'Long live Attila! Blessings!'

In my eyes he was a barbarian chief no longer, but life-giving sunshine, the source of my fortune, my king forever!

After Attila returned inside, the people went on celebrating in smaller groups. I went to the Chaths' house, where Italian singers and Kvad dancers were performing with tambourines.

As I stood there, I noticed all Chath's servants standing in a group, Djidjia among them. She stood in front beside Jonji, and the flames of the torches cast their light on her face. The girl's beauty surprised me.

I had first seen her a dusky, immature child. Now her face was pink and white, and her eyes were dark, like two black butterflies. She had lovely thick hair and a good figure. My gaze stayed upon her; I could hardly believe my eyes.

Uzura saw me then, and hailed me over to join them, which I did gladly.

A Kvad dancer, a young man with a supple body, was just beginning his torch-dance. He spun and leaped with ease, weaving the torches around him like snakes. But perhaps for the special festive occasion he had put a little too much grease on his head, for the flames caught his hair, and to the great merriment of the Huns the dance came to an abrupt end.

'Let's go somewhere else!' shouted Uzura. He grabbed Raba by the arm and dragged her with him.

'Let's go!' Lado took Jonji by the arm.

Djidjia was left for me. She clutched my arm tightly and we meandered through the noisy city.

They could rarely get away from the house, poor souls. Now that there was no one at home, they all took their chance of an evening out.

We walked among the bright lights and merry-makers, stopping now and then to watch the revery. It was wonderful to see the way the lads made the young girls spin and dance.

'Hooy! Hooy!'

Then we heard some songs about the expedition to Italy. One of them I can remember even now. It told of finding a place for Attila's tent on the vast Italian plains where there were no hills.

'Well, one hill there shall be!' cried the commander-in-chief. 'Let each of you bring a hatful of earth!'–and so a mountain was born.

We walked on. Suddenly I felt Djidjia's arm trembling.

'Are you cold?' I asked gently. It was only early spring.

'No,' she replied, and looked at me happily.

'How beautiful you are, Djidjia!' I said, staring at her. 'Just now I was absolutely astonished by it.'

Blushing, she smiled and shrugged her shoulders. 'What's the use of my being beautiful?' she whispered. 'It's no use to me.'

'Oh, come, come! I've never heard of people feeling sorry for someone because she was beautiful! Have you? Don't expect any pity on that account!'

And as her arm was resting on mine, I noticed that her hands were beautiful too.

We were silent.

'If Emmo didn't exist,' I thought, 'this would be just the girl for me!'

But it was only a fleeting thought. By the time we arrived back home, and I took my leave of them all, my mind was already on tomorrow and the hopes that glittered before me: At last I too would have cause for celebration!

I couldn't go to sleep for a long time for speculating on my future hopes.

What could I expect from Attila?

One thing was certain: he would give me my freedom. After each of his weddings Attila set free his prisoners of noble birth so that the day would live in their memories. The freed slaves could return home if they so desired, but only rarely did anyone leave. That handshake which pledged freedom usually made people stay with Attila.

Well, he would shake hands with me too. But what else would I get?

What if I got no more than an ornate sword and a hat? No, no: of course I'd get a nice tent and some land with horses, cows and servants. Maybe he'd even suggest I get married before the campaign. No, he wouldn't do that just yet–perhaps afterwards. By then I would receive ten portions when they dealt out the plunder.

This kept me turning and tossing in bed. In the morning, when I woke up, mixed feelings of happiness and doubt sent shivers down my spine. I dressed with a trembling heart, like a bride on her wedding day. I fastened the gold spurs on my sandals; I combed and scented my hair.

The sky was slightly cloudy, and the air was chilly, turning to cold. Music could still be heard in parts of the city.

The nobles began to gather and talk quietly on the spacious porch of the palace. The commander-in-chief was there, wearing a blue velvet hat, and his sword slung behind him. My master was there also, twirling his handspan-long moustache. Free Greek too was around with old Barcza. Orestes, a few officers, King Ardaric, Berki, Orgovan, Dorog, Macha, Kason, Upor–some fifty noblemen stood there in little groups, awaiting the horn signal that would invite them to enter the hall.

There was a lowing and bleating in the courtyard from the gift animals: seven white cows with gilded horns; seven white horses with gilded hoofs; seven white lambs; seven white goats, also with gilded horns; seven white hens; seven white peacocks; seven white doves; seven white cranes–in short, lots of white things, all in sevens.

Four sleepy guards stood by the open door. In the dim corridor within, Captain Edecon's red cloak could be seen. He had probably stood watch throughout the night, and, befitting his status, wanted to be first to wish Attila good morning, luck, strength and health.

Free Greek spoke to me.

'Well, boy, how much would you sell this day for?'

'If I could get for it all the wealth in the world outside the Huns' lands, I wouldn't sell it, no, not for all the Roman Empire because what I want is the king's to give. And if I can't get what I am hoping for, then my freedom, all the king's gifts and my head as a bonus I'll give to the devil for nothing.'

Free Greek laughed.

'I like puzzles, but this I couldn't possibly solve! What are you talking about?'

'Well, if the king gave me all his gold, and the sun and the moon, and all the stars of heaven in sacks, all that would be nothing compared to what I expect of this day.'

He laughed.

'I still don't understand.'

Kason, the chief bugler, stepped up to our group; he was dressed in unusually fancy clothes, and his eyes were bloodshot and sleepy. He asked if the king were up yet, shook hands with a few lords, and took a drink out of Kamocha's wine flask.

'Why did you bring your horn?' asked Vachar. 'You don't think we'll start out today, surely!'

'I wouldn't put it past Attila,' replied Kason. 'The weather has warmed up early this year.'

But a noise interrupted him. Edecon came running along the corridor towards us without his helmet, and his face was contorted in agony. He was utterly beside himself, and could hardly speak to the bodyguards.

'Get the commander!...' He was choking on the words and waving his arms. 'The commander-in-chief!... Run to him!... get the head shaman!... get all the doctors!...'

We were stunned.

The commander-in-chief was standing right in front of him in one the groups, but Edecon was so confused he didn't see him.

'What has happened?' everyone asked, dumbfounded.

Edecon fell against the wall as if he were drunk. Tears poured out of his eyes and he beat his forehead with his fists.

'This is the end of us!' he cried. That made our blood freeze.

The commander-in-chief grabbed him by the shoulders.

'I am here! Now, what has happened?'

'He's dead!' The words burst out of the man in such a horrible voice that it was as if his heart had broken.

Everyone seemed struck by lightning. People lost all power of thought. No one dared ask who it was who had died. Such an unimaginable horror suggested itself we couldn't think of it.

At last the lips of the commander-in-chief moved.

'He was killed...' he said, as though speaking in a nightmare.

'I don't know anything,' Edecon answered. 'The woman screamed, and I rushed in. Attila...lay there...on his back... I called to him: "My lord!..." I shook him...' And he leaned against the wall and sobbed.

We started to move like sleepwalkers, without a word, jostling one another–through the door, along the dim corridor, and up the stairs leading to the second floor and Attila's bedroom. But all this happened so mechanically and in such silence that it was as if everyone moved in the grip of a horrible dream.

The room had no doors, only a thick blue silk curtain down to the floor.

The lords swarmed in and I was swept along with them. Ildiko was kneeling in a dim corner of the room, shaking and crying: her hair was tousled, and she was wrapped in a veil. Attila lay on his back in the great

walnut bed, covered up to his chest. He was motionless, and yellow as silt. I thought I saw some blood around his half-open mouth.

'My lord!' Macha whispered in a trembling voice.

'My lord!' yelled the commander-in-chief shaking Attila by the shoulder.

'He's dead! He's dead!' they whispered all around me, paralysed with fright.

'They've murdered him!' shouted old Barcza. He grabbed Ildiko by the hair as if she were an animal. '*You* killed him!'

The woman screamed and pushed his hand away, burying her face in her hands. She couldn't understand the words, but his wild voice had made her tremble. Her face was like a mad woman's.

Barcza too shook the king.

'Attila!' he cried, with an old man's, a father's grief. 'Attila!'

The king's hand was resting on the covers. He took hold of it, then let it drop again, and fell to his knees, weeping violently.

'He's dead!'

Every face was wet with tears. The commander turned his head to the wall and sobbed.

'Oh, my good lord! My good king!'

'We are done for!' a voice cried out.

Some fell to their knees, some threw themselves on the bed; everyone moaned and wept with convulsive sobs.

I left the room, choking on my tears. Pale, moaning people swarmed in and out in the corridor. Squeezed into a corner near the steps that led to the steeple, I went up to get some air.

All was still quiet in the vicinity of the palace. Sounds of music drifted from the city. The sun broke through the clouds and gilded the peaks of tents and the copper roofs of the palaces.

I could see horsemen galloping away in all directions. The music in the distance stopped and a suffocating stillness settled over the city.

Then from everywhere people came hurrying towards the palace–men on horseback, and women and children running beside the horses. More and more came; the crowd kept pouring in and surrounded the palace. Master and slave, woman and man thronged shoulder to shoulder as they came through the gates of the palace; the air trembled with a great buzz and murmur of voices.

I felt as if the sky and the earth had crashed together. The air was stifling, as it is before a storm. I felt a sudden impulse to ride out into the fields so as not to see, not to hear anything.

As I came down I was stopped by guards; they had cordoned off the corridor. Queen Rika came running towards Attila's room just then, screaming and tearing her hair.

'He was killed! He was murdered!' she kept shrieking.

Close on her heels came Prince Aladar, head bent and hat in hand. He was as white as the walls.

Then came the other wives and children.

'I cannot bear to hear any more of this heart-breaking crying!' I told Balassa, one of the bodyguards. 'Let me through!'

'Who could have murdered him?' the guard asked with tears in his eyes. 'No one was here–no one but us.'

Then came the shamans and doctors. Everyone was talking about Attila having been murdered, and saying that the Greek court was to blame. The people were overcome with anger and despair. In fifteen minutes the doctors came out, reporting that there was no wound to be found anywhere on Attila's body, and that he had died in exactly the same way as Buda had.

This was formally announced in front of the palace; a great sad murmur rose from the crowd.

The noblemen were on the porch, weeping. Chath pulled out his dagger and cut his clothes to shreds, slashing his face with it too. He wailed aloud, sat down on the ground and then collapsed.

'Everything is over now! Even God is finished!'

Kason was about to help him up when the spear was brought out–Attila's gilded spear, covered in black felt–to be mounted on top of the palace.

Kason turned away, then untied the beautiful ivory horn from his neck and smashed it against a pillar with such force that it broke into a thousand pieces.

By the afternoon Attila was lying in the main square on a tall catafalque, under a black silk tent adorned with silver stars. The sides of the tent had been drawn up to allow people to see him.

The head shamans sacrificed a black horse behind the catafalque, and the blind Kama questioned the departed Hunnish souls as to how Attila should be buried.

'Put him in a triple coffin,' was the reply. 'Let the first coffin be made of gold, like sunshine, for he was the sun of the Huns. Let the second coffin be made of silver, like the tail of a comet, for he was the comet of the world. Let the third coffin be made of steel, for he was strong as steel.'

While the coffins were being prepared, the Hunnish nobility had to decide where to bury Attila. They stayed up all night discussing this, for the Huns were a travelling nation, and it was possible that a future king would move on to other territories, the way bees will sometimes swarm. Or a band of thieves from one of the many allied nations could decide to take the golden coffin. Or possibly after many centuries, another powerful people would be born who would dig it up and desecrate it.

Old Kama answered, following the heavenly counsel.

'The River Tisia is full of tiny islands. Divert the water from the narrower branch in one of the places where the river divides. Dig the grave there very deep in the exposed bed, then widen that bed so that *it* will be the greater. After the king has been buried, let the water flow back again. After a time memory fades, and silt will quickly cover the coffin–no one will know where Attila is buried.'

A hundred thousand spades and hoes began their work the next morning. A dam of sacks filled with earth was built across a branch of the Tisia where it divided and flowed around a small islet. By that evening the grave was dug, so deep that no man would ever be able to find it again.

They sprinkled the bottom with flowers and foliage.

On the third day the triple coffin was completed. Attila was once more lifted up so that everyone could see him for the last time. Then amid the wailing of the people they placed him inside the gold coffin. They set the sword, bow and gilded spear beside him, and put on his head the helmet he had always worn in battle.

Something peculiar happened to me the night before the funeral. As I was standing there stupefied among those who were keeping an all-night vigil, listening numbly to the prayers of the shamans, someone touched my shoulder. I turned and saw that it was Djidjia.

'What do you want?'

'Come!'

I could only guess that Emmo must have sent a message. I followed her listlessly like a thing without feeling. We cut through the multitude and arrived in the courtyard. The place was deserted. She pulled me aside, against the wall, into the darkest shadow. Then she began to whisper mysteriously.

'I ask you not to go to the funeral.' I caught a whiff of Emmo's perfume on her, and this made me furious.
'Why?'
'Because. I ask you, I implore you! Just do this one thing for me!'
'But why? Tell me the reason!'
'I had a horrible nightmare last night! I dreamed that Attila was flying in the clouds on horseback, followed by a small group of people. The horses were blood-drenched and so were the men... You were among them.'
'Oh, go on! Go to hell!' I bawled at her.
She knelt down and put her arms around my legs in the gesture of a suppliant.
'Zeta, don't go! I ask you only this one thing! There was a time when I thought that I could ask you more. You were kind to me, and gentle, and once I dropped a rose from the window for you. You picked it up and kissed it. I thought then that rose was my heart...'
The blood rushed to my head.
'Did *you* give me that rose?
'Are you angry with me because of it? Did I do something wrong? I didn't mean to! Please forgive me! I will never cross your path again! But don't go to the funeral!'
My first impulse was to kick her, trample her, I felt outraged! But even while I was still stunned by the shock, a milder thought held me back: the silly girl hadn't known what she was doing!
'Calm down,' I said. 'I too have had a dream–a pleasanter one than yours, and no doubt it makes more sense.'
And I left her there.
At noon a list was brought around by a morose bodyguard; those whose names were on the list were to remain in their rooms until the funeral. Some forty names were on the stick; mine was among them. The three scribes who lived with me were also listed.
An hour later Mena-Sagh entered our room. Two apprentice shamans followed him, one carrying some clothes, the other torches.
He gave his orders in a sombre voice. 'Men, put on these mourning sacks for the funeral. You will proceed beside the horses in a line. Zeta, you will lead. When the coffin is taken from the cart to the bottom of the Tisia, all of you who wear these clothes will throw yourselves around the grave when my horn sounds the call. Remain like that until the funeral dirge is over!'
'As you command, my lord.'
He left.

We examined the clothes–sacks made of thin black felt. Some were long enough to reach to the heel, some reached just to the knees. They were all loose, and had holes only for the eyes and arms.

Shortly after Mena-Sagh had departed, a woman clad in mourning apparel appeared in the doorway. She threw back her black veil; it was Emmo. She looked at my fellow slaves and in a commanding tone told them to leave us, and they obeyed.

I was amazed at her looks. She was like a marble statue clad in a mourning dress. Her face was coolly serene, her gaze piercing and cold.

'I see you already have your mourning sack, Zeta,' she said in a husky quiet voice.

'They were brought a little while ago.'

'I came to ask you something. I know you would do anything I ask. When it is time for you to leave, dress up, but lag behind a little. Wait until your companions have left the room. Wait until I come here.'

She lifted her finger, and whispered even more quietly, 'Until I come here.'

I accompanied her to the outer door, but in silence–I didn't dare say anything. By then the palace people were all wearing black; they had the black horses ready too...

I returned, wondering. I didn't understand what Emmo wanted. Had Djidjia spoken to her too, perhaps? How deadly pale her face was! And how mechanical her movements! Everyone else's eyes were red, but hers weren't though there were deep blue shadows round them, giving her haggard, haunted look.

Around four in the afternoon the wail of the funeral bugle began. It was such a powerful sound that even the walls of the palace shook. We donned the peculiar funeral clothes and set out.

When we reached the exit, I called out to my fellow slaves closest to me.

'I forgot my belt. You go ahead!'

I didn't have to wait many minutes before the door opened and Emmo came in.

She hesitated and looked at me. 'Is that you?'

'Yes, it's me. Tell me what you want!'

'Take off your funeral sack and help me into it! Quickly!'

She tore off her veil and threw it on the ground. She pulled the pin from her hair and threw it into a corner, her hair fell loosely, now her face was as white as wax and her lips were almost blue.

'My young lady!' I whispered, uneasily.

'Quiet! Not a word!'
'My young lady!...'
By then I had taken off the sack and was holding it on my arm, but the leaden stare of eyes frightened me.
'Help me into it!' she whispered.
'But please–'
'Do you love me?'
'Oh, God!...'
'Then help me into the sack!... No, wait a moment... Kiss me... You deserve it... I know what you have suffered! I know, I know what it is...'
And she offered me her pale lips. That could have been my moment of joy! But–her lips were cold; it was as if I had kissed a corpse.
'Don't ask questions!' she whispered. 'Don't say a word!'
So I didn't say anything, but as I helped her into the sack I felt a shudder of reluctance run through me.
Then she was gone like a shadow, and I stayed in the room.
I had to do what I had done–because she asked me. If she had asked me to jump into a well, I would have done it because it was her wish. And yet I found it very strange that she should want to take my place in the procession of torches. I didn't understand.
Outside the dirge began; the sound of weeping mingled with the song and the priests' exhortation to their god; while I sat on in my room with dark thoughts going round my head.
Why should she have wanted to take my place? Women are often touchy–had someone hurt Emmo's feelings? Perhaps she hadn't been allotted a place for the ceremony in keeping with her rank. Or perhaps it was patriotic feeling that made her want to express her grief for the king's death in this way.
The thought that I could be hanged for disobeying orders flashed through my mind only for a moment. Emmo's wish was my command. I picked up the torn veil and hid it in my crate. I put her hair pin there too, thinking to return these things next day.
When I left the palace, Shaman Gyorhe was standing beside the coffin. He and the other priests were wearing large sheets sprinkled with blood; their heads were shaved smooth, and had been slashed till they bled. Old blind Kama stood at the heap of the coffin with his face raised to heaven. The sad forest of people listened in suffocating silence to Shaman Gyorhe as he turned to them and, in his deep voice, intoned a farewell in Attila's name.

This world has never had another king more loved than I; and yet I now desert my faithful nation!

I, who often walked the lands of Death, had never met him face to face, treacherously he attacked me while I slept, my head on the heart of my lovely bride. God bless you, Rika, farewell my wife; you were my dream in wars, salvation at home, fruit tree of my two golden apples, the melancholy flower in my royal palace.

The royal lady raised herself with a heart-rending scream and threw herself on the coffin. The two princes, Chaba and Aladar, dressed in black, fell down with loud sobbing.

The shaman continued.

I speak to you for last time now, Chaba, my flower. You were dearest to my heart in all my earthly life. Never again will you look at me with your smiling eyes, never will you say these words: my father. But whenever you sense trouble, look up in the skies; lightning will flash, and you will know your father's soul is there.

The people wept with the royal family. The shaman spoke Attila's farewell to each of the sons; the commanders, nobles, allied kings and at last the people were named, whom he enjoined to live in harmony. The valediction closed with these lines:

God bless you, beautiful country, land of the
Maros and Tisia,
eternal home of my most valiant people.
My body now enters Mother Earth's lap;
my soul this night will gallop amid the stars.

Then old Iddar stood beside the coffin, and in a carrying, sing-song voice he began to lead the lament.

'Oh, we are lost! Our sun has fallen from the sky! Our beautiful sun has fallen from the most brilliant of heights!'

'Our sun has fallen!' murmured the people, weeping.

'Why did you leave us, Attila? Is there another place in the world where you could be better loved than you are here? There is no other place anywhere in creation! Why did you leave us, Attila?'

The people repeated the shaman's last words, sobbing, and the men kept slashing their faces with their knives so that their tears mingled with blood. For common tears were not enough for mourning Attila.

Iddar continued.

'Whenever we saw your royal face, our hearts beat with the greatest joy. Every sword stirred in its scabbard. Fire shot through our veins. Mothers lifted their babies and told them, "Look, there goes Attila!" '

And he went on, amidst general sobbing.

'Attila! Attila! You were our joy. Such joy we never possessed before; now you are our grief–such grief we never felt before. Your name was our pride, our luminous tower shining into the distance; now your name is our humility, the cause of mourning and grief.' His voice broke and shook with sobs. 'There were kings in this world–famous, notorious, powerful–but a king like you, Attila . . . there was none!'

'A king like you . . . there was none!' repeated thousands of people, crying.

'And there will be other kings, but no king will ever be like you!'

'No king will be like you!' repeated the people.

'Your name shone forth like the rising sun after a dark night. Why do you return into the darkness, Attila? The setting sun takes all its rays with it; you take away with you the glory of the Huns!'

'The Hunnish people are lost!' the commander-in-chief burst out.

The people repeated the commander's words with loud weeping, and it was some time before the shaman could continue.

'How could you leave your army, the strongest this earth has ever seen? Why did the sword of God drop from your hand? Oh, why have you left your nation fatherless?'

He could not go on. A fit of delirious madness seized the people; with the blood pouring down their faces, they began to slash at their arms and chests as well. The commander-in-chief thrust his dagger into his left arm. Women fainted. Old King Ardaric staggered and fell beside the coffin.

The shamans lifted the coffin onto the funeral cart, and the twelve black horses began to move in the direction of the River Tisia.

Lightning, Attila's favourite horse, was led in front, saddled and covered completely with a black veil. Behind the horse, fourteen crowned kings followed on foot, veiled as well. Then came the priests, some in white, some in black–about a hundred of them–with an army of young boys, all singing the Hunnish psalm for the dead to a melancholy tune on the fifes. The sound went to the very marrow–I've never heard anything like it outside the land of the Huns.

The family followed the coffin on foot–all the queens, Attila's sons, and the nobles and commanders, all bareheaded and in torn clothes. It was flanked on either side by Attila's bodyguards. Their helmets were covered with black veils, their uniforms hung from them in shreds, and their faces were so bloody that they couldn't be recognized. From time to time there was a roll on the drums.

It was terrifying to watch this multitude. Gepids, Saraguri, Ugors–every nation within three days' riding distance was there. These followed the coffin on horseback in an endless crowd. They brought along their flags as well as if going to war. But this time each wore something black which lent them a somber aspect.

My gaze sought out the group clad in mourning sacks: they were beside the bodyguards. I thought I would make my way through the crowd, find Emmo and stay close to her to watch lest she get hurt in the melee. But I looked for her in vain. Though they were close I couldn't recognize anyone in those black sacks. Emmo was somewhere among them: perhaps I would recognize her if I joined them, I thought. No one had such fine white hands as hers, I would know them among a hundred.

I had to return to get a torch, for in an hour it would be dark; everyone carried torches. Attila was buried at night so that the grave might never be found again.

So I went back to the deserted palace. In the courtyard the previous day I had seen a heap of torches the size of a haystack; now I could find not a single one, not even a handful of straw.

Meanwhile the funeral procession had advanced, and when I rejoined them I was among the common people. All my pushing was in vain; the people followed so thickly behind the nobles that it was impossible to get through.

As we left the city, the setting sun covered the clouds with a veil of gilded scarlet. Soon the yellow waters of the Tisia lay before us. Tired of the pushing and jostling of the crowd I stood for a while beside an ancient poplar, thinking at first that I'd wait for most of them to go by. Then I decided I wouldn't go any farther, I would only get trampled and crushed to no purpose. If I was too late to get close to the bodyguards, I couldn't possibly see Attila's coffin lowered into the grave.

I climbed the tree and viewed the rest of the procession from there. Then I climbed higher–no one paid any attention to me–and now I could see the island and the branch of the Tisia which had been drained. The water in the other branch had flooded the surrounding fields.

The sun had gone down, and more and more torches lit up the darkness of evening. It looked as if there were millions of them. No moon or stars could be seen in the sky; it seemed to me that all the stars had come down to earth to follow Attila to his grave.

The procession was over. No one passed below me any more; they had all gathered on the banks of the river. I could hear their dirge in the distance and the dry rattle of drums. Then for a short time there was silence–perhaps the shamans were praying.

I climbed down from the tree and joined some men who were leading the horses of the queens and noblemen who had gone on foot. When we reached the river, the bugles were calling: the last post.

Sleep Attila! Good night!

Then suddenly there was a noise in the distance like heavy rain. They had begun to dismantle the dam, so that the water might cover the grave.

Torches flew up into the air in great arcs of light, then went out – the people had all thrown them into the river. Now they started back to the city in silence.

I waited, thinking I'd let them go by and wait for Emmo. I had to return to the tree and wait there, though, to avoid being pushed along by the crowd.

I recognized Balassa, one of the bodyguards, by his voice. He stopped under the tree and I heard him say to his companion, 'The horse shouldn't have been left like that.'

'It wasn't,' someone contradicted him.

'But it was.'

I didn't understand what 'left like that' meant; I could only surmise that Attila's horse had been put to the sword at the graveside and laid beside the coffin.

I thought this proper. Every Hun was buried like that – head due west, feet due east, and his horse on his left side. Horses too had souls; at midnight both souls would stir and rise, the Hun would mount his horse and ride into the starry skies.

But by now the servants should have been coming by. I strained my eyes, but couldn't see any of them anywhere. The princes appeared, walking slowly, and the queens passed on horseback, a shield-bearer leading each horse.

I recognized groups of noblemen too, and the voices I heard were gruffer and louder than usual; they seemed to be arguing, quarrelling.

'The sword must go to Aladar!'

'He designated Chaba before he died!'

'Chaba is still a child! You cannot entrust to a child the leadership of the Hunnish nation!'

'There's always the commander-in-chief!'

The dispute grew more and more heated, and hundreds and thousands of people were talking of nothing else.

For hours the multitude kept passing by me, but where were my companions who had worn the funeral sacks? They must have stayed behind till the very end, for they had to lay flowers and leaves and wreaths on the coffin. But even so, they should have been here by now.

I climbed down from the tree but went on waiting. The moon came out from behind some clouds, but it was a thin crescent, giving hardly any light. Some women passed – A child cried. . .

Then fewer and fewer people came.

I approached everyone who came on foot and looked remotely like Emmo.

All in vain – she didn't come. They must have taken off their sacks, throwing them on the grave among the wreaths and torches, and Emmo must have joined the queens.

*I*t was about midnight by the time I entered the city. People were milling around the streets, and here and there were groups of horsemen around a torch, talking, sometimes arguing loudly.

I saw bards standing on horseback, singing of Attila's deeds and playing lutes. The songs were all old – often repeated, and known to all–but that night it was different; people listened to them with a new feeling.

Bonfires were lit in several places, and in the attentive silence priests prophesied what the future would bring.

Near the palaces there were even more riders, and the people were even louder. Only a few torches shed light on the blood-smeared faces. At any other time the palaces would have been all lit up by torches at every entrance and a bonfire beside the well to light the square.

Now the square was dark, and the palaces also.

Why was this? I wondered. Always when a nobleman died the funeral was followed by a great feast. Friends who had loved the deceased would sit with the mourning family around a table, talking quietly over supper of all his merits. At the head of the table would be an empty chair and an unused plate. The dead man's soul was supposed to sit there; it was reserved for him.

I expected to see an even greater feast in Attila's honour. Why was it not being held? Perhaps they didn't know who should give the feast . . . The entire nation? Attila had no governors, no cabinet; he himself was everything. But his family could have organized it! Were they afraid of public disturbances?

Or perhaps it was simply that nobody had thought of the feast; the blow was so great that everyone had been stupefied. Who could occupy the throne which Attila had left so empty? And who was great enough to pick up his sword? Everyone was preoccupied with this question, not with the feast.

I was so tired I could hardly stand on my feet. I walked round the palace to where my room was. Our quarters had no oil lamp. I listened. There was no snoring. No one was there! My fellow scribes must be still out somewhere among the groups of excited talkers.

So I went to bed. I dozed off a little, but people kept thumping back and forth in the corridor, and talking loudly. Now and then I heard shouts from outside, or the song of a lute player. It was impossible for me to sleep so I dressed and went out again.

In the square Almad, an old lute player was standing on the rim of the well, singing to a large, sad crowd.

As I stepped outside the palace I bumped into Macha. He stared at me for a moment as if he were seeing a ghost. I stared back, not knowing what was the matter.

'You!' he blurted at last. *'You* here!'

'Yes, I'm here,' I replied, not quite understanding the question.

He stuttered something, blinking and looking almost apologetic, but just then some noblemen came by and took him with them.

Then I heard a shout some way off: 'Chaba is king!'

I went round to the back, to the stable, found my horse, mounted without a saddle, and rode out among the people.

As I passed Almad, he was singing:

His remains we sealed into a triple coffin,
Then we put him in the earth and under water.
Bowstring twanged; arrows flew whistling through the air:
All your faithful servants fell down around you.

On hearing this sentence my heartbeat faltered. I froze, and my heart felt like a stone. Oh, good God! What had happened?

The bard continued, gesturing with his right hand.

With a slow gush the flow of Tisia started,
And covered the tomb with a glittering wave.
Torches extinguished–the stars tumbled down:
Your dear, faithful servants fell down around you.
Black darkness engulfed the Hunnish nation;
A blacker darkness still is the grief in our hearts.

I looked around me. Sabolch was near and I grabbed his arm.

'What is he saying about the servants?' I said, almost choking on the words.

He was completely taken aback. His eyes opened wide. 'You weren't there?'

'No.'

'How is that possible?'

'It was orders. What is the lute player talking about? I don't understand!'

'He is singing about the servants. Don't you know that the faithful servant dies with the master? They shot every servant who was dear to him. But you...'

'Those who were in the mourning sacks?'

'Those too.'

I almost collapsed; I felt as if someone had struck me on the head with a club.

I don't know when I got off my horse, or what was said to me, or who passed by me, or who talked to me, or who jostled me. At times I sat down and screamed out Emmo's name, then I lurched on. In the first light of dawn I found myself down by the Tisia where Attila had been buried. I sat and stared into the yellowish waves in the very stupor of madness.

My reverie was interrupted by the touch of a hand on my shoulder, and a gentle, sad woman's voice.

'Zeta.'

I looked up and saw Djidjia beside me, pale and sad.

'Take flight!' she whispered. 'Take flight at once. There is horrible bloodshed in the city!'

I realized only then that for a long time I had been hearing a noise in the distance, a noise that reminded me of the battle on the plains of Catalaunum.
'The people have divided into two camps!' Djidjia whispered. 'All around the palaces, the Huns are killing one another! You must escape, Zeta. You must flee from this hell!...'
(Oh, you blessed soul! You angel. You had always been near me, protecting me with your wings, and yet I never saw you until now. Weren't you always the one who loved me, who was faithful to me, suffered because of me–and was always meant for me? And yet I never noticed you. I had eyes only for the one who now was lying with an arrow in her heart, beside her secret idol at the bottom of the Tisia.)
I rose like a sleepwalker and took the girl by the hand.
'Djidjia!'
'Take flight, Zeta! take flight!'
'Will you come with me?'
She bowed her head humbly.
'If you'll let me.'
I took only one look back: the city was burning, the steeple of the royal palace glowed yellow in the scarlet sea of fire, till it seemed that the sun was rising from the west.

And we set out.

POSTSCRIPT

Hungary is situated right in the centre of Europe. While its internal population exceeds ten million, some five million more native speakers of Hungarian can be found beyond its borders in the neighbouring countries, in Western Europe and in America. In addition, there are still a few million more people, scattered all over the world, who are conscious of the fact that their closer or more distant ancestors emigrated from this part of Central Europe, and for whom the Hungarian language, so different from all Indo-European languages, may continue to have a ring of familiarity. The Hungarian language is somewhat isolated among the Latin, Germanic and Slavic languages of Europe. According to its grammatical structure, Hungarian belongs to the Finno-Ugrian family of languages, along with Finnish and Estonian, and the languages of several smaller peoples living in the Asiatic regions of the Soviet Union. Due, however, to several thousand years of separation these linguistically related peoples are unable to understand one another's respective languages. The Hungarian nation, the largest of the above in population, has been forced to survive in linguistic isolation in Central Europe for more than a thousand years, surrounded by Germanic, Romanic and Slavic neighbours and situated in the centre of their sphere of cultural influence. Its conquering forefathers reached the territory of present-day Hungary at the very end of the ninth century, arriving from the East on one of the last waves of the Great Migrations. Ever since the first year of the eleventh century the Hungarians have been living in this area as an organised state. In the course of their thousand-year history they established a powerful medieval kingdom, witnessed, like most other European nations, the great struggles between kings and powerful nobles, and produced a glittering Renaissance culture of international significance. This, however, was to be followed by a state of wellnigh non-existence over the next two hundred odd years when the concept of the "Hungarian nation" represented little more than a geographical label for a population broken into three parts under the sovereignty of the Habsburg Emperor, the Turkish Sultan and the Prince of Transylvania. Due to Turkish decline at the end of the seventeenth century, the Austrians were able to extend their rule over nearly the whole territory, Hungary becoming a subject state within the Habsburg Empire. From the end of the eighteenth century onward growing national consciousness led to increasing conflict with Vienna, culminating in revolution in 1848. Although this and the ensuing War of Independence ended in defeat and was followed by a period of ruthless absolutism, Habsburg power was on the wane and in 1867 a compromise was reached securing Hungary's domestic independence within the Austro-Hungarian Monarchy, which survived as a significant European power until its dismemberment at the end of the First World War. Two revolutions in 1918 and 1919 could not avert the fate inflicted upon Hungary by the Treaty of Trianon where the nation was reduced to one third of its former size. Between the two wars the, at least partial, repossession of lost territories became the principle object of Hungarian foreign policy leading inevitably to an alliance with Nazi Germany. Only after their liberation in 1945 were Hungarians once again able to set to work on national renewal in their, albeit considerably truncated, homeland. Here the Hungarian people continue to preserve and enrich their national culture whose language remains equally alien to the closest of neighbours and farthest of friends. This must surely count as one of the main reasons why Hungarian literature is so little known to the outside world.

In the course of its stormy history Hungary has nevertheless produced an impressive poetic tradition accompanied, since the end of the eighteenth century, by a significant body of major prose. One after the other, all the intellectual trends known to Europe over the last two hundred years have found their way to Hungarian readers and writers. Ever since the invention of printing educated Hungarians have always held the printed word in high esteem, and over the last forty years the active reading public has increased at such a speed that the number of novels printed per reader tends to be higher in Hungary than in most of those nations who enjoy a higher standard of living and a more fortunate past. In recent decades, the re-publication of certain classic works by earlier novelists has resulted in the printing of more copies in a single edition than ever appeared throughout the whole of the last century. Among such celebrated Hungarian authors one would have to include Géza Gárdonyi – novelist and short story writer – one of whose most popular works, *Slave of the Huns (A láthatlan ember),* the reader now has before him.

Géza Gárdonyi (1863–1922) was born into a large country family, the son of a locksmith and agricultural engineer. He began his career as a teacher and taught for some years in a village elementary school before his restless critical spirit came increasingly into conflict with both the clerical and secular authorities. His breadth of reading, his lively interest in philosophy and his sympathy with not only the natural sciences in general but also with the ideas of the notorious Darwin in particular, all served to arouse the suspicion of his superiors. He gave up teaching to become a provincial journalist, also trying his hand at literature at an early age, alternating between short educational pieces and cheap popular novels. Although he was later to feel somewhat ashamed of these early attempts, it was during precisely this period that certain distinctive traits of his mature style began to emerge. His first published stories concerning village life introduced an entirely new voice into Hungarian literature and won him immediate popularity. Even the best of his predecessors had tended to idealise the extremely hard life of the peasantry, and the naturalistic trend which had come into fashion at the end of the nineteenth century as a reaction to this had only emphasized the darker and more alarming sides of village existence. Gárdonyi's presentation was more balanced: village life is depicted not only with harsh realism but also with an affectionate understanding of its brighter and warmer sides. Maintaining a fine equilibrium between realism and romanticism, Gárdonyi's language is richly poetical without ever ceasing to be simple and straightforward. He was popular throughout his lifetime and his popularity only increased with every decade after his death. After the short stories came a series of masterfully composed novels in which the images of peasant life gradually gave way to a preoccupation with the lifestyle and characters of the urban bourgeoisie. Then, at around the turn of the century (when Gárdonyi was in his forties) he wrote three historical novels which rank among the most widely read and most frequently reprinted works of Hungarian literature ever to have been written since.

When speaking of Gárdonyi's ever increasing popularity it is interesting to remember that both before and after his death his ideas were always a source of controversy and disagreement. Although passionately anti-Habsburg during the long years of Viennese rule, he did not believe in political activity and remained isolated, refusing to identify himself with any of the oppositional movements of his time. His antipathy towards any form of church or religious organisation alienated the pious, while non-believers would often find themselves disturbed by his sympathy with various forms of contemplative philosophy which occasionally even included mysticism. He sought God without religion, while periodically expressing enthusiasm first for materialism, then for the pessimism of Schopenhauer, later for Buddhism and at one point even for Tolstoy's heretic belief in Christ. All these ideas, however, appear in his novels with such freshness that even those who disagree with him are overwhelmed by the beauty of his writing.

It is characteristic of Gárdonyi's position within Hungarian literature that his works have found a cherished place in contexts as different as the Hungary of his lifetime, steeped in noble traditions, and the socialist Hungary of the present. The fact that Gárdonyi himself, a critic of both the nobility and the bourgeoisie, but certainly no socialist, is somewhat difficult to place, is equally true of his literary style. His writing is too romantic for the realists and too realistic for the romantics. He does not describe great social conflicts and interrelations, but rather concentrates on the finer points of individual psychology, highlighting not the terrifying depths of the human soul, but individual tenderness and humanity. He is captivated by the beauty of nature and by the potential goodness that can always be discovered in the depths of the human heart. In the bitter struggles of life he is always able to uncover elements of love and joy and to give these expression in finely controlled and poetic prose. In his historical novels these qualities are supplemented by a richly insightful vision of ancient times and it is not surprising that these form his most popular works. Between the appearance of two novels focusing ostensibly on the Hungarian past, *Stars of Eger (Egri csillagok,* 1901) and *Prisoners of God (Isten rabjai,* 1908), he published a third classic, *Slave of the Huns* (1902) which, although world historical in subject matter, is nonetheless interpreted by Hungarian readers as a work of specifically national interest. To understand the popularity of *Slave of the Huns* in Hungary we need to look more closely at the fusion of world historical fact and national mythology which informs its plot.

The novel is set in the ancient world of the Huns during the reign of King Attila, its epic prose style recalling the animated flow of image and action so characteristic of traditional heroic poetry. Its plot, based on real historical events, embodies elements of archaeologically verified fact with aspects of the author's inventive and playful imagination. The unrequited love of the leading character Zeta for the Hun Emmo along with that of the maid Djidjia for Zeta are of the author's own invention, but the historical events in which they are situated are entirely authentic. Attila, the king of the Huns before whom the whole world trembled in fear, Priscus rhetor, the Greek scribe from Byzantium, Aetius, the last of the great Roman military leaders, and some of the more important characters of the court are all authentic historical figures. This historical method of reanimating the past through a fusion of imaginary and authentic historical characters was first introduced to the novel in the work of Walter Scott. When romanticism was at its height in the 1830s the whole of Europe from France to Russia came under Scott's powerful influence, Hungary being no exception. Scott's method of intertwining the lives of imaginary characters with real historical figures had a profound influence on Hungarian novelists for generations to follow. The most popular author to adopt this technique was Mór Jókai (1925–1904), who ranks as the most widely read Hungarian romantic novelist to this very day. Jókai was still active when Gárdonyi first appeared on the literary scene, and even lived to see the publication of the latter's two most important historical novels in 1901 and 1902, which were to become Jókai's most serious rivals.

There are two main reasons why *Slave of the Huns* is read in Hungary primarily as an imaginative evocation of the national past. Firstly, the heart of Attila's short-lived empire was located in an area geographically identical with that of present-day Hungary. Secondly, and far more importantly, according to a common belief which originated in the Middle Ages the original Hun people and the early Hungarians (who arrived to occupy the same territory more than four hundred years later) were closely related in ethnic terms. Indeed, it was even said that the Hungarian forefathers simply reoccupied the territory which was no less than their due inheritance from Attila. There were various historical reasons for this long-held belief. It can be traced back to the early stages of the Great Migrations when in the fifth century the Huns arrived in Central Europe from the East. Their language, belonging to the Ural-Altaic family, was as fundamentally different from that of the wandering Germanic and Slavic peoples as from the languages of the Celtic, Greek and Latin peoples who had been living in the western and southern parts of Europe long before their arrival. The fact that the Ural-Altaic languages do not in any way belong to the great Indo-European family only made the terrifying Huns even more alien in the eyes of their neighbours. When, therefore, during the turmoil of the following centuries, another wandering people appeared on the scene whose language was similarly Ural-Altaic in origin, it was commonly believed that they were the descendants of the terrible Huns, representing yet another menace to the whole of Europe. When these rumours finally reached the new arrivals themselves, their leaders were only too willing to consider themselves the descendants of Attila, as this meant that they could justify their occupation of this new territory as the legal successors of the Huns. Two distinct branches of the Ural-Altaic language group were spoken by the tribes moving westward during the Great Migrations: the Turkish-Tartar and the Finno-Ugrian forms. Between the disappearance of the Huns and the arrival of the Hungarians, the Avars (whose language was related to Turkish) established a short-lived state on the same territory. They too considered themselves to be the descendants of Attila and were likewise regarded as Huns by their neighbours. The Avar state was crushed by Charlemagne at the end of the eighth century. It was here, however, that the Hungarian tribal confederation was to emerge two centuries later, consisting of a mixture of Finno-Ugrian (and perhaps even Turkish-Tartar) linguistic elements. They soon managed to organise themselves into a kingdom powerful enough to survive the storms of the centuries. Naturally the belief that they were the descendants of Attila and had simply reconquered their rightful homeland grew even stronger in the consciousness of the people and their leaders. During the first three centuries of the Hungarian Kingdom (from 1001 to 1301) the members of the royal family were the direct descendants of Árpád, the leader of the conquering tribal confederation, and they are recalled in Hungarian history as the Árpád dynasty. The official political line adopted by the kings of the House of Árpád was that the Huns of Attila were the first people to conquer this territory and that the tribes of Árpád were their legal successors. Writing in Latin, the early Hungarian chroniclers recorded this belief as historical fact. The chronicles had such a profound effect on Hungarian historical thinking that gradually even the legends of Hungarian folklore became inextricably mixed with imaginary Hun sources. Even those scattered and fragmented peoples who were either already living in the area at the time of the Hungarian conquest or who arrived later on, soon intermixed with the Hungarians and adopted their historical legends as their own.

Although extensive scholarly research in later centuries has been able to separate the Huns from the authentic traditions of Hungarian prehistory, the awesome image of Attila has never been erased from the national memory as a pertinent symbol of ancient Hungarian glory. Even in the middle of the last century János Arany, Hungary's greatest epic poet, chose the Hun legends as the theme of one of the finest epic poems ever written in the Hungarian language. Thus when Gárdonyi wrote his historical novel about Attila at the beginning of this century, Hungarian readers had every reason to identify this massive historical figure with the traditions of their own ancient past.

Although the emphasis of Gárdonyi's writing only strengthens this identification, the author himself was well aware of the world historical scale of his subject. Rather than rely upon the Hungarian chronicles written in Latin during the Middle Ages, he chose as his primary source the only genuinely authentic material available – the account of the Byzantian scholar Priscus rhetor who had actually served on a legation to Attila's court. Working from this material Gárdonyi produced a fine description of a period which can be considered both as an epilogue to the ancient world and an overture to the Middle Ages.

The middle of the fifth century saw the last generation of the Western Roman Empire, the fall of which is traditionally considered to represent the end of the ancient world. In response to the Hun threat, Aetius, the last of the great Roman military leaders, organised the last effective Roman army in the Empire's defence. The two great powers clashed on the plains of Catalaunum (Chalons-sur-Marne, France), the site of so many crucial battles in the history of the world. Although successfully stopping Attila's army in its tracks, Aetius was unable to score the decisive victory which would have allowed him to march on to conquer the Empire of the Huns. The third major power in the area, the Eastern Roman Empire, governed by Theodosius from Constantinople, had for a long time been using all available diplomatic means to encourage the Huns to press westwards rather than in their direction. Theodosius was prepared to make all kinds of compromises, including the provision of large sums of money, to preserve his artificial friendship with the notorious barbarian Attila. In 448 a delegation set forth from Constantinople, among whose members was the talented and observant scholar Priscus rhetor, who recorded his experiences in his famous memoris. Gárdonyi made comprehensive and faithful use of this source; the description of Attila, his household and numerous Hun customs are based directly upon the observations of Priscus. Zeta, "the invisible man" (the literal translation of the Hungarian title) and the central character of the novel, is a fine example of literary invention who narrates the story in the first person. Arriving at the Hun court with Priscus as the latter's young and literate protégé, he falls in love with Emmo, the daughter of a high-ranking Hun lord, who is, however, secretly in love with Attila himself. Meanwhile Djidjia, a quiet and bashful maidservant, is in love with Zeta.This private narrative – which ends tragically for Emmo, but happily for Djidjia – is built into a massive historical panorama. Zeta, who remains in Attila's court, becomes a hero of the Hun army, taking part in an epically described military procession, and in the battle of Catalaunum. He witnesses and narrates the collapse of the Hun Empire: the death and burial of Attila and the failure of his great dream of world domination. Finally Zeta withdraws from the world of great ambitions to enjoy the more modest and peaceful pleasures of family life, leaving the dramatic story of his experiences, struggles and miraculous survival to posterity.

It is here that the ancient world of the Roman Empire comes to an end, the Middle Ages begin. Priscus rhetor's delegation set out in 448, the battle of Catalaunum was fought in AD 451 and the Western Roman Empire collapsed in 476, not long after the fall of the Huns. Attila died in 453, Aetius in 454 – the failure of both leaders opening the way for the next wave of migrants to begin reshaping Europe. Not long after Attila's death Theodoric, who learnt the art of war from the Huns, establishes a Gothic kingdom; Vandals, Gepids and Longobards pour into Central Europe. At the time of the Battle of Catalaunum and Attila's death Gorlois still rules in the North from the Castle of Cornwall in Tintagel, but he will soon be defeated by Uther Pendragon who will also kidnap his wife. From this new marriage King Arthur is born, who will go on to lead his legendary knights against their own Germanic invaders, the Anglo-Saxons. This life and death struggle will prepare the way for the eventual amalgamation of these two antagonistic peoples, resulting in the birth of England. Bearing this in mind, the English reader may perhaps find it easier not only to understand, but also more vividly to feel, the significance of this imaginative account of the bloody history of the Huns.

Géza Hegedűs